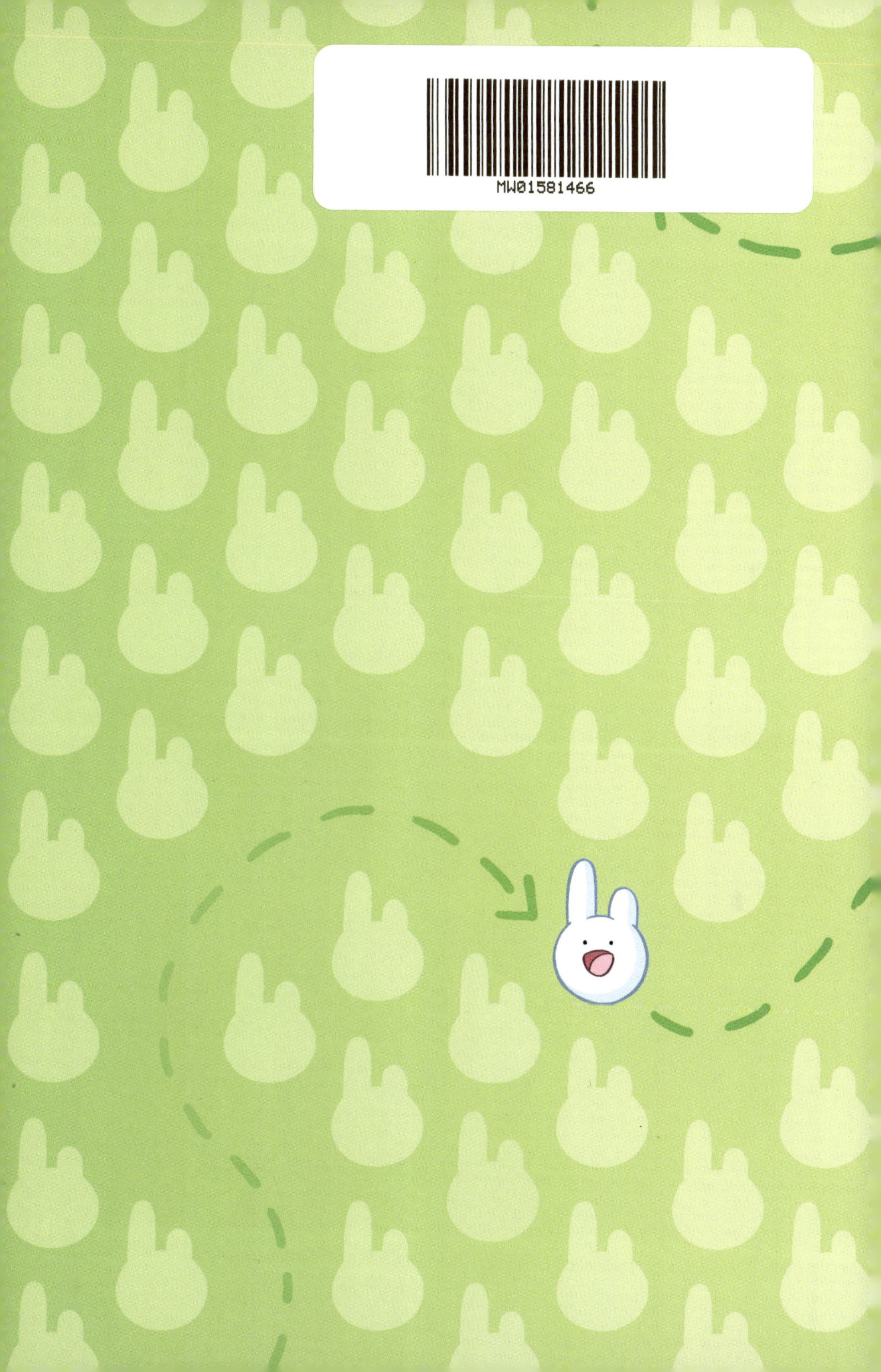

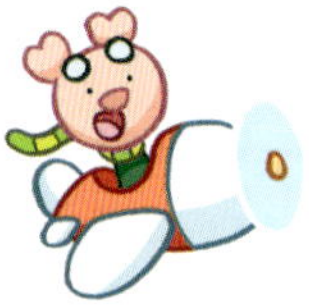

Jamie Smart's

Max & Chaffy

Welcome to Animal Island!

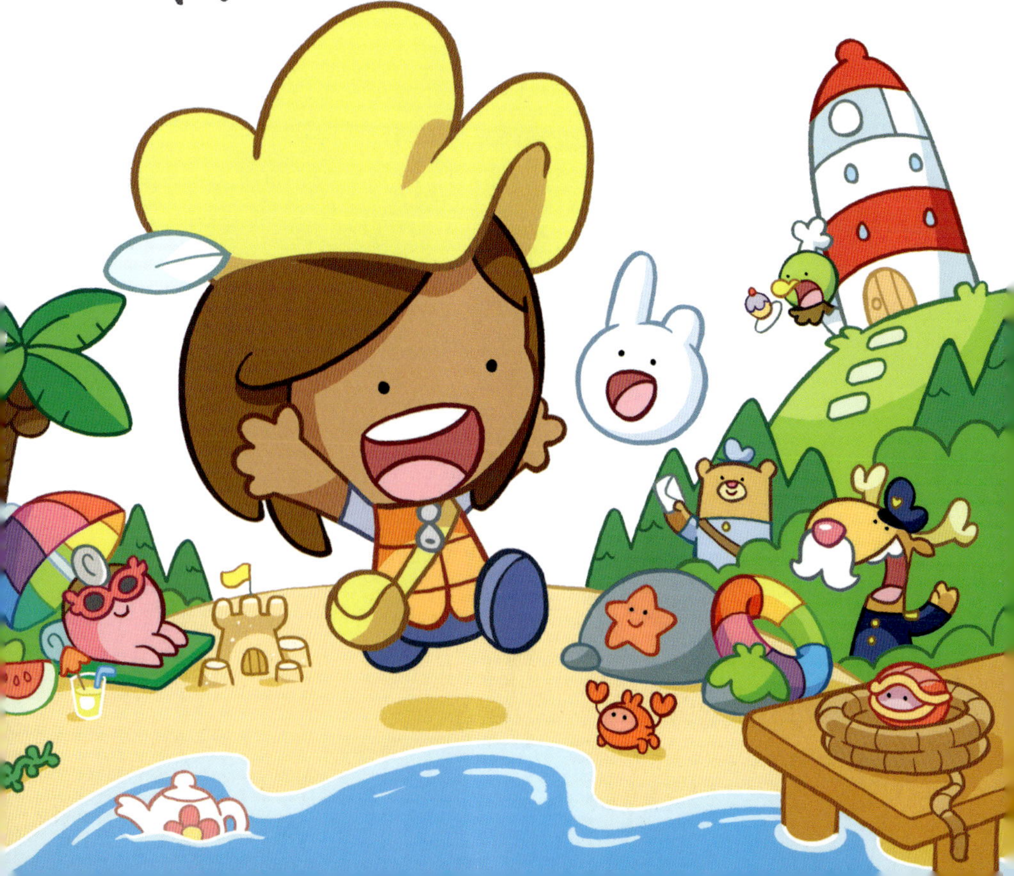

First American Edition, 2025
Published in the United States by DK Publishing,
a division of Penguin Random House LLC
1745 Broadway, 20th Floor, New York, NY 10019

Text and illustrations © Fumboo Ltd 2023

The right of Jamie Smart to be identified as the author and illustrator of this work has been asserted in accordance with the Copyright, Designs and Patents Act 1988.

DK, a Division of Penguin Random House LLC
25 26 27 28 29 10 9 8 7 6 5 4 3 2 1
001–345663–May/2025

All rights reserved.
Without limiting the rights under the copyright reserved above, no part of this publication may be reproduced, stored in or introduced into a retrieval system, or transmitted, in any form, or by any means (electronic, mechanical, photocopying, recording, or otherwise), without the prior written permission of the copyright owner.

Published in Great Britain by David Fickling Books.

A catalog record for this book is available from the Library of Congress.
ISBN 978-0-5939-6529-0 (Paperback)
ISBN 978-0-5939-6530-6 (Hardback)

DK books are available at special discounts when purchased in bulk for sales promotions, premiums, fund-raising, or educational use. For details, contact: DK Publishing Special Markets, 1745 Broadway, 20th Floor, New York, NY 10019
SpecialSales@dk.com

Printed and bound in China

www.dk.com

MIX
Paper | Supporting responsible forestry
FSC™ C018179

This book was made with Forest Stewardship Council™ certified paper – one small step in DK's commitment to a sustainable future.
Learn more at www.dk.com/uk/information/sustainability

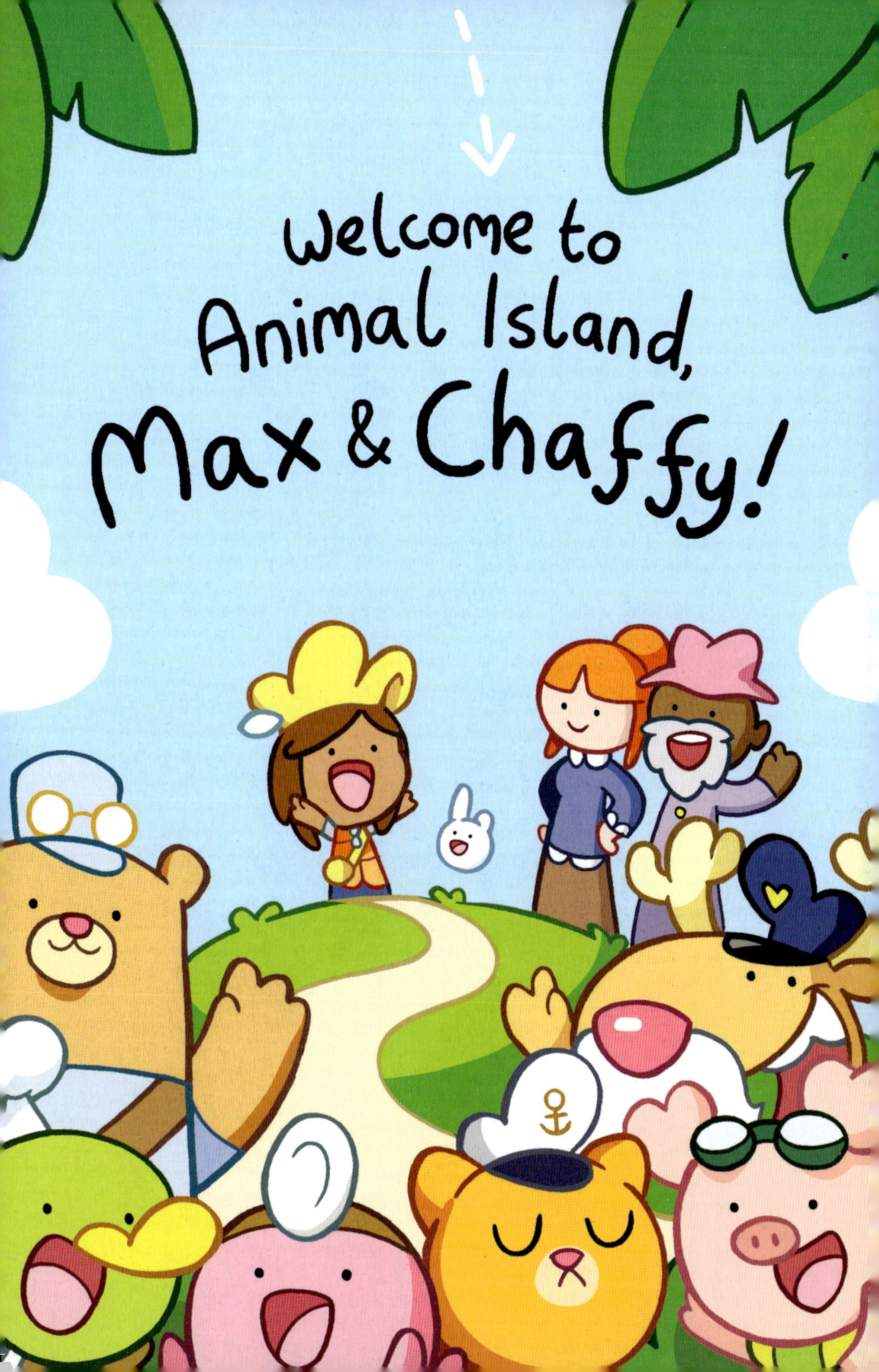
Welcome to
Animal Island,
Max & Chaffy!

Far, far across the ocean . . .

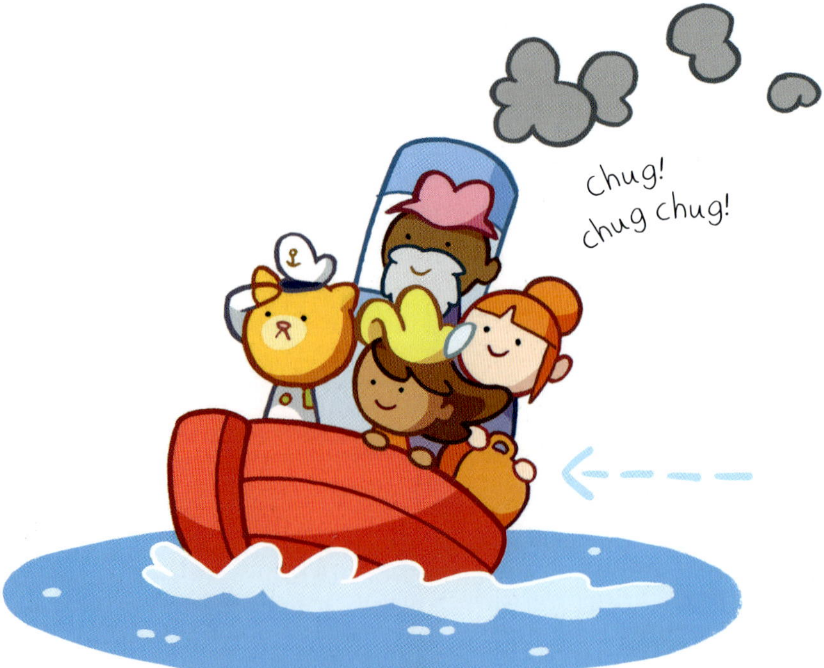
chug!
chug chug!

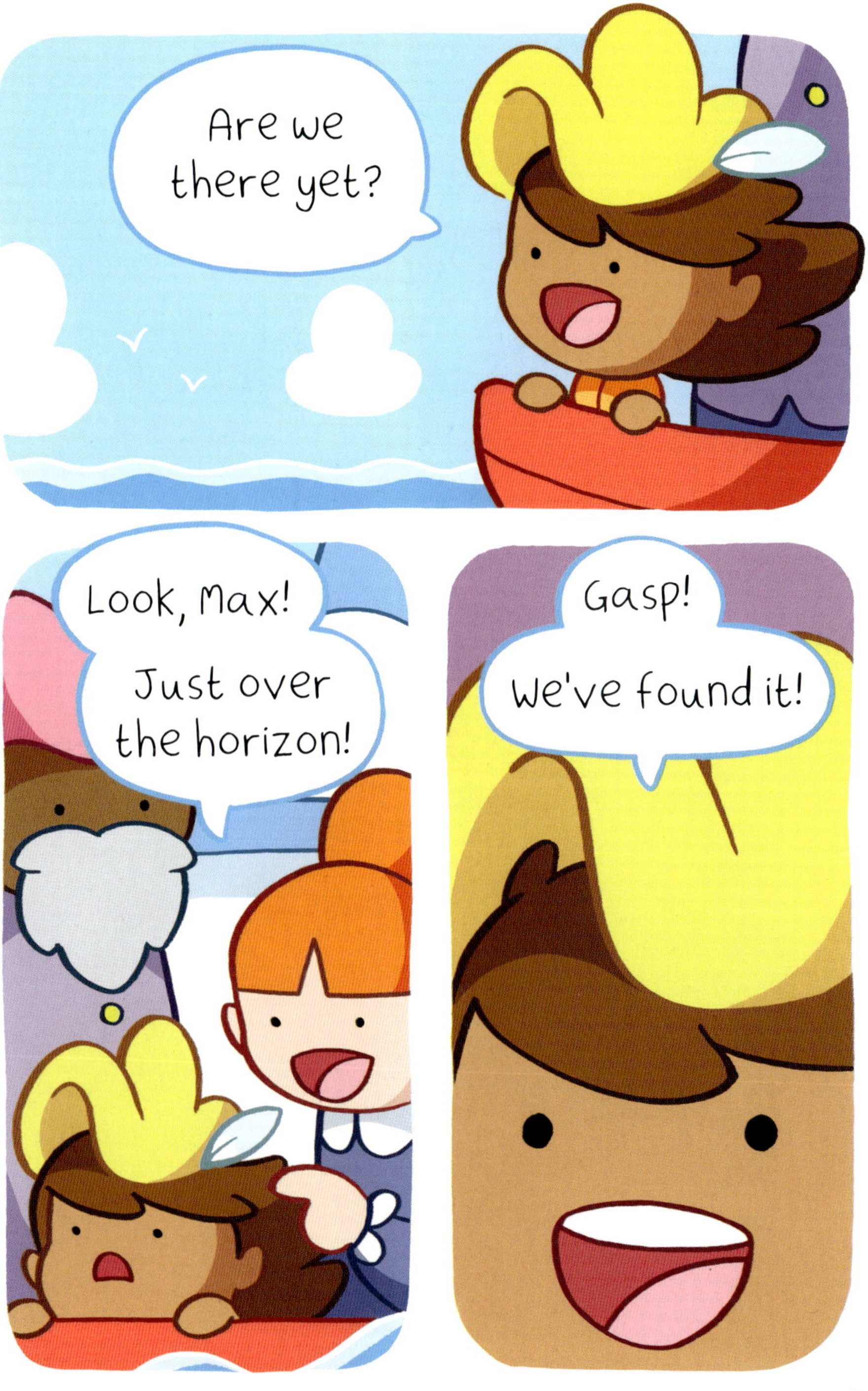
Are we there yet?
Look, Max!
Just over the horizon!
Gasp!
We've found it!

welcome to Animal Island!

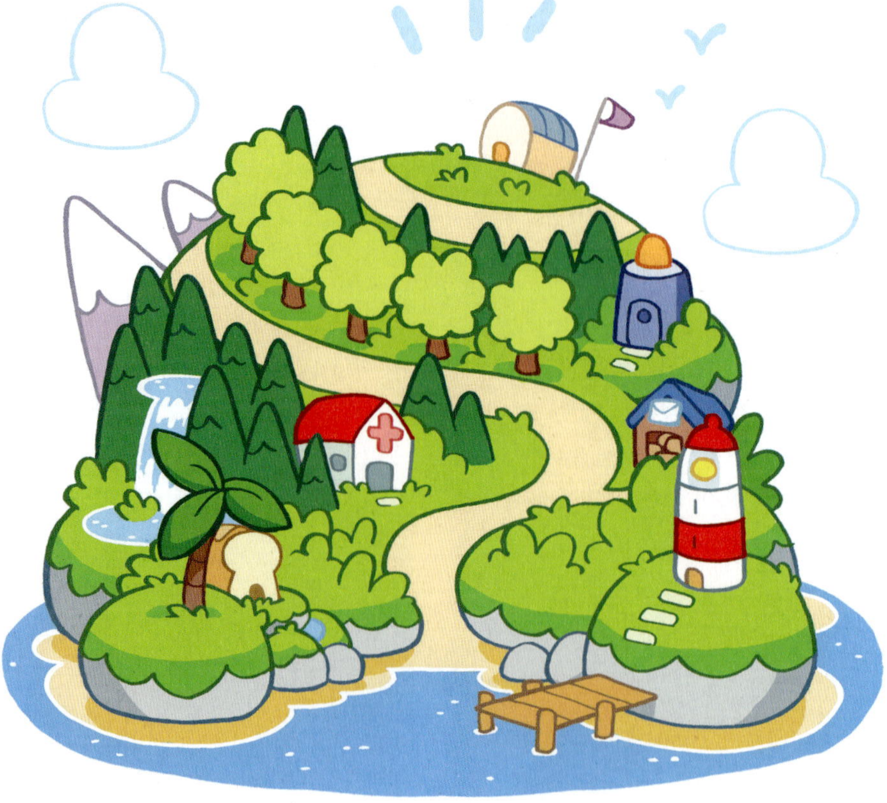

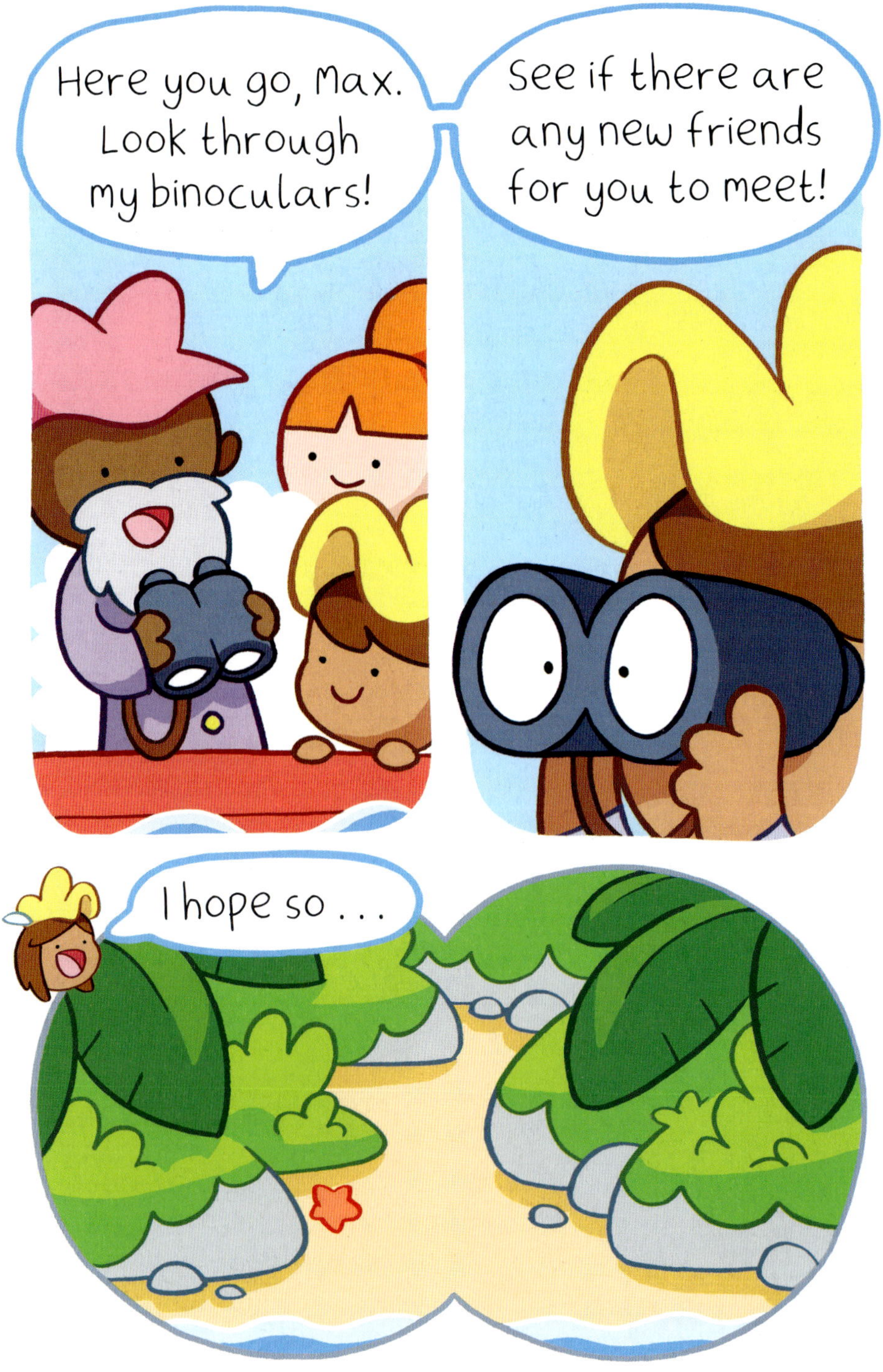
Here you go, Max. Look through my binoculars!
See if there are any new friends for you to meet!
I hope so . . .

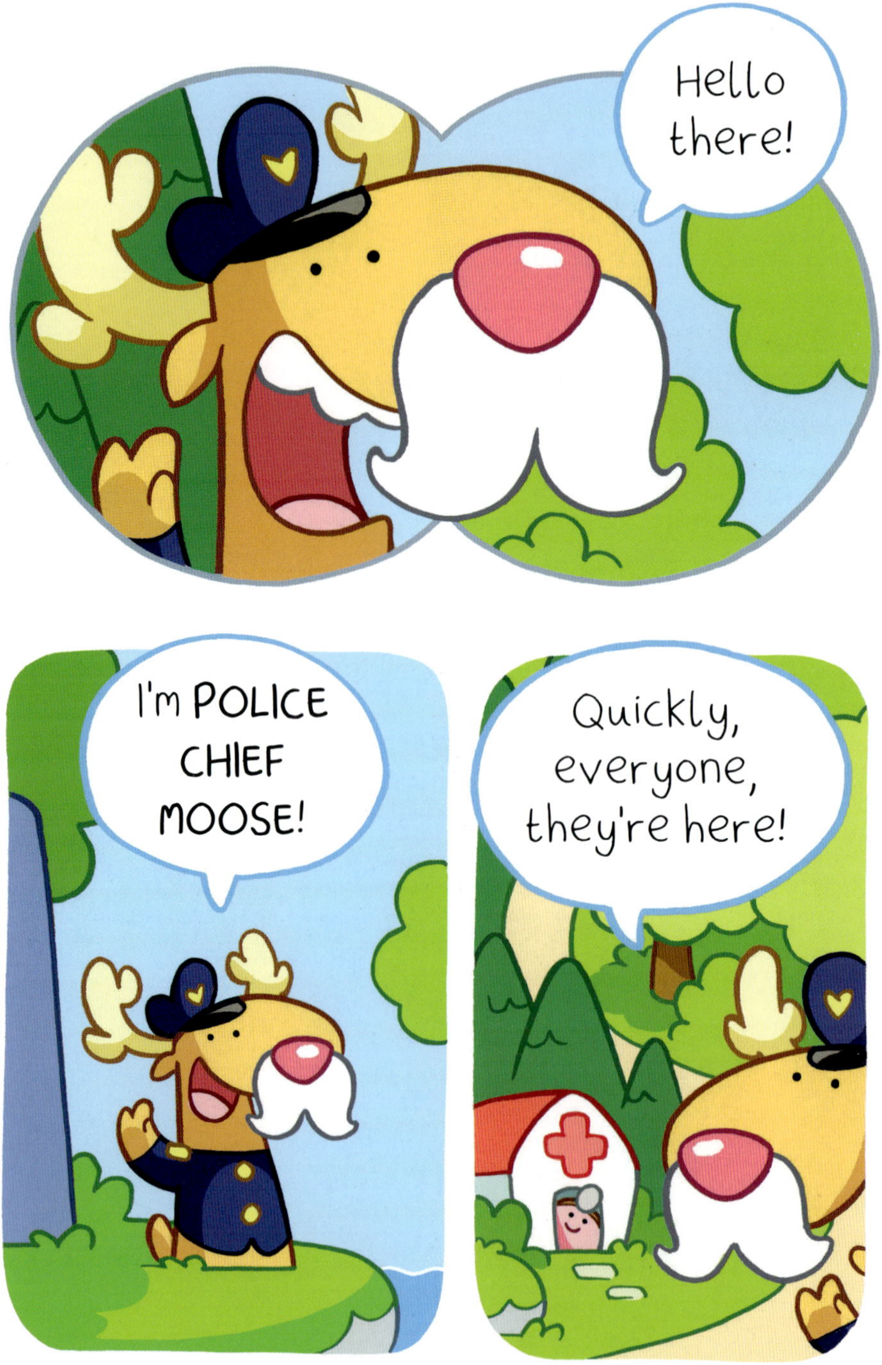
Hello there!
I'm POLICE CHIEF MOOSE!
Quickly, everyone, they're here!

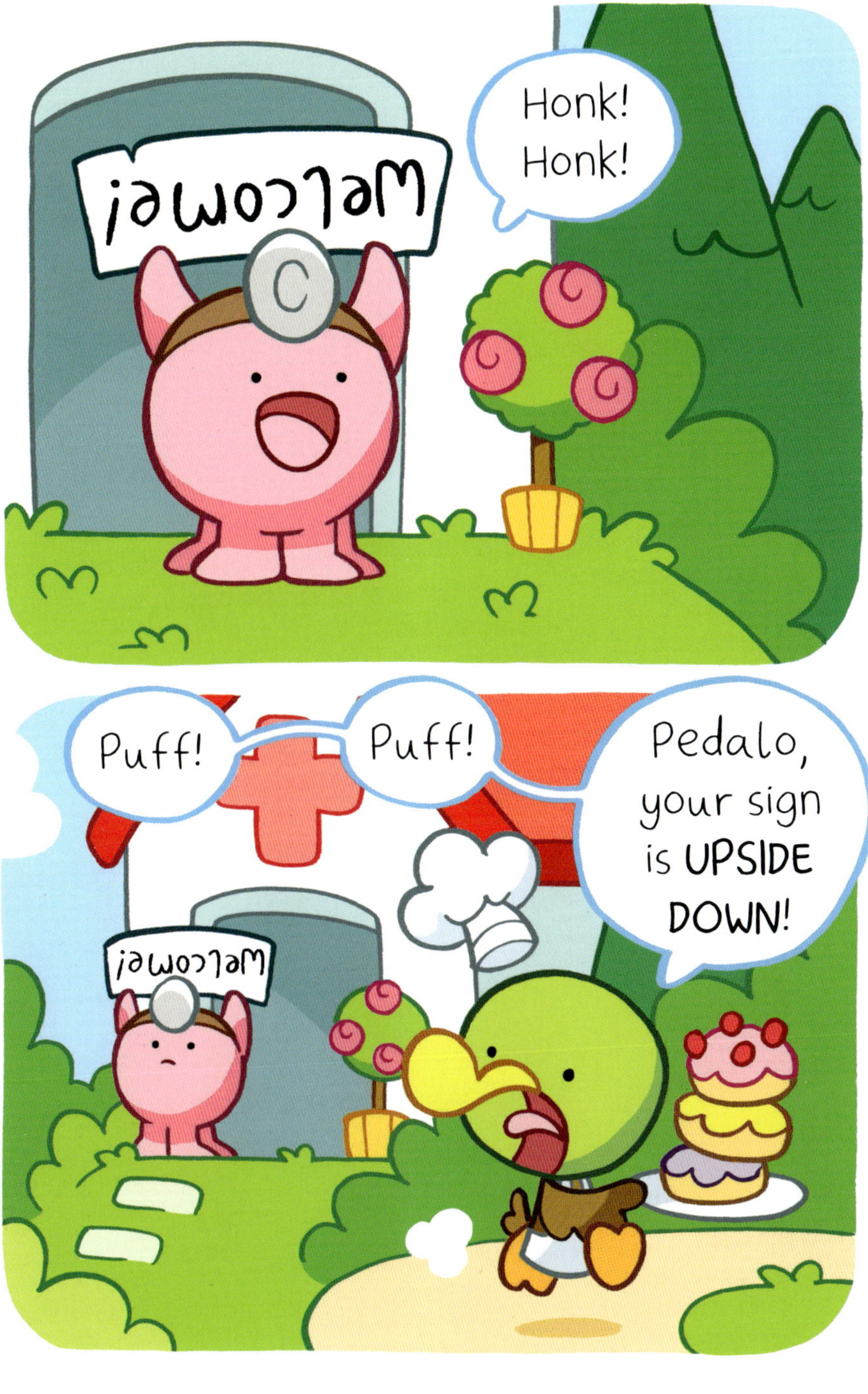
Welcome!
Honk! Honk!
Puff!
Puff!
Pedalo, your sign is **UPSIDE DOWN!**
Welcome!

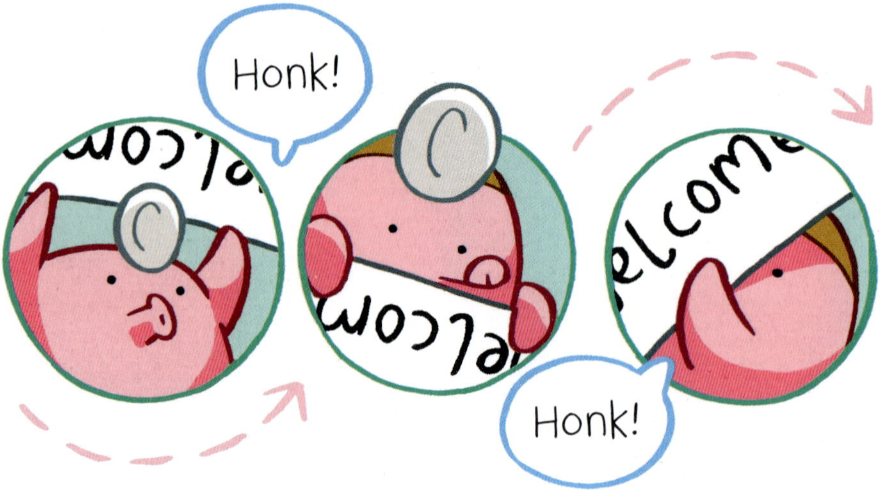
Honk!
Honk!

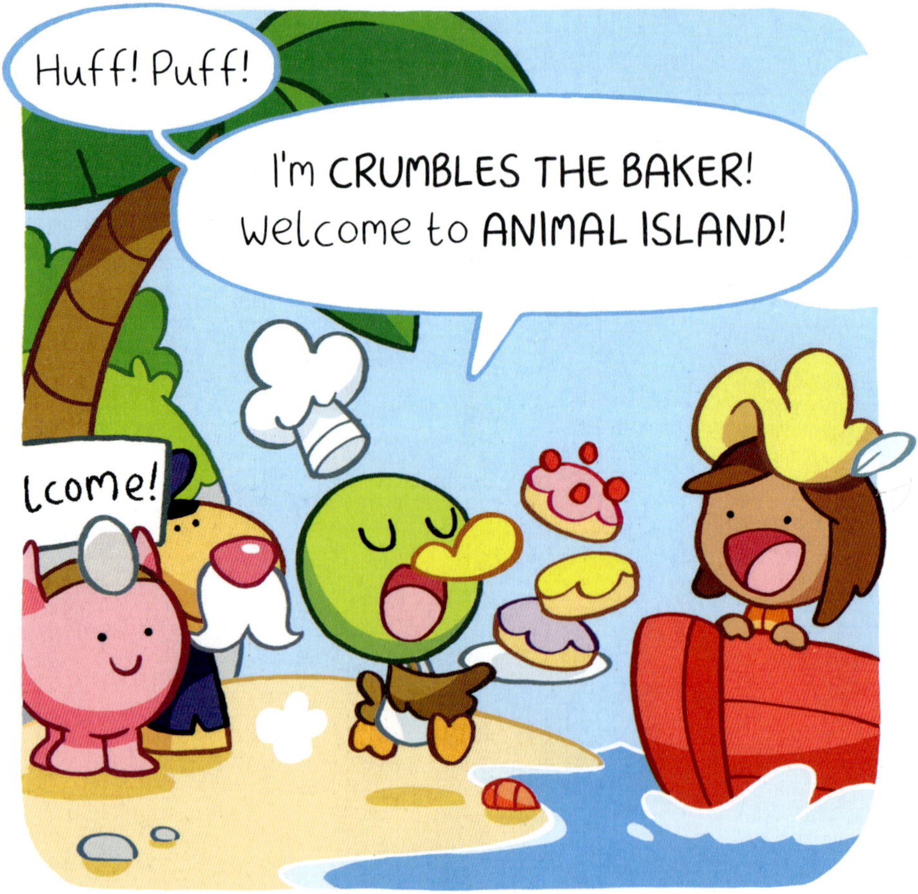
Huff! Puff!
I'm CRUMBLES THE BAKER! Welcome to ANIMAL ISLAND!
lcome!

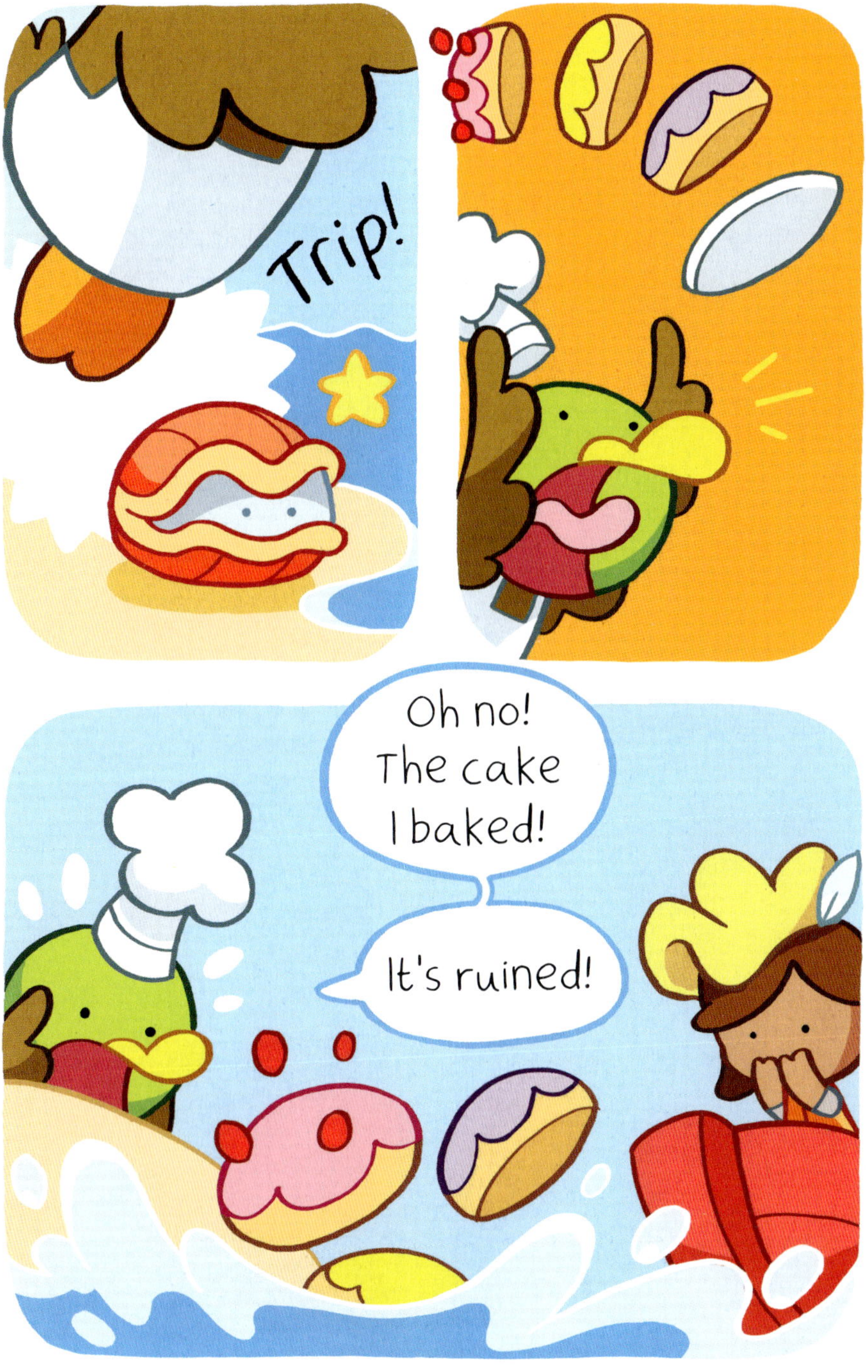
Trip!
Oh no! The cake I baked!
It's ruined!

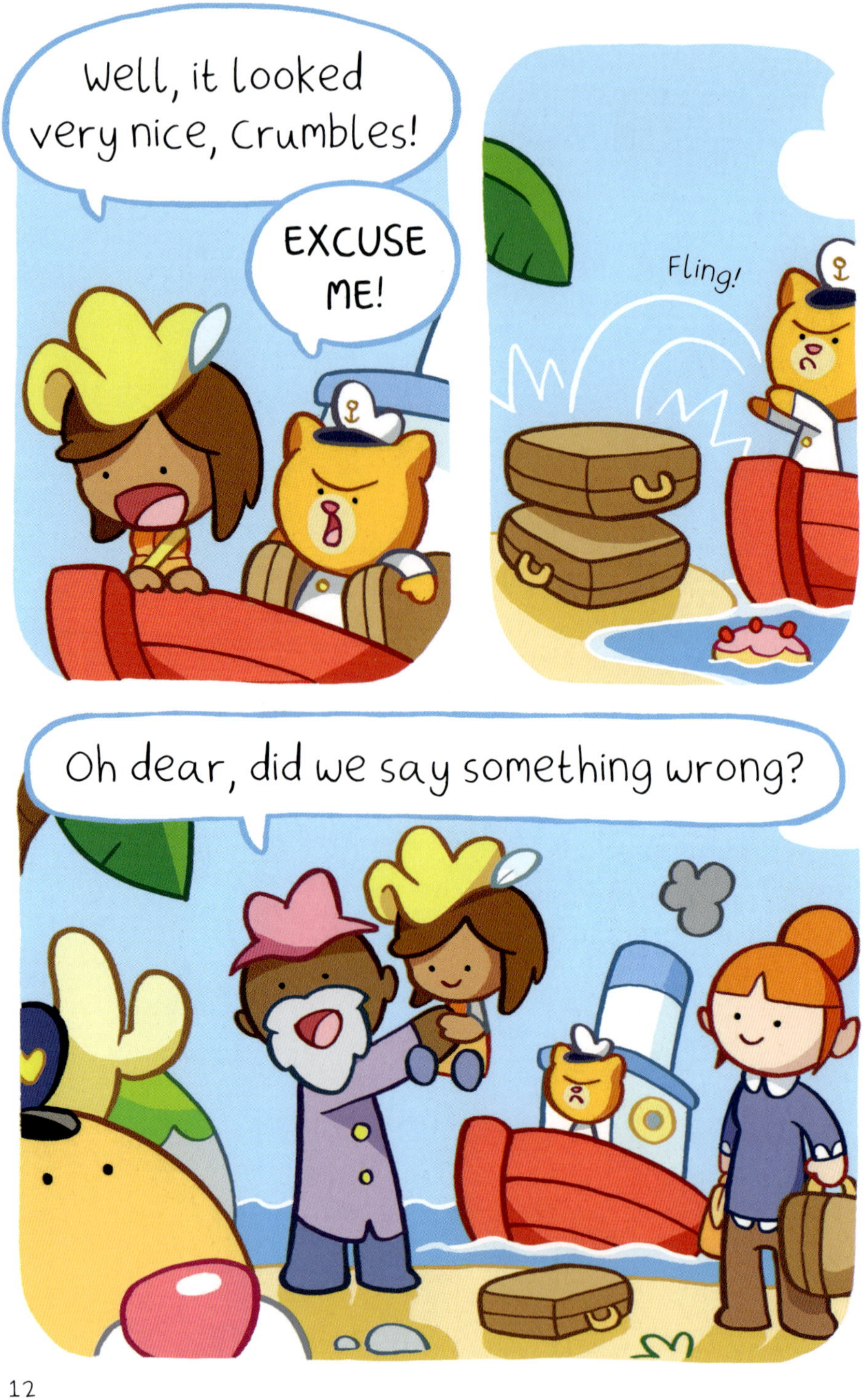
Well, it looked very nice, Crumbles!
EXCUSE ME!
Fling!
Oh dear, did we say something wrong?

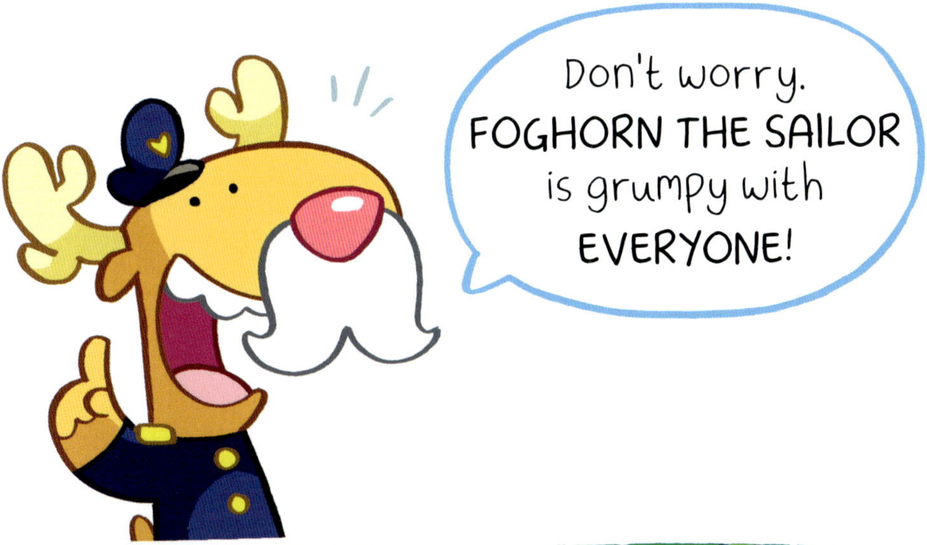
Don't worry. FOGHORN THE SAILOR is grumpy with EVERYONE!

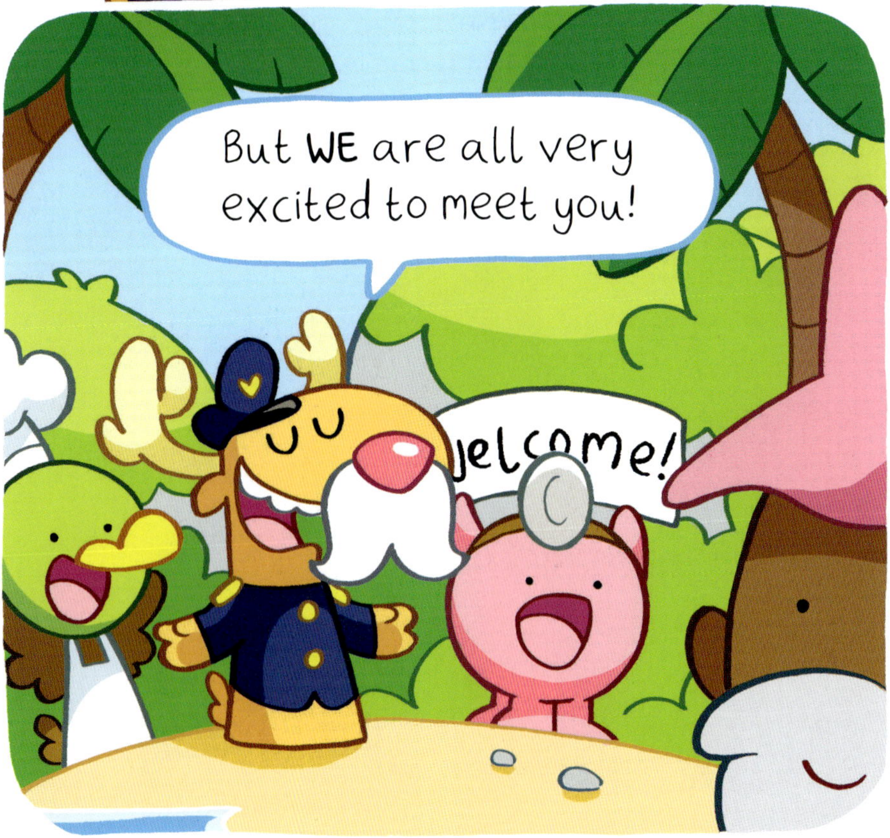
But WE are all very excited to meet you!
elcome!

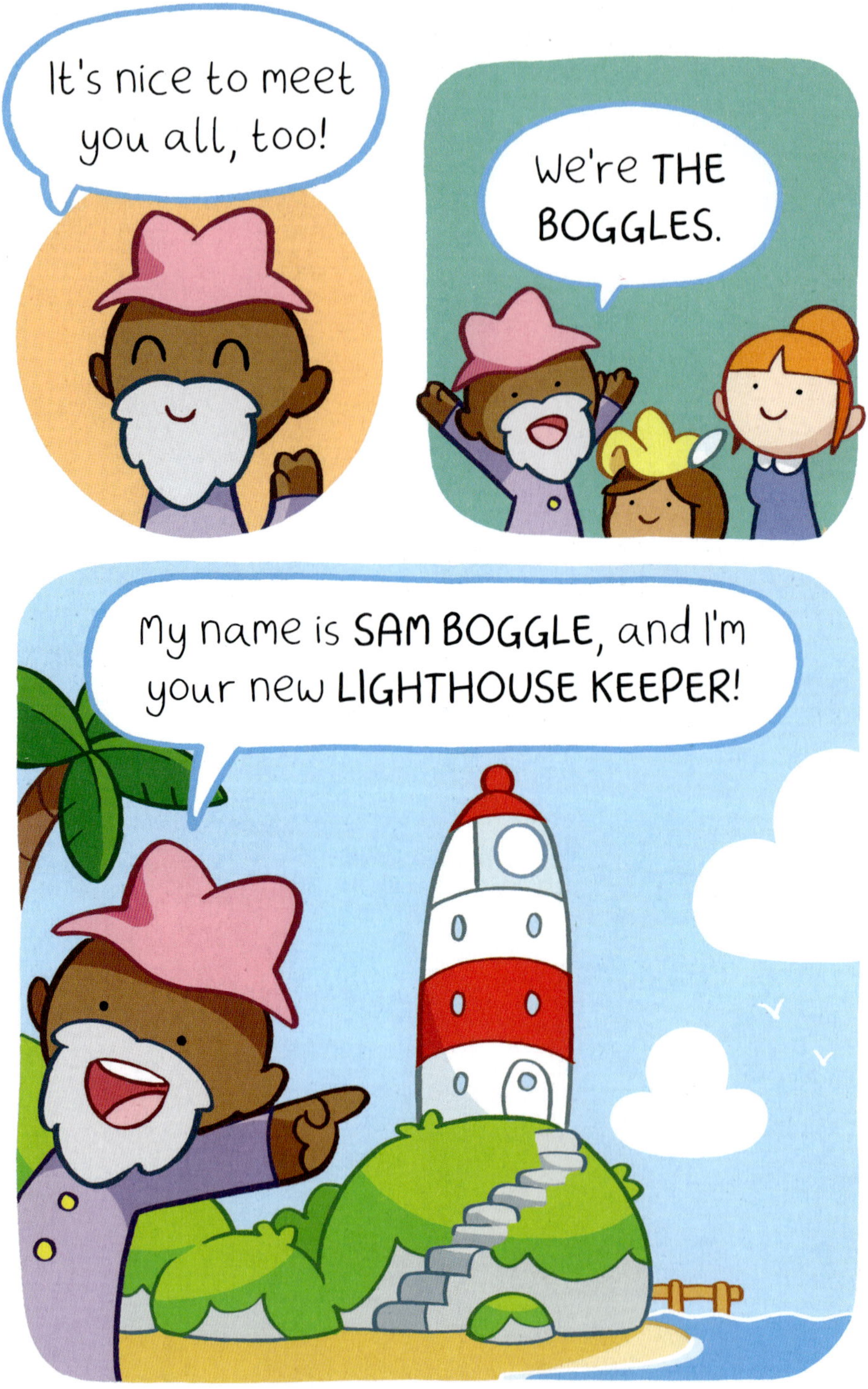
It's nice to meet you all, too!
We're THE BOGGLES.
My name is SAM BOGGLE, and I'm your new LIGHTHOUSE KEEPER!

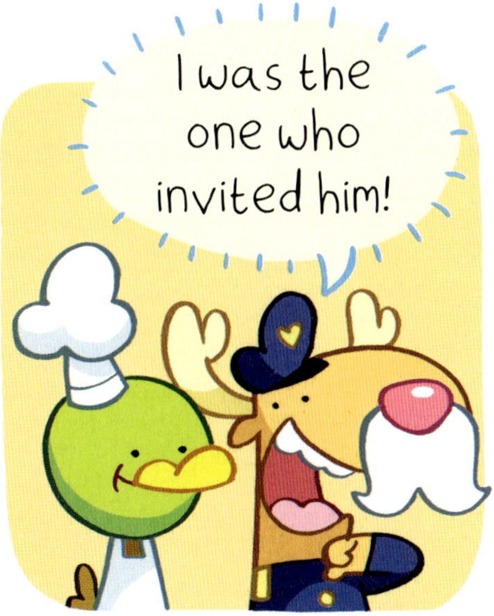
I was the one who invited him!

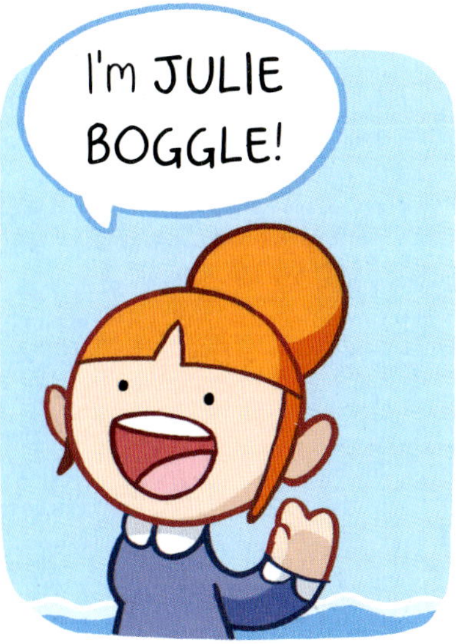
I'm JULIE BOGGLE!

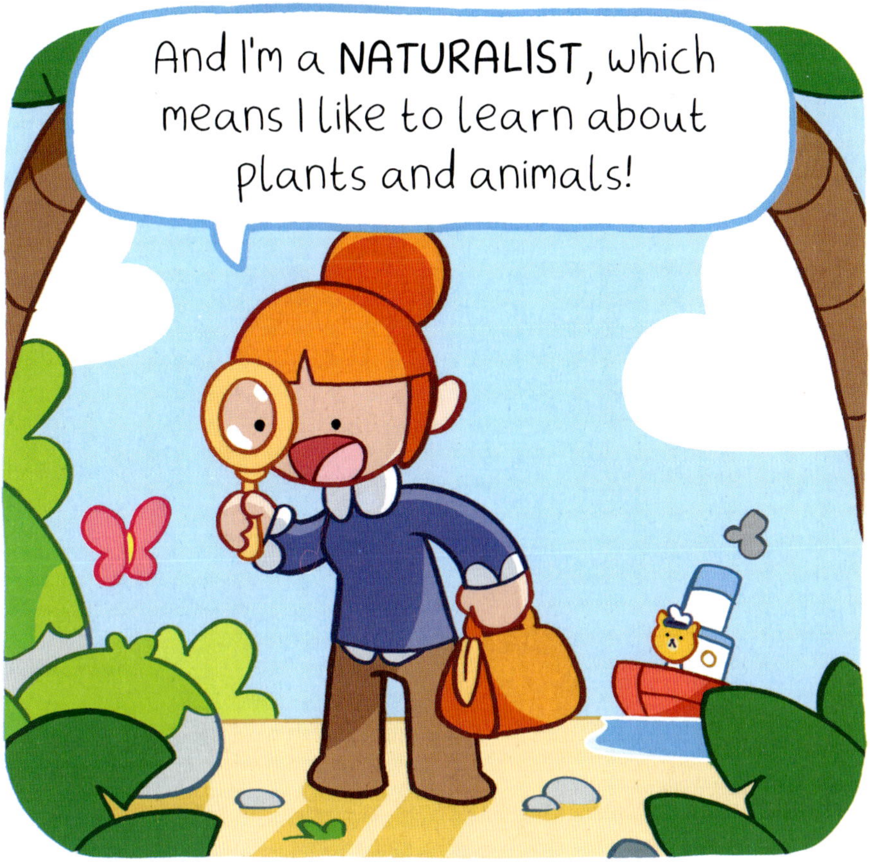
And I'm a NATURALIST, which means I like to learn about plants and animals!

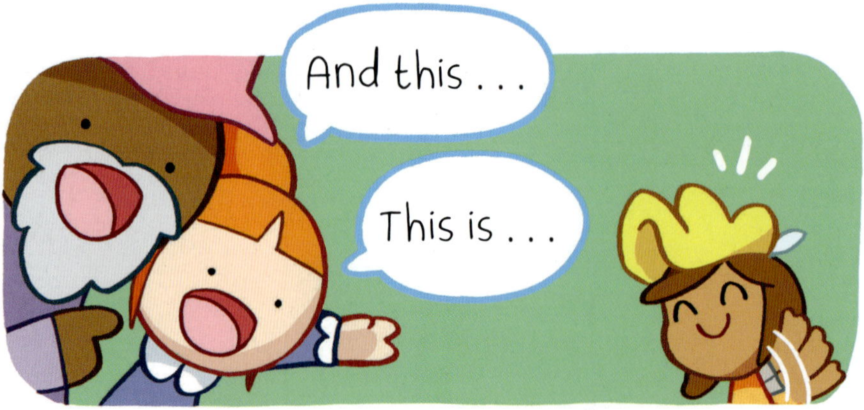
And this . . .
This is . . .

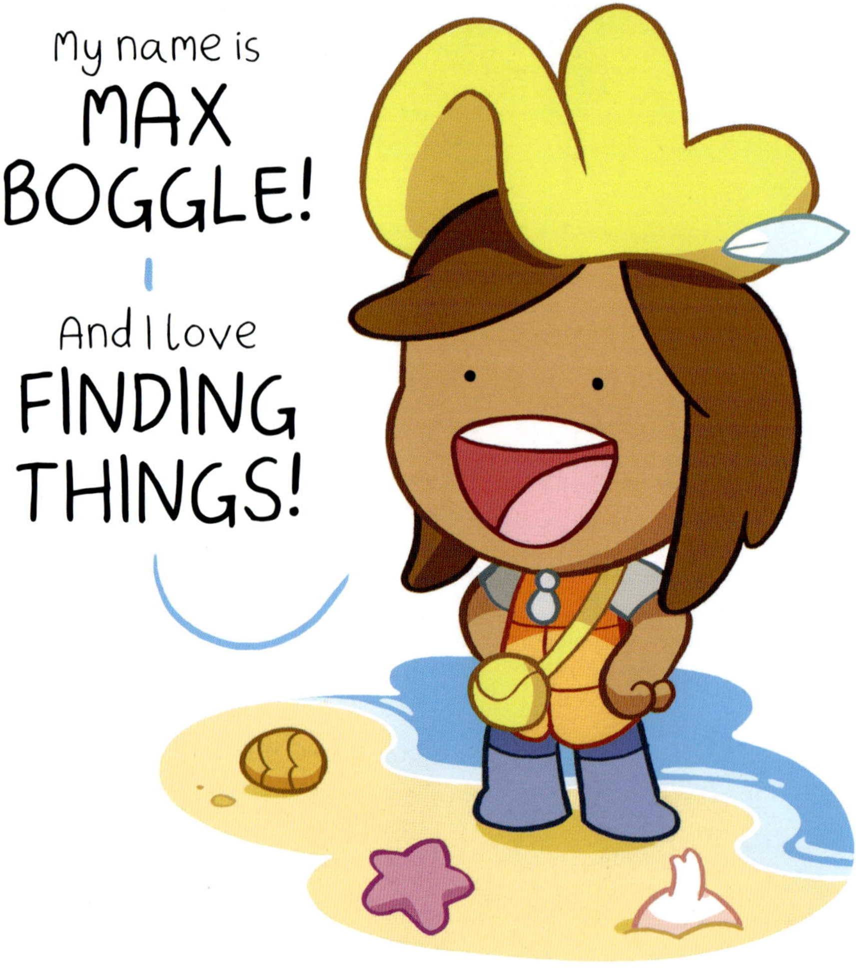
My name is
MAX
BOGGLE!
And I love
FINDING
THINGS!

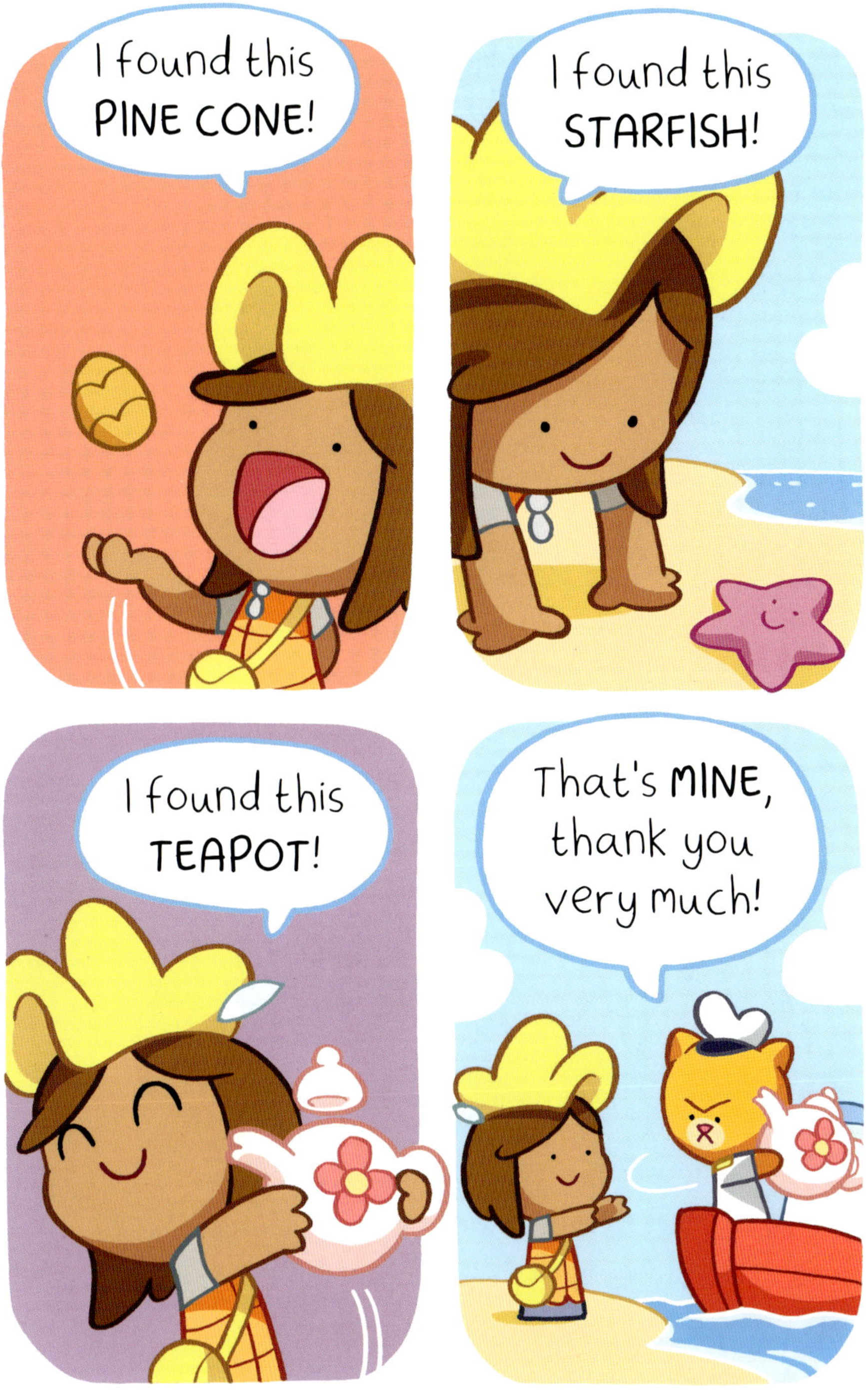
I found this PINE CONE!
I found this STARFISH!
I found this TEAPOT!
That's MINE, thank you very much!

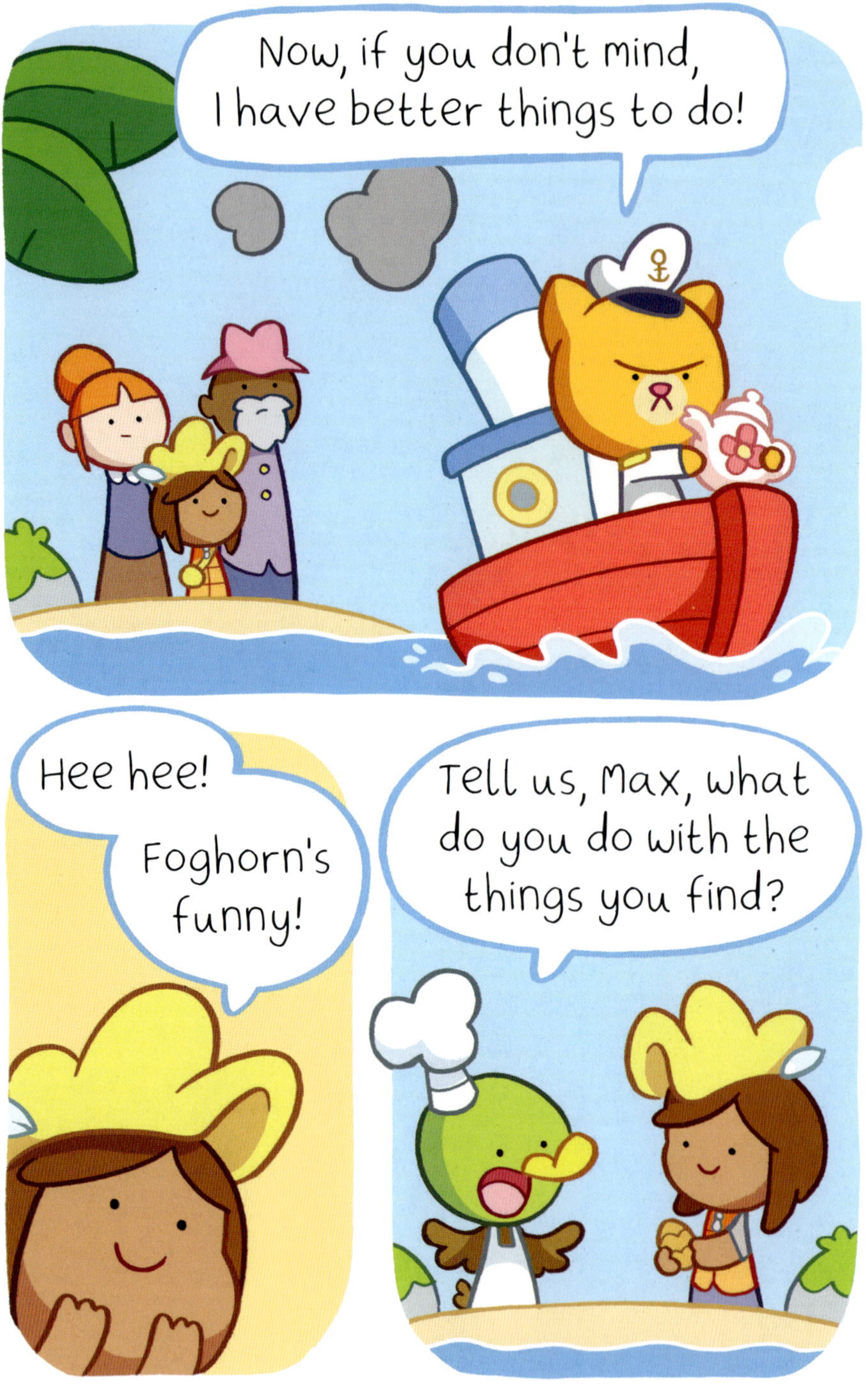
Now, if you don't mind, I have better things to do!
Hee hee!
Foghorn's funny!
Tell us, Max, what do you do with the things you find?

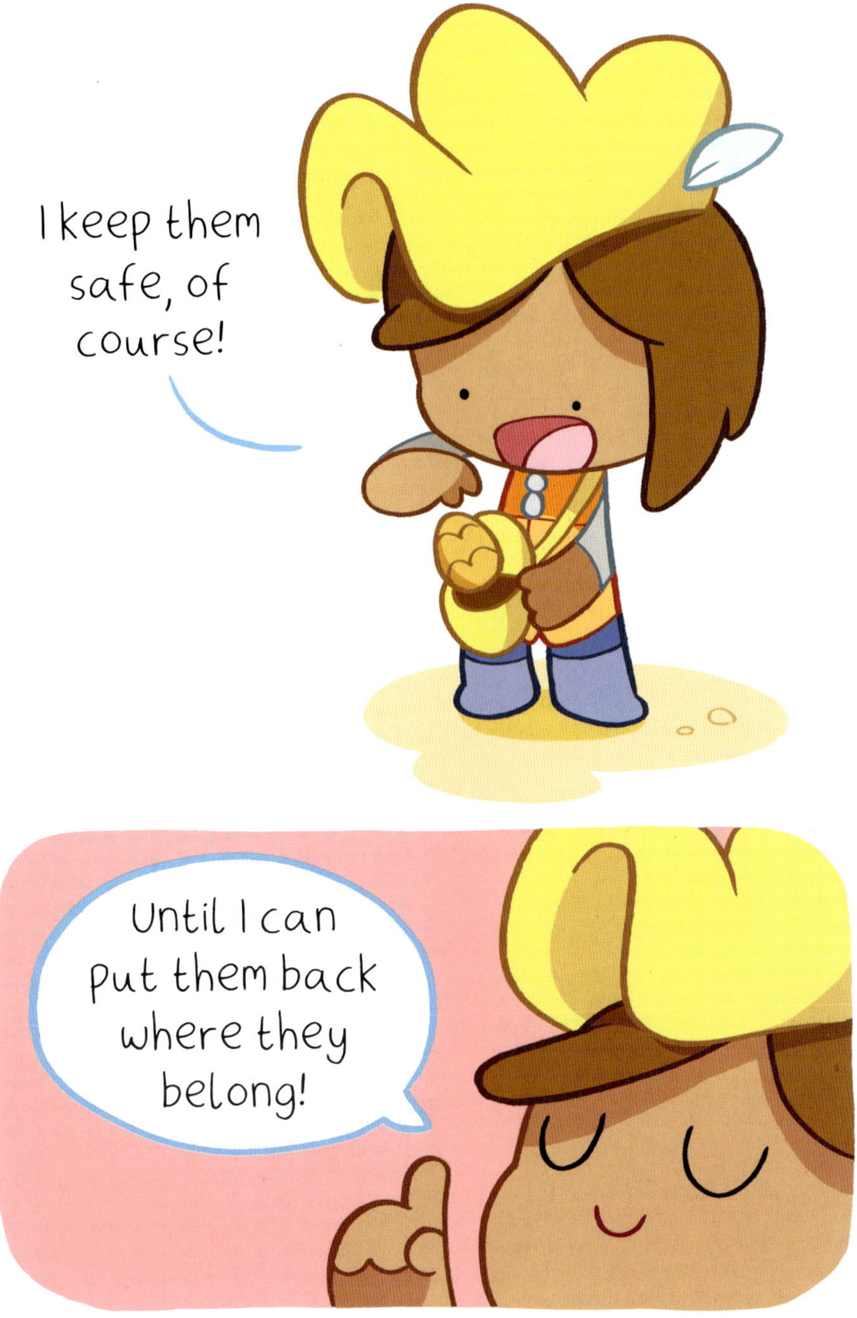
I keep them safe, of course!
Until I can put them back where they belong!

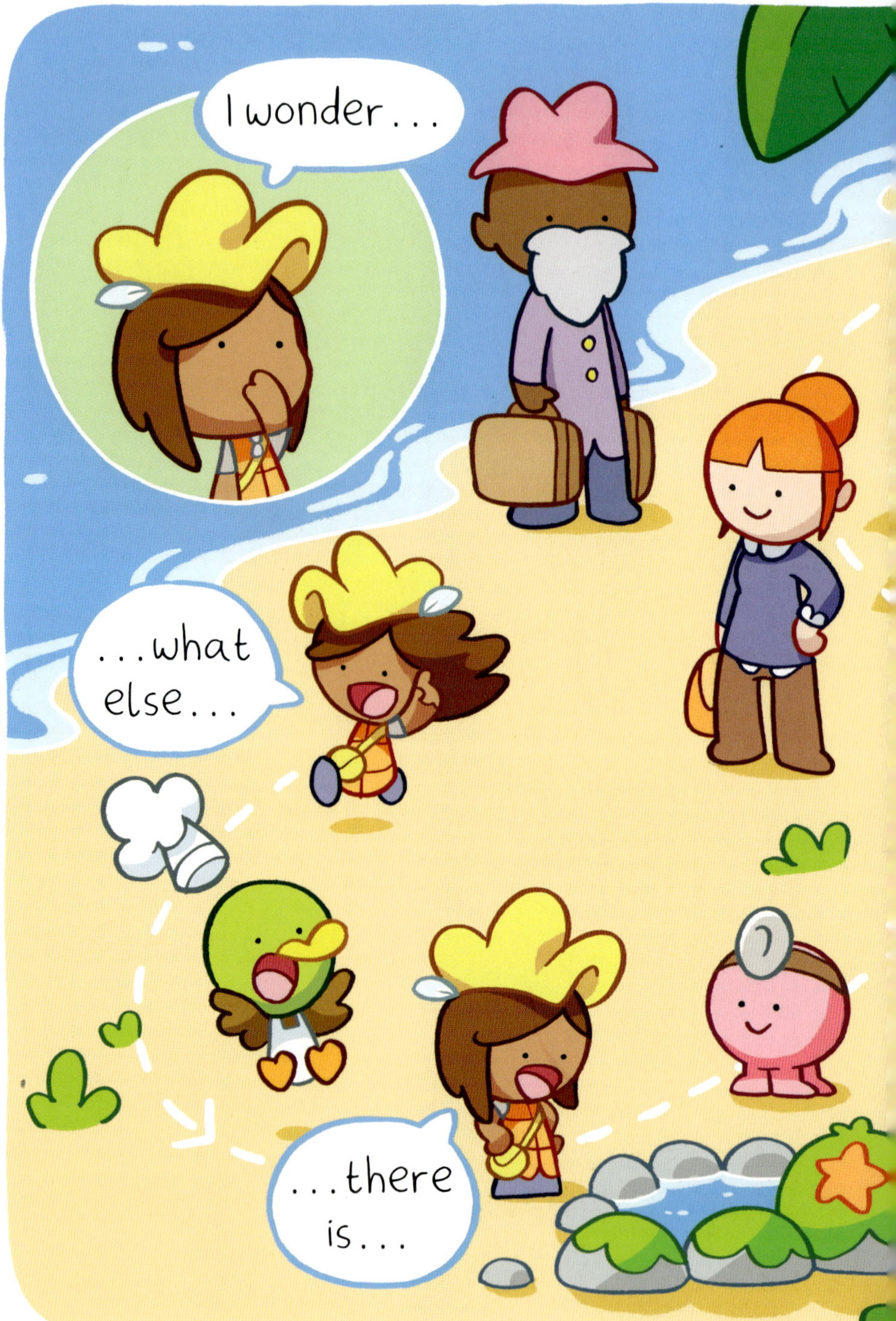
I wonder...
...what else...
...there is...

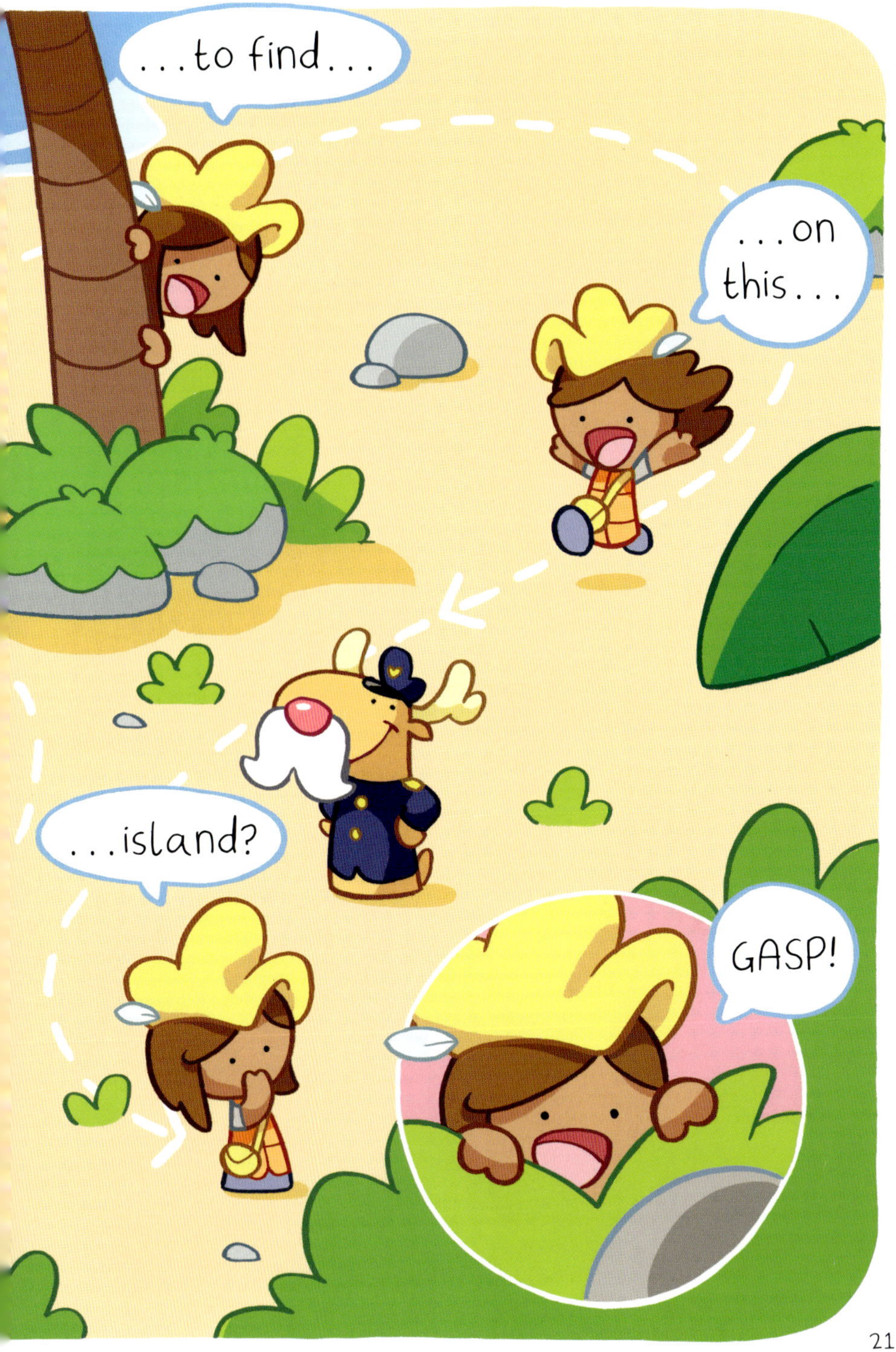
...to find...
...on this...
...island?
GASP!

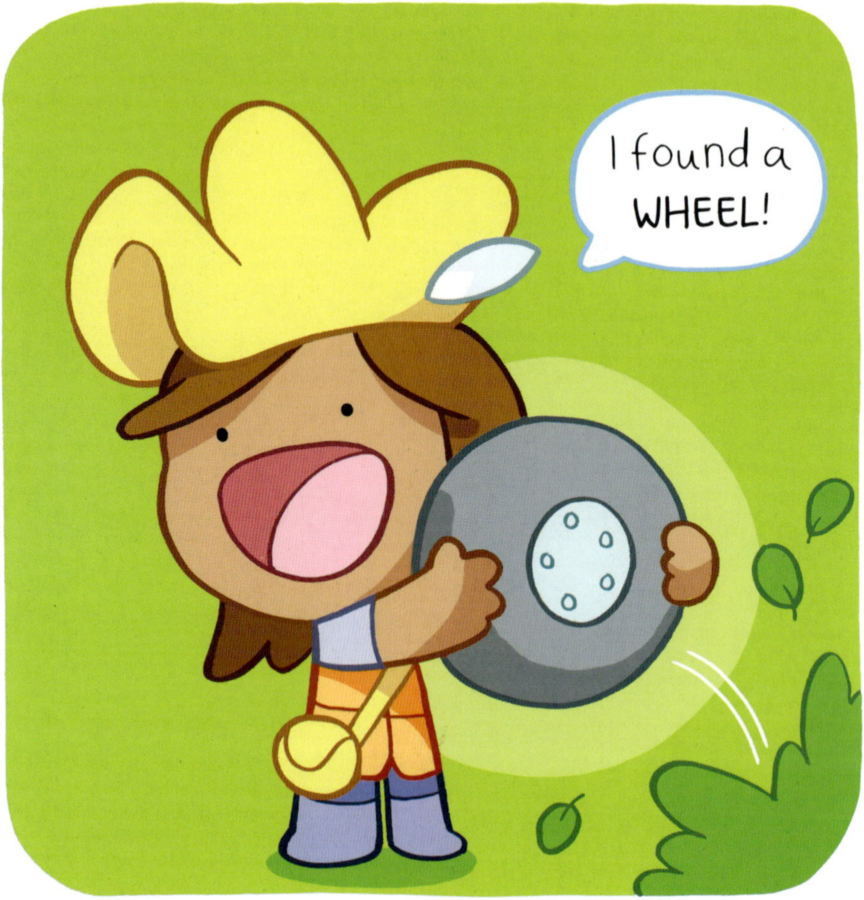
I found a WHEEL!

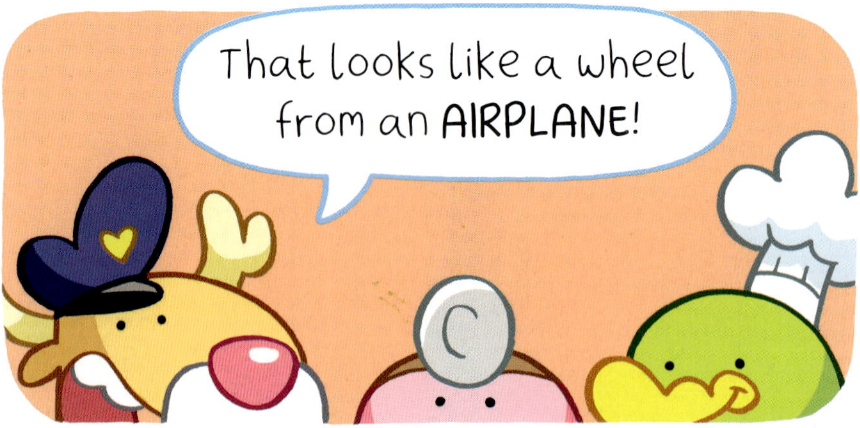
That looks like a wheel from an AIRPLANE!

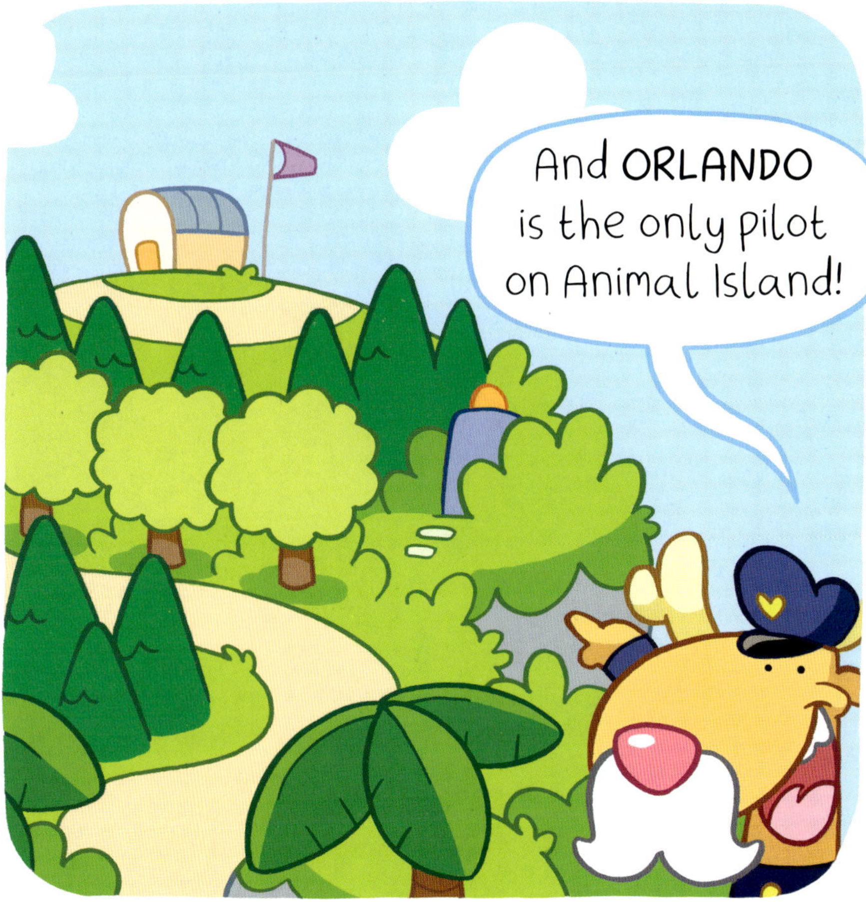
And **ORLANDO** is the only pilot on Animal Island!

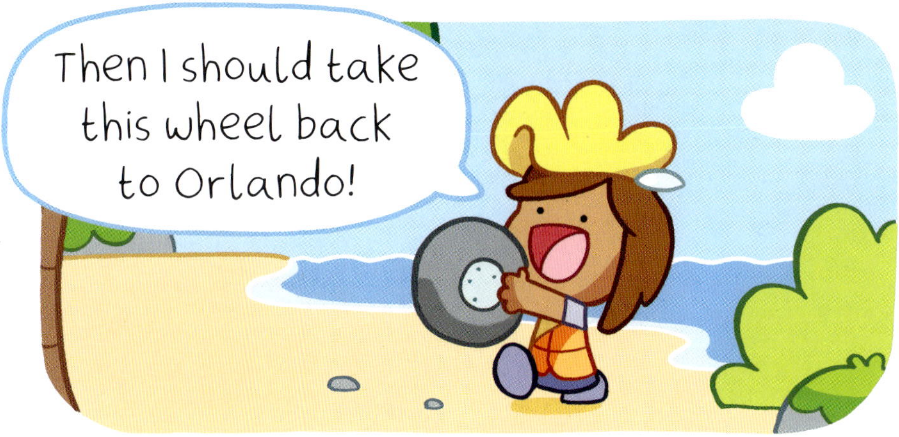
Then I should take this wheel back to Orlando!

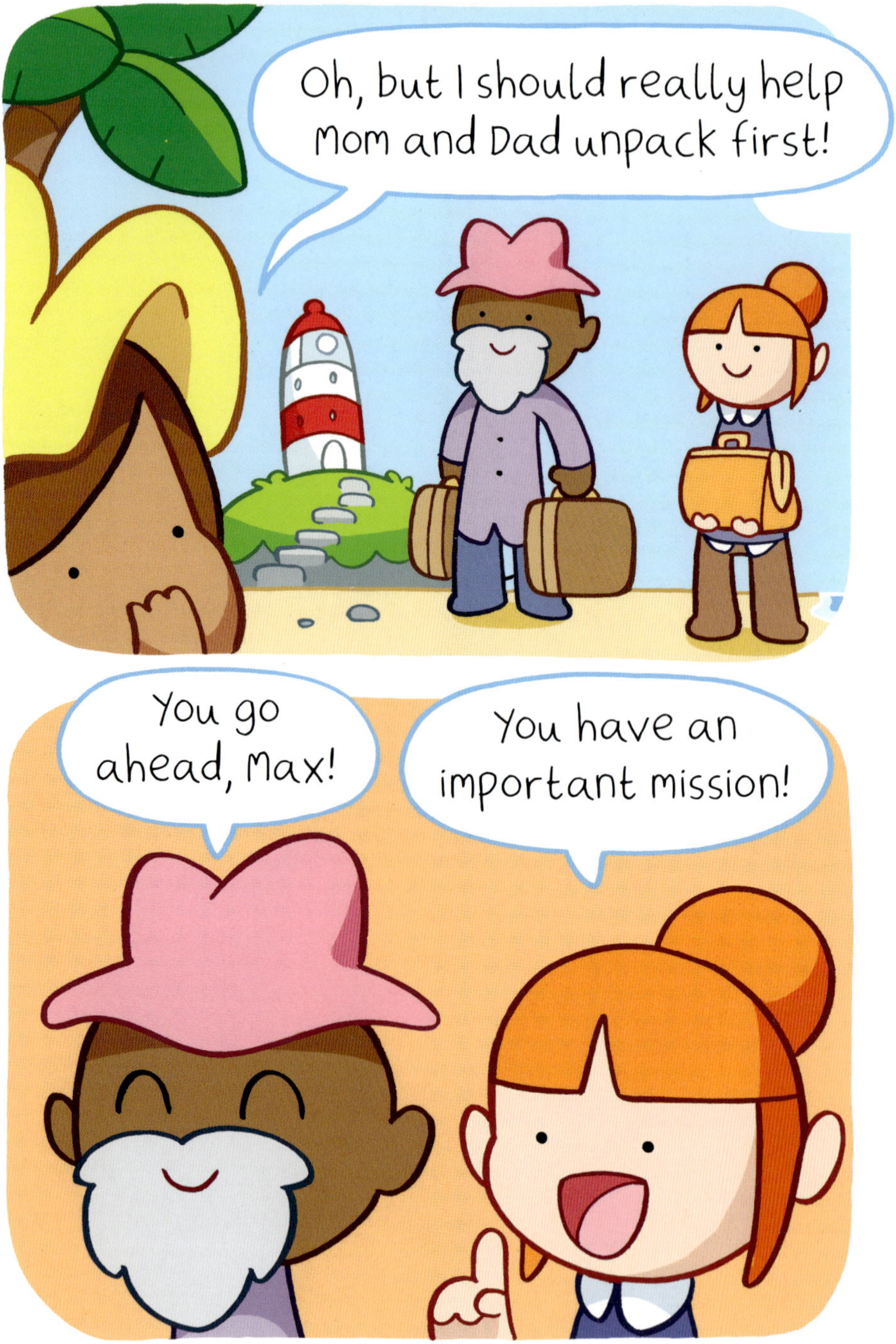
Oh, but I should really help Mom and Dad unpack first!
You go ahead, Max!
You have an important mission!

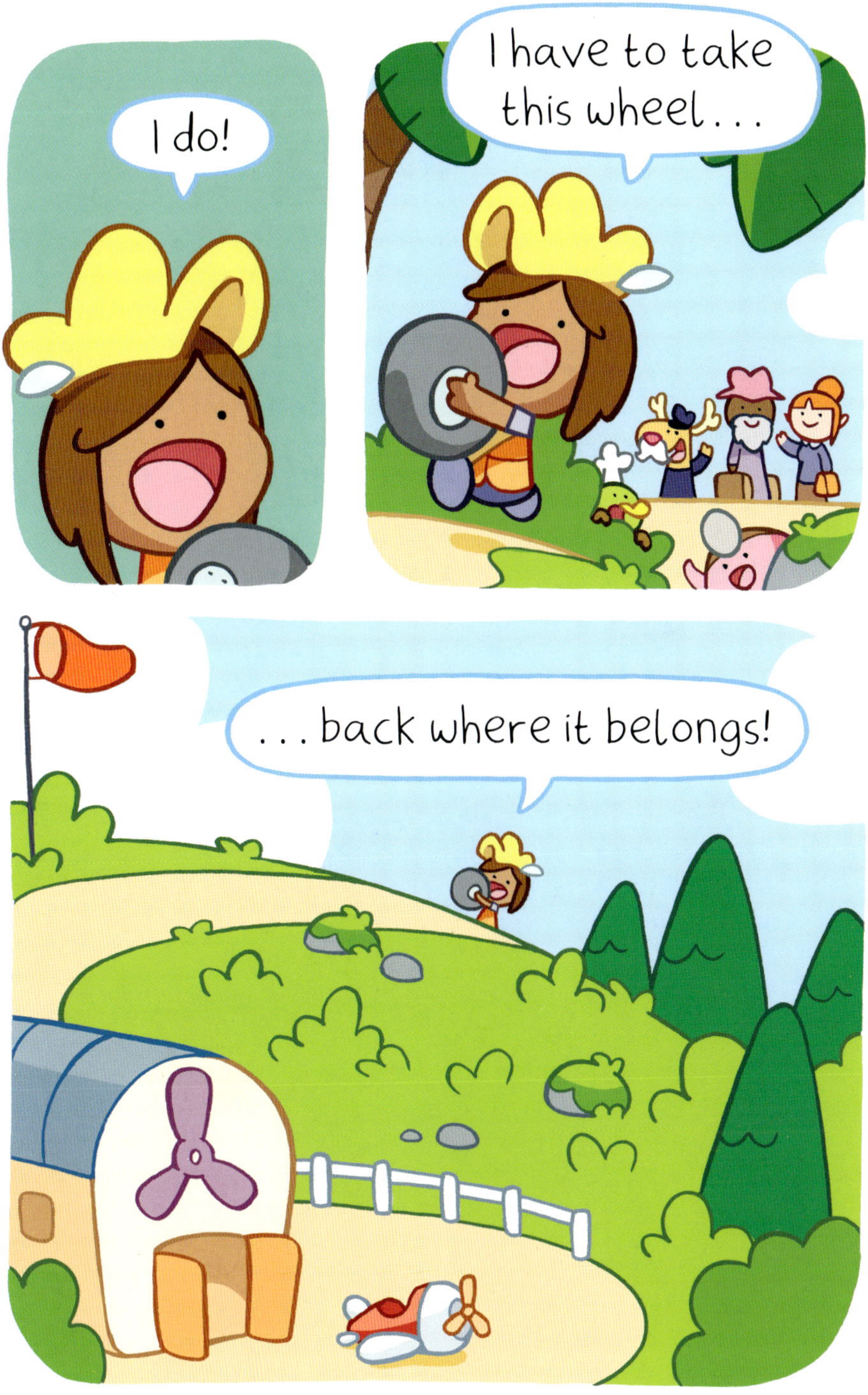
I do!
I have to take this wheel...
...back where it belongs!

Orlando's Hangar!

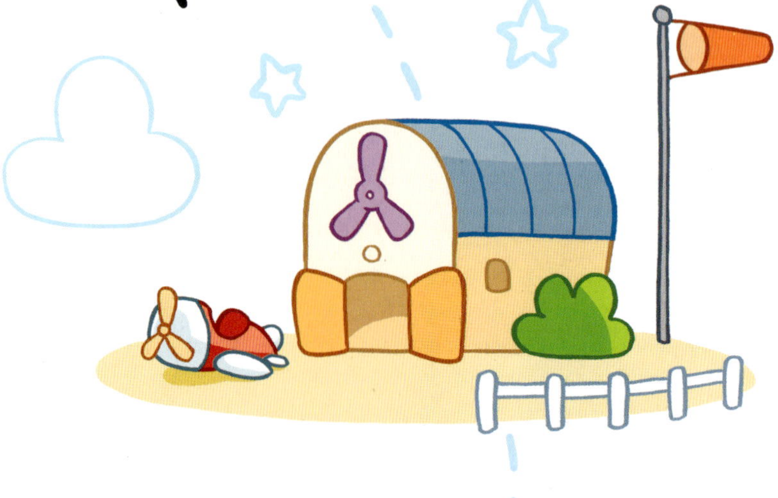

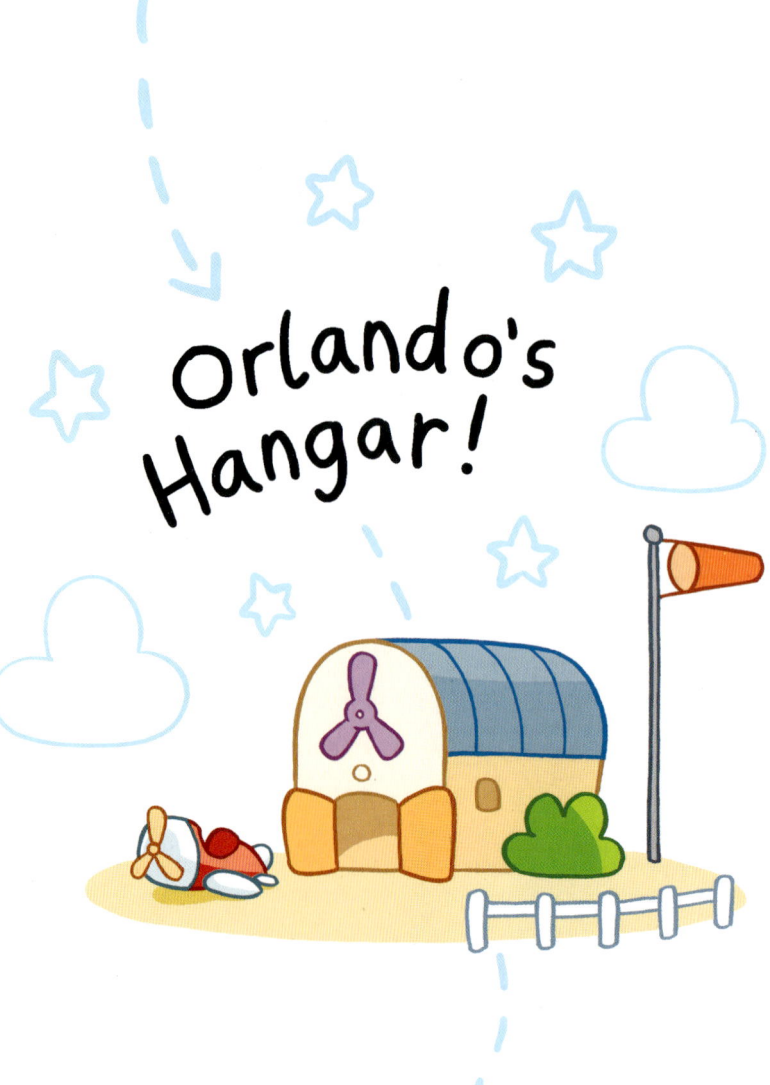

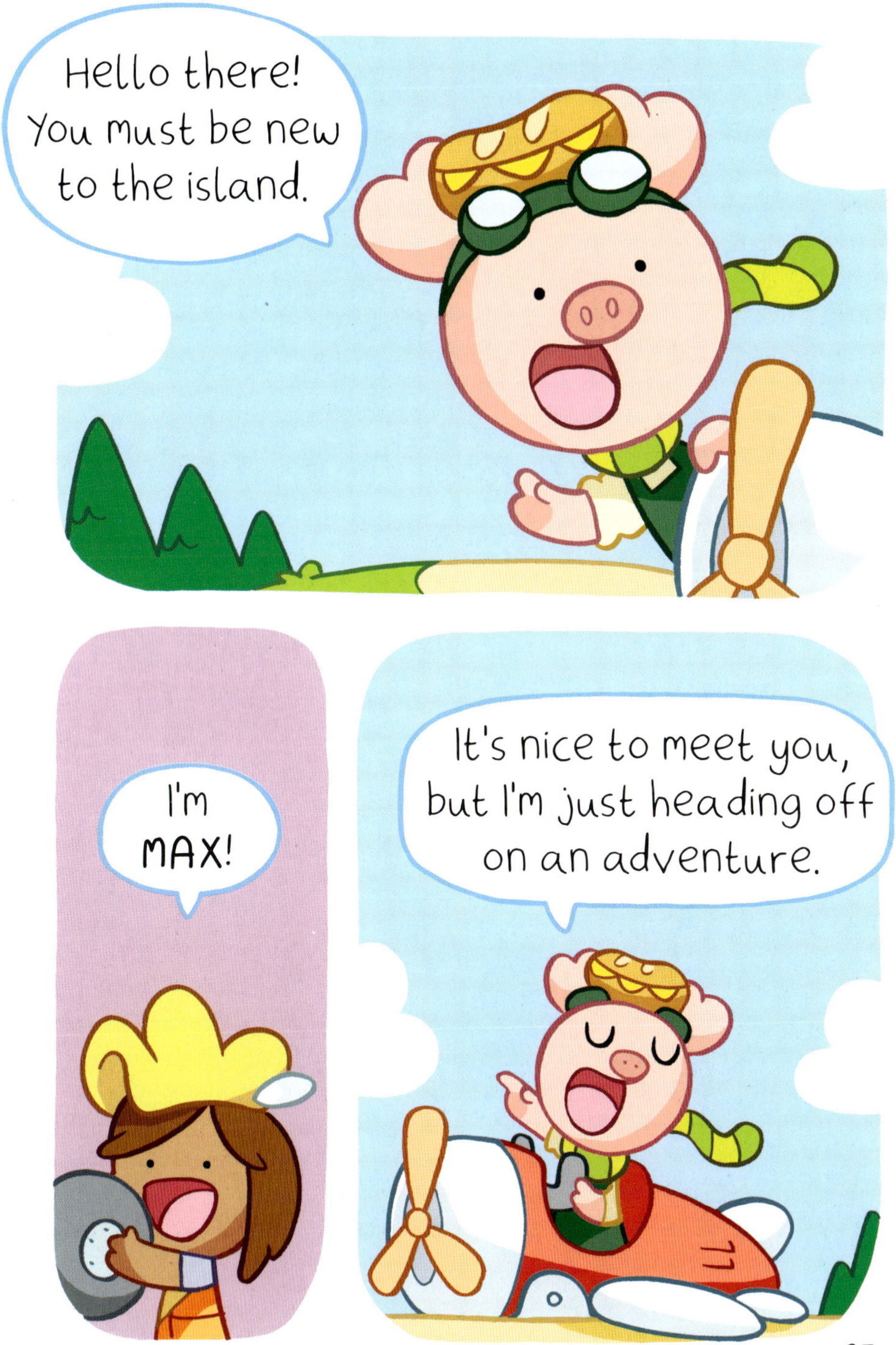
Hello there! You must be new to the island.
I'm MAX!
It's nice to meet you, but I'm just heading off on an adventure.

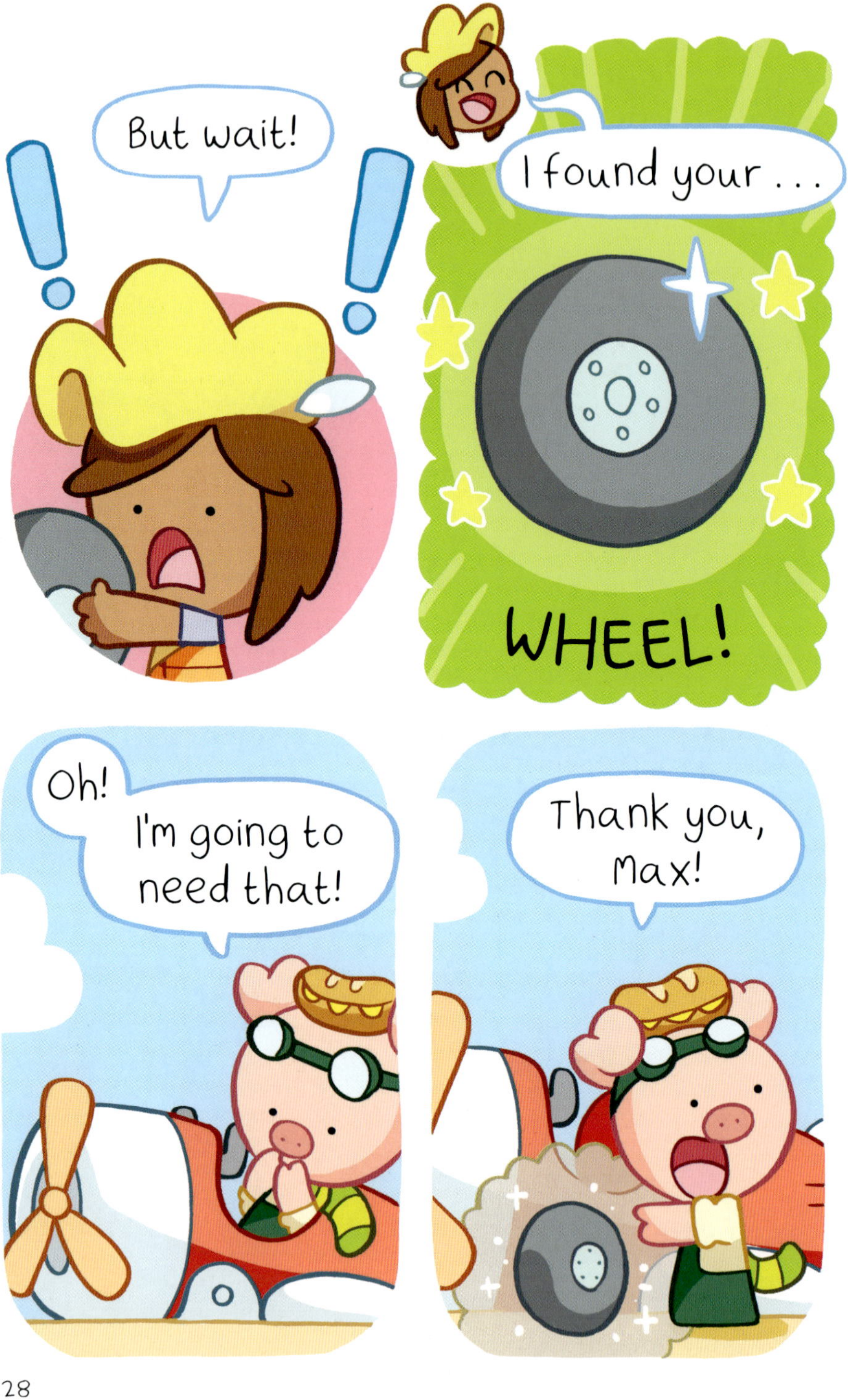

But wait!
I found your . . .
WHEEL!
Oh!
I'm going to need that!
Thank you, Max!

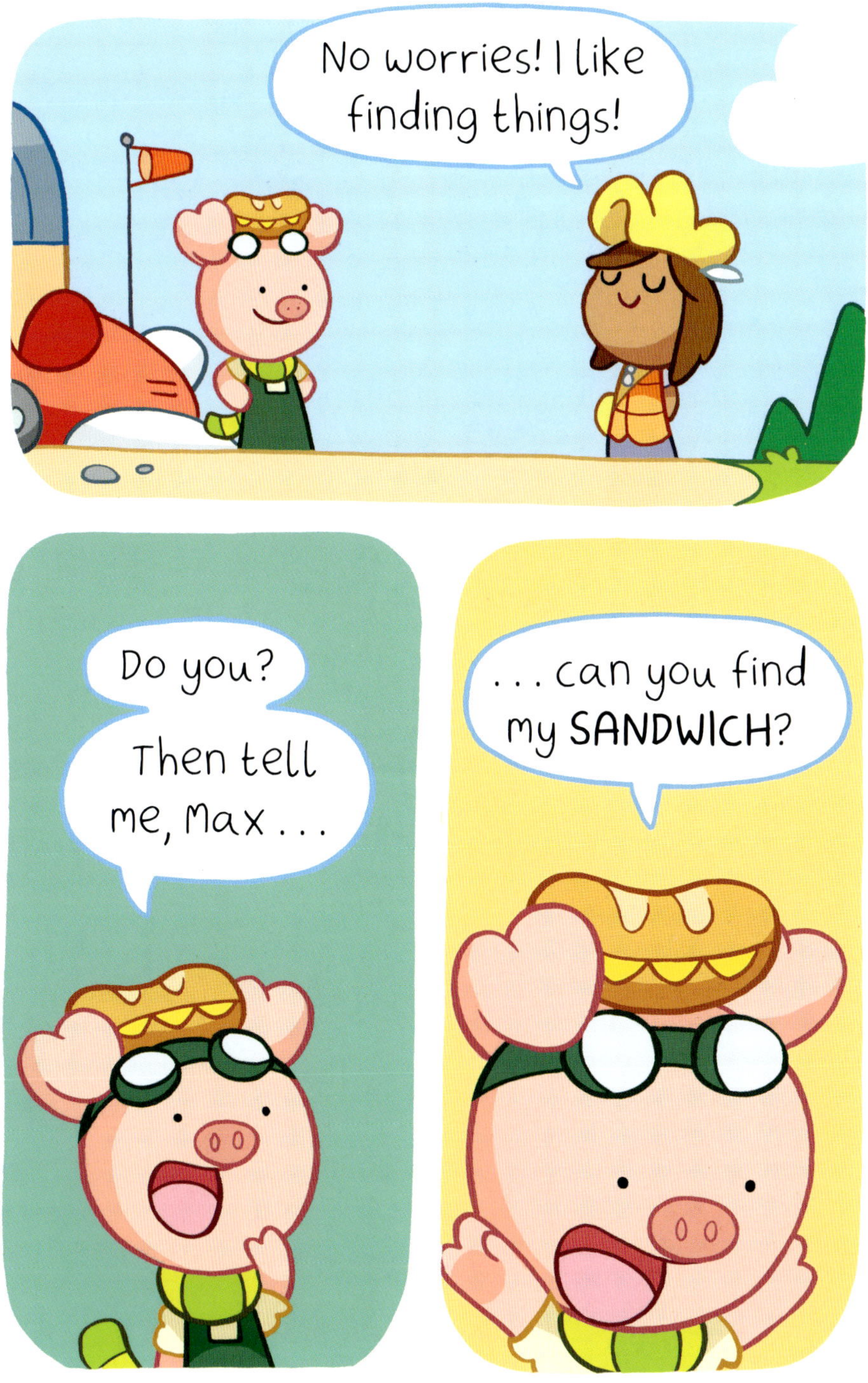
No worries! I like finding things!
Do you?
Then tell me, Max . . .
. . . can you find my SANDWICH?

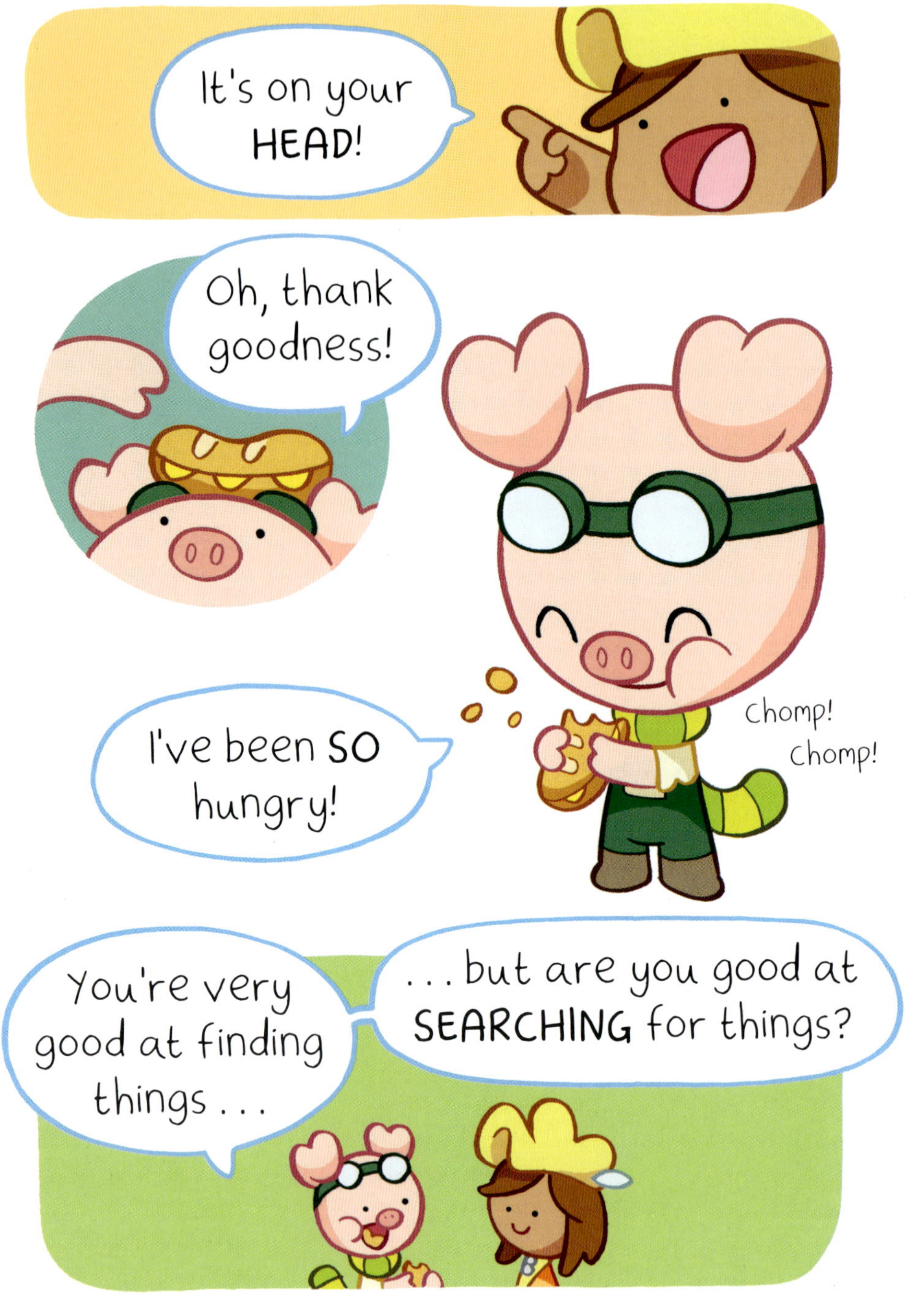
It's on your **HEAD!**
Oh, thank goodness!
I've been **SO** hungry!
Chomp!
Chomp!
You're very good at finding things . . .
. . . but are you good at **SEARCHING** for things?

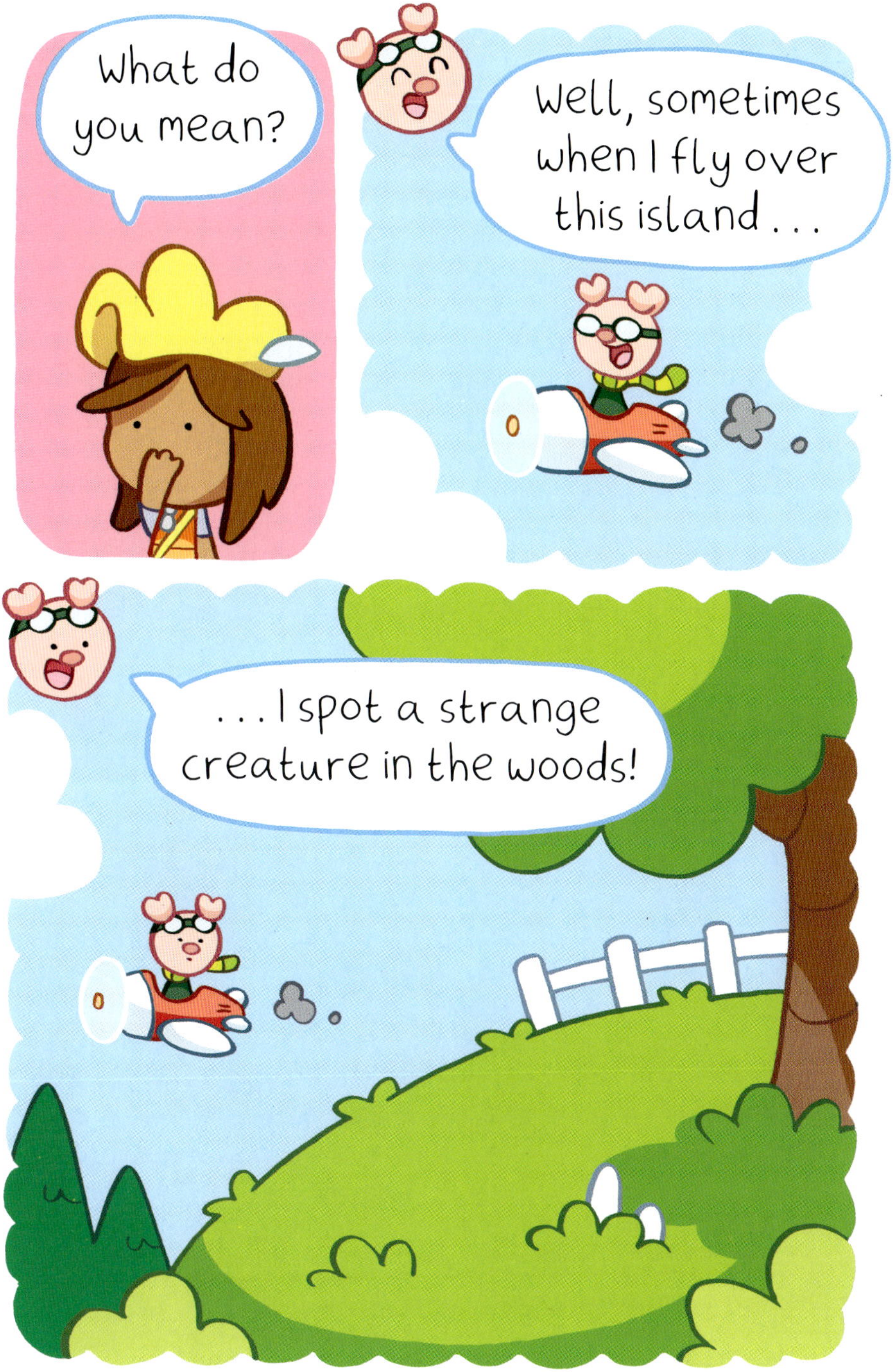
What do you mean?
Well, sometimes when I fly over this island . . .
. . . I spot a strange creature in the woods!

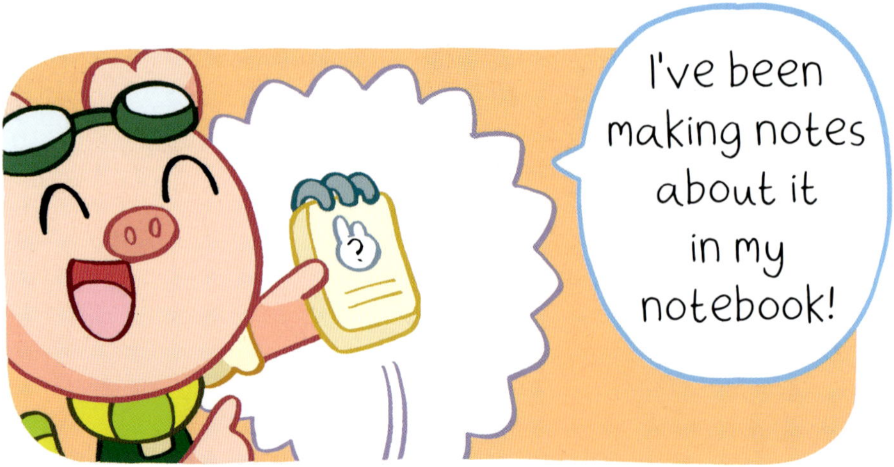
I've been making notes about it in my notebook!

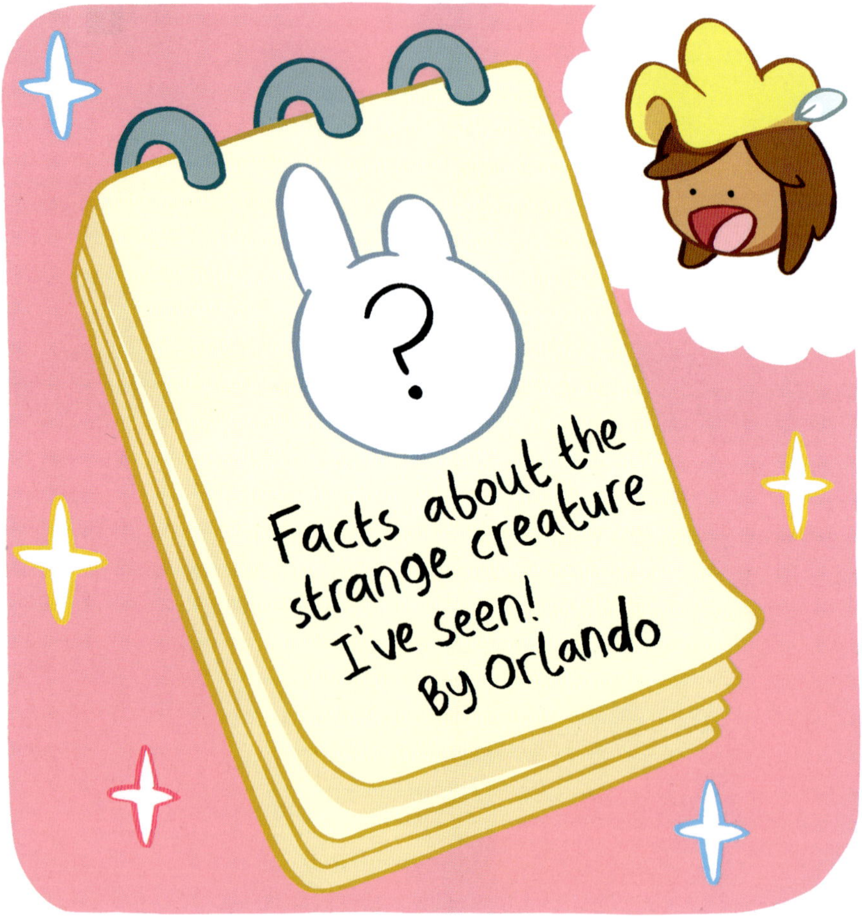
Facts about the strange creature I've seen!
By Orlando

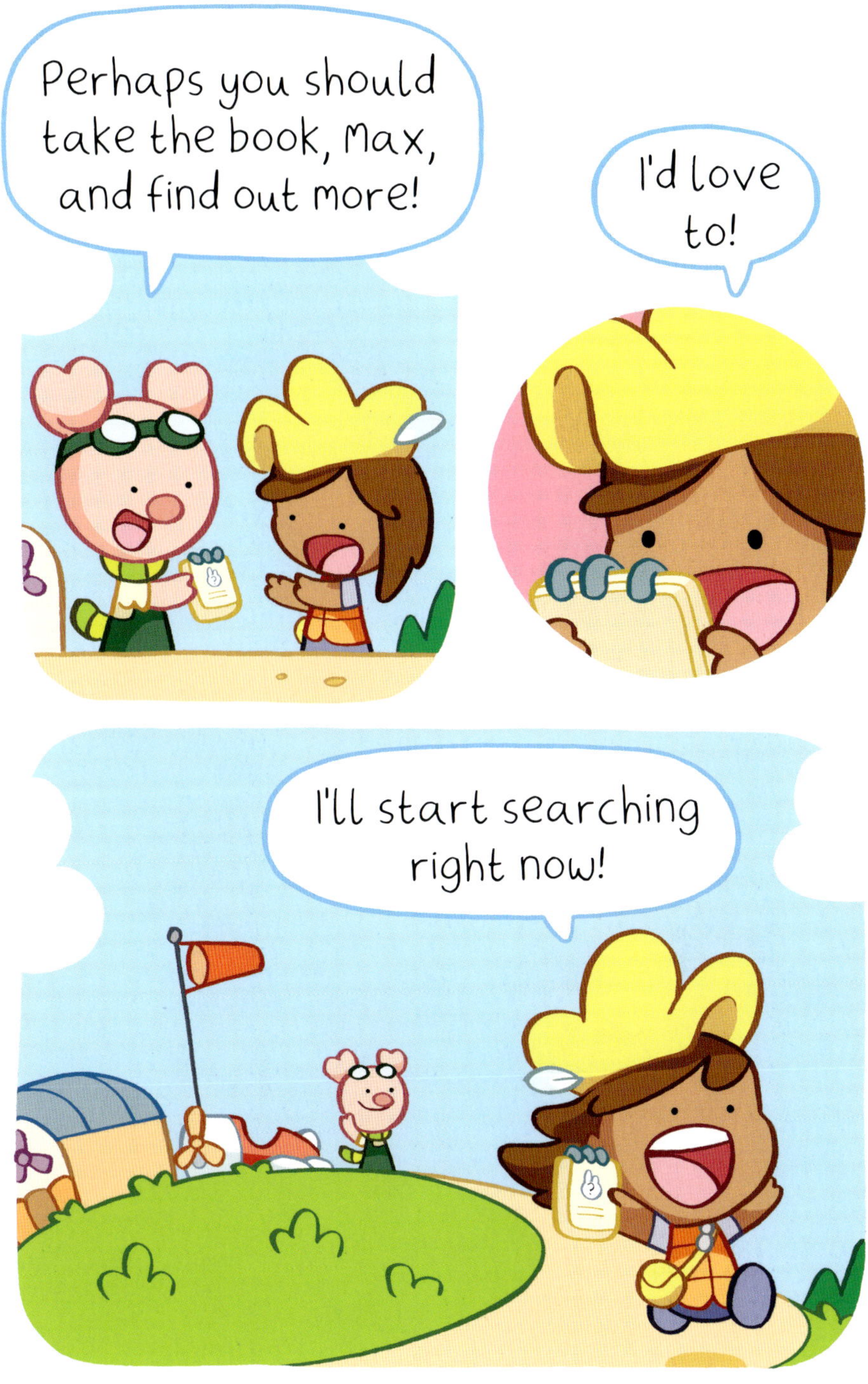
Perhaps you should take the book, Max, and find out more!
I'd love to!
I'll start searching right now!

The Woods!

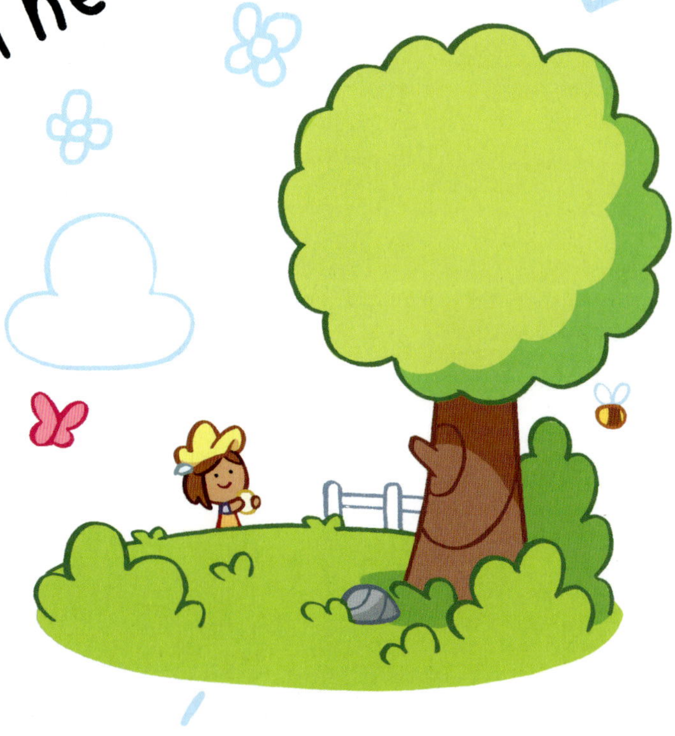

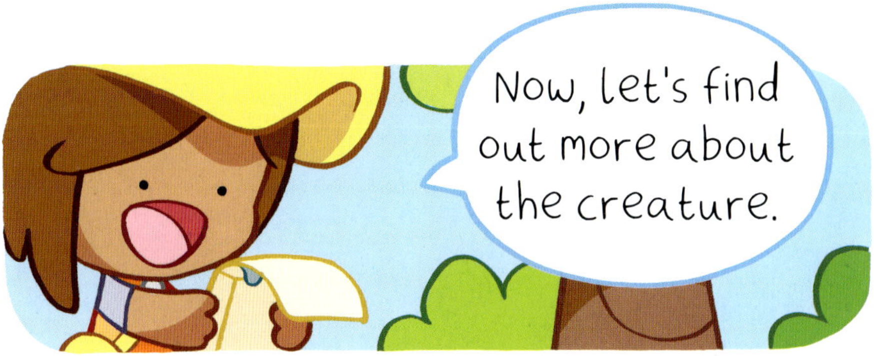
Now, let's find out more about the creature.

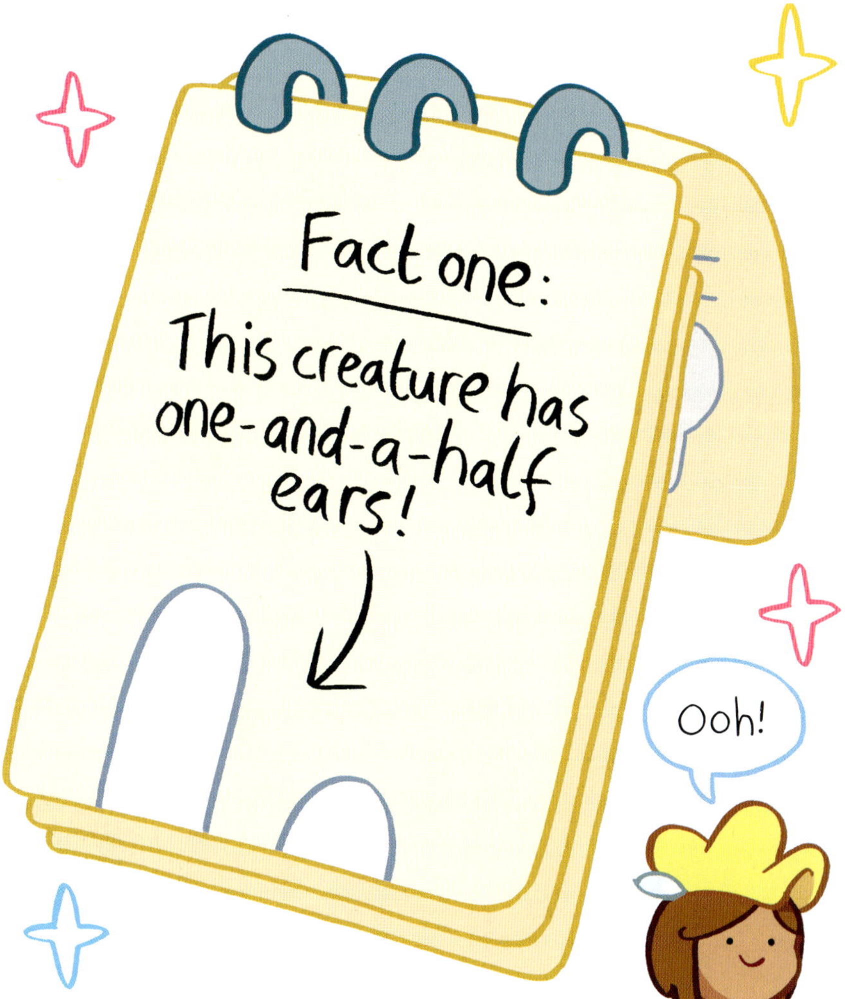
Fact one:
This creature has one-and-a-half ears!
Ooh!

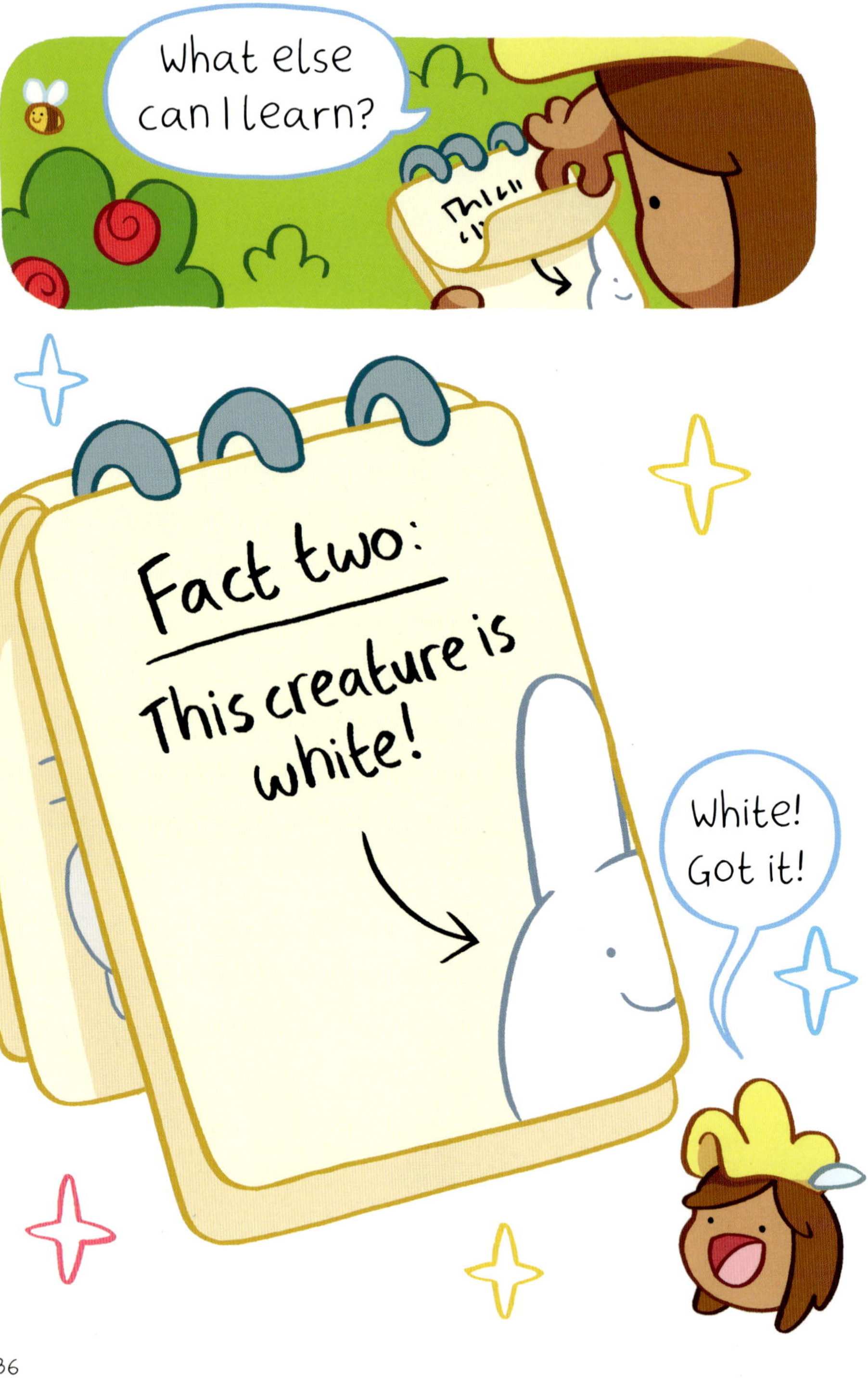
What else can I learn?
Fact two:
This creature is white!
White! Got it!

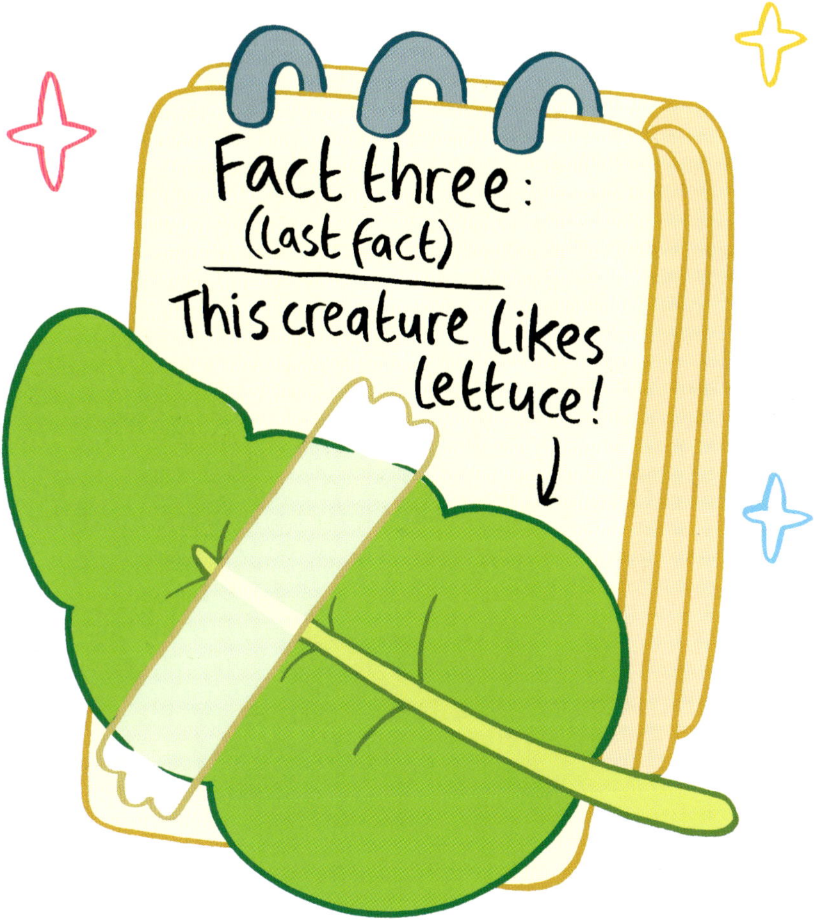

Fact three:
(last fact)
This creature likes lettuce!

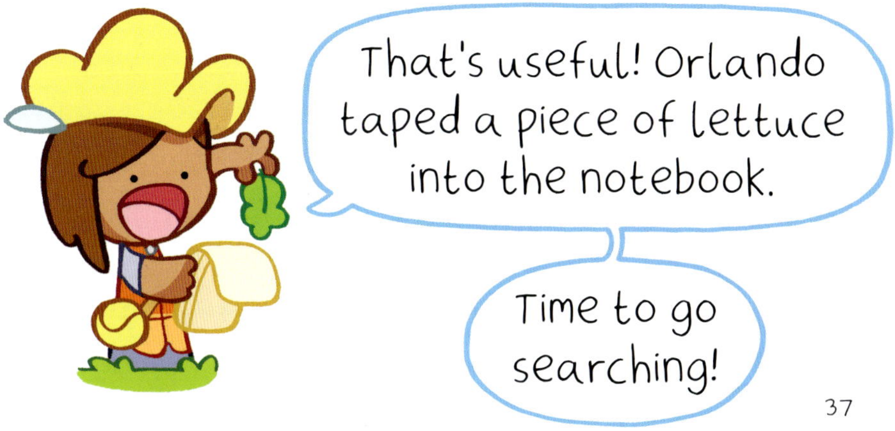

That's useful! Orlando taped a piece of lettuce into the notebook.
Time to go searching!

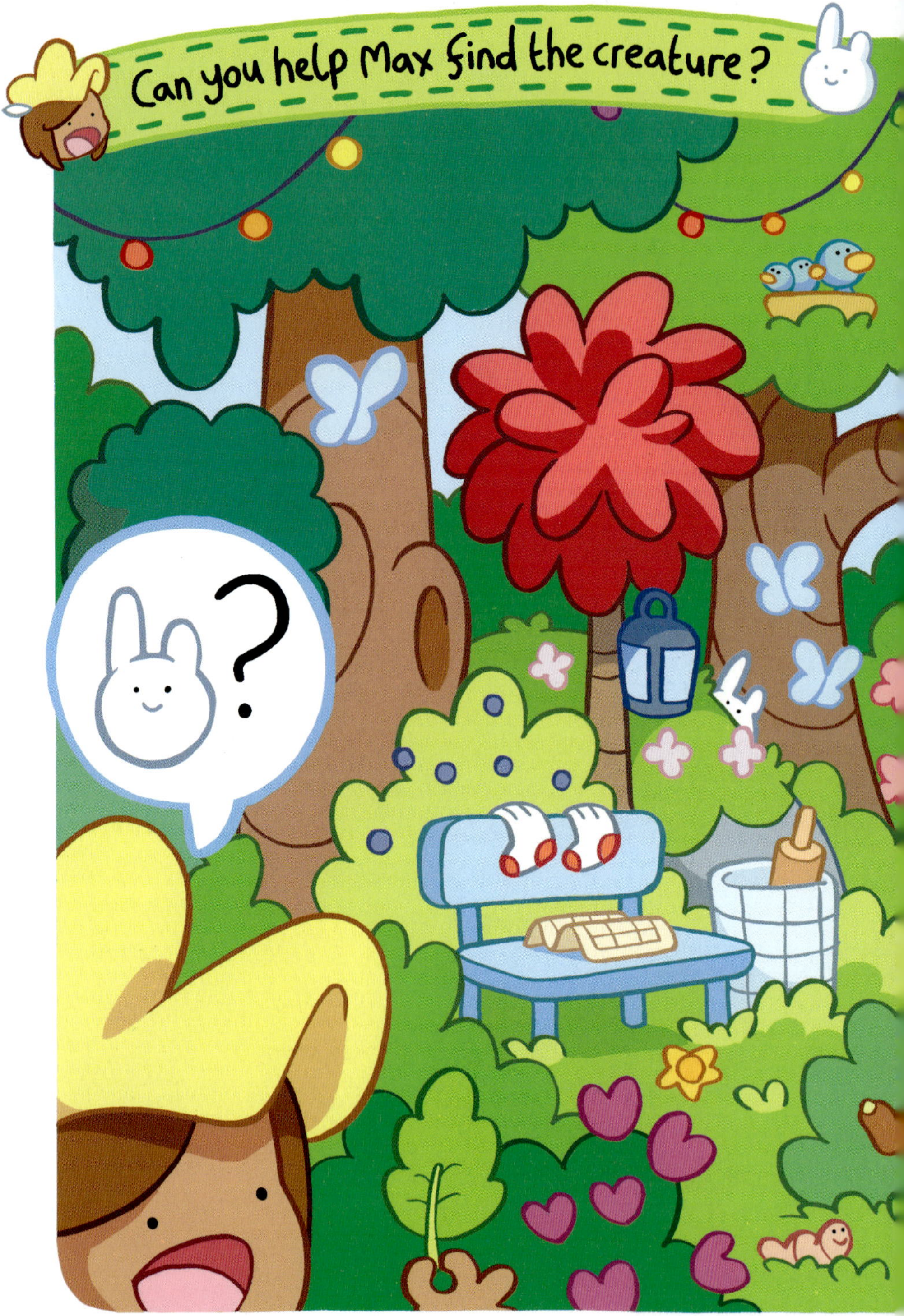
Can you help Max find the creature?
?

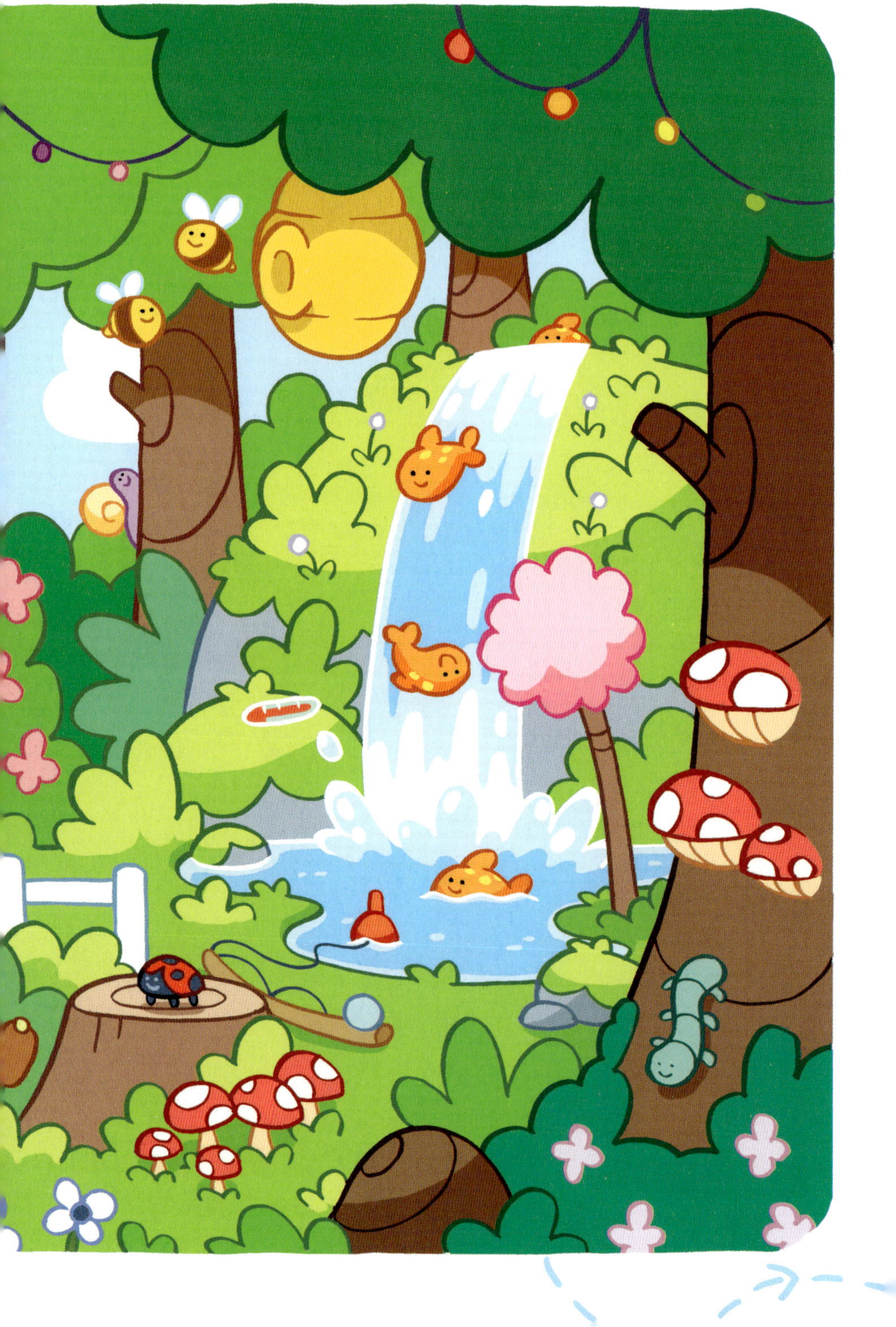

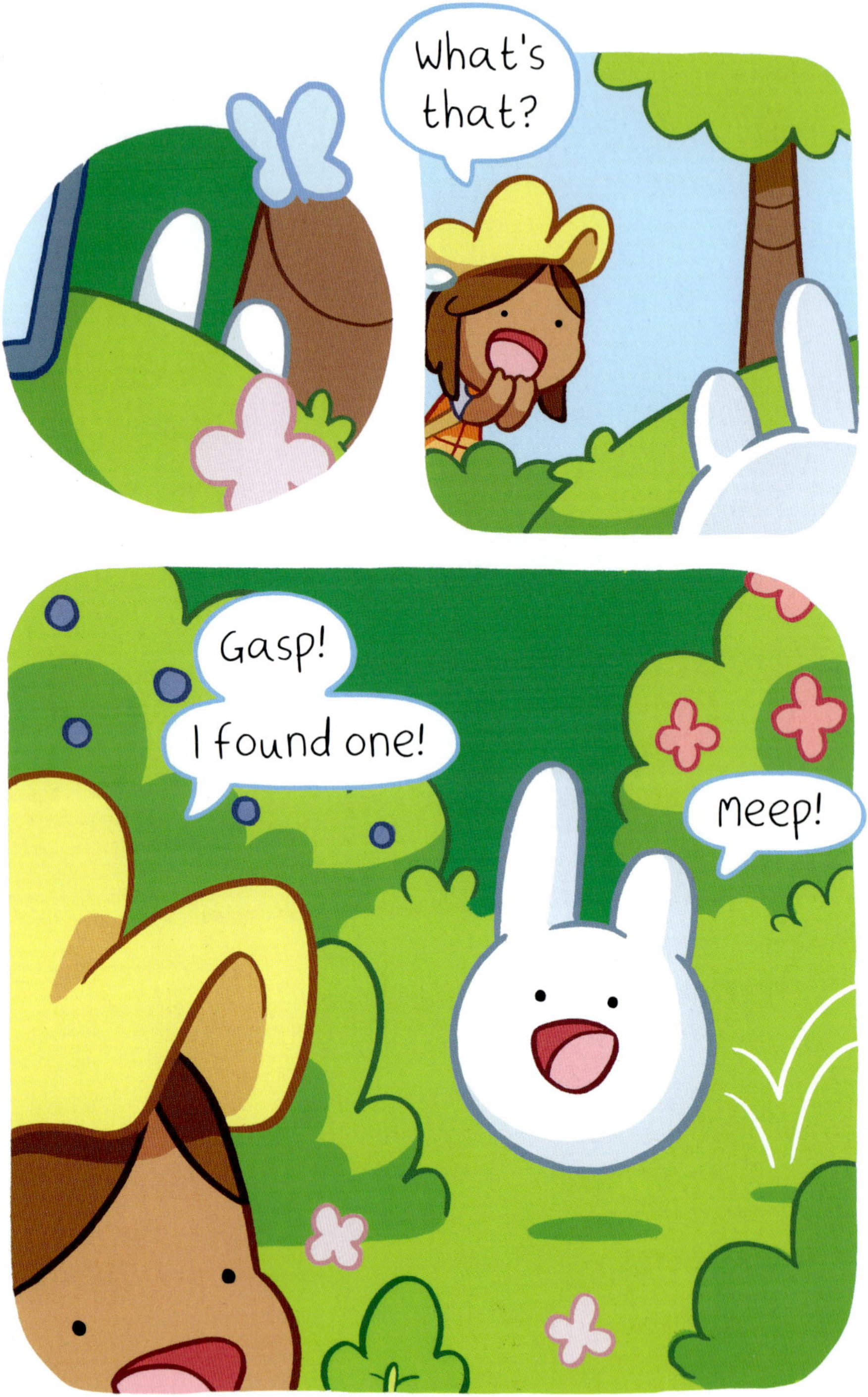
What's that?
Gasp!
I found one!
Meep!

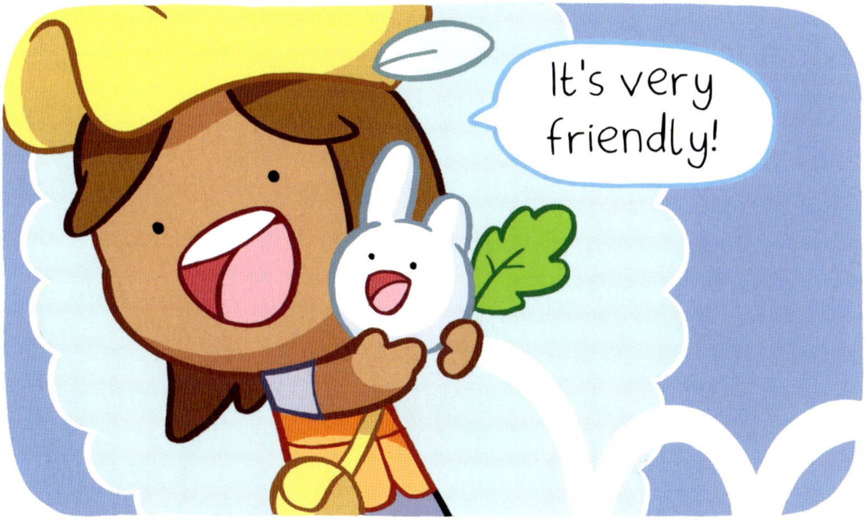
It's very friendly!

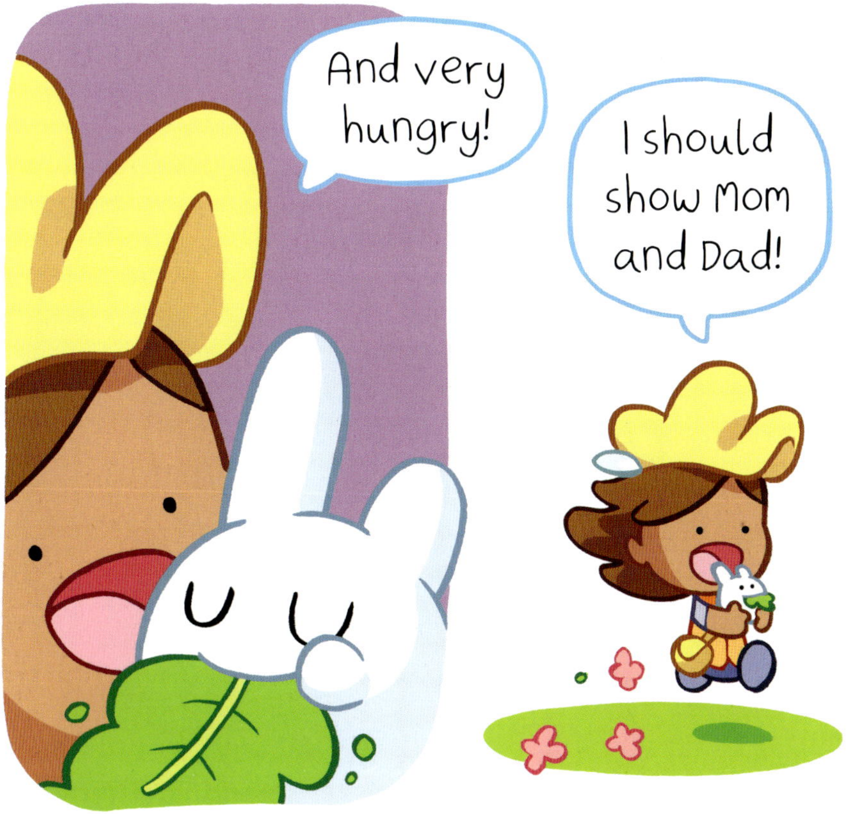
And very hungry!
I should show Mom and Dad!

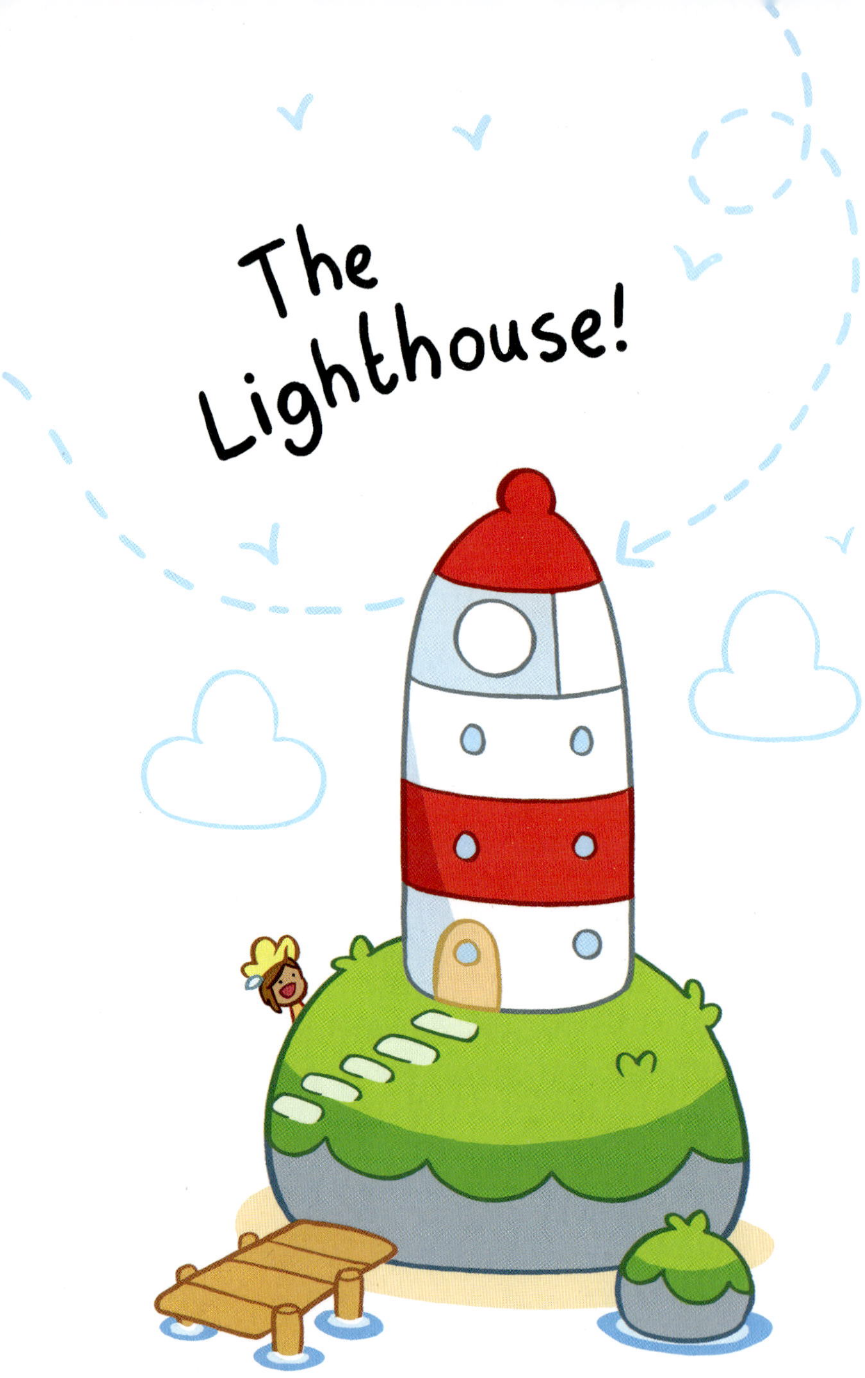
The Lighthouse!

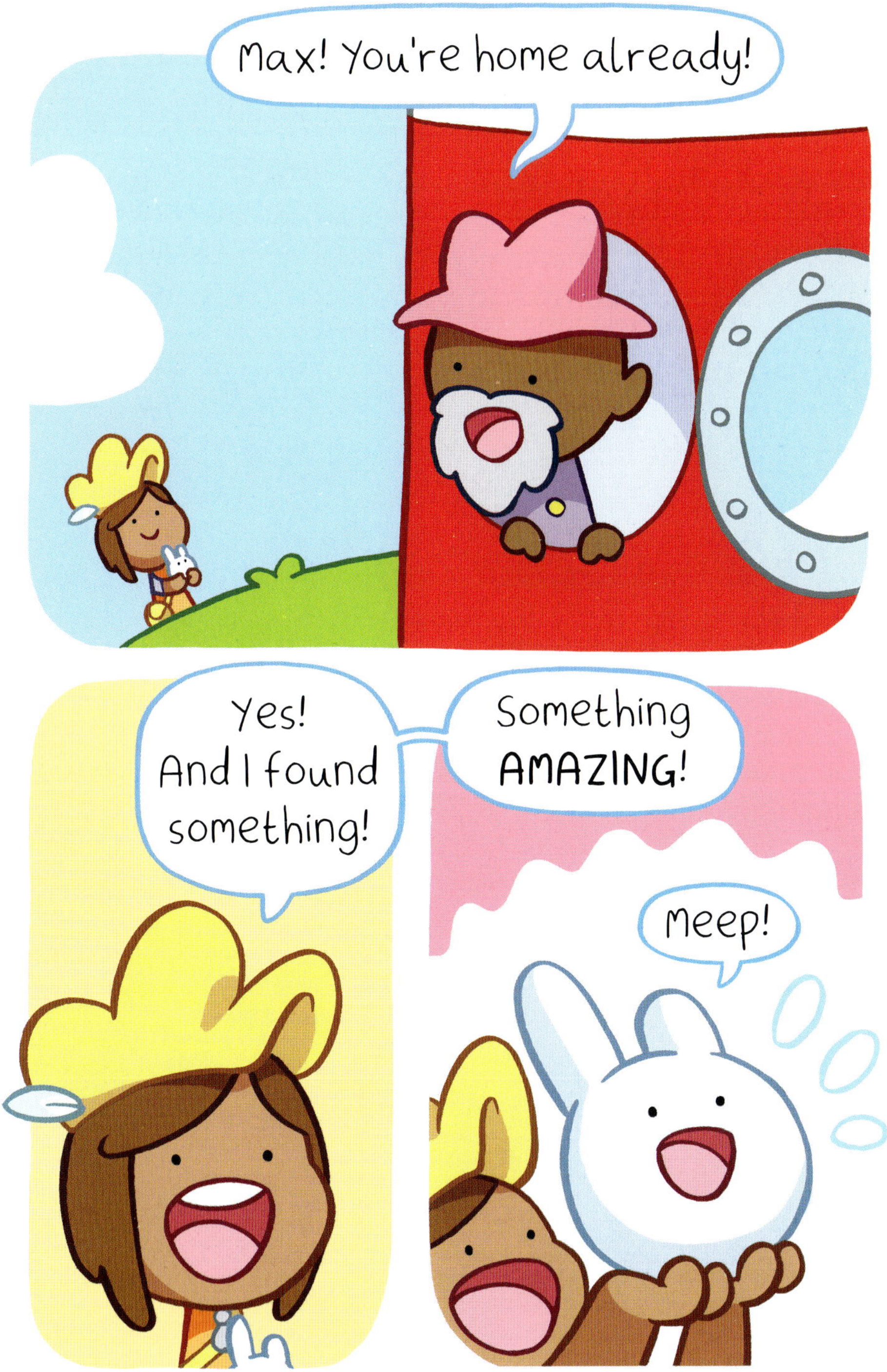

Max! You're home already!
Yes! And I found something!
Something AMAZING!
Meep!

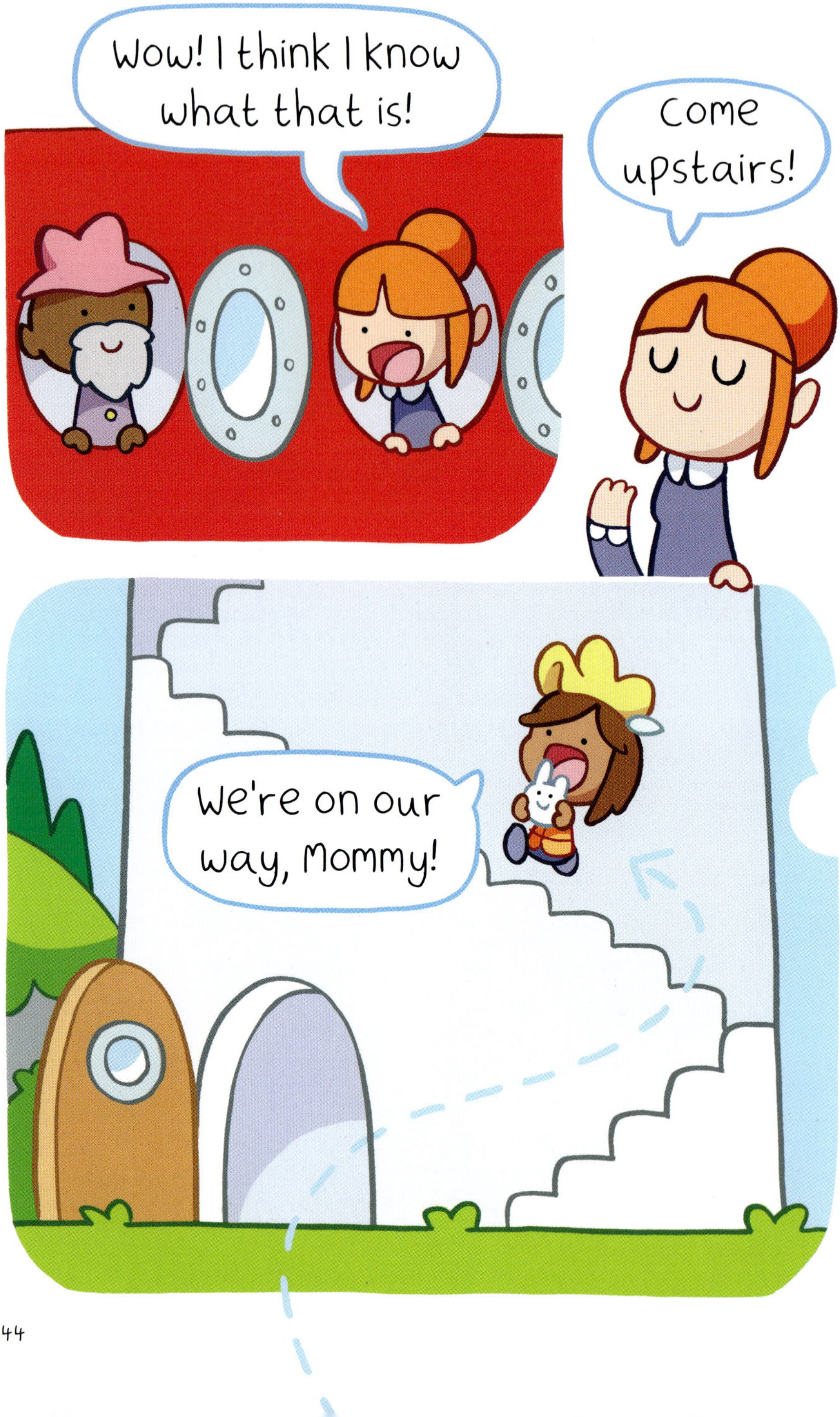
Wow! I think I know what that is!
Come upstairs!
We're on our way, Mommy!

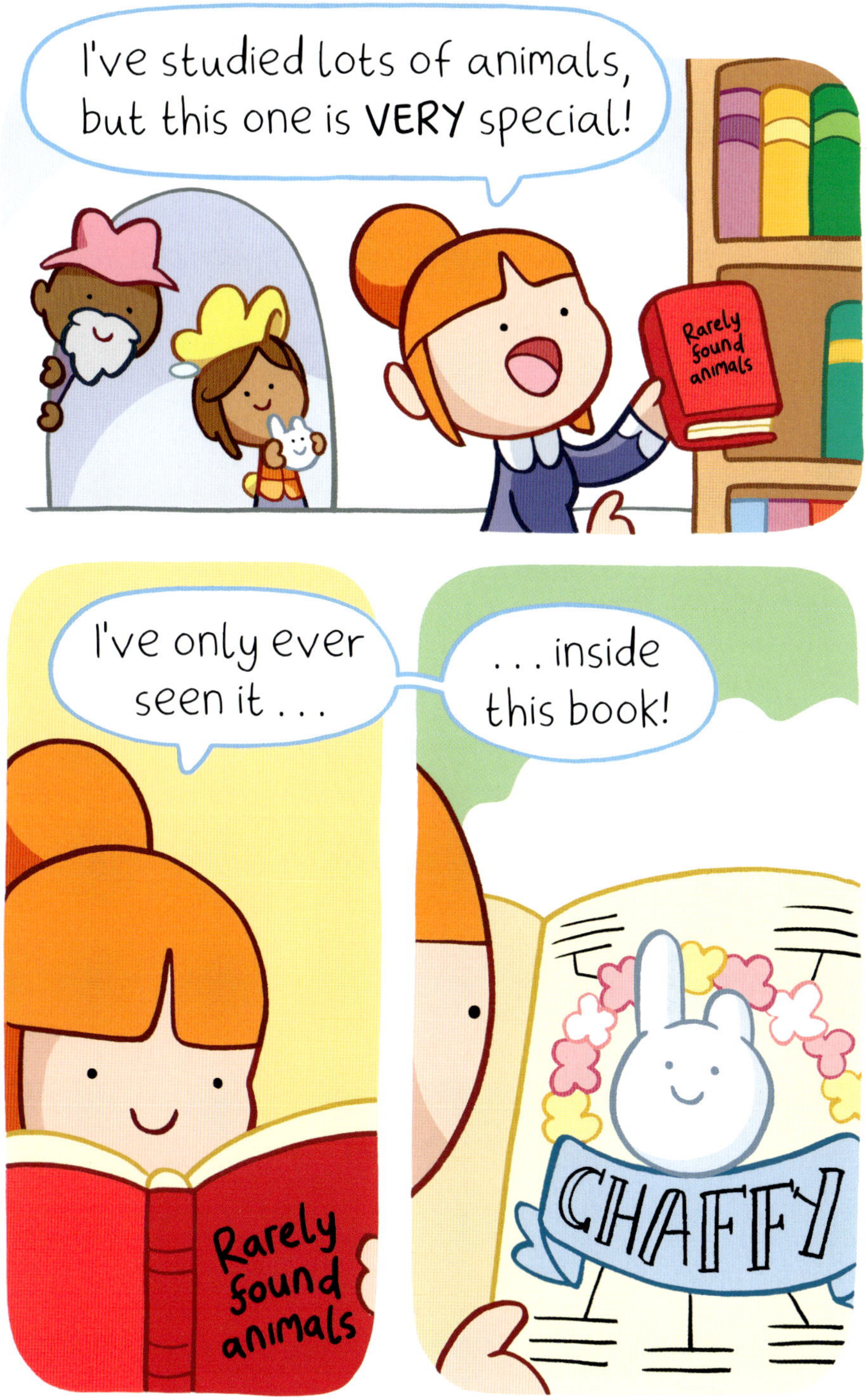
I've studied lots of animals, but this one is **VERY** special!
Rarely found animals
I've only ever seen it . . .
. . . inside this book!
Rarely found animals
CHAFFY

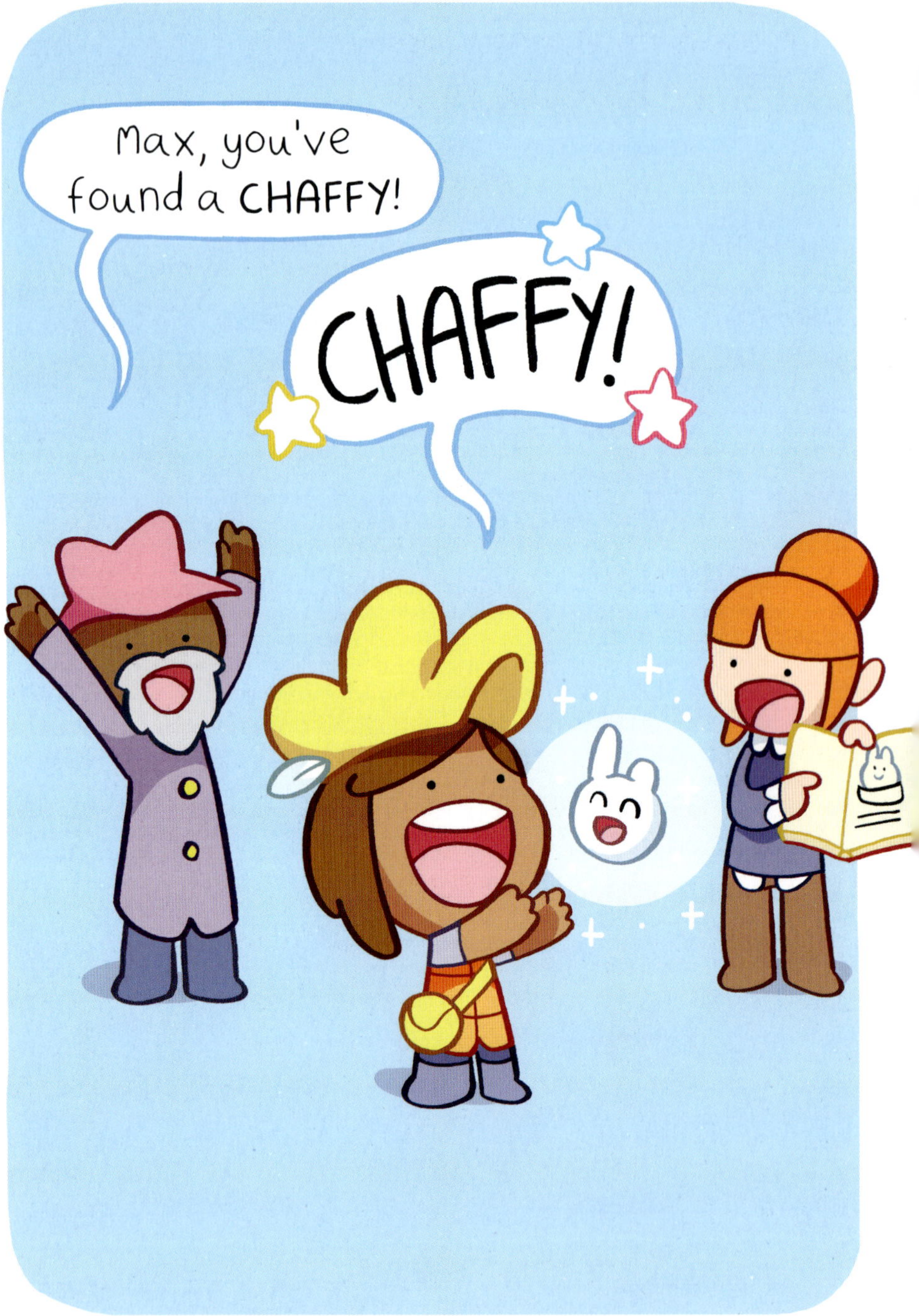
Max, you've found a CHAFFY!
CHAFFY!

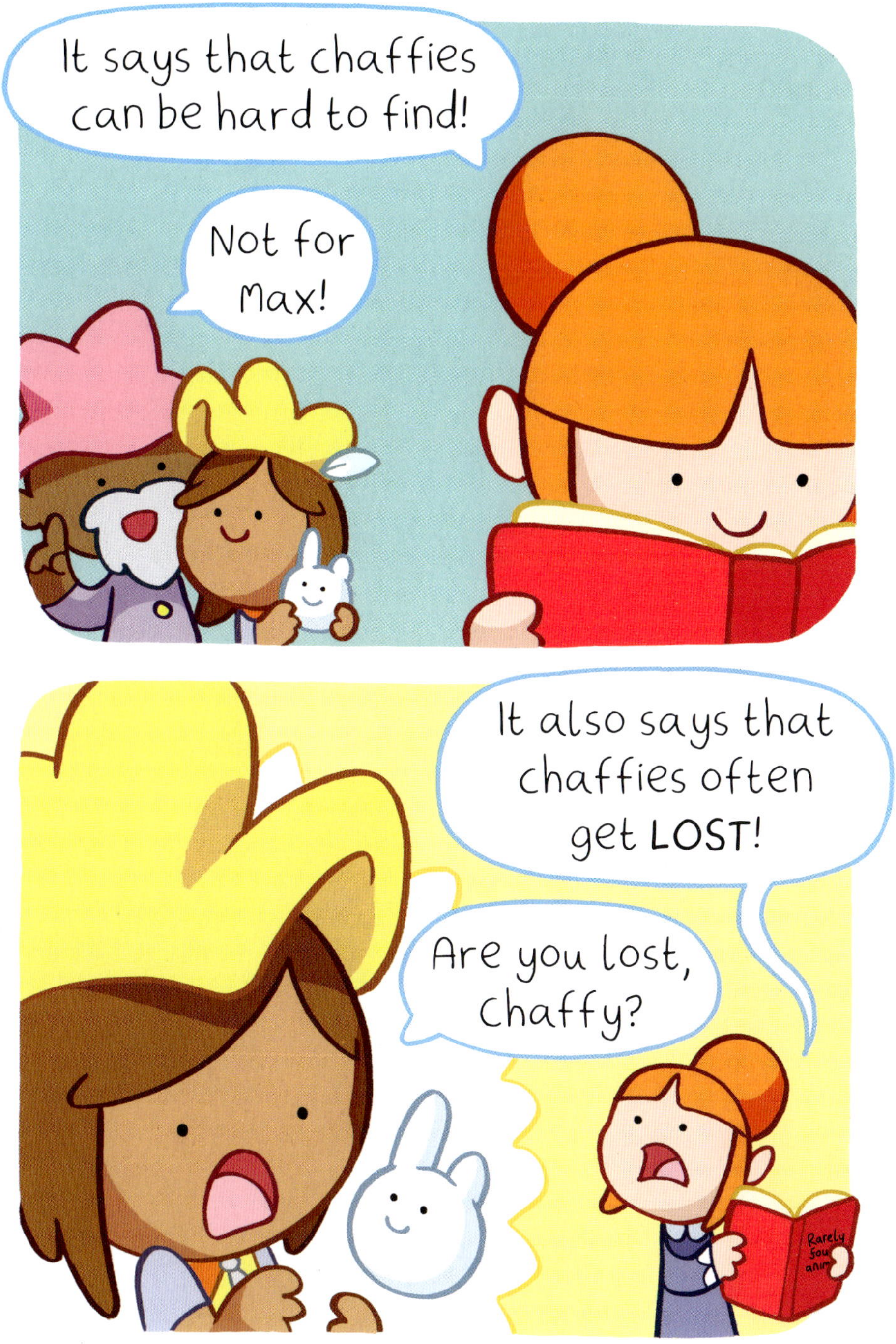
It says that chaffies can be hard to find!
Not for Max!
It also says that chaffies often get **LOST**!
Are you lost, Chaffy?

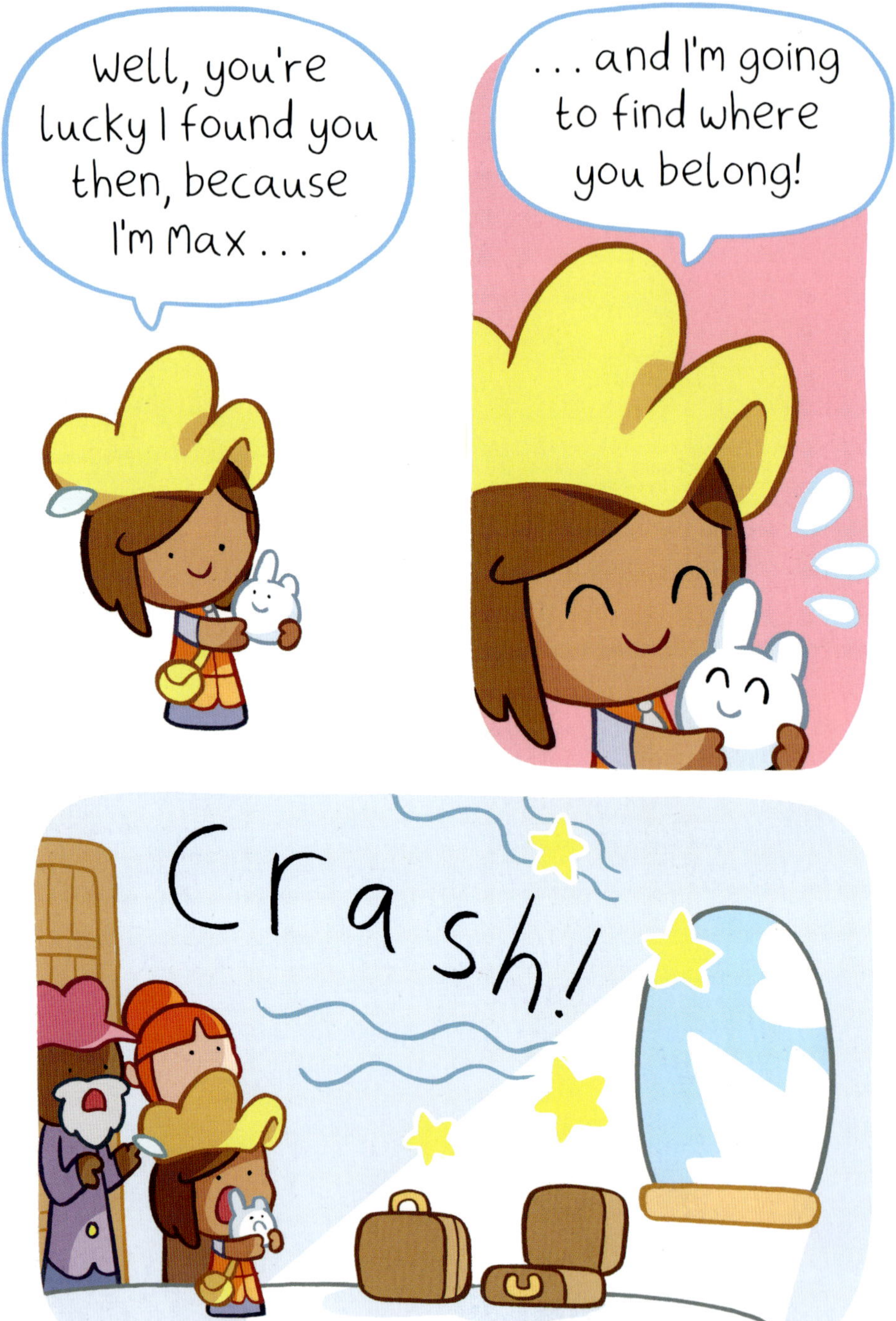
Well, you're lucky I found you then, because I'm Max . . .
. . . and I'm going to find where you belong!
Crash!

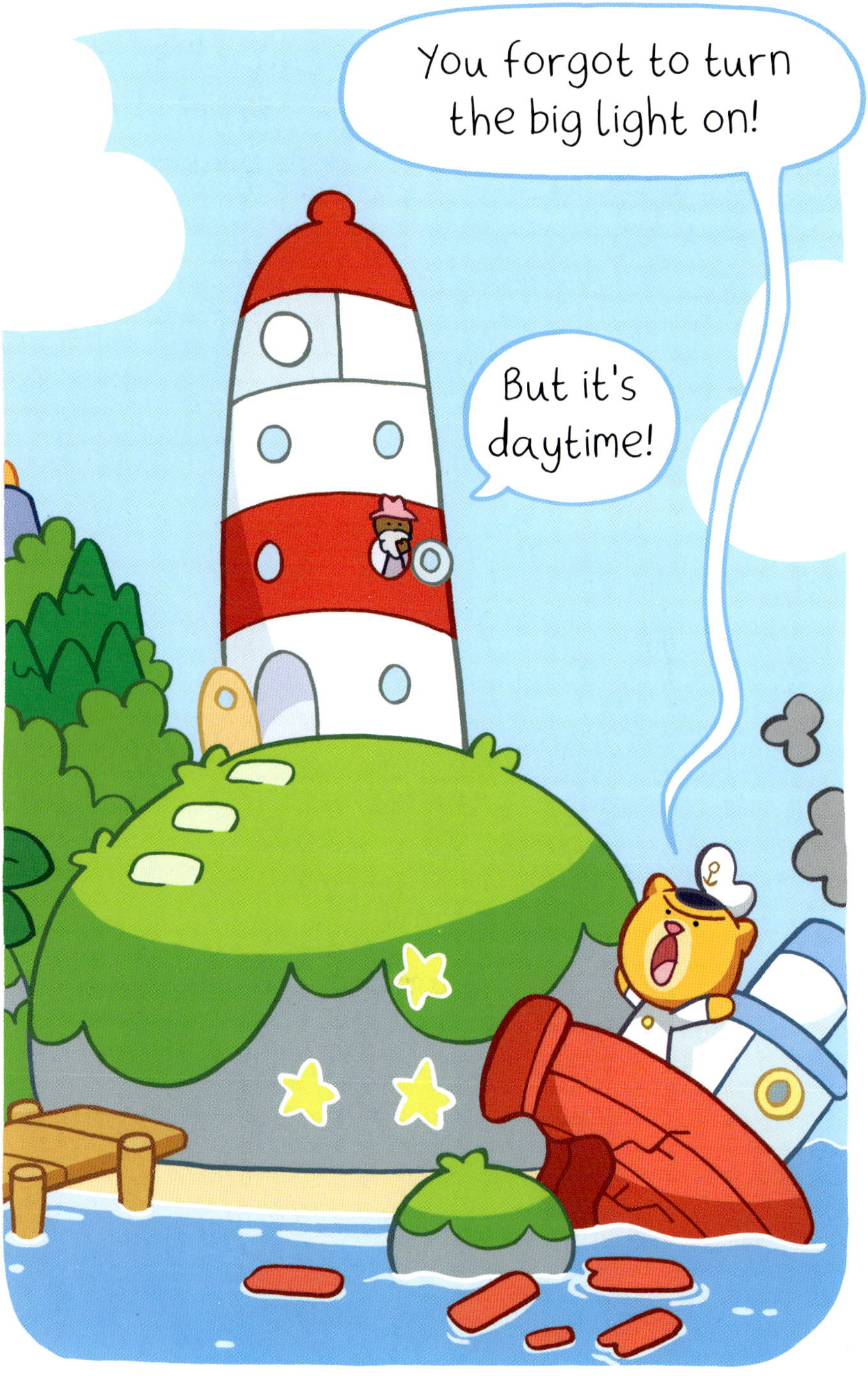
You forgot to turn the big light on!
But it's daytime!

Foghorn's Boat!

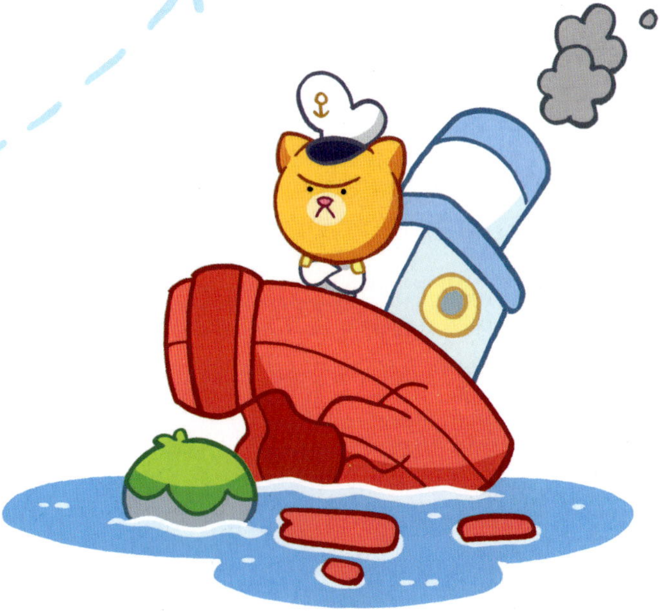

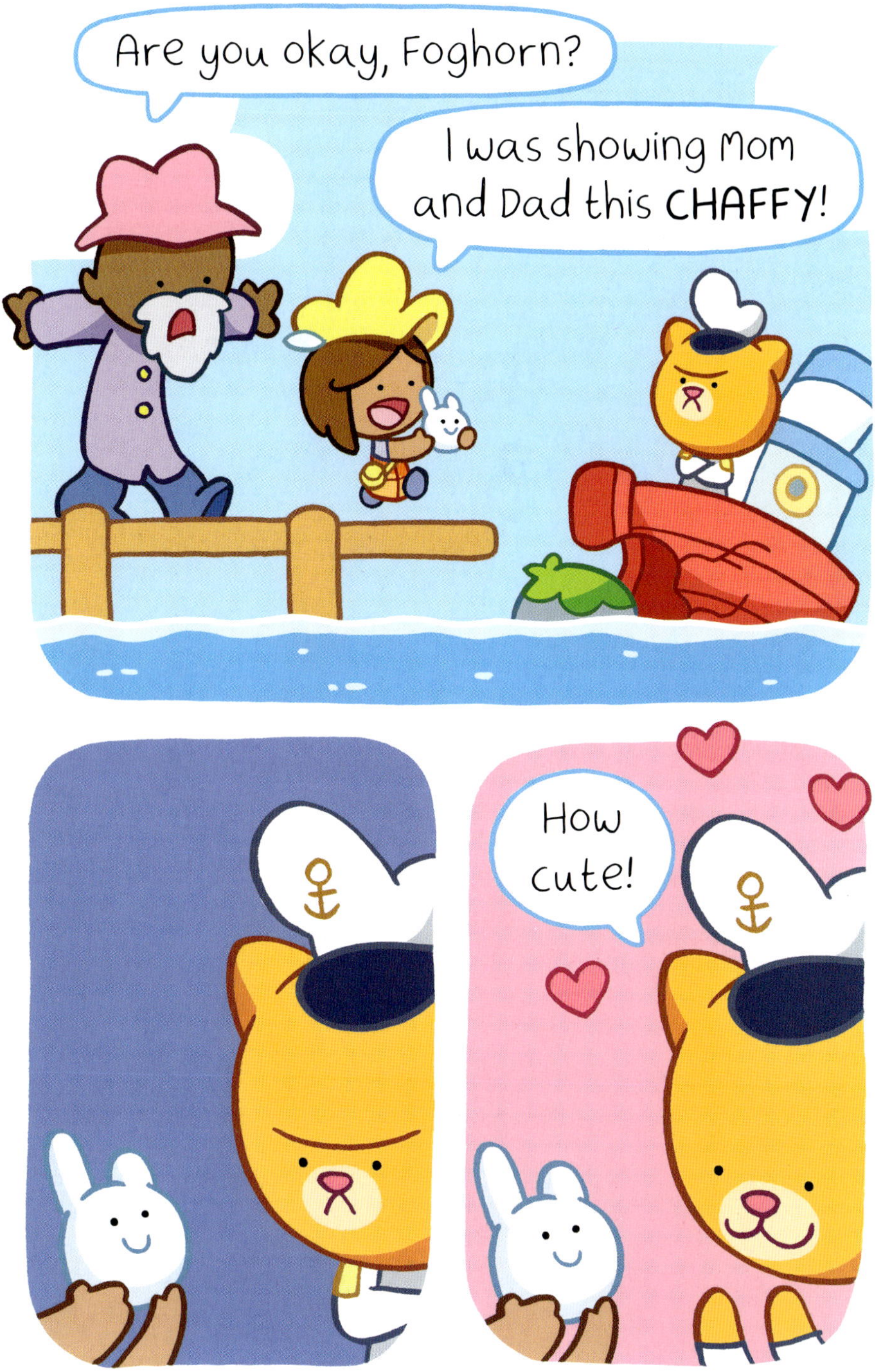
Are you okay, Foghorn?
I was showing Mom and Dad this CHAFFY!
How cute!

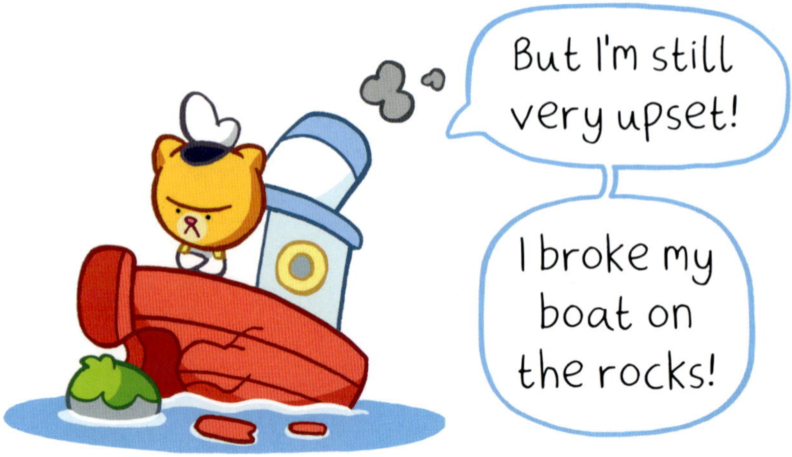
But I'm still very upset!
I broke my boat on the rocks!

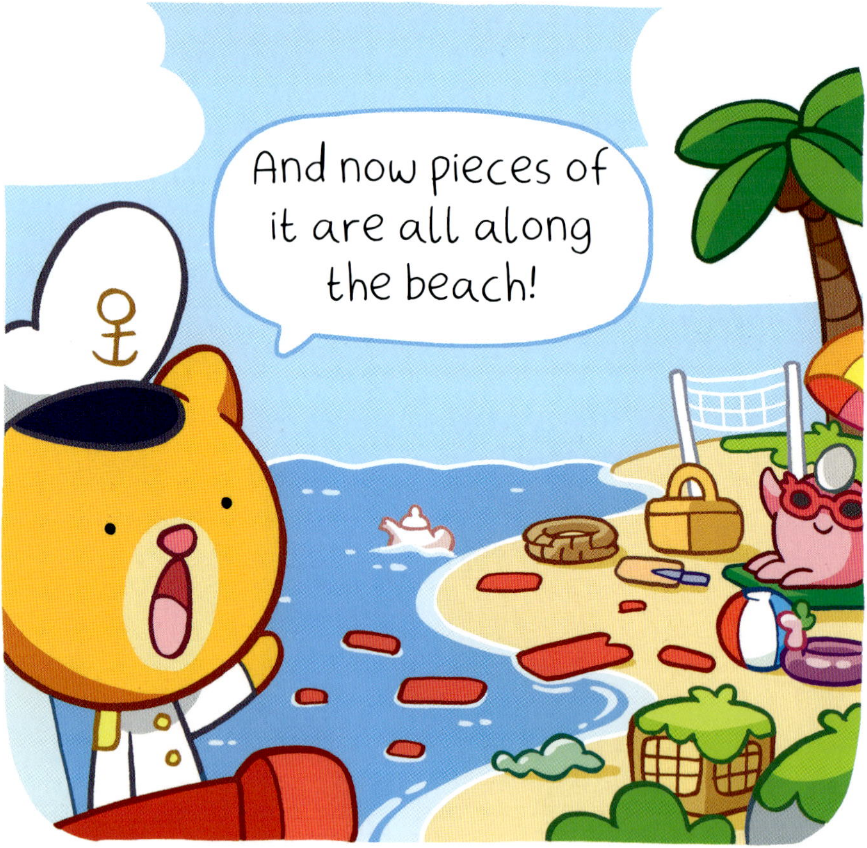
And now pieces of it are all along the beach!

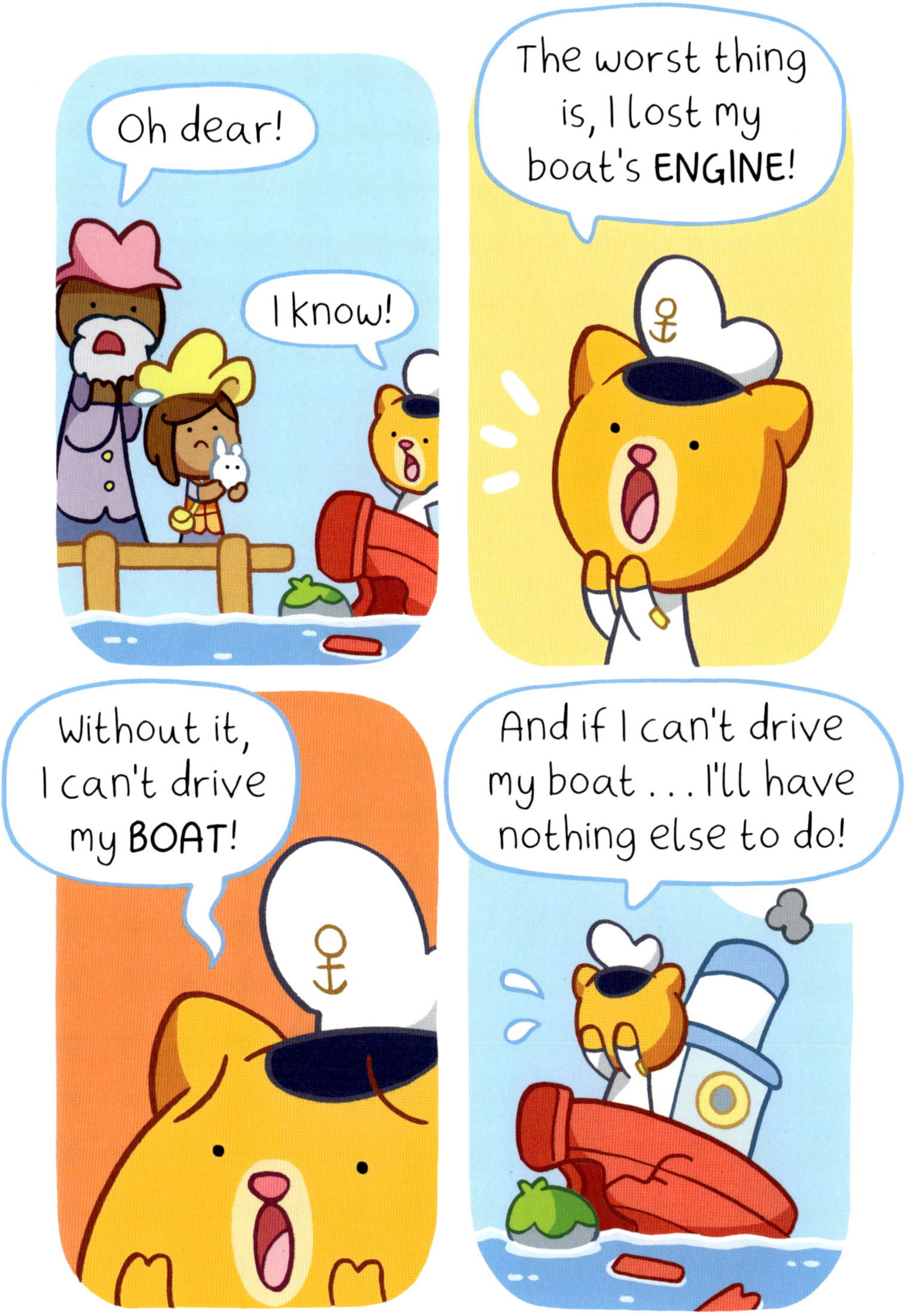
Oh dear!
I know!
The worst thing is, I lost my boat's ENGINE!
Without it, I can't drive my BOAT!
And if I can't drive my boat . . . I'll have nothing else to do!

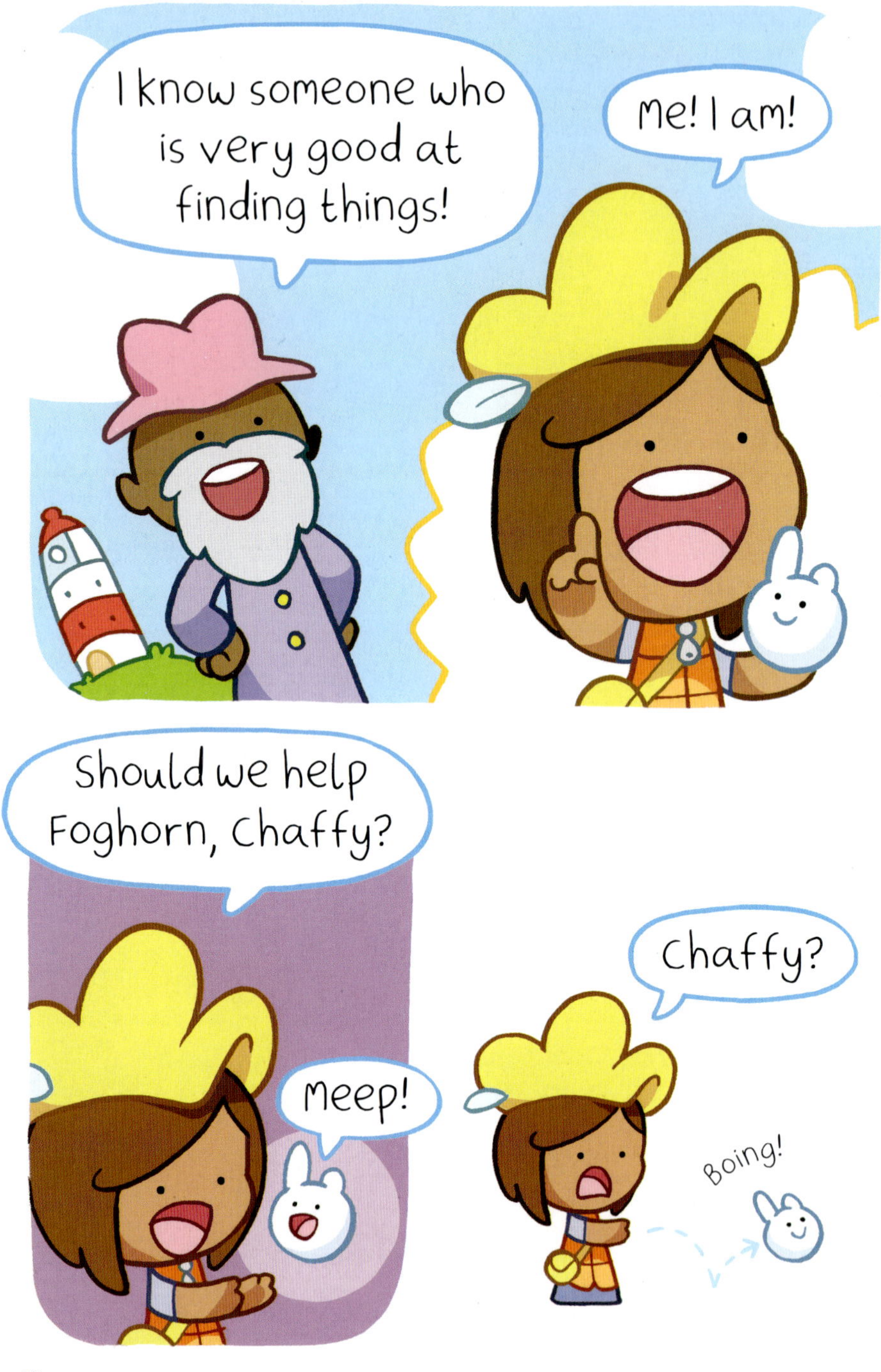
I know someone who is very good at finding things!
Me! I am!
Should we help Foghorn, Chaffy?
Meep!
Chaffy?
Boing!

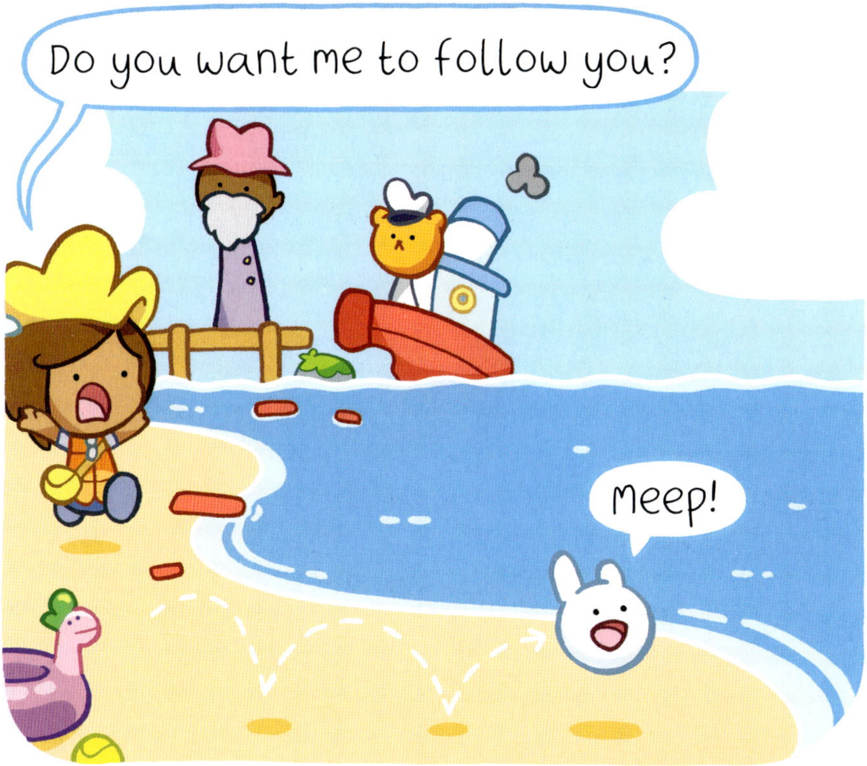
Do you want me to follow you?
Meep!

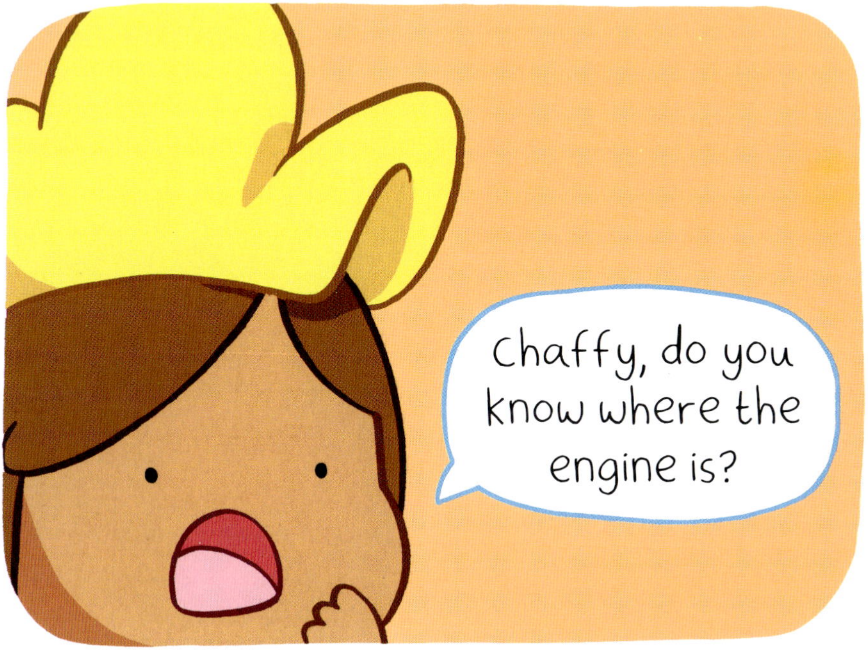
Chaffy, do you know where the engine is?

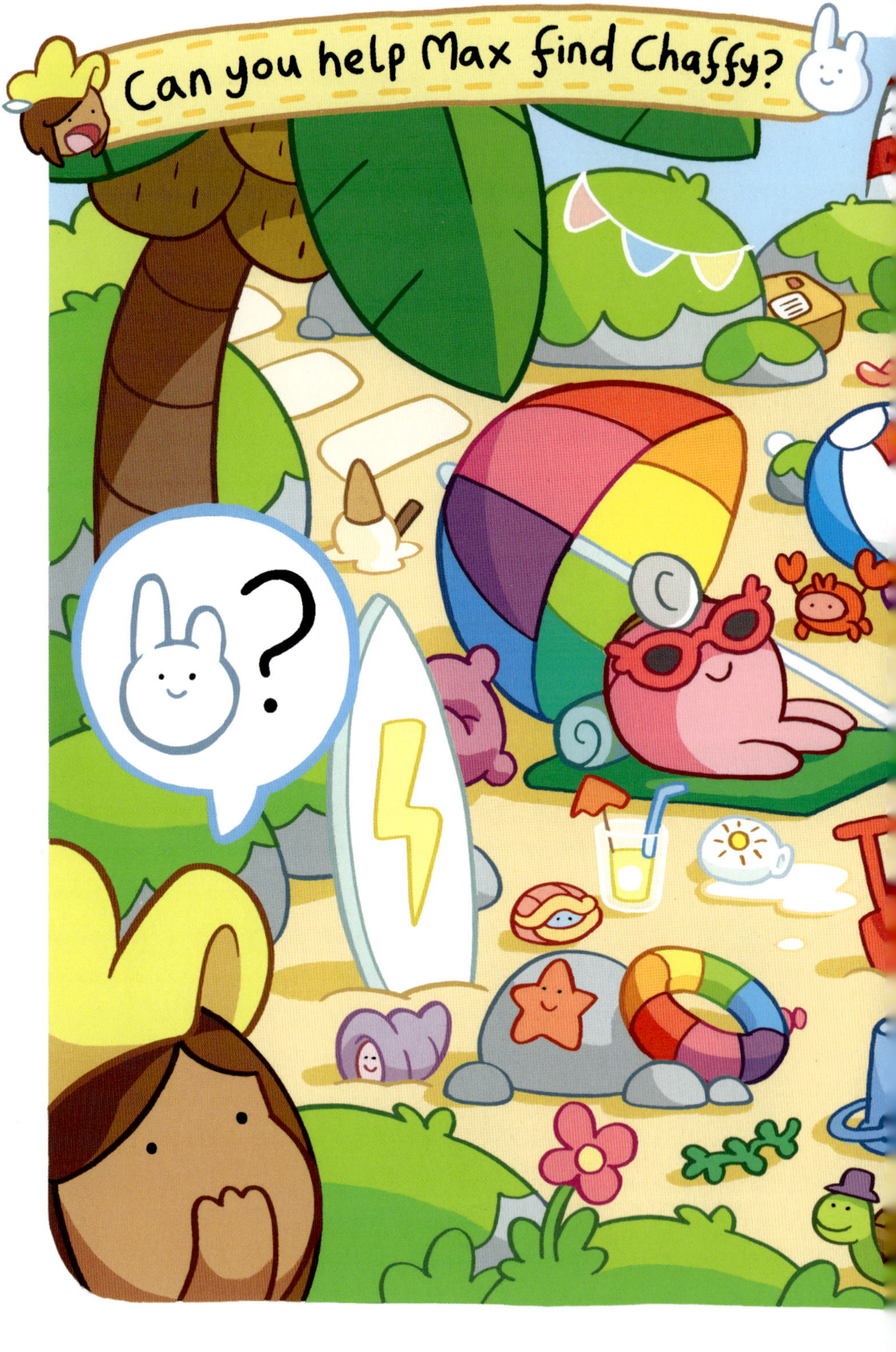
Can you help Max find Chaffy?
?

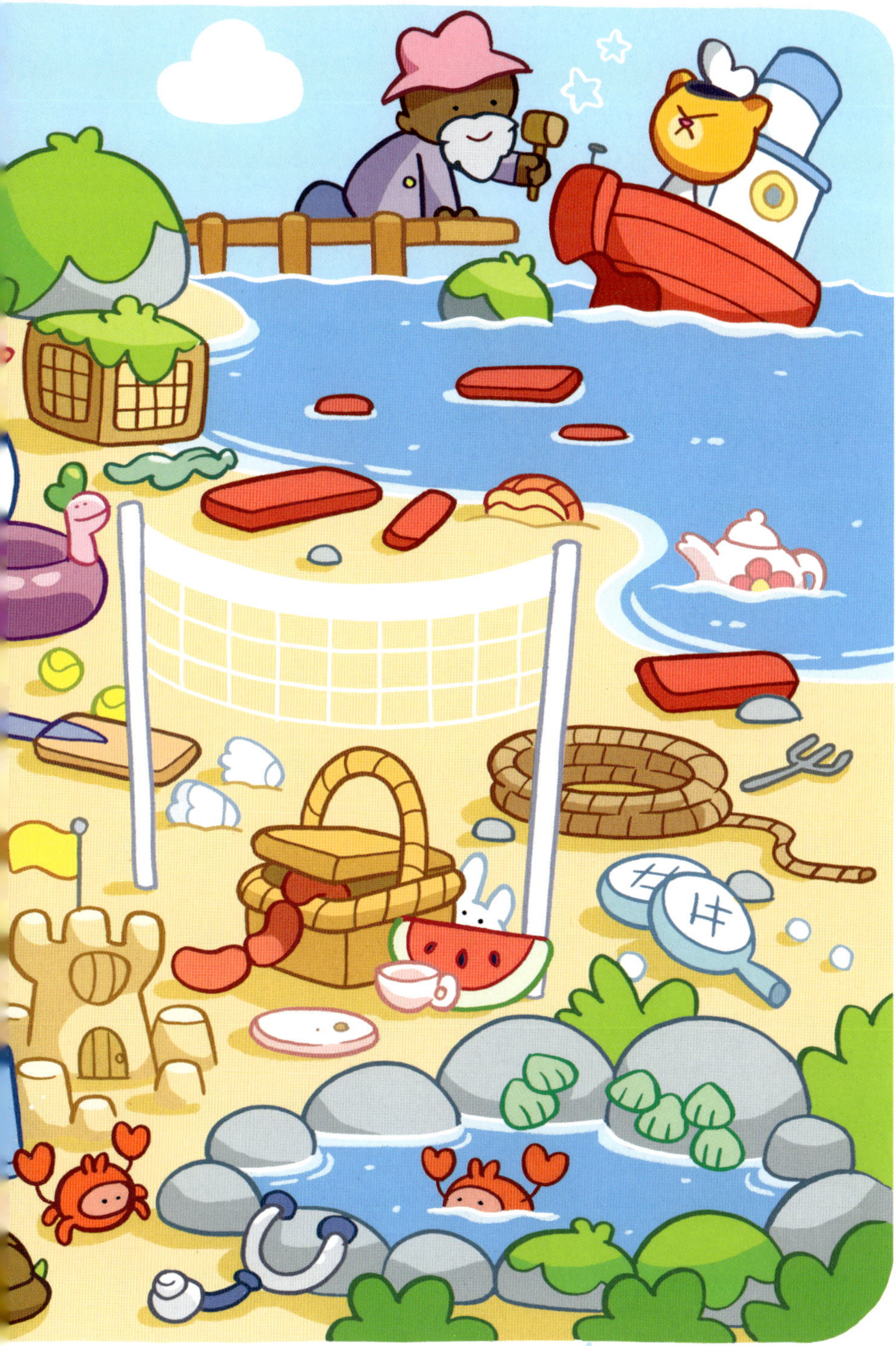

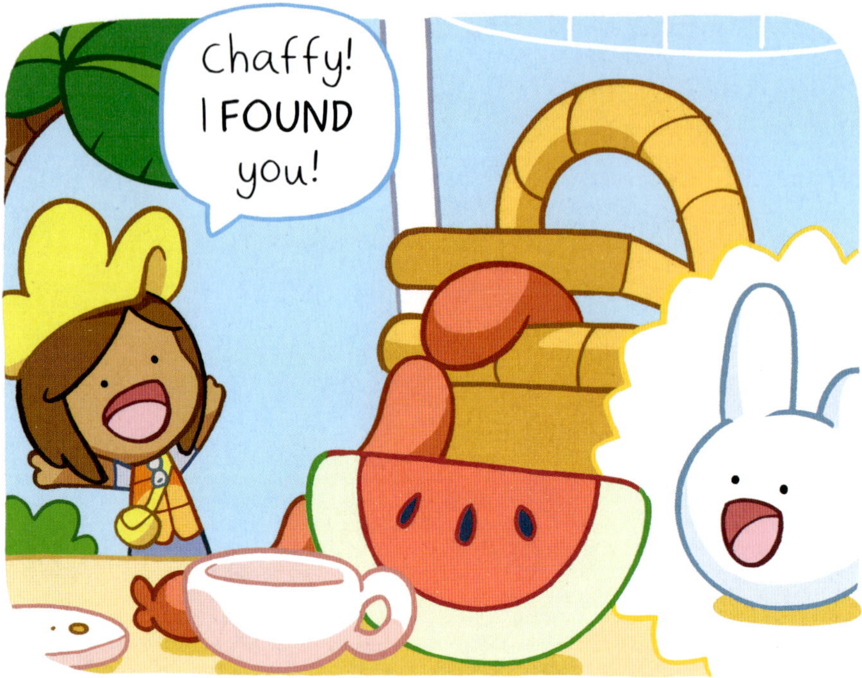
Chaffy! I **FOUND** you!

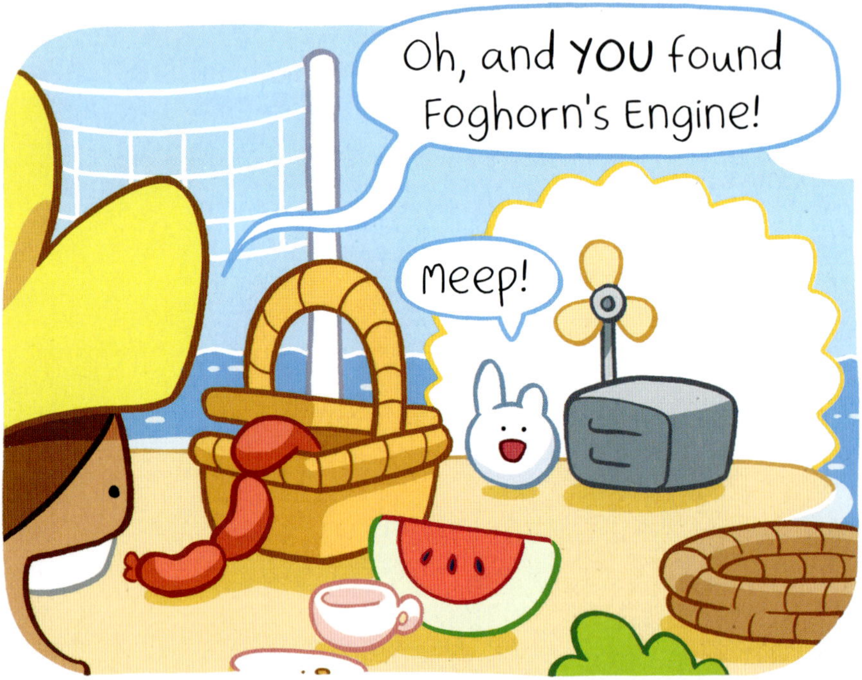
Oh, and **YOU** found Foghorn's Engine!
Meep!

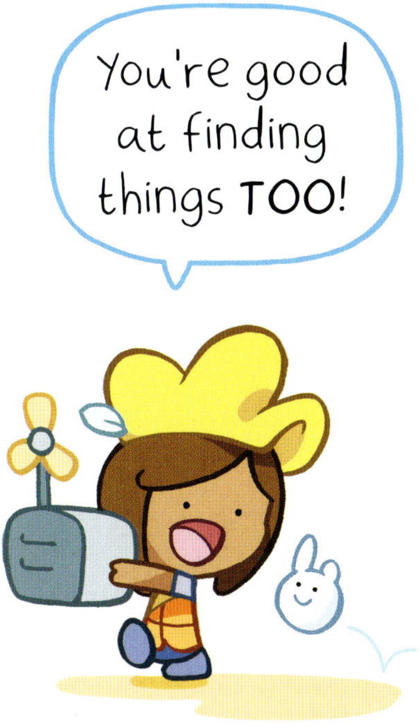
You're good at finding things TOO!

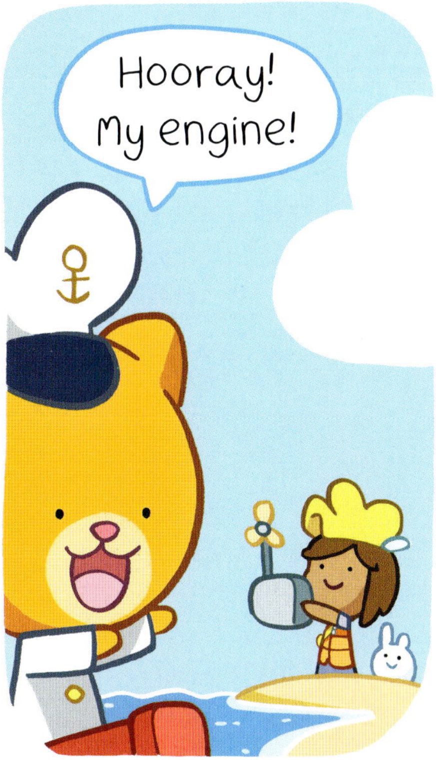
Hooray! My engine!

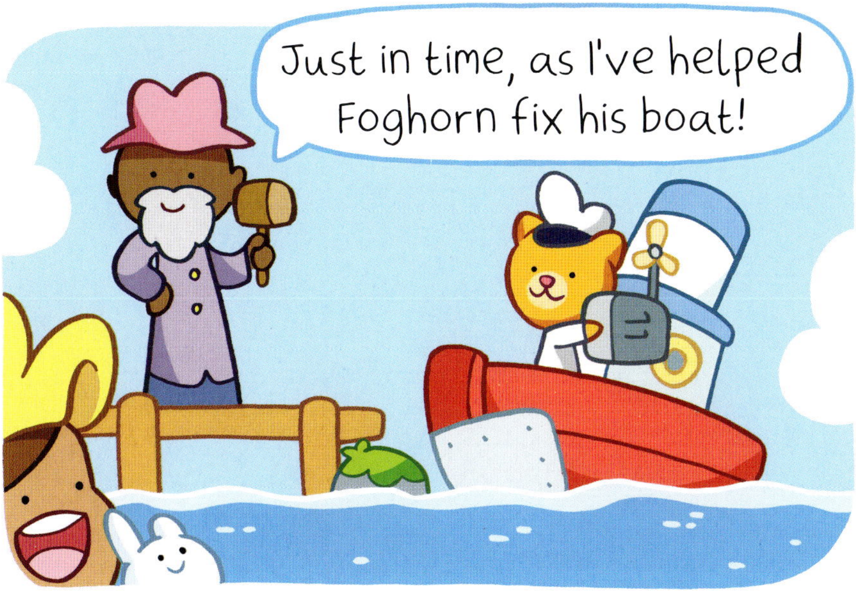
Just in time, as I've helped Foghorn fix his boat!

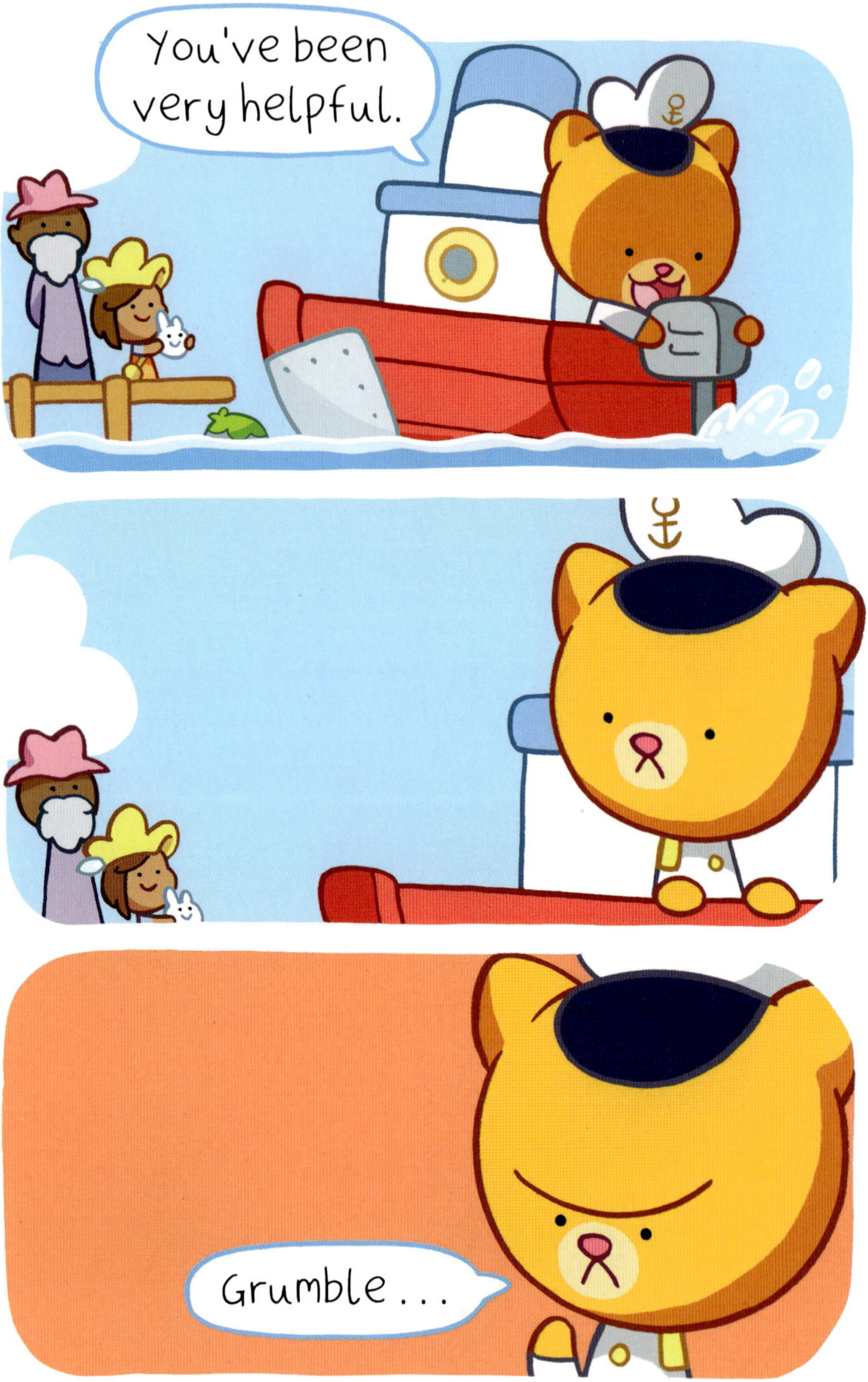
You've been very helpful.
Grumble...

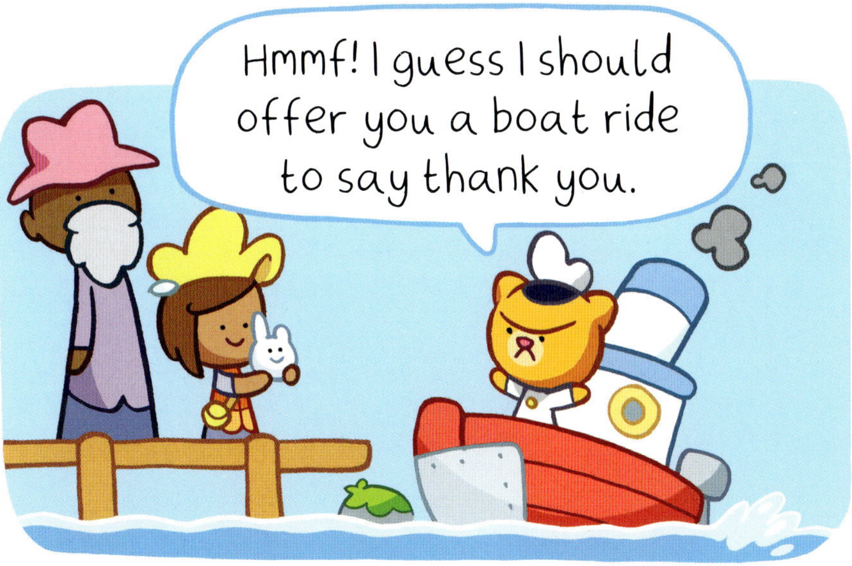
Hmmf! I guess I should offer you a boat ride to say thank you.

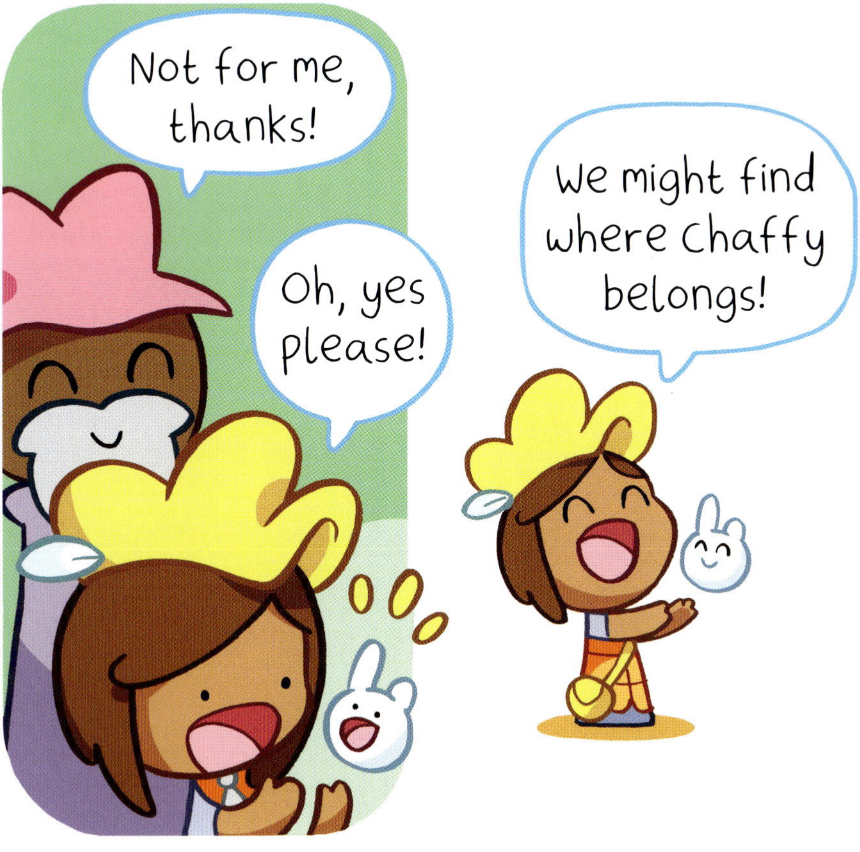
Not for me, thanks!
Oh, yes please!
We might find where Chaffy belongs!

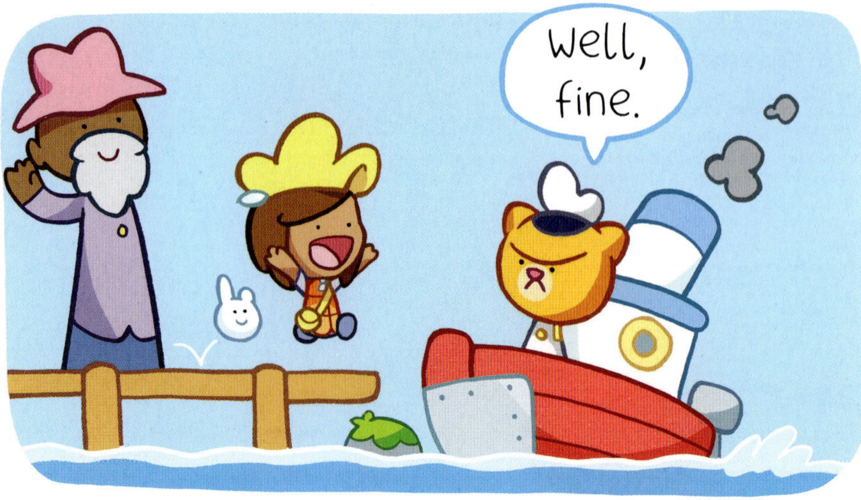
Well, fine.

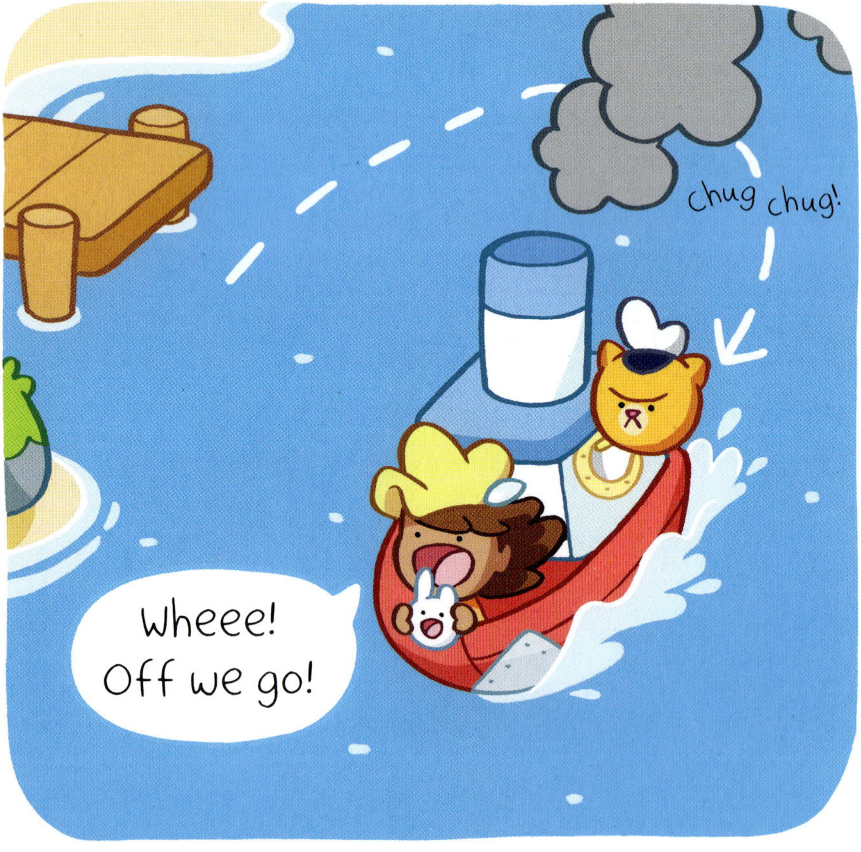
chug chug!
Wheee! Off we go!

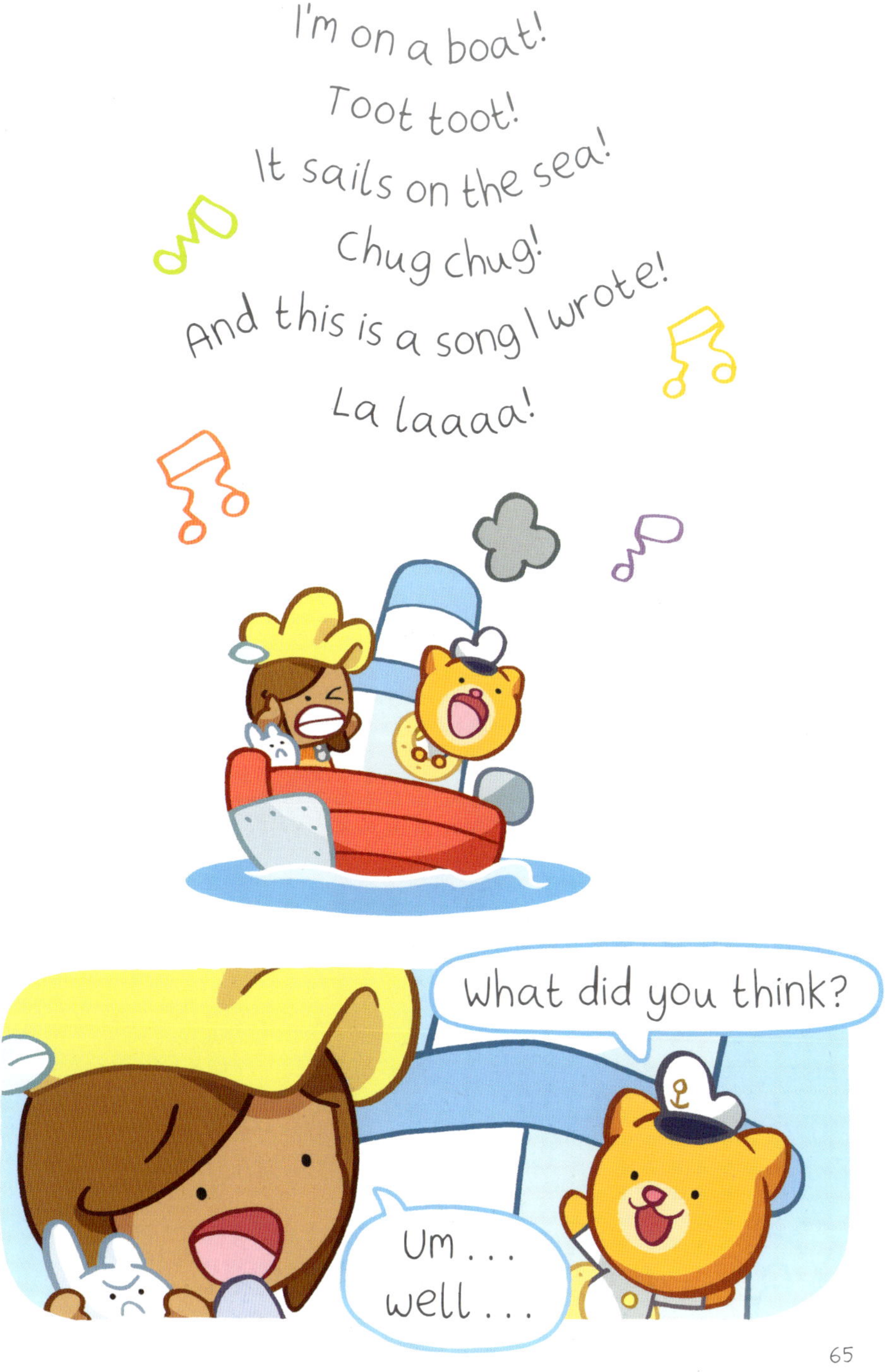
I'm on a boat!
Toot toot!
It sails on the sea!
Chug chug!
And this is a song I wrote!
La laaaa!
What did you think?
Um . . .
well . . .

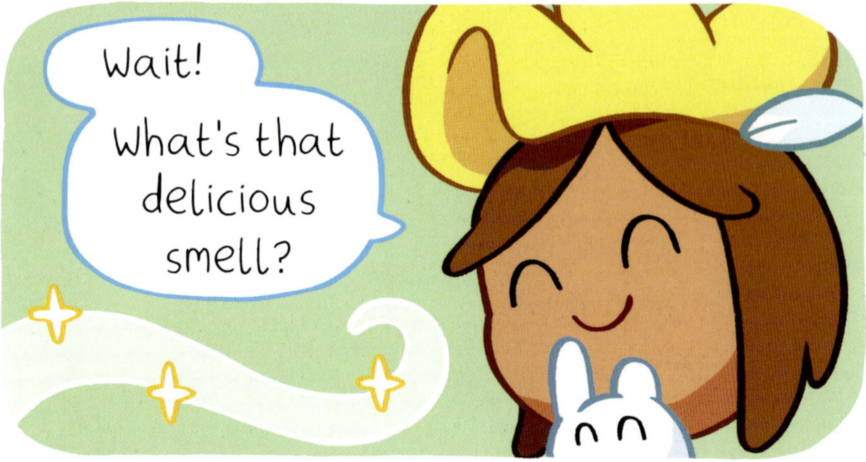
Wait!
What's that delicious smell?

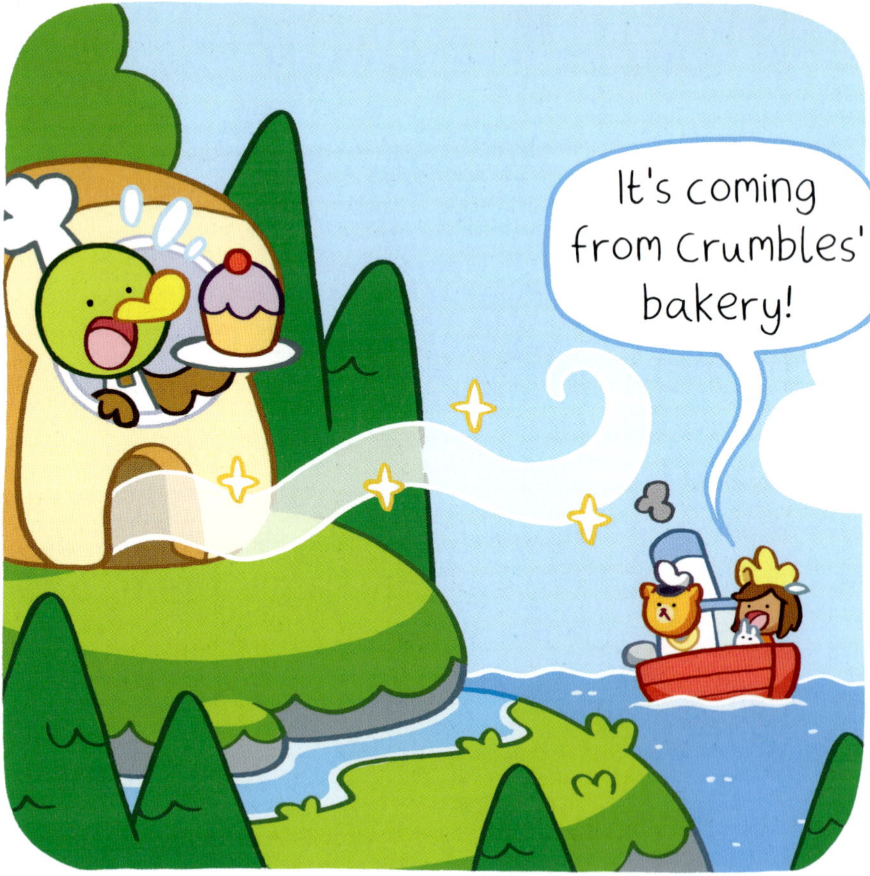
It's coming from Crumbles' bakery!

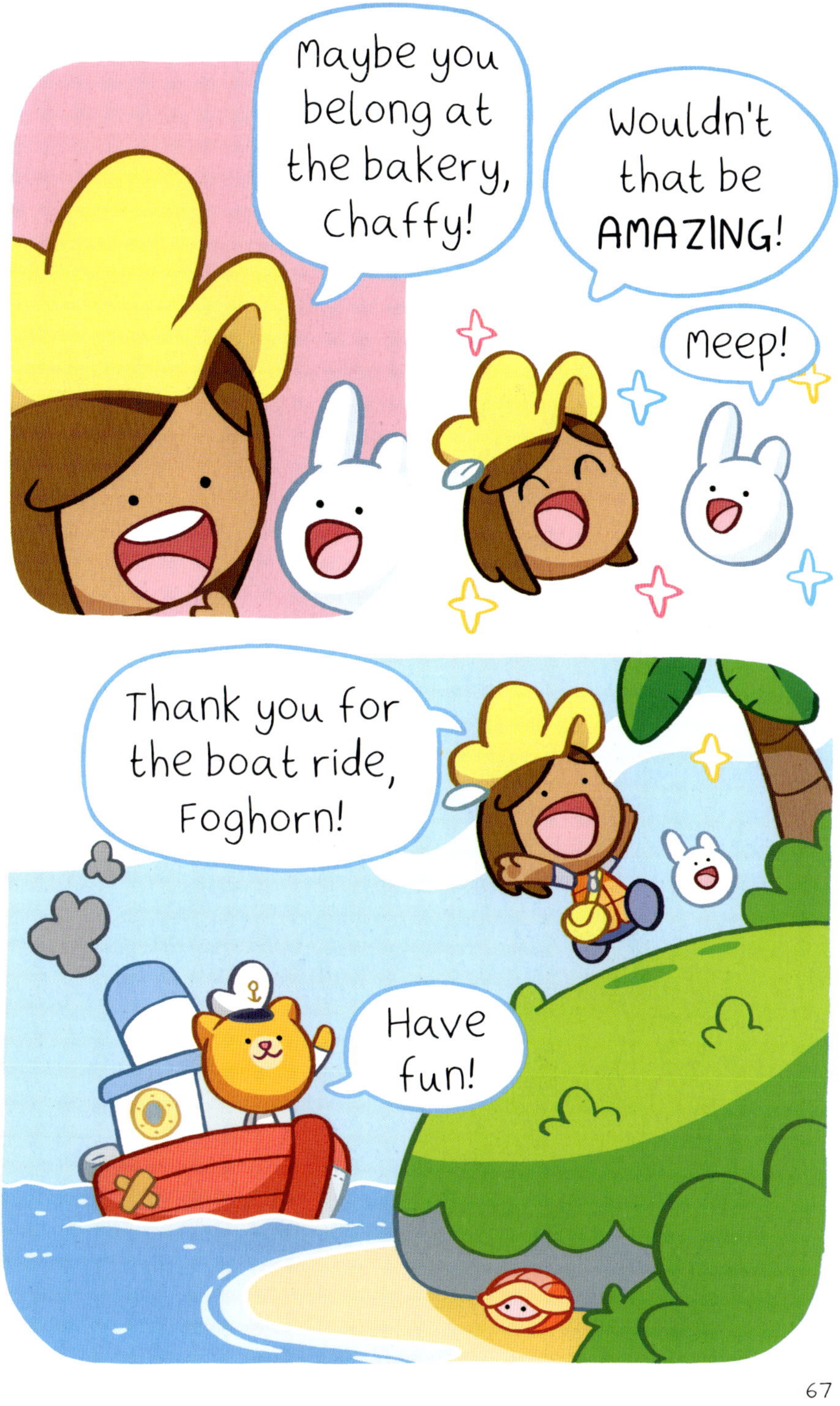
Maybe you belong at the bakery, Chaffy!
Wouldn't that be AMAZING!
Meep!
Thank you for the boat ride, Foghorn!
Have fun!

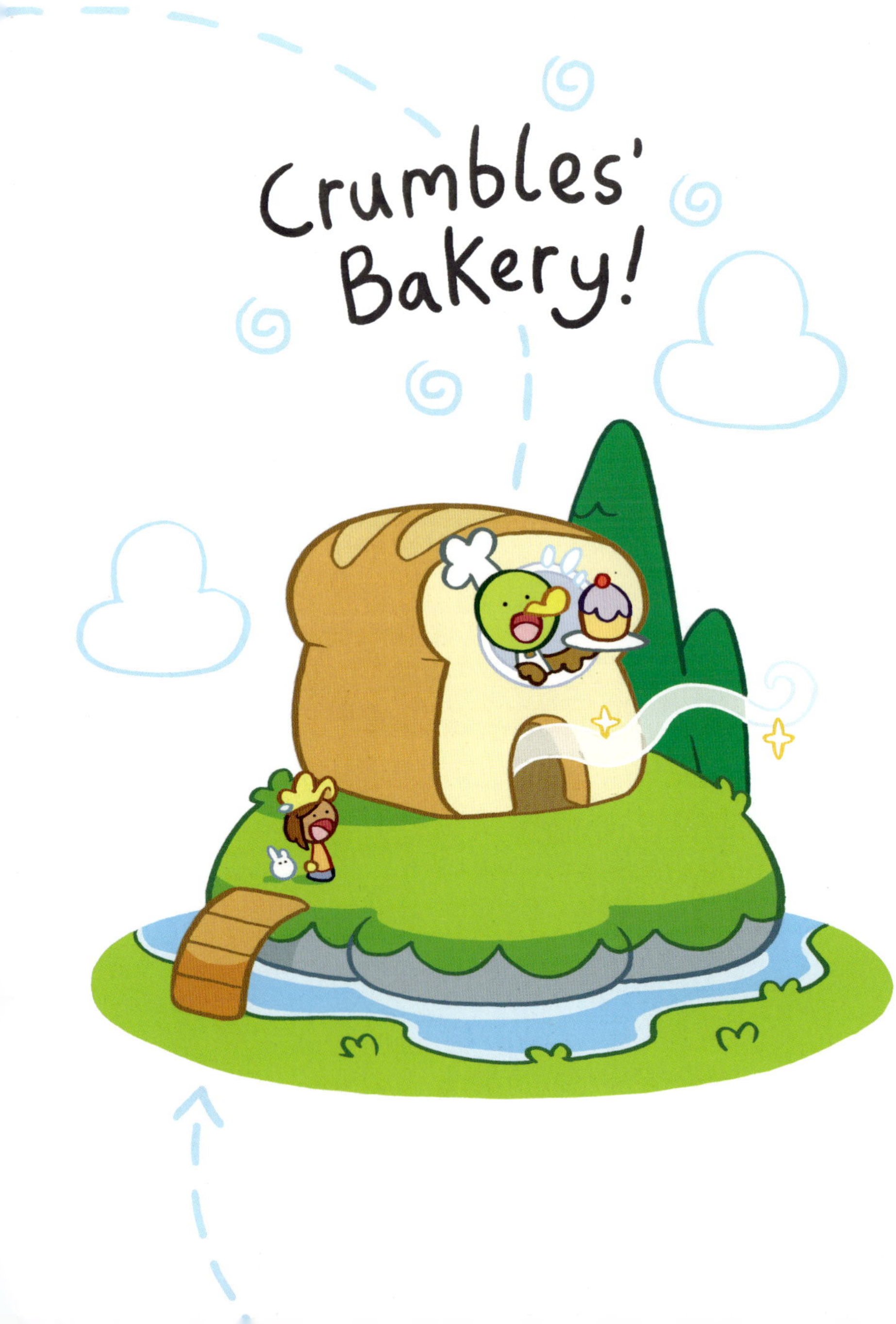
Crumbles' Bakery!

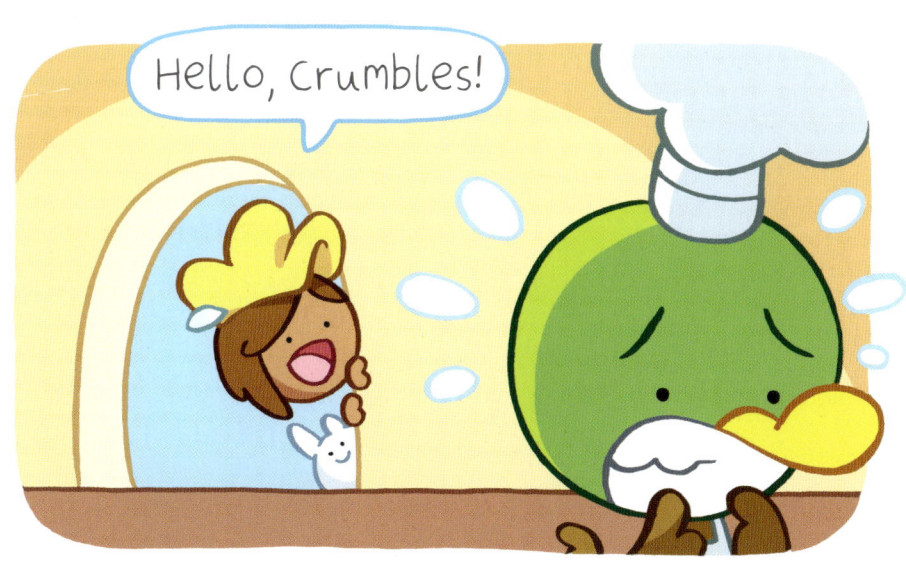

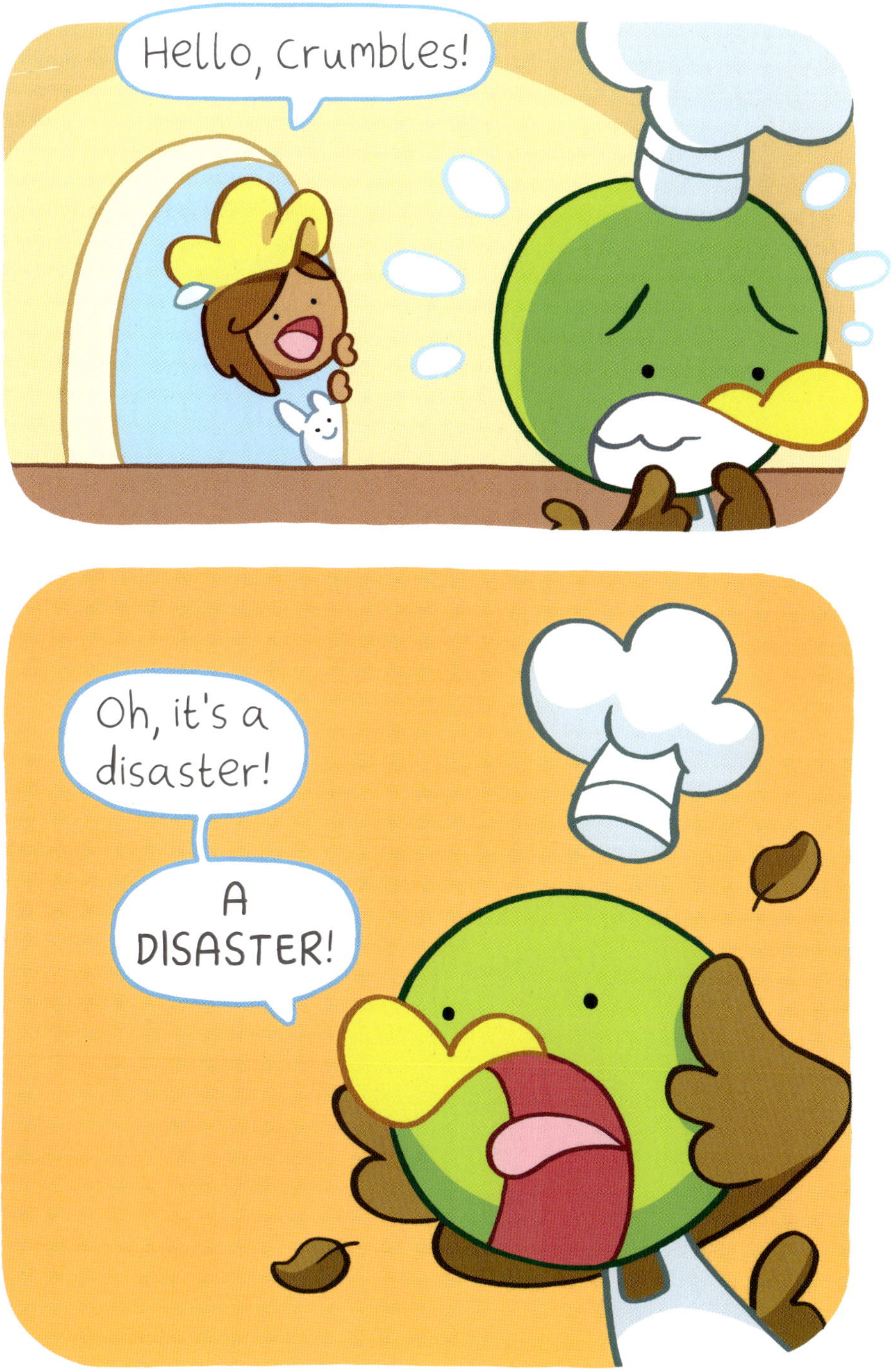
Hello, Crumbles!
Oh, it's a disaster!
A DISASTER!

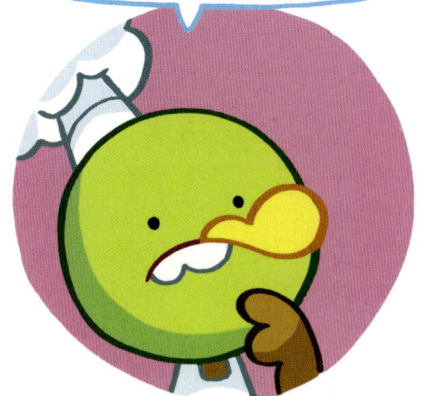

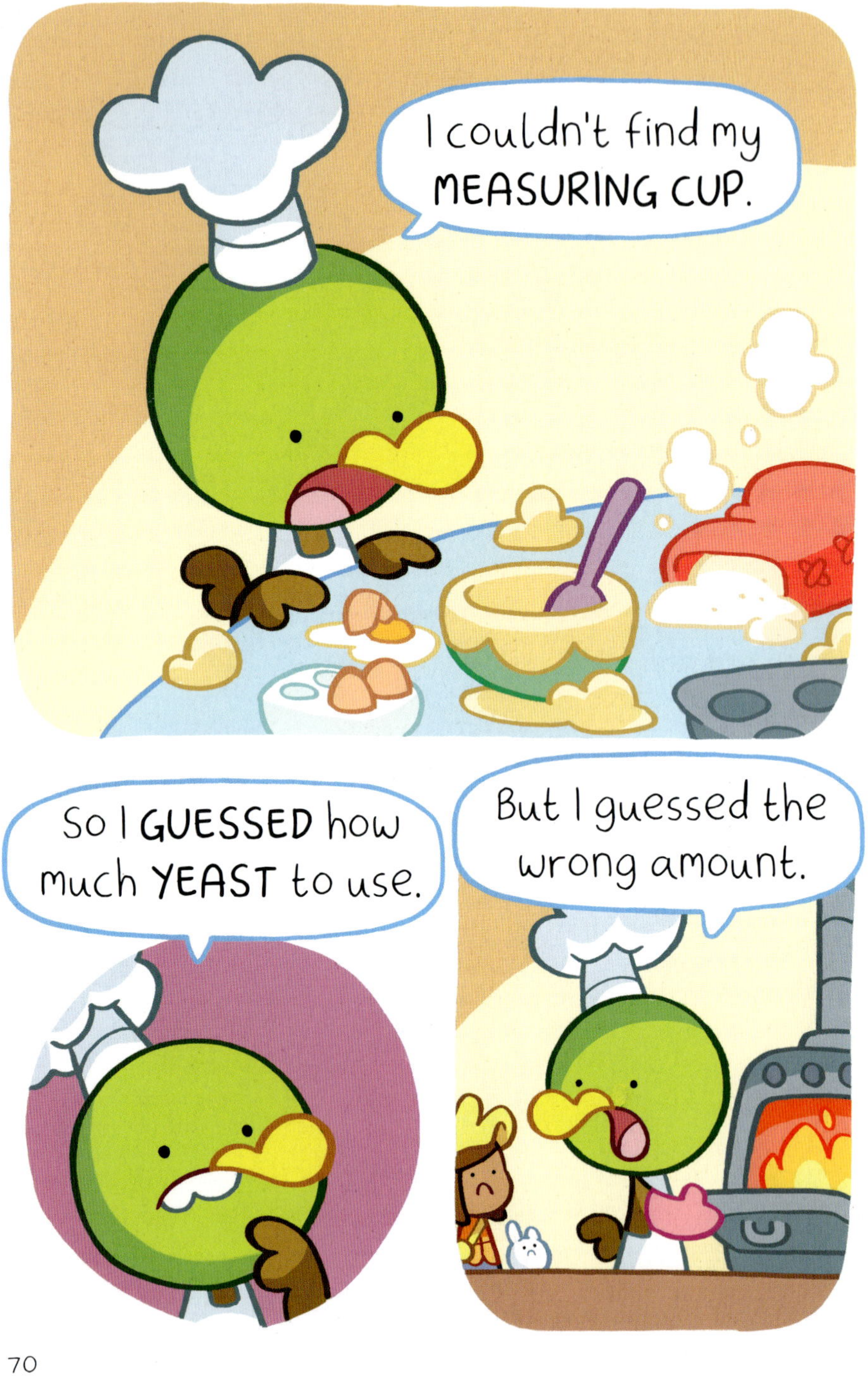
I couldn't find my MEASURING CUP.
So I GUESSED how much YEAST to use.
But I guessed the wrong amount.

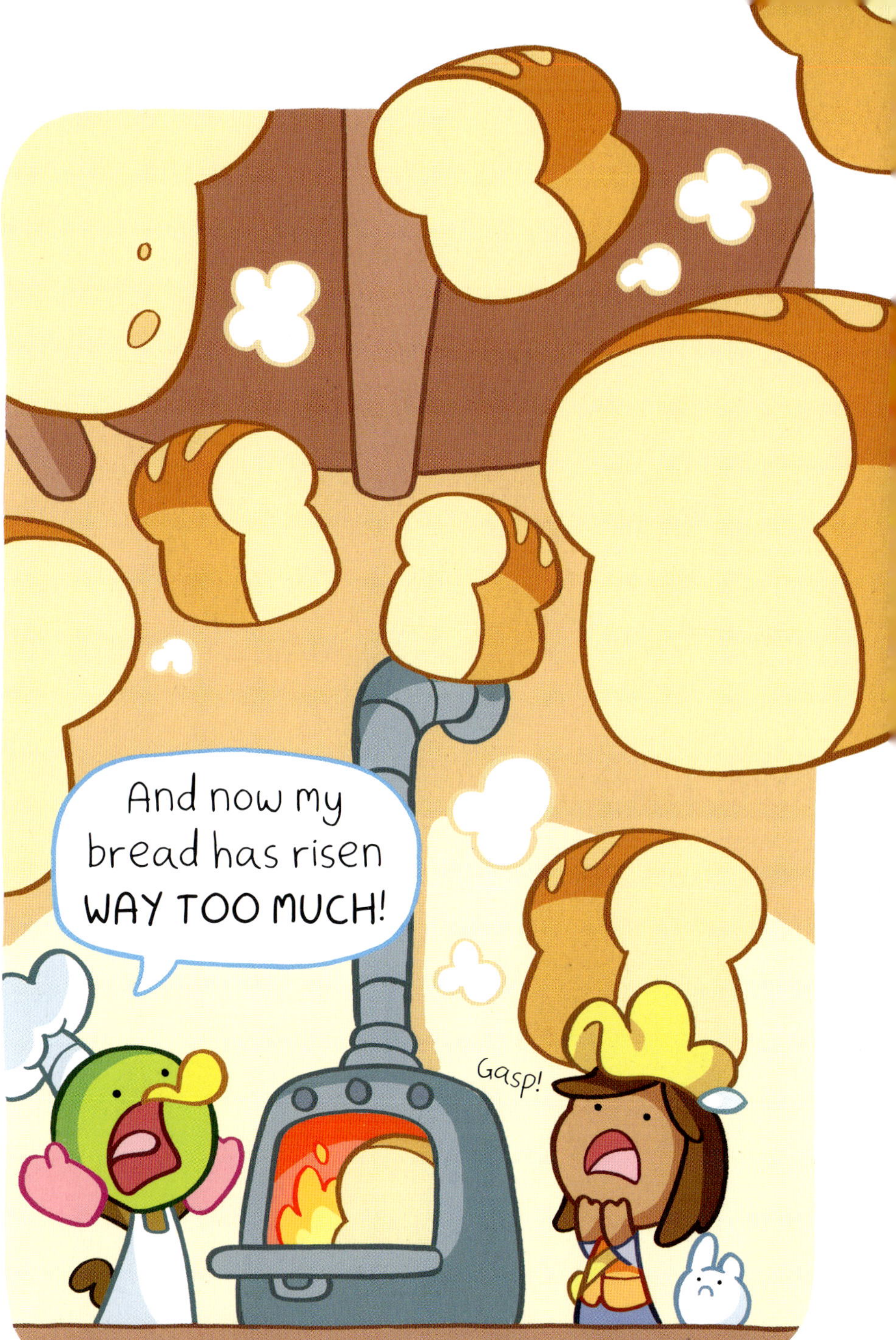
And now my bread has risen WAY TOO MUCH!
Gasp!

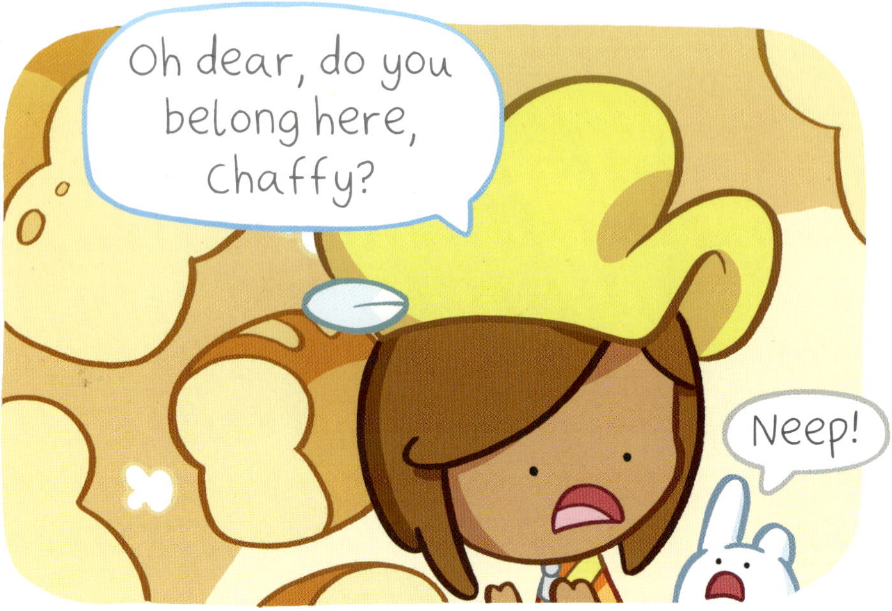
Oh dear, do you belong here, Chaffy?
Neep!

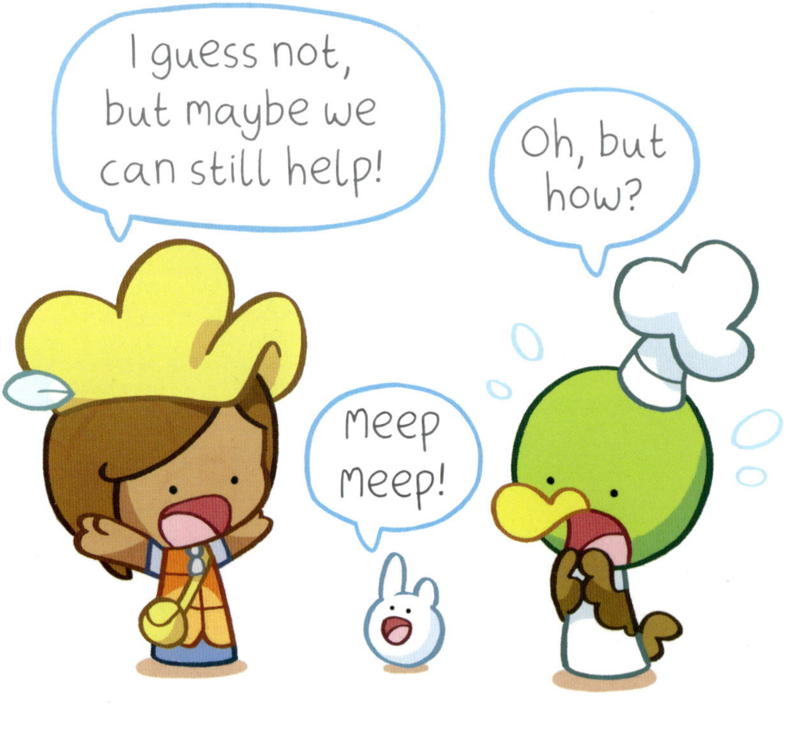
I guess not, but maybe we can still help!
Oh, but how?
Meep Meep!

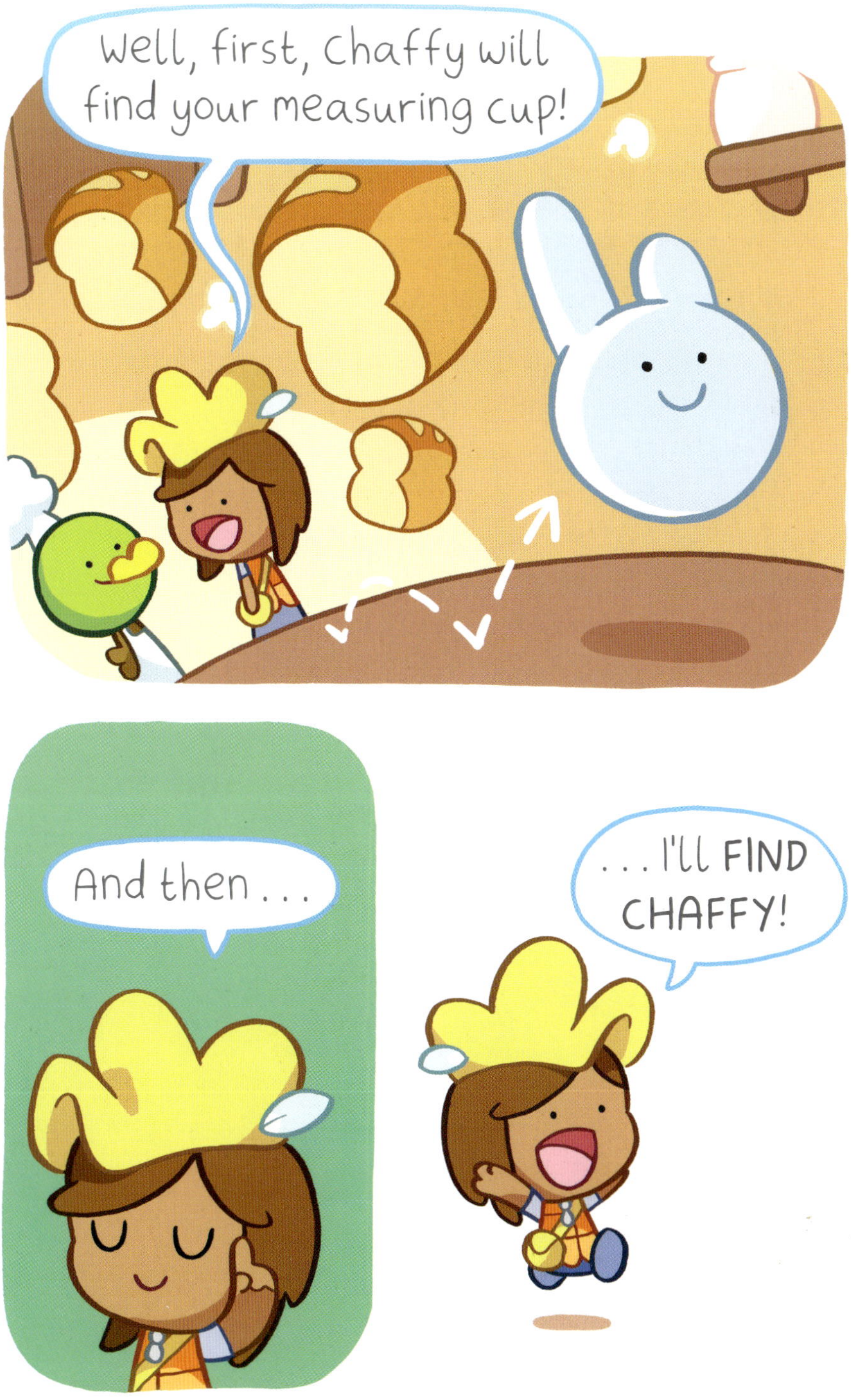
Well, first, Chaffy will find your measuring cup!
And then . . .
. . . I'll FIND CHAFFY!

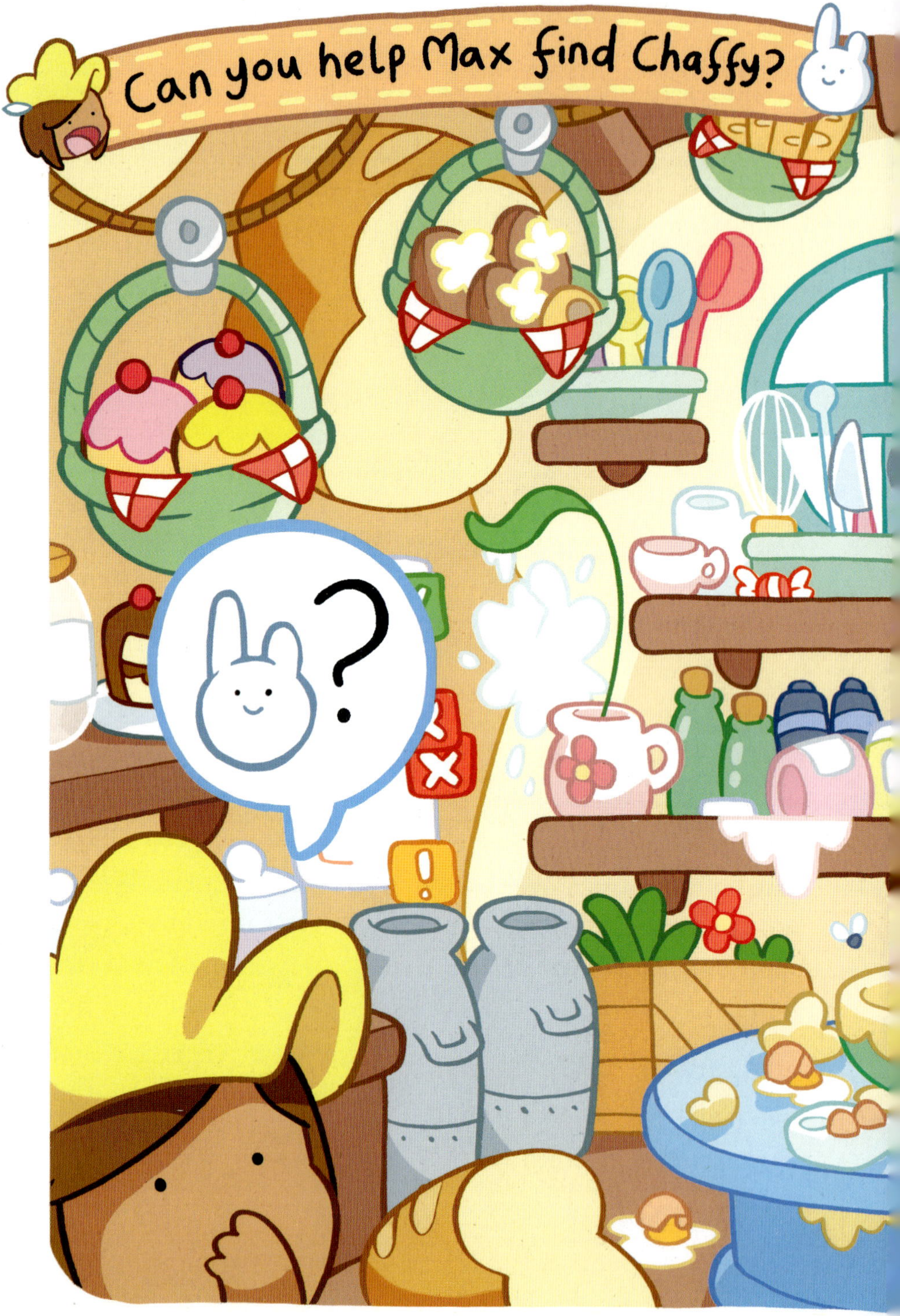
Can you help Max find Chaffy?
?

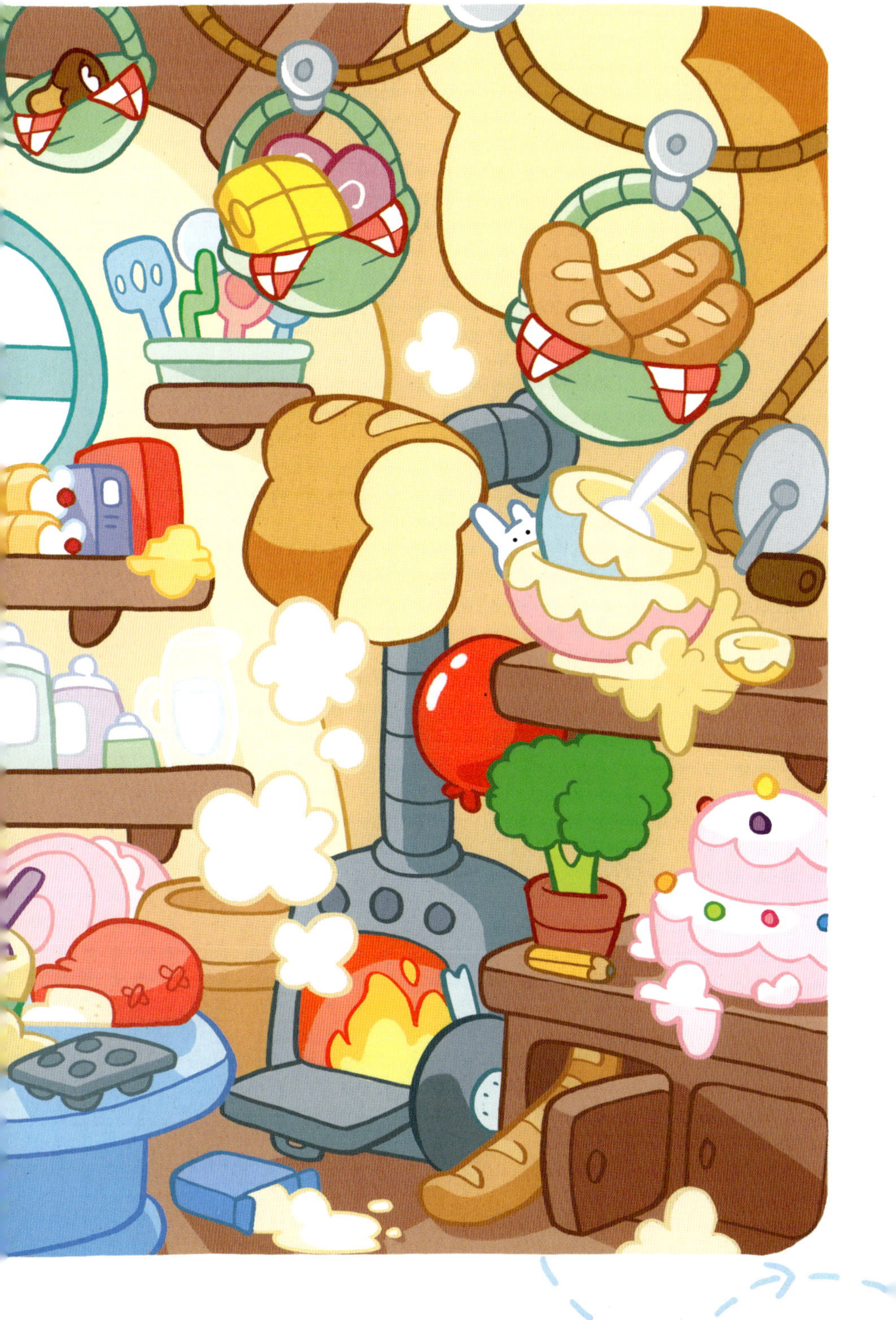

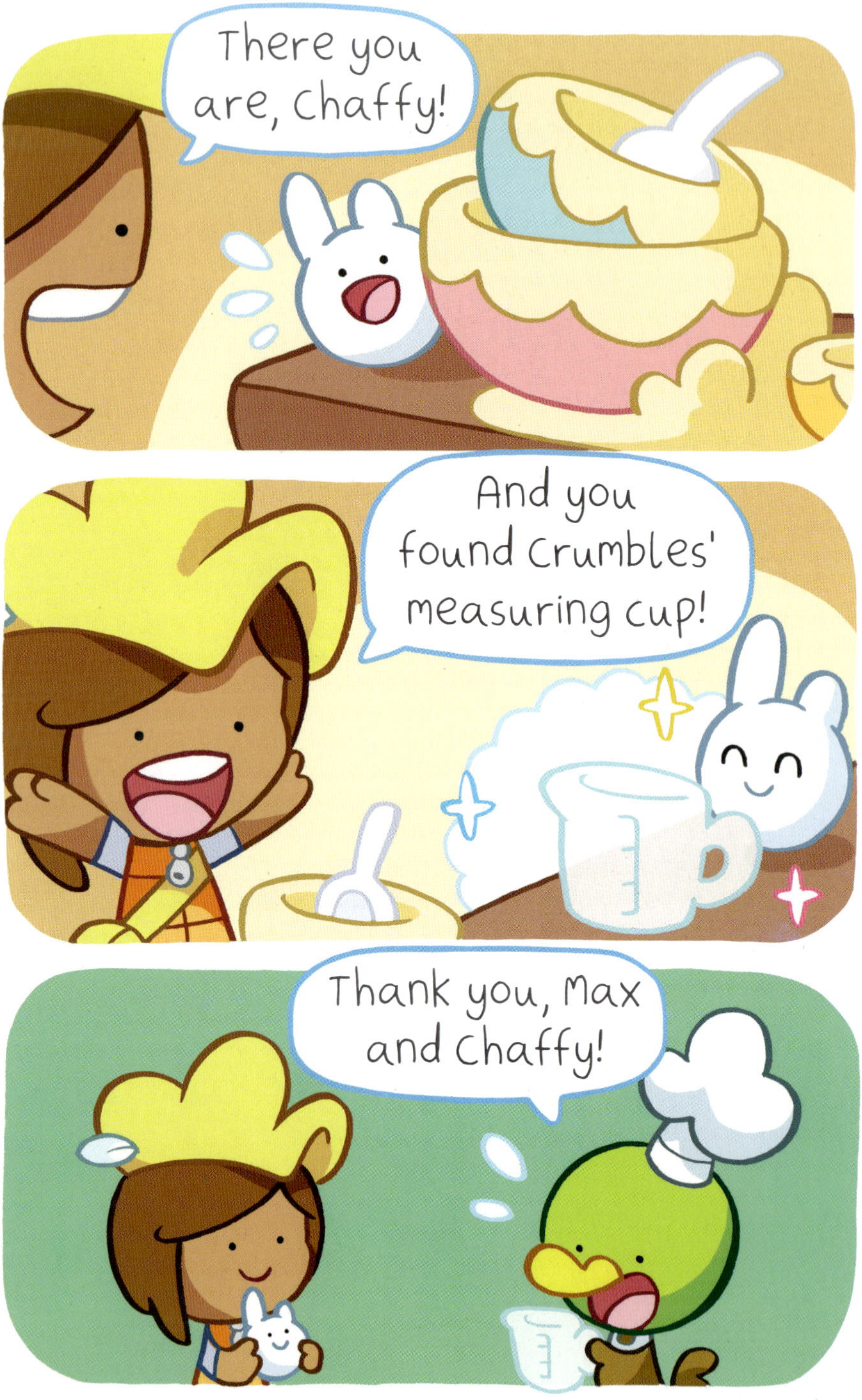
There you are, Chaffy!
And you found Crumbles' measuring cup!
Thank you, Max and Chaffy!

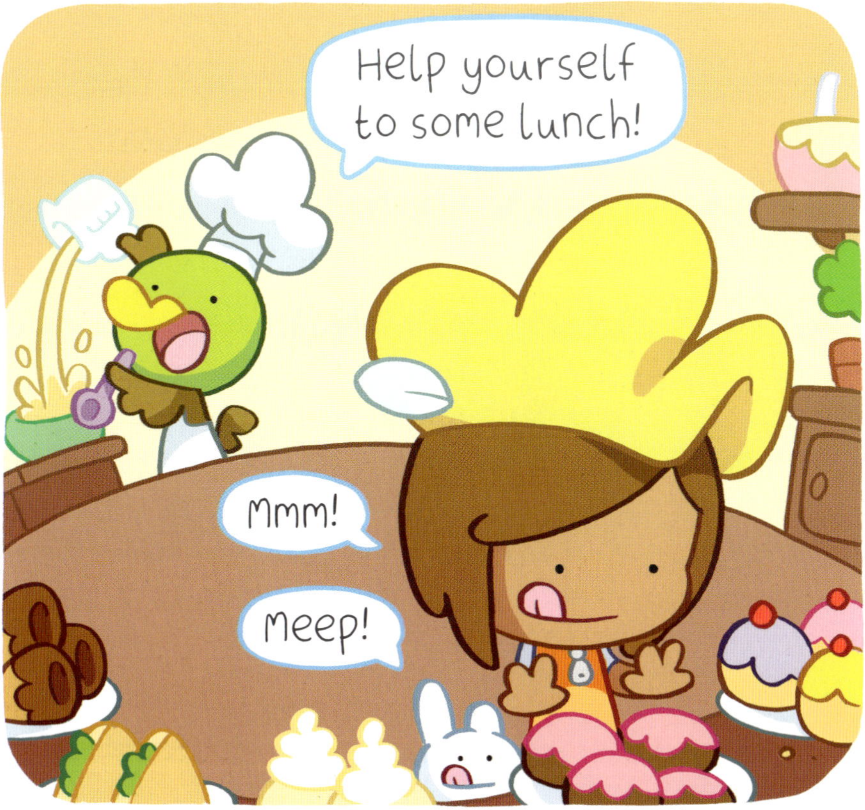
Help yourself to some lunch!
Mmm!
Meep!

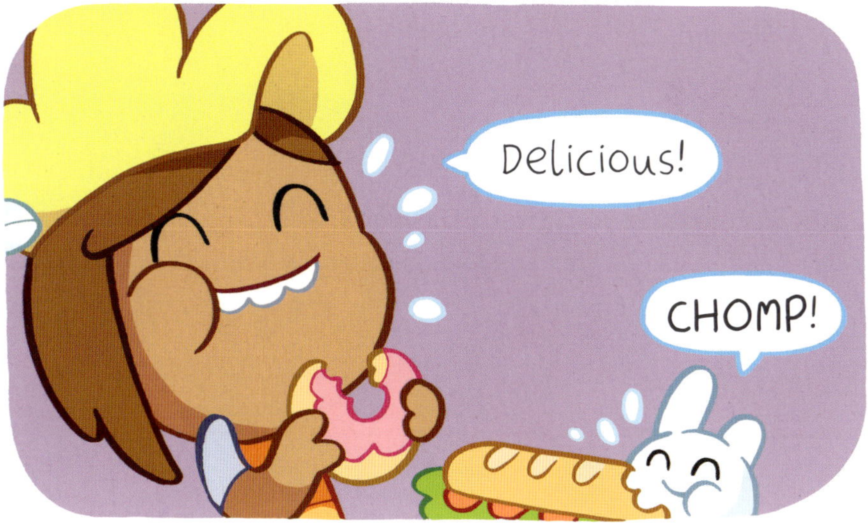
Delicious!
CHOMP!

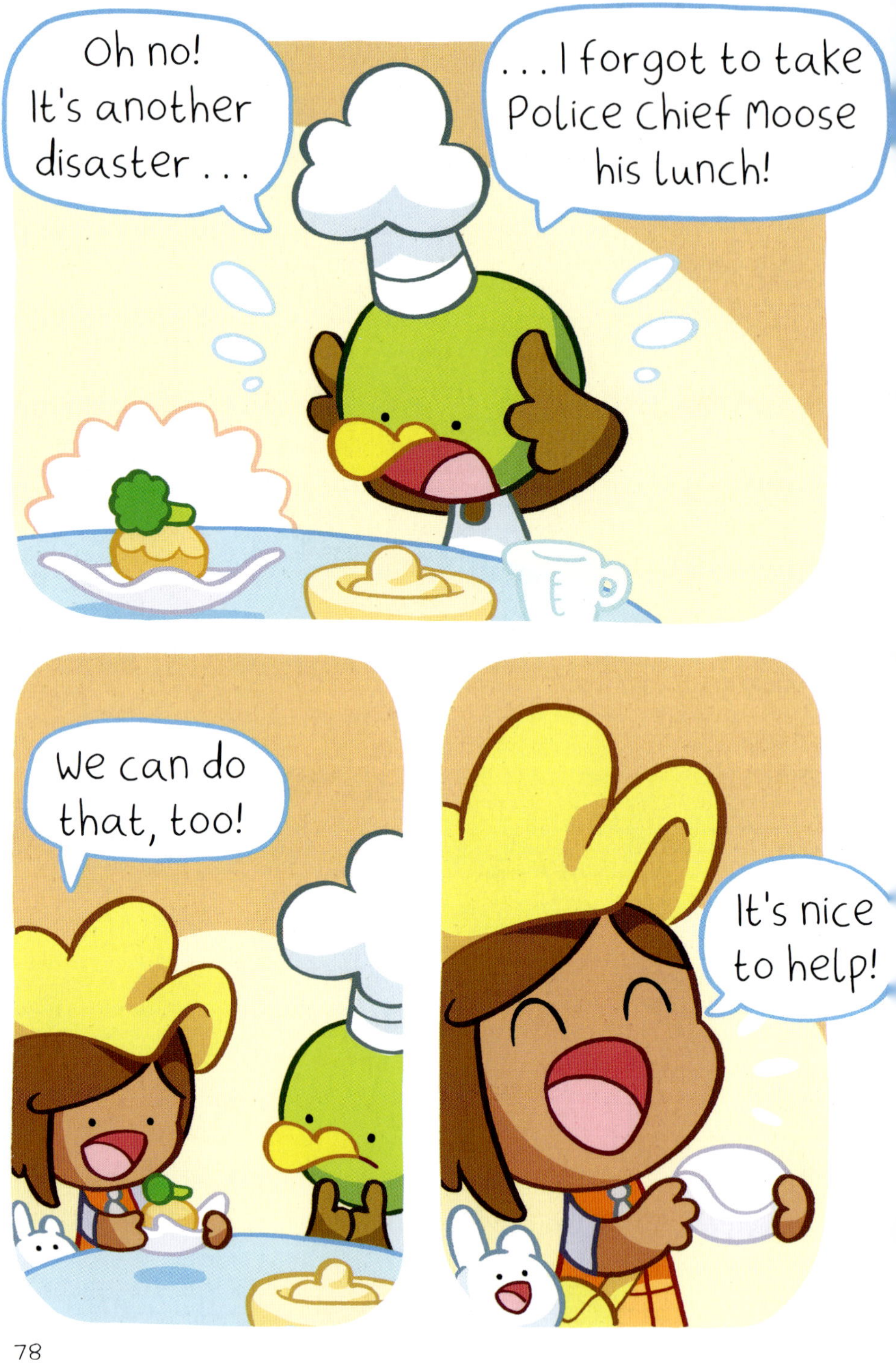
Oh no! It's another disaster . . .
. . . I forgot to take Police Chief Moose his lunch!
We can do that, too!
It's nice to help!

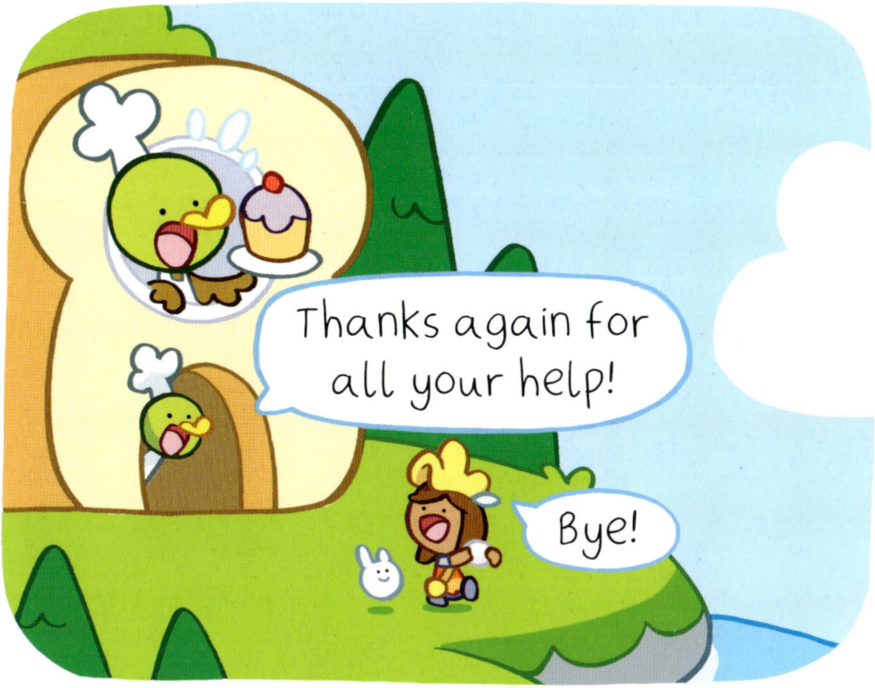
Thanks again for all your help!
Bye!

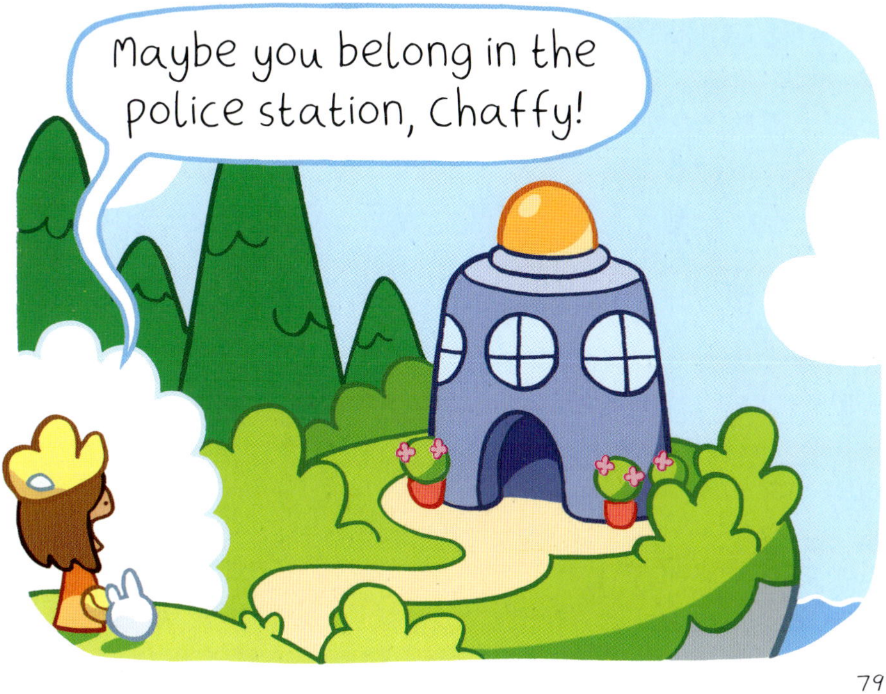
Maybe you belong in the police station, Chaffy!

Police Chief Moose's Police Station!

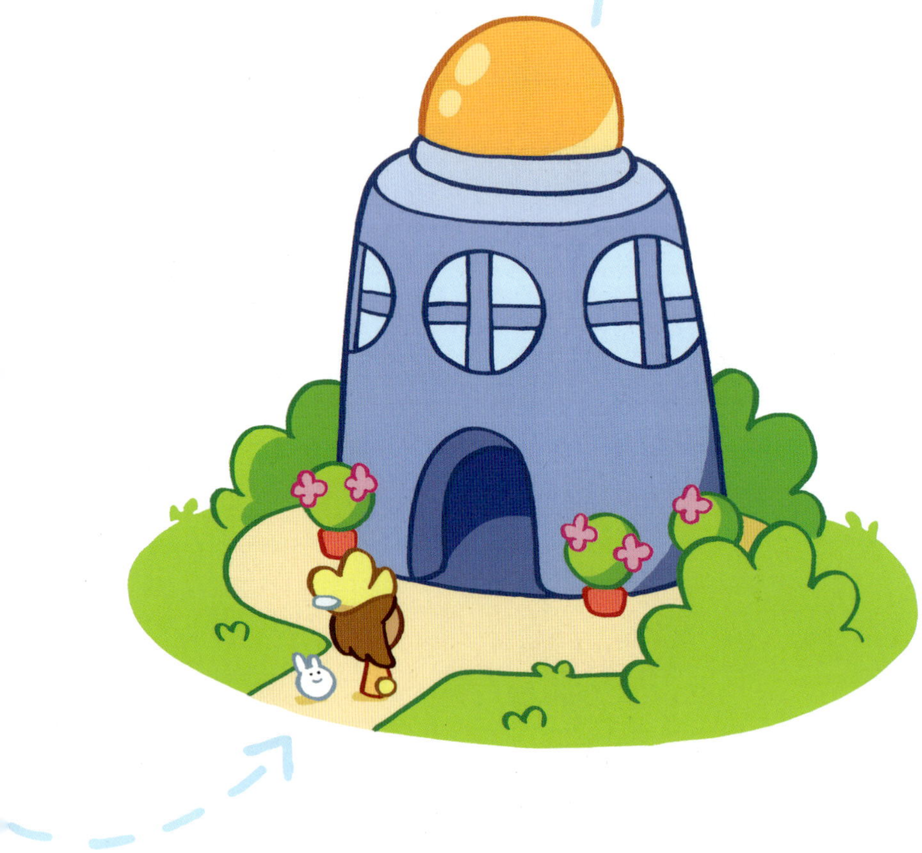

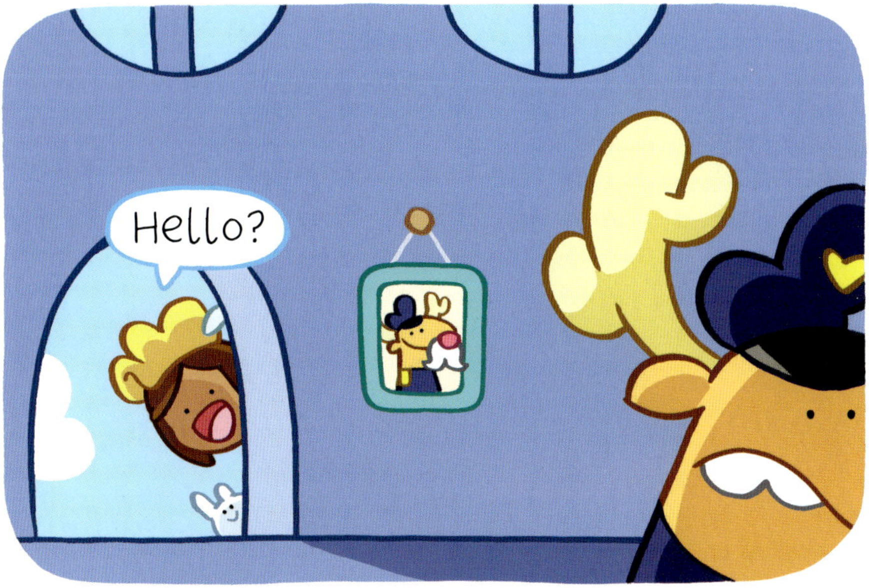
Hello?

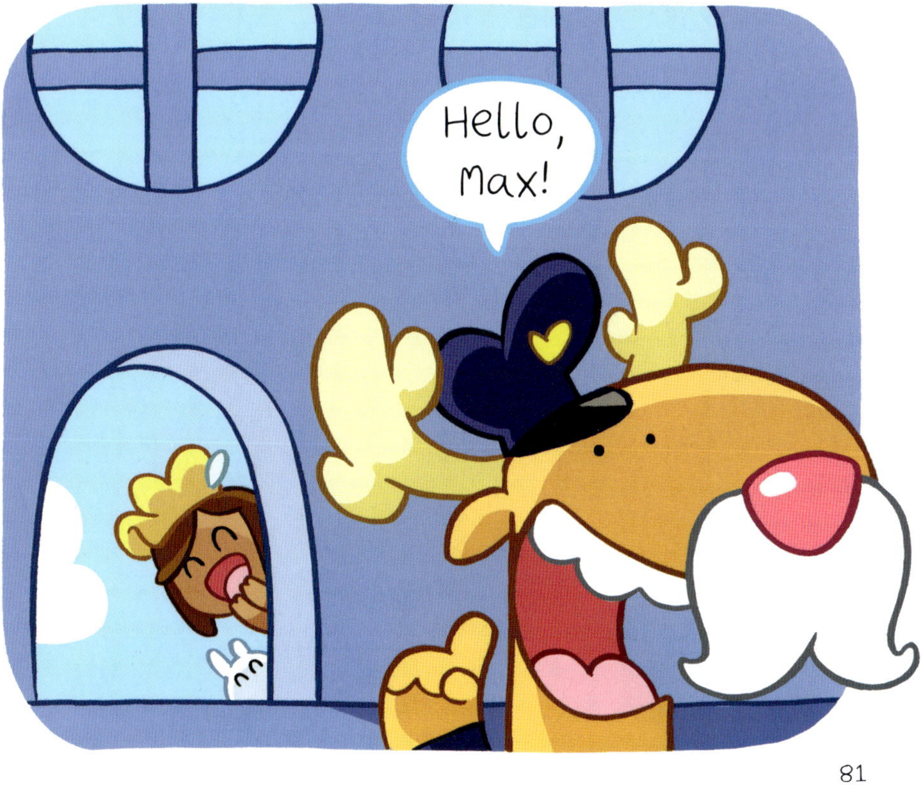
Hello, Max!

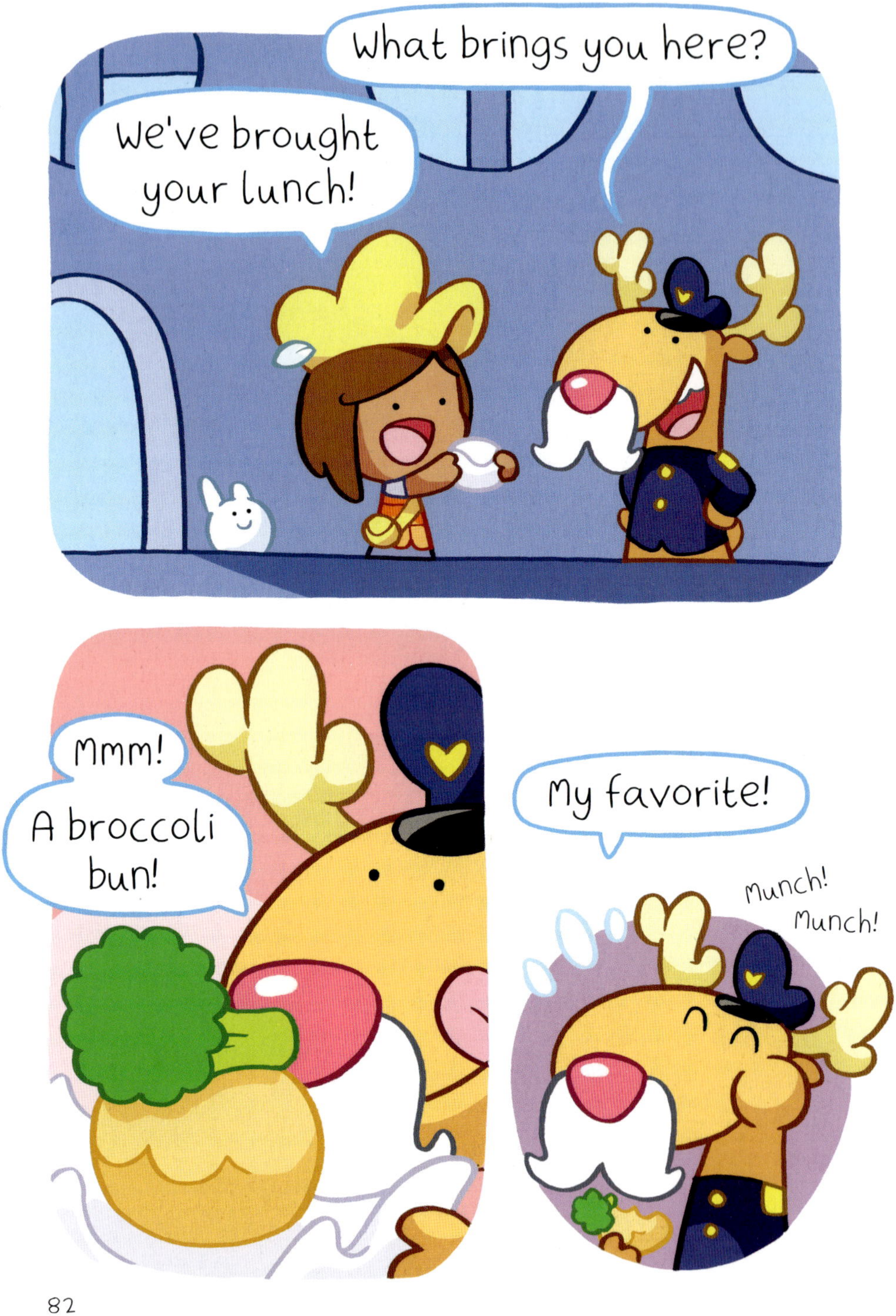
What brings you here?
We've brought your lunch!
Mmm!
A broccoli bun!
My favorite!
Munch!
Munch!

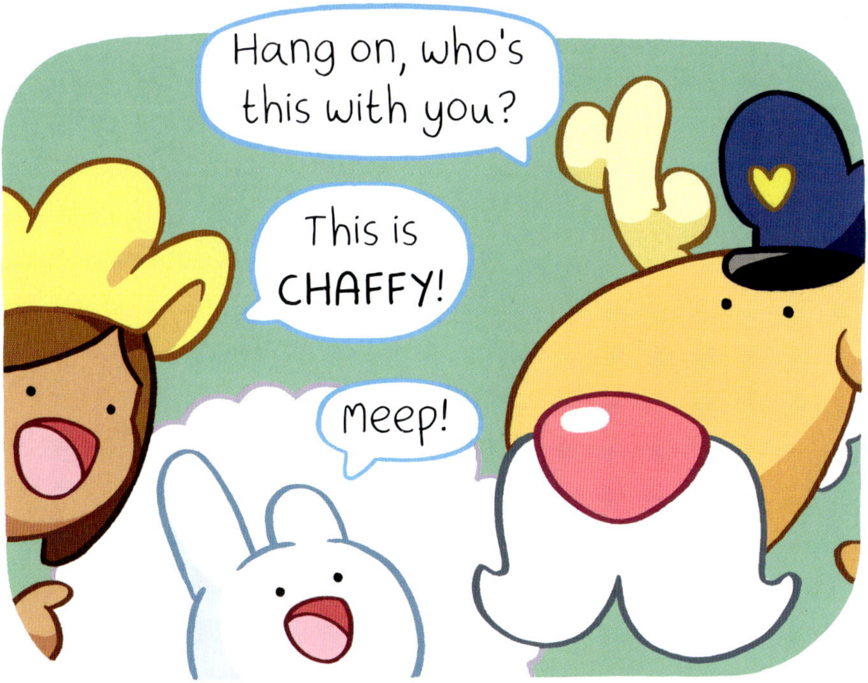
Hang on, who's this with you?
This is CHAFFY!
Meep!

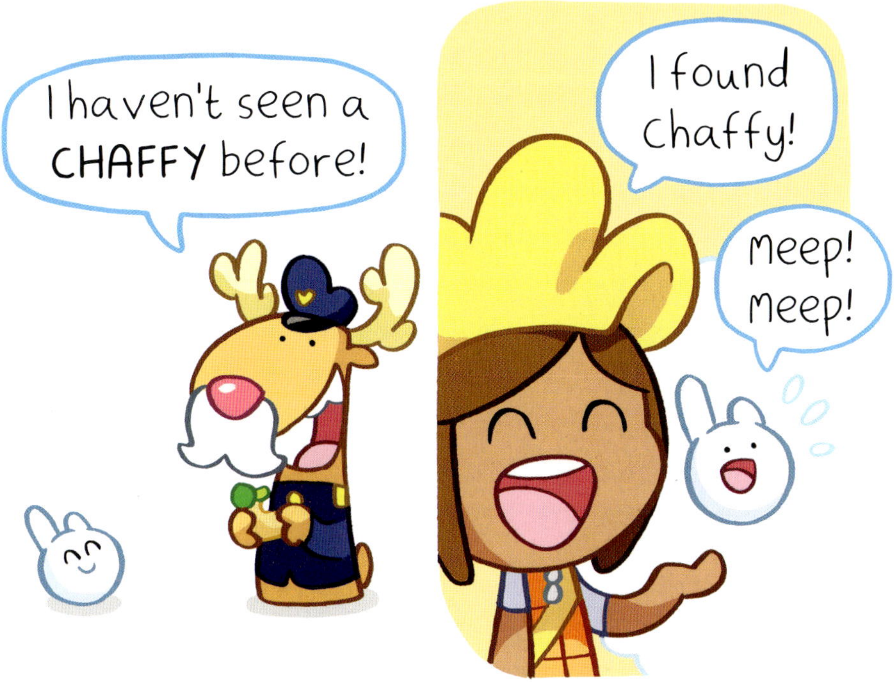
I haven't seen a CHAFFY before!
I found Chaffy!
Meep! Meep!

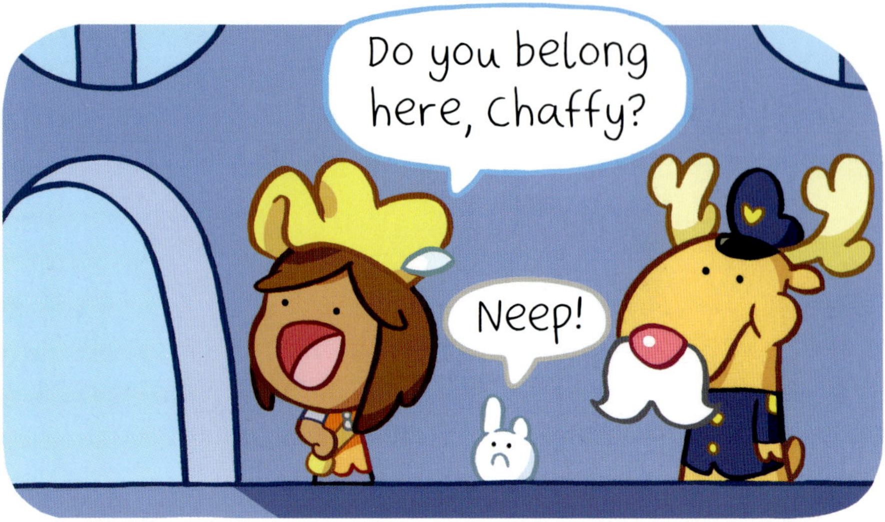
Do you belong here, Chaffy?
Neep!

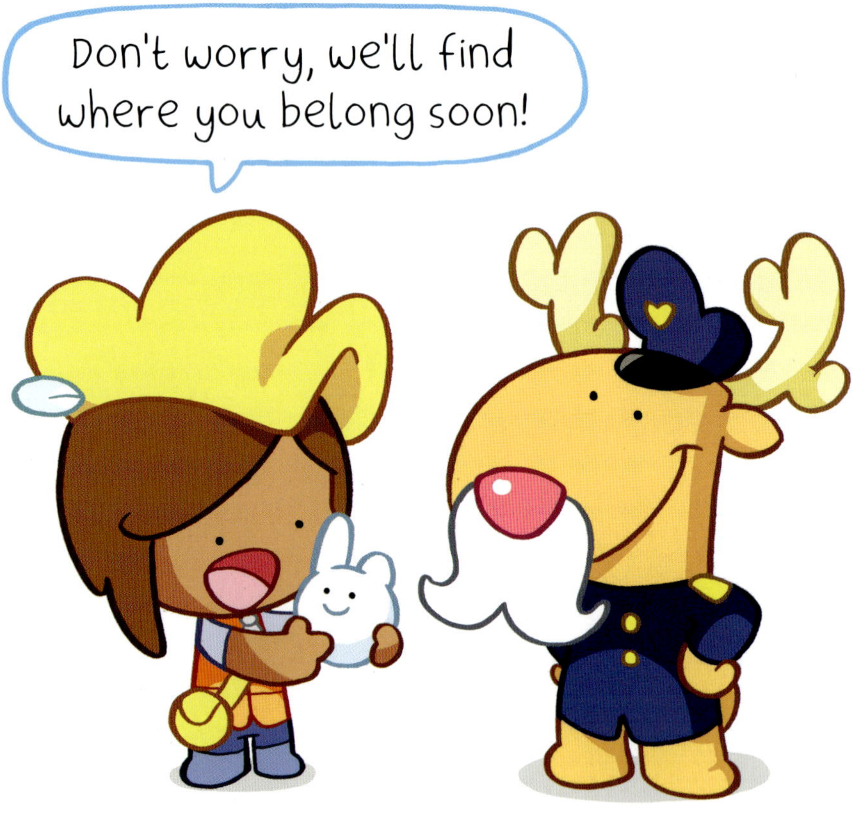
Don't worry, we'll find where you belong soon!

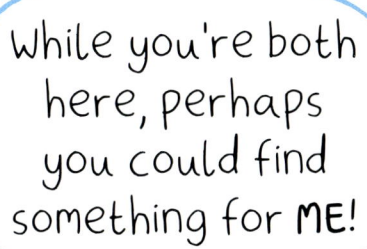

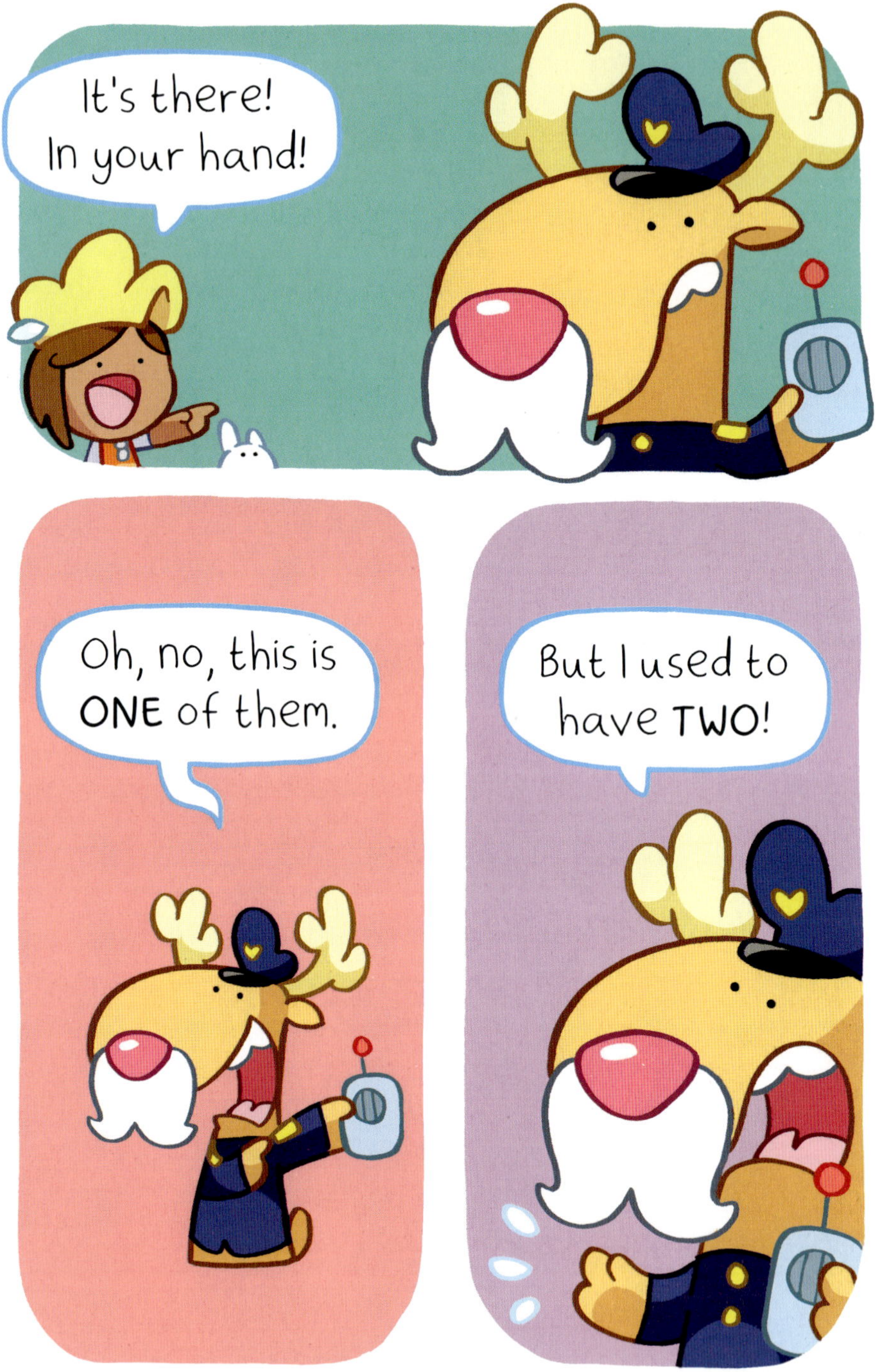
It's there! In your hand!
Oh, no, this is **ONE** of them.
But I used to have **TWO**!

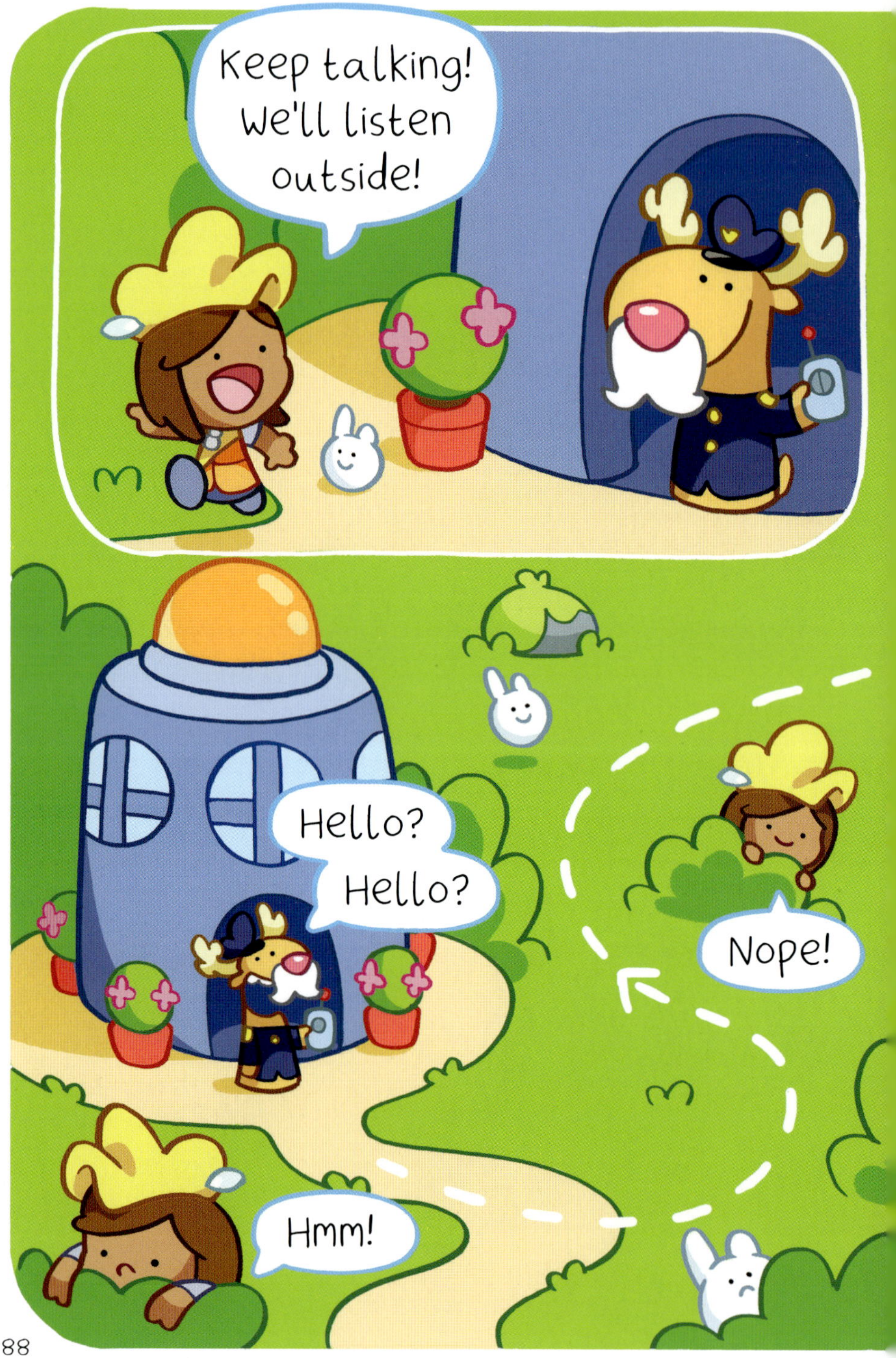
Keep talking! We'll listen outside!
Hello?
Hello?
Nope!
Hmm!

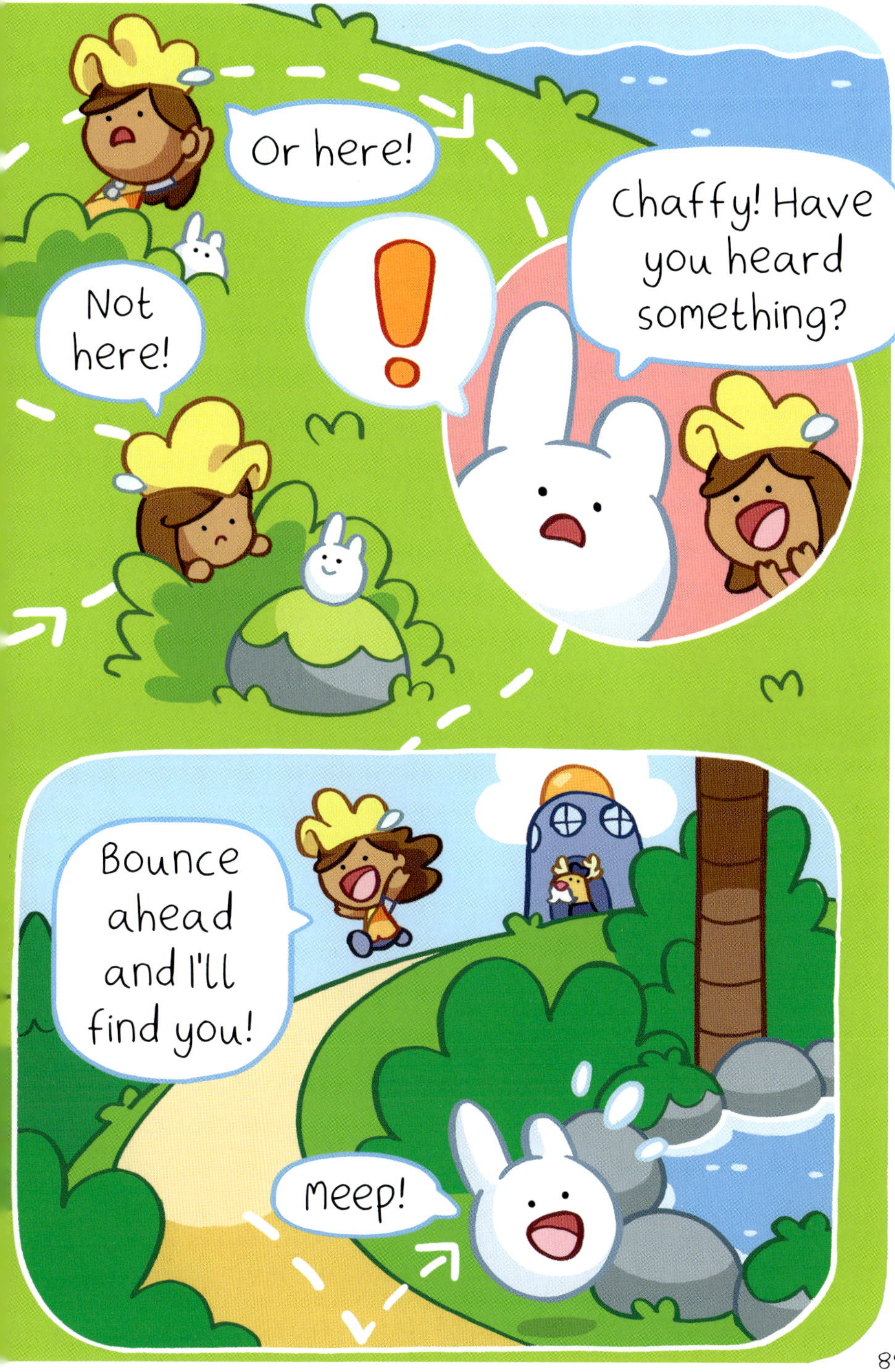
Or here!
Not here!
!
Chaffy! Have you heard something?
Bounce ahead and I'll find you!
Meep!

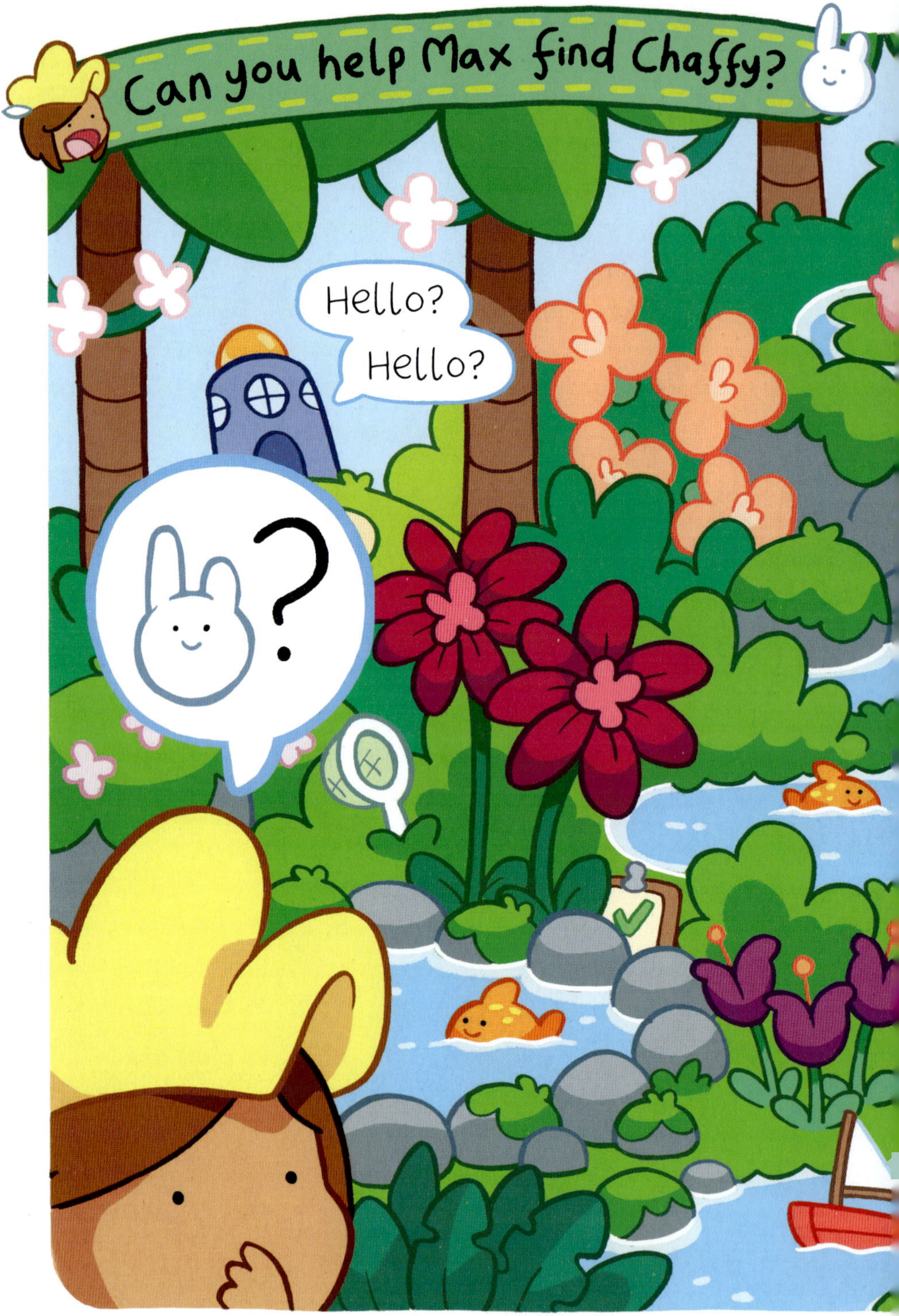
Can you help Max find Chaffy?
Hello?
Hello?
?

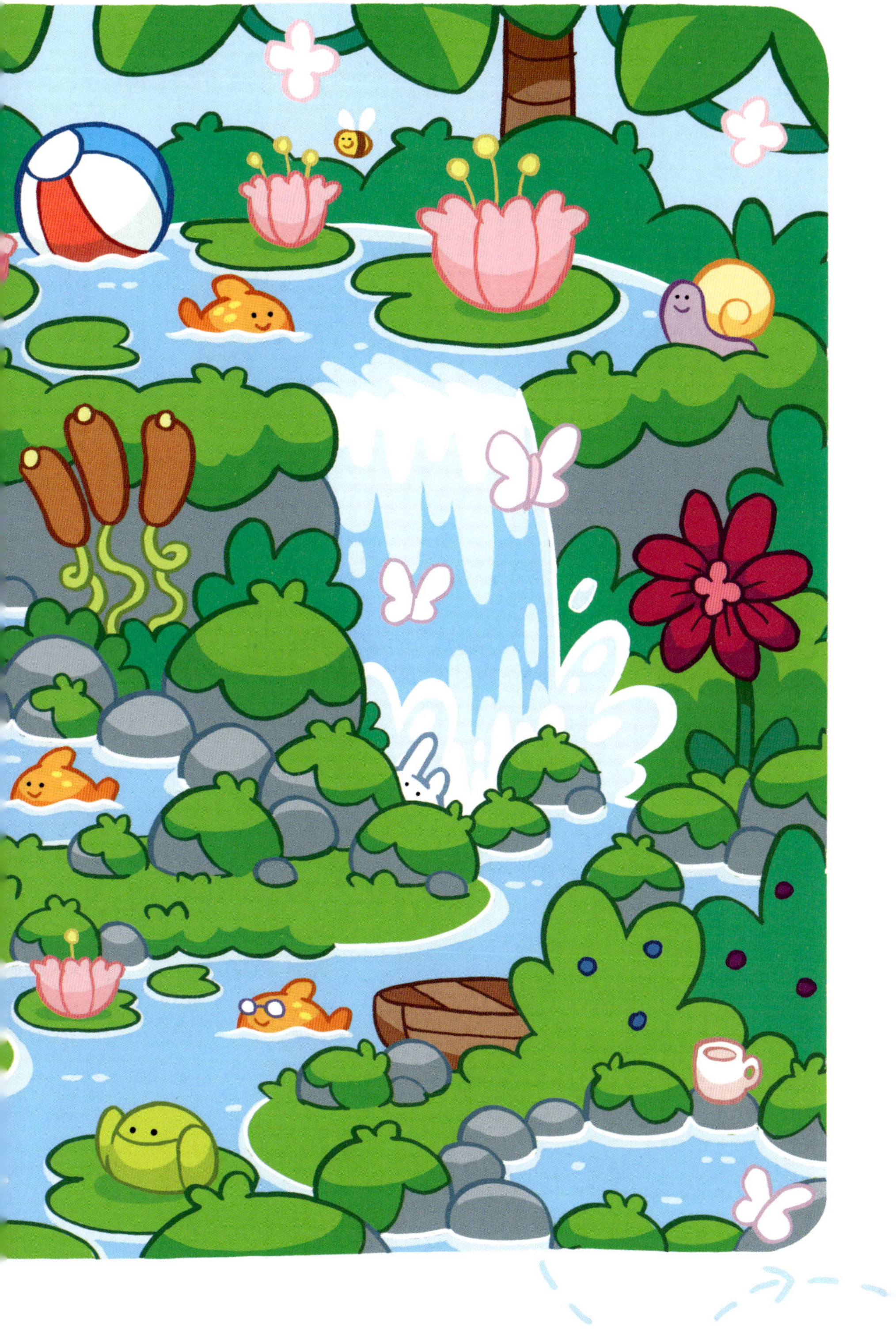

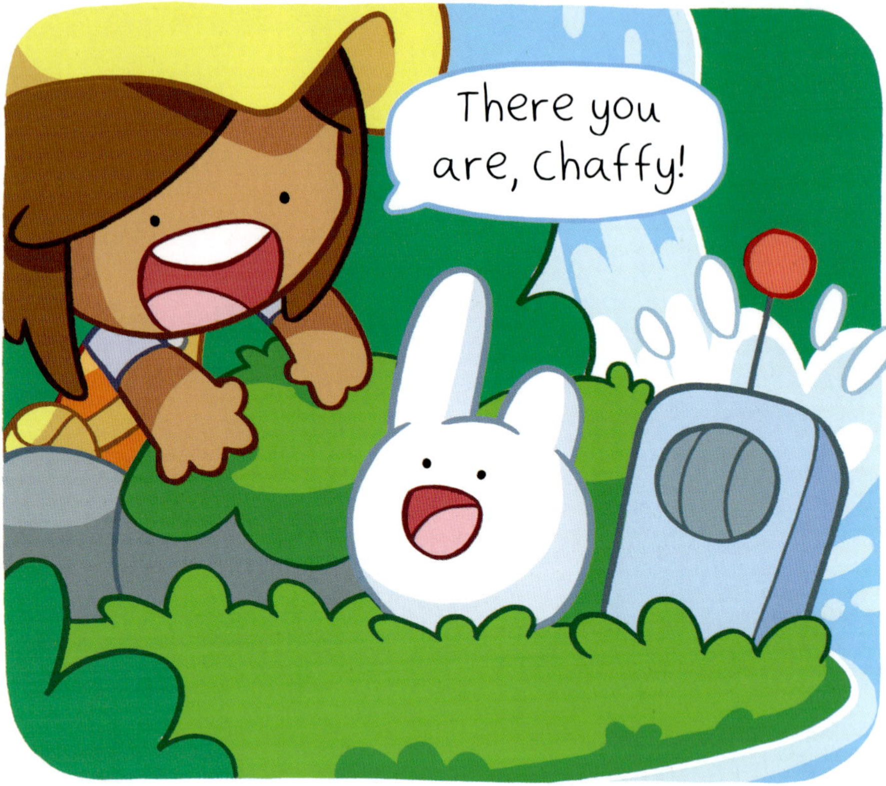
There you are, Chaffy!

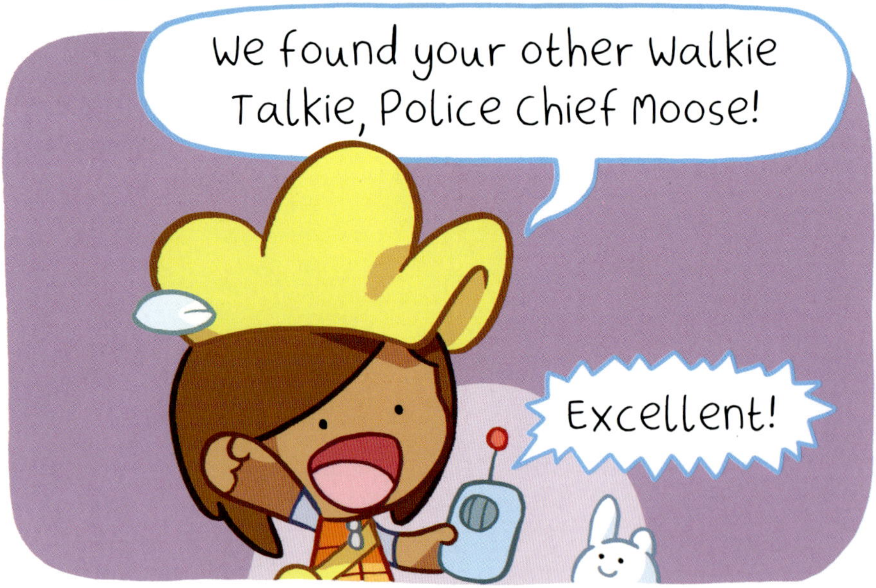
We found your other Walkie Talkie, Police Chief Moose!
Excellent!

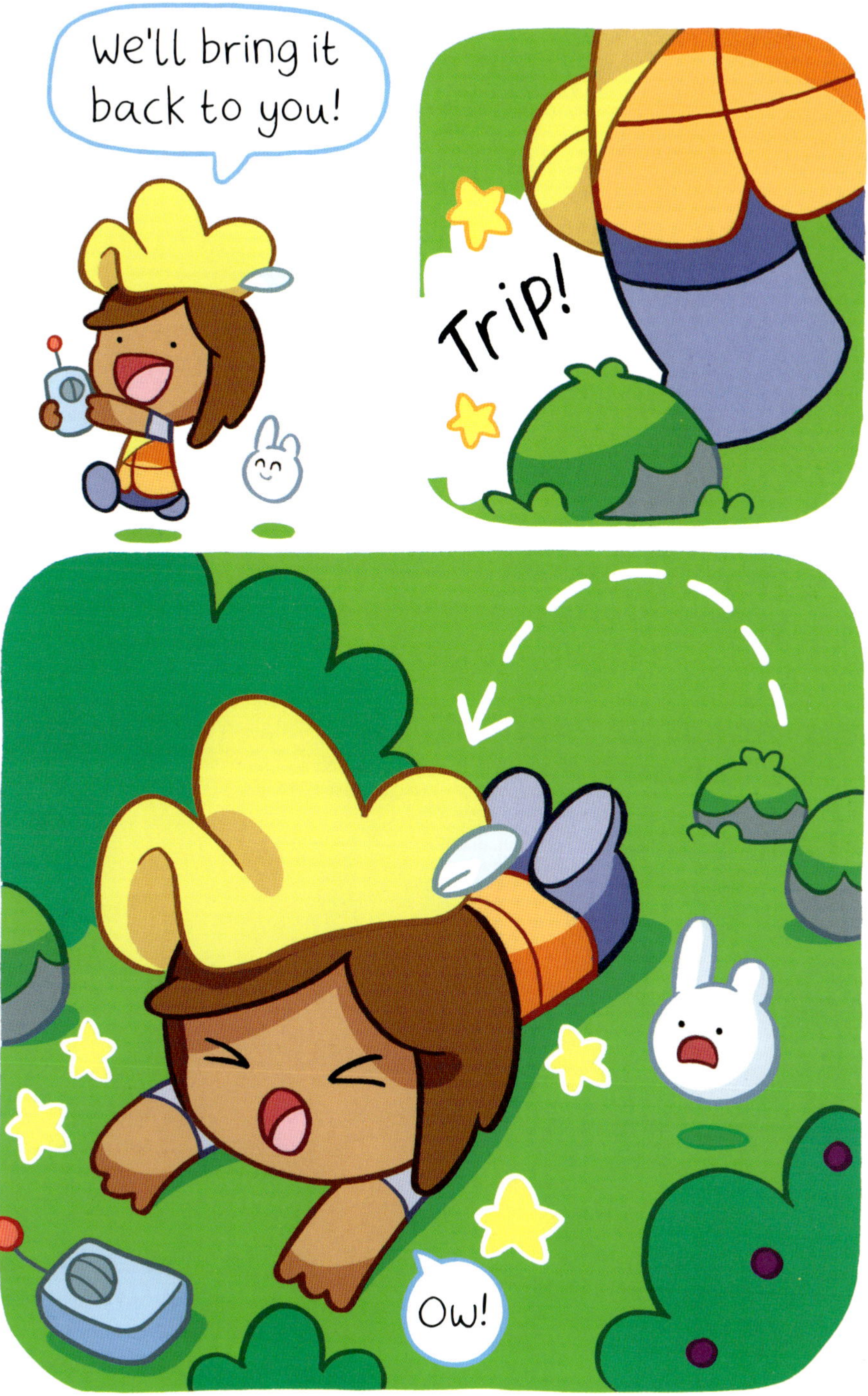
We'll bring it back to you!
Trip!
Ow!

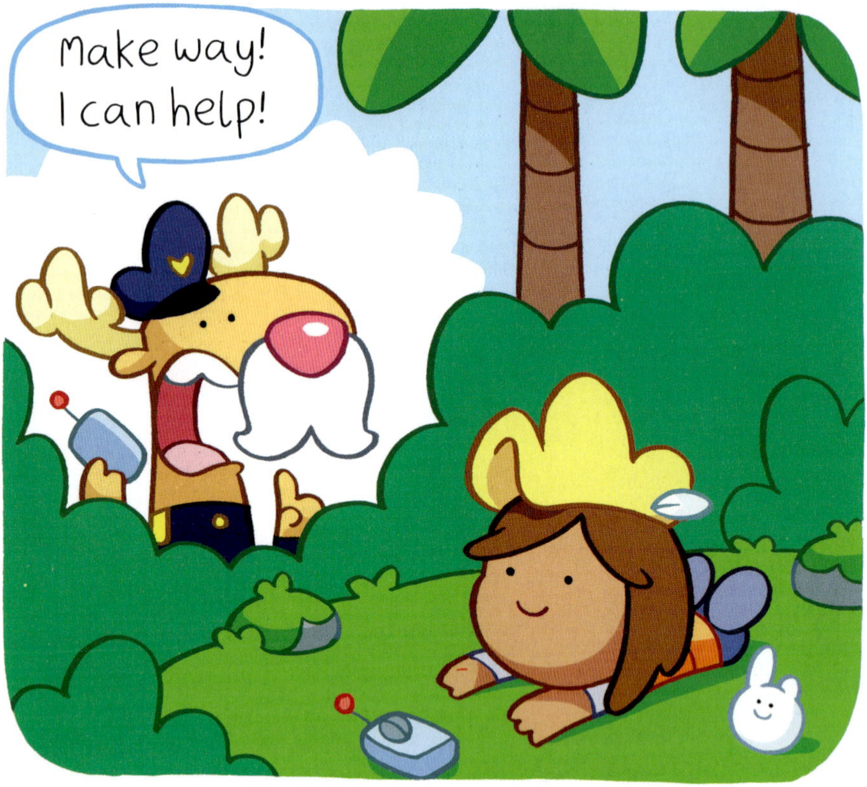
Make way!
I can help!

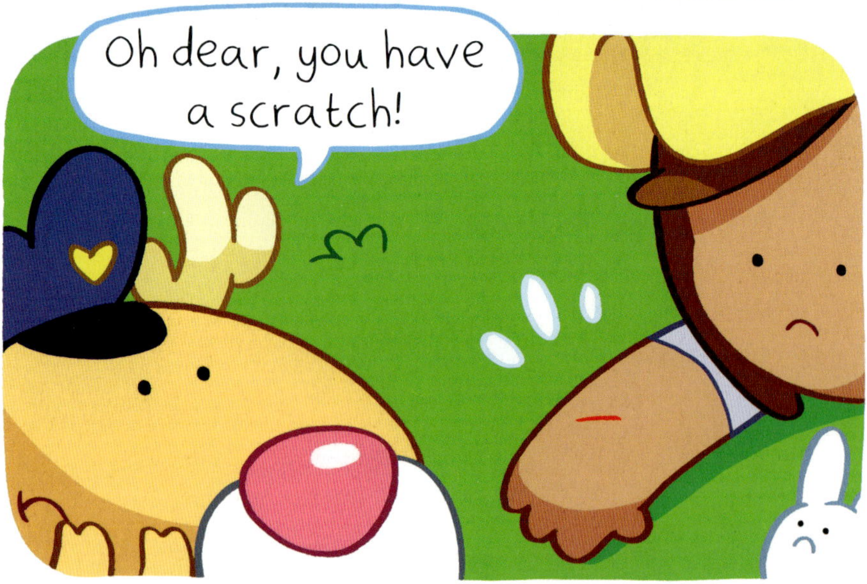
Oh dear, you have
a scratch!

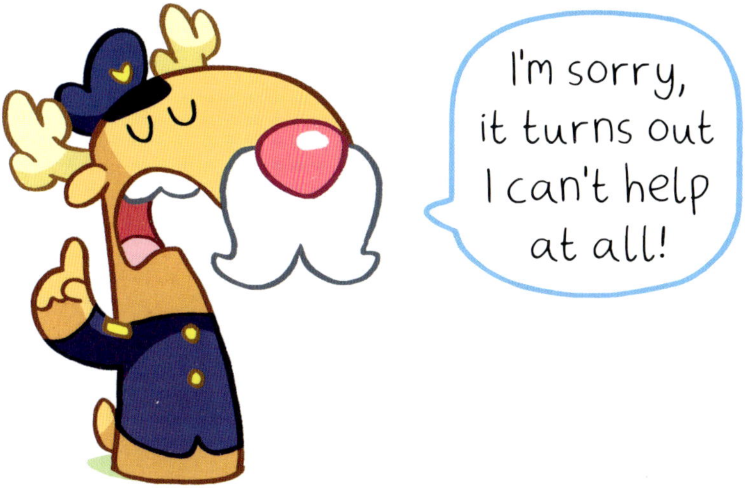
I'm sorry, it turns out I can't help at all!

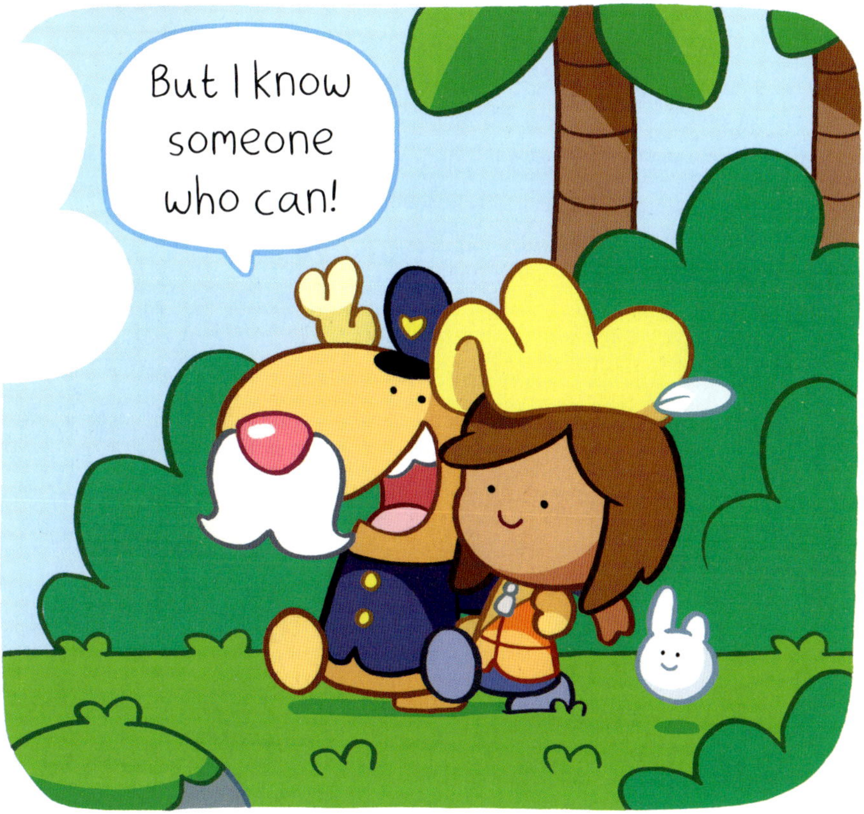
But I know someone who can!

Doctor Pedalo's Hospital!

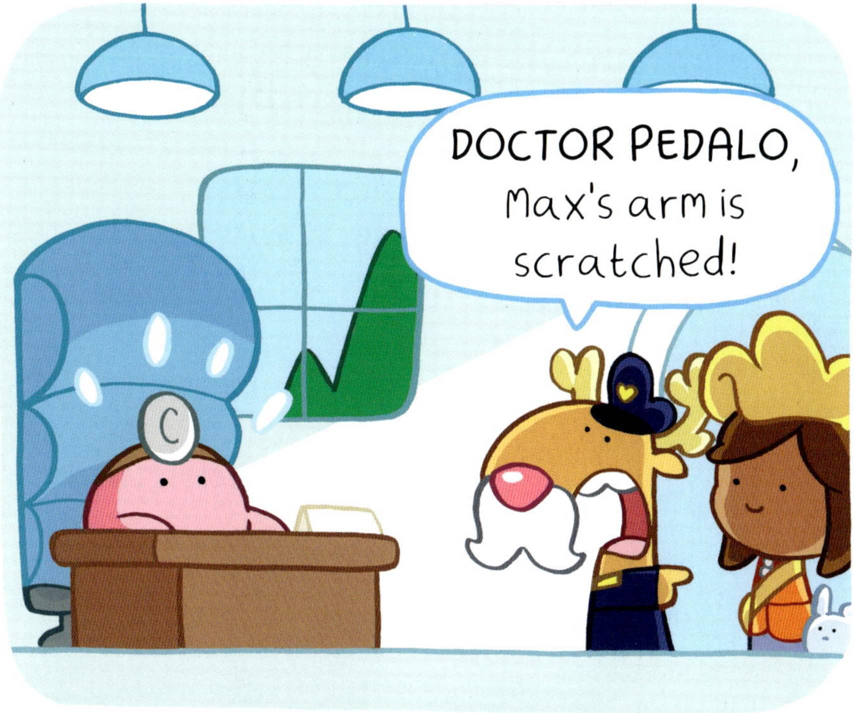
DOCTOR PEDALO, Max's arm is scratched!

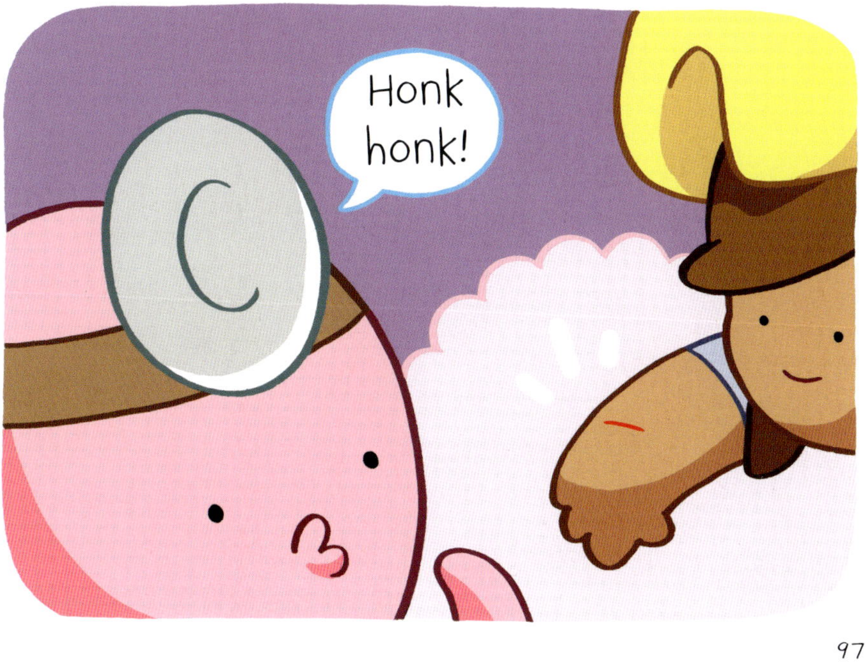
Honk honk!

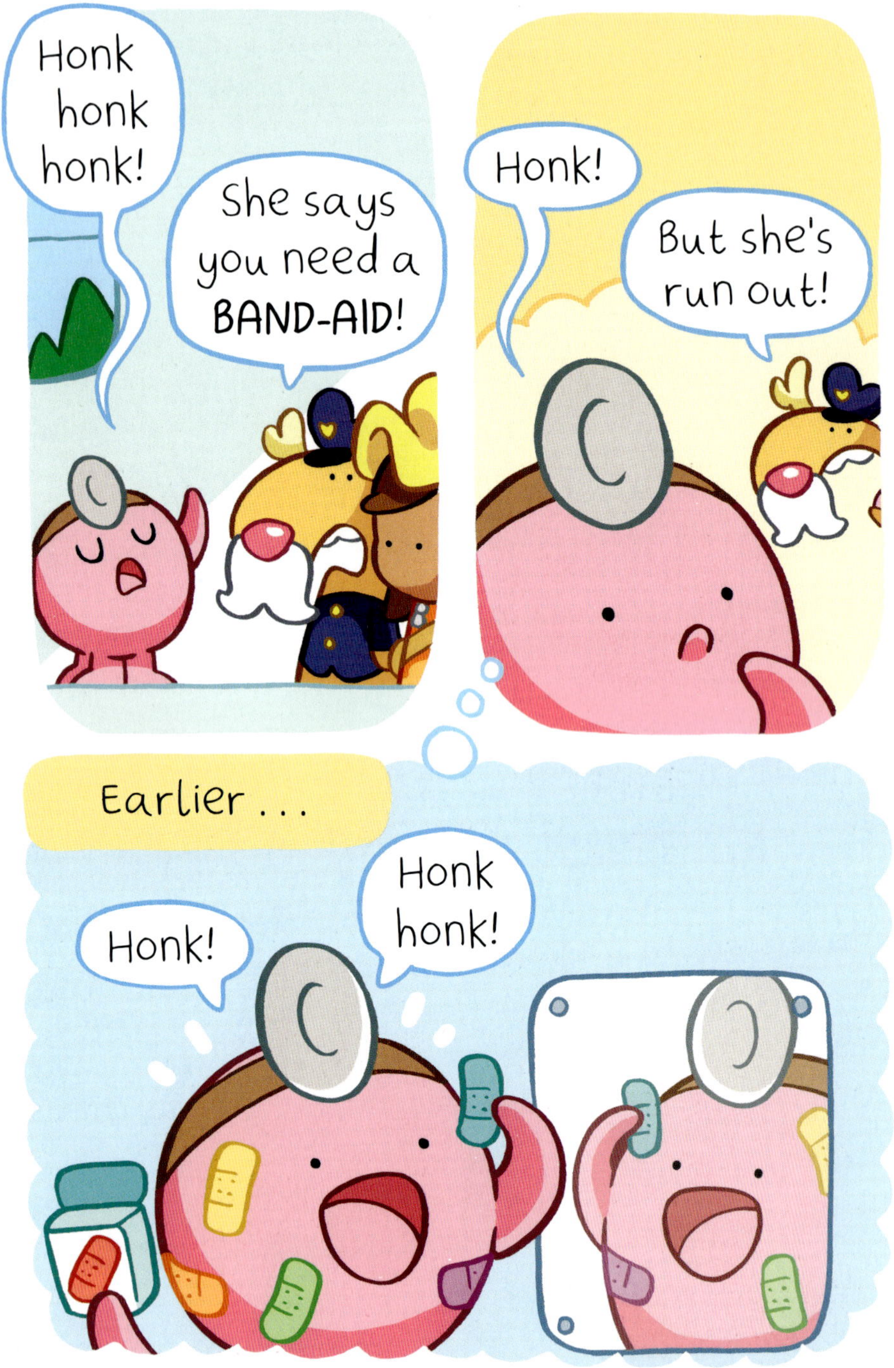
Honk honk honk!
She says you need a BAND-AID!
Honk!
But she's run out!
Earlier . . .
Honk!
Honk honk!

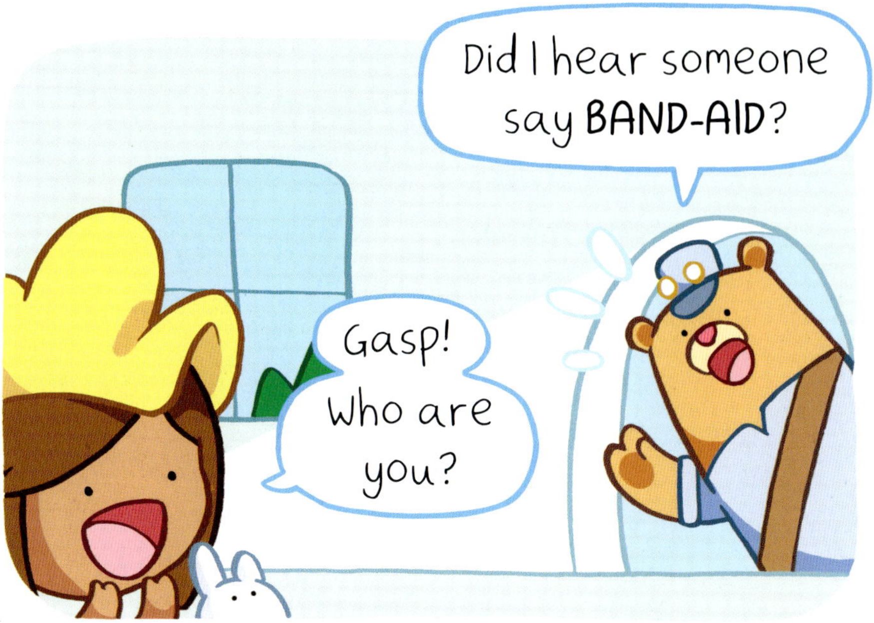
Did I hear someone say BAND-AID?
Gasp! Who are you?

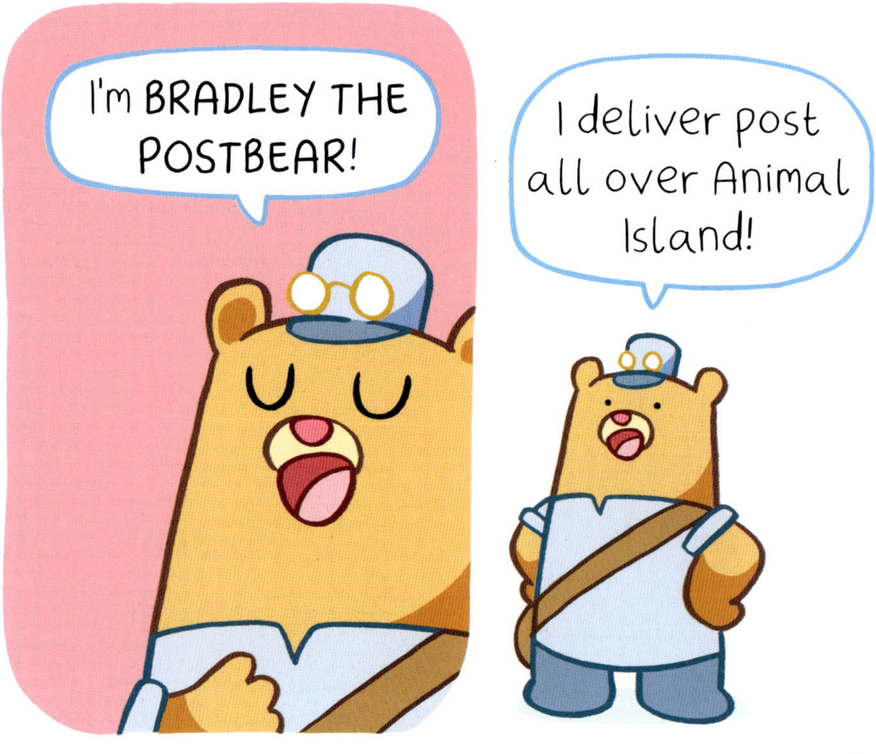
I'm BRADLEY THE POSTBEAR!
I deliver post all over Animal Island!

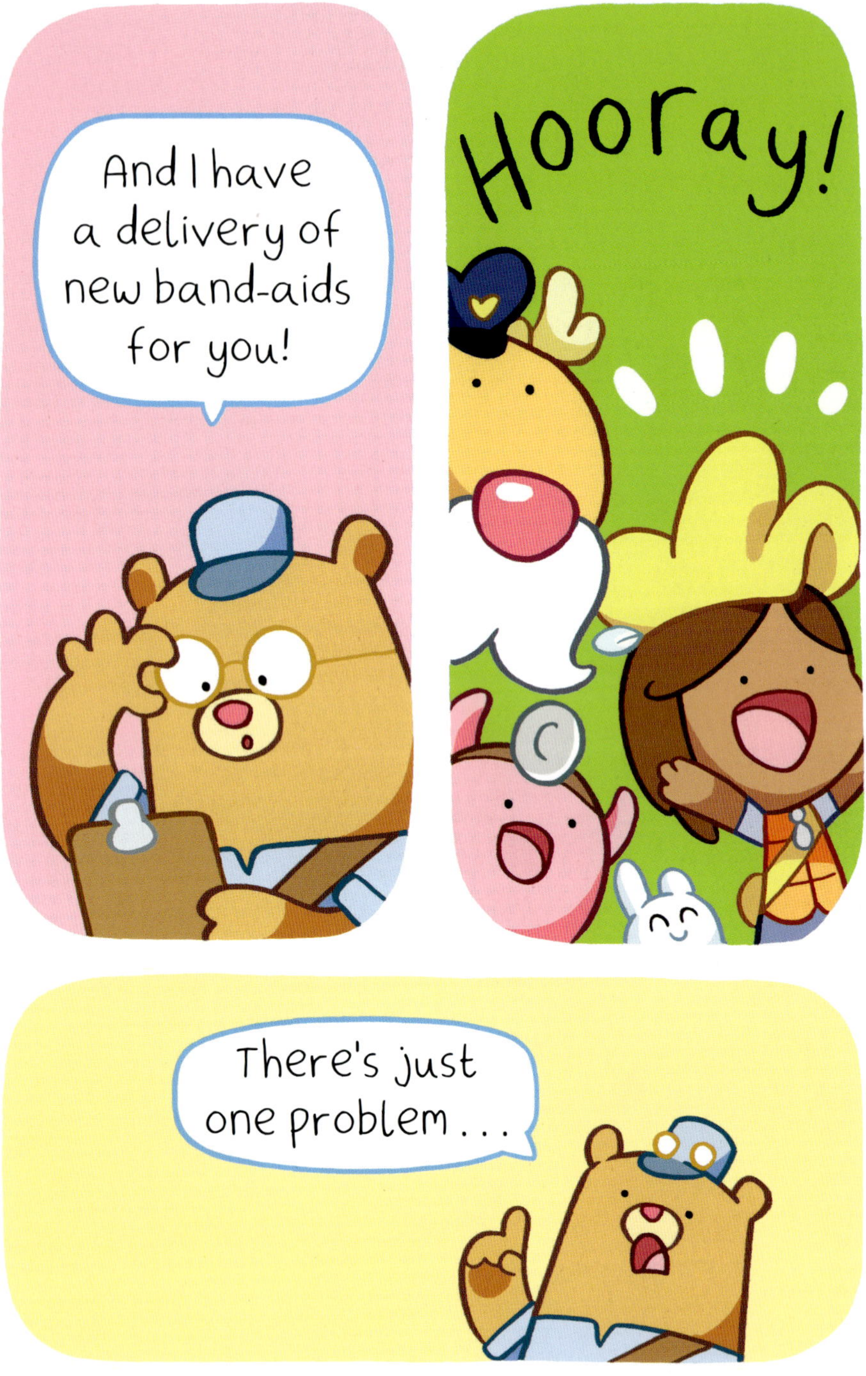
And I have a delivery of new band-aids for you!
Hooray!
There's just one problem . . .

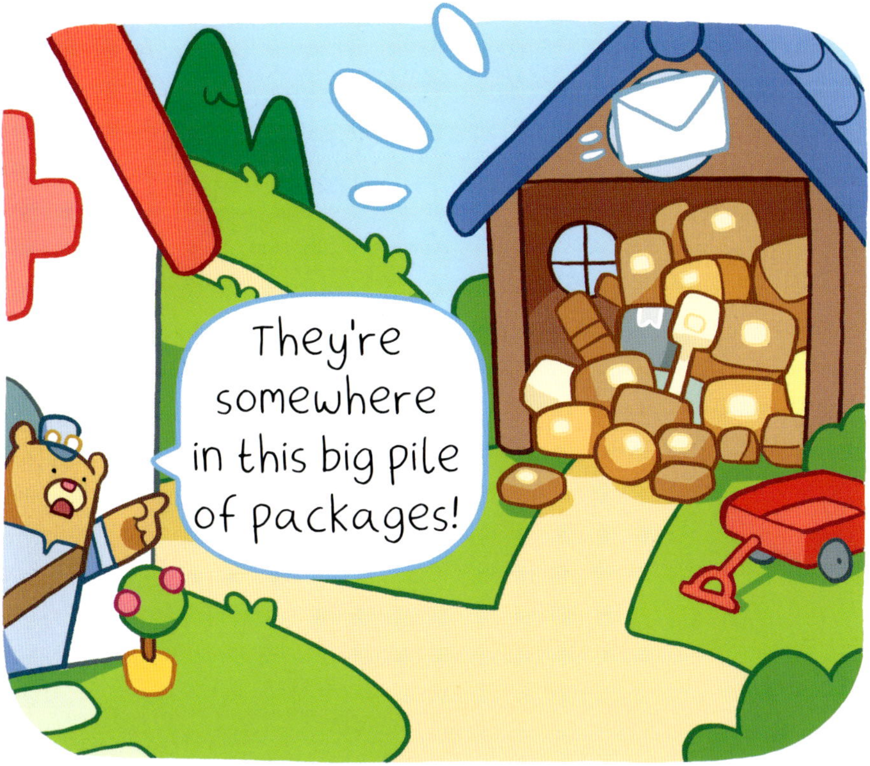
They're somewhere in this big pile of packages!

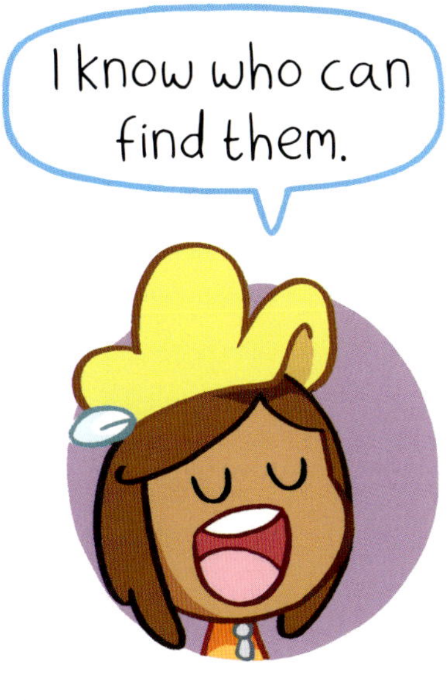
I know who can find them.

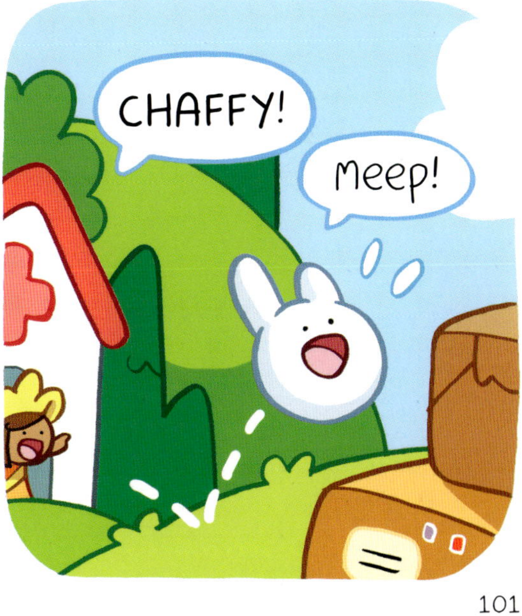
CHAFFY!
Meep!

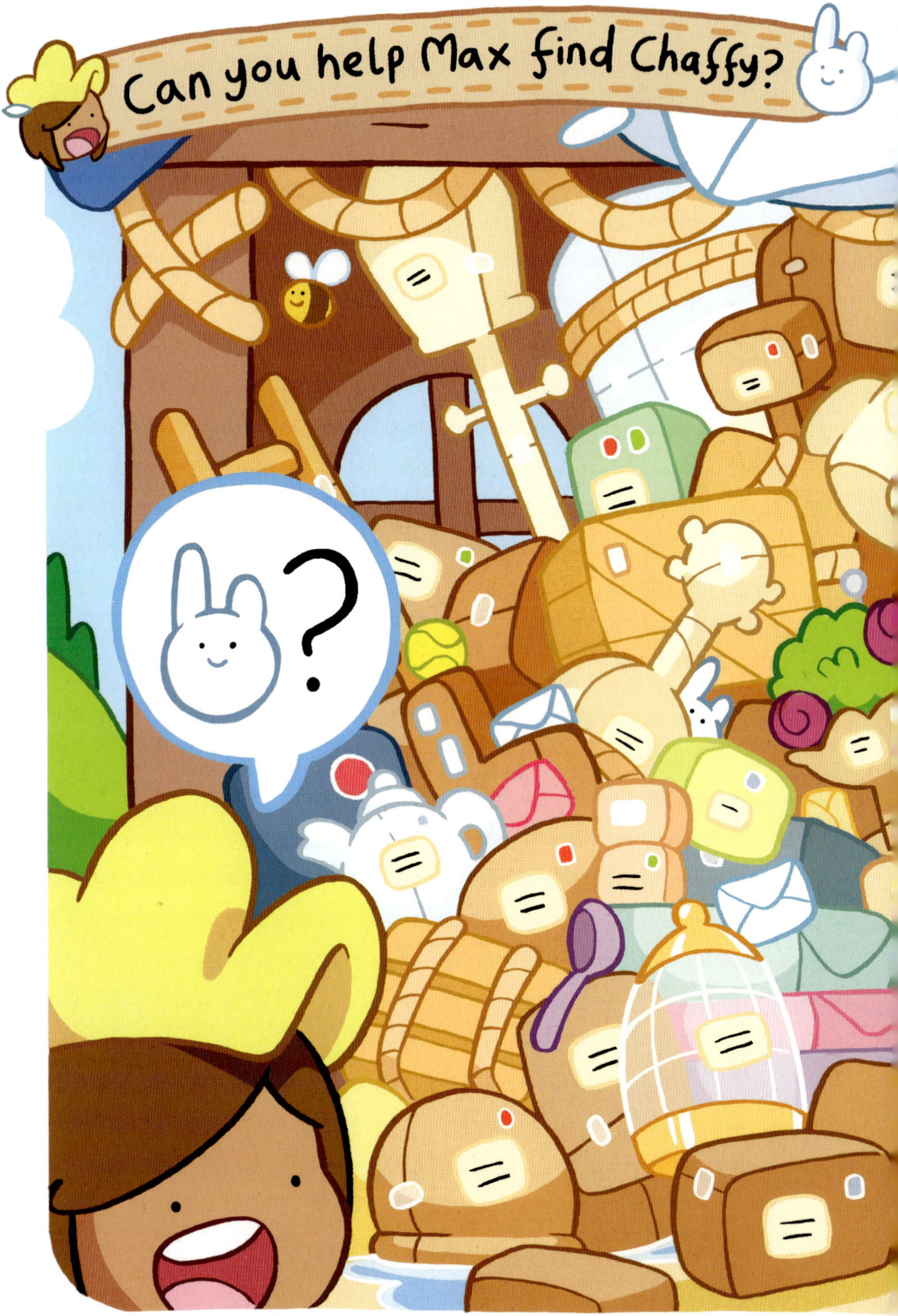
Can you help Max find Chaffy?
?

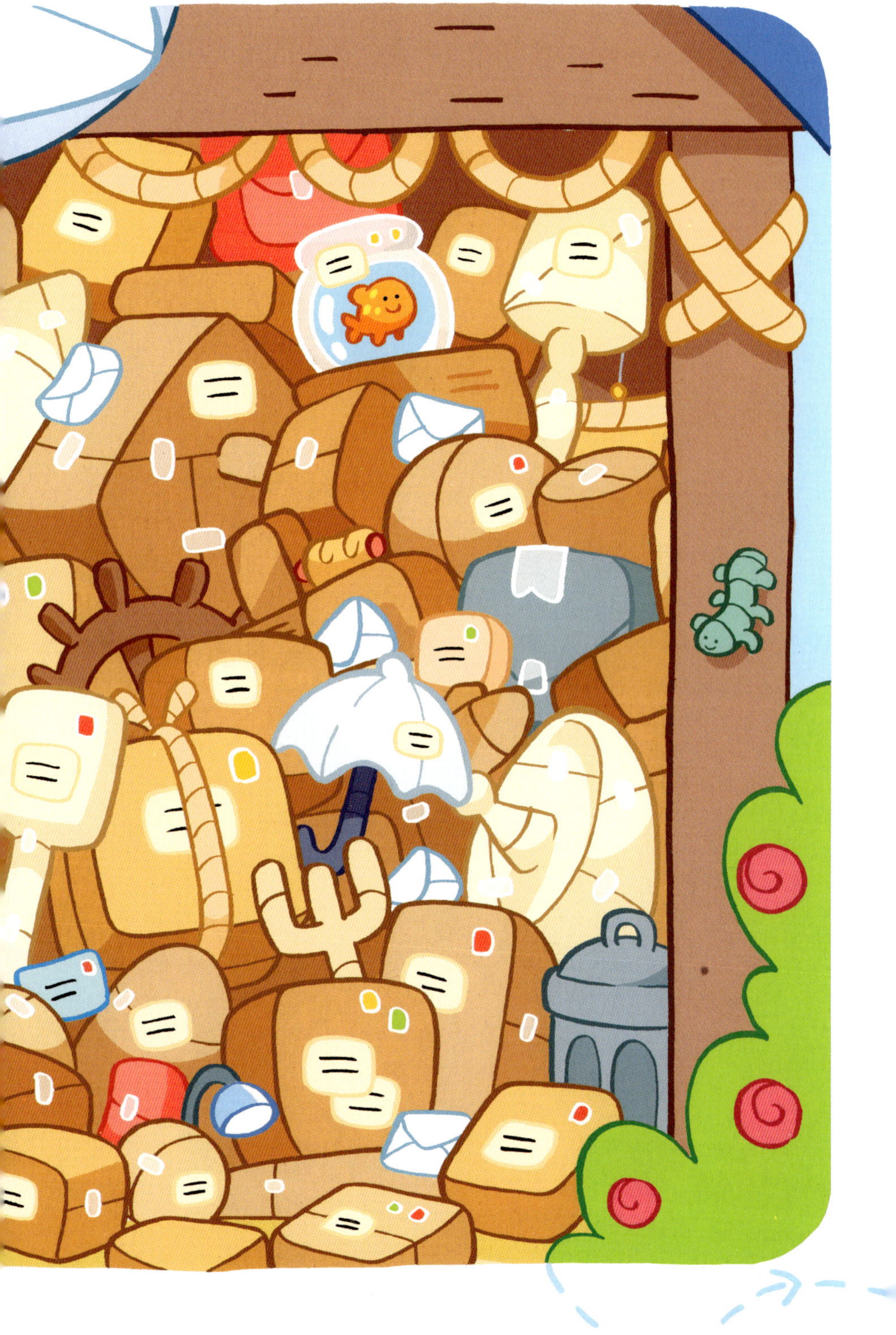

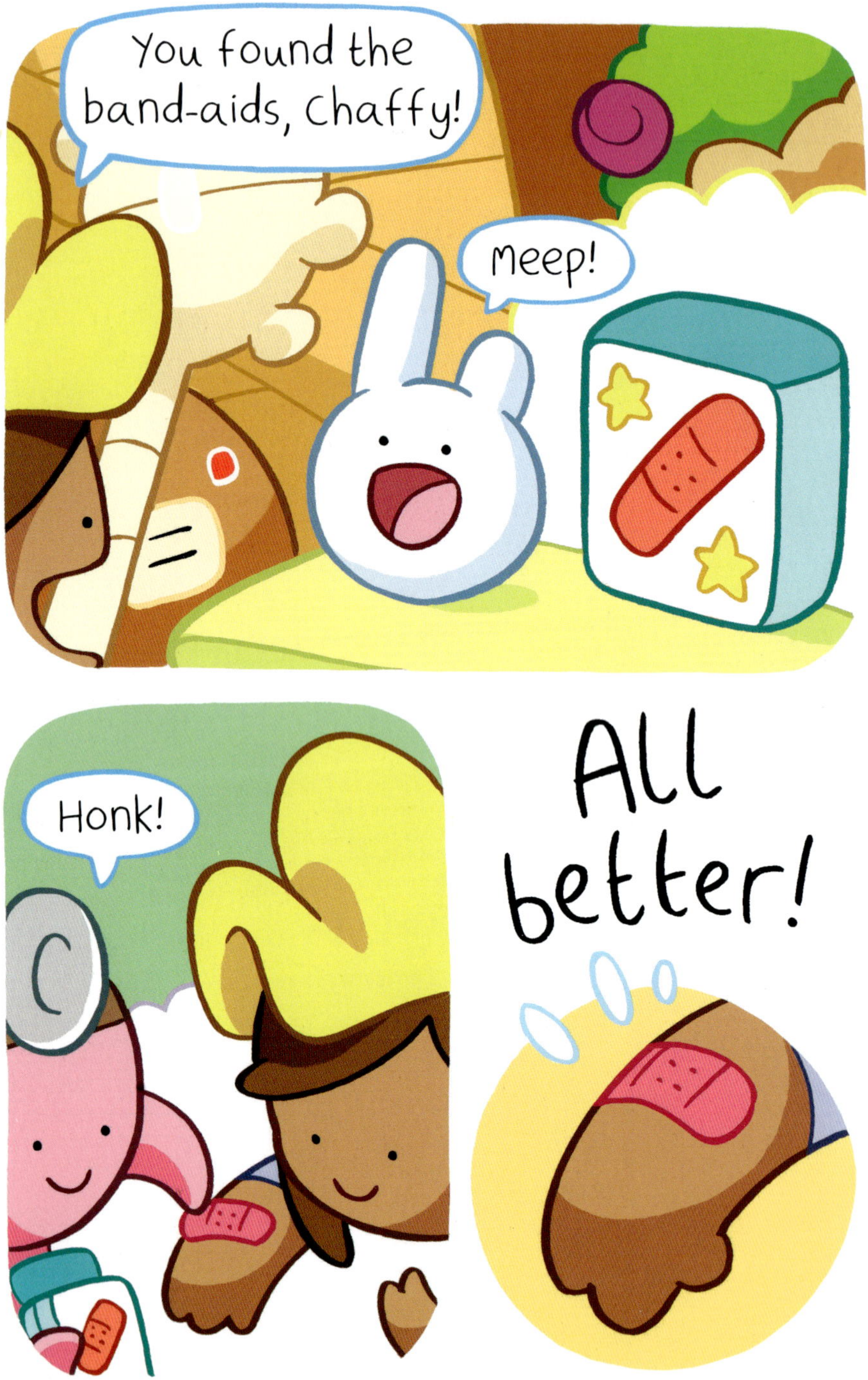
You found the band-aids, Chaffy!
meep!
Honk!
All better!

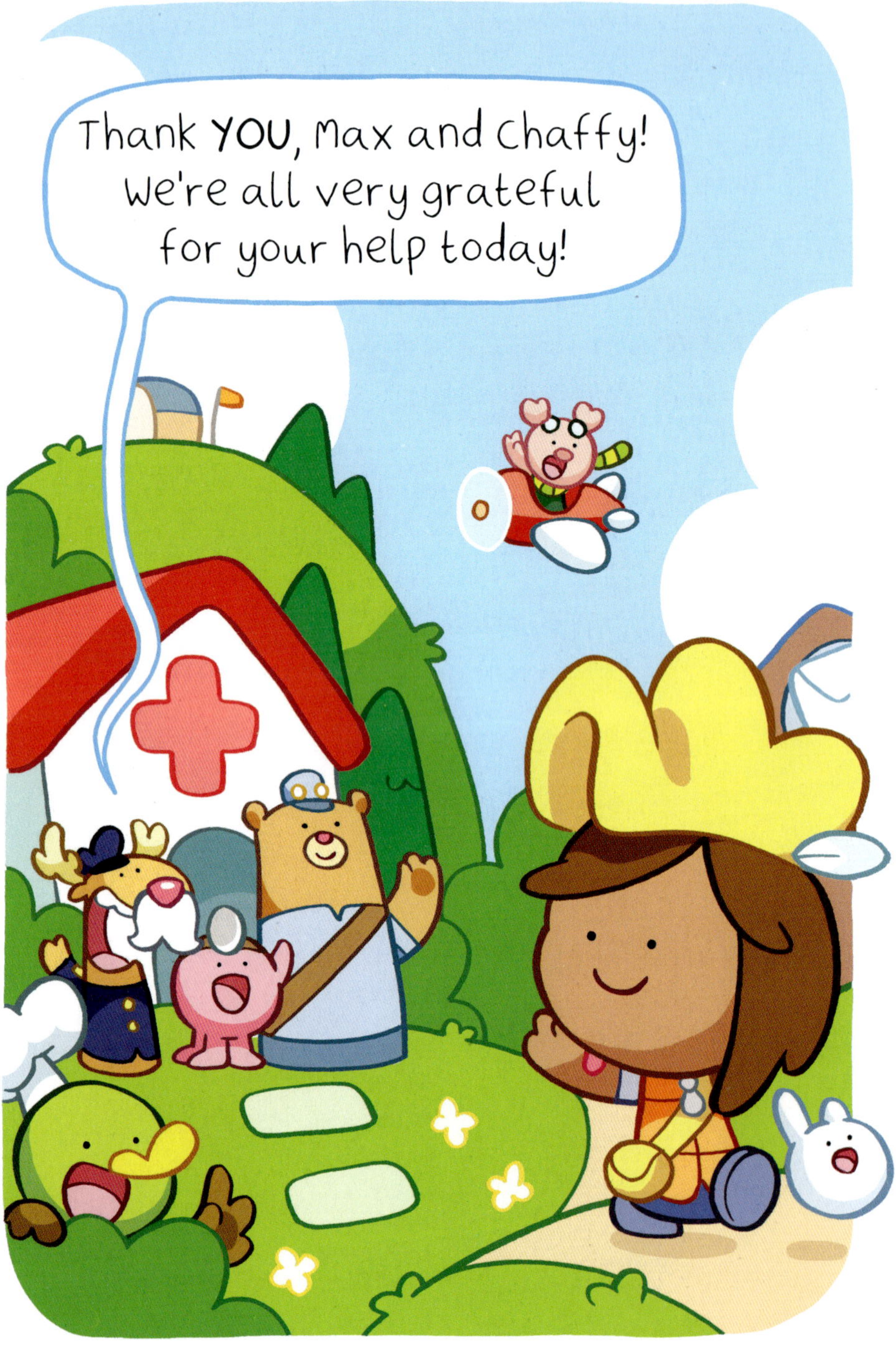
Thank **YOU**, Max and Chaffy! We're all very grateful for your help today!

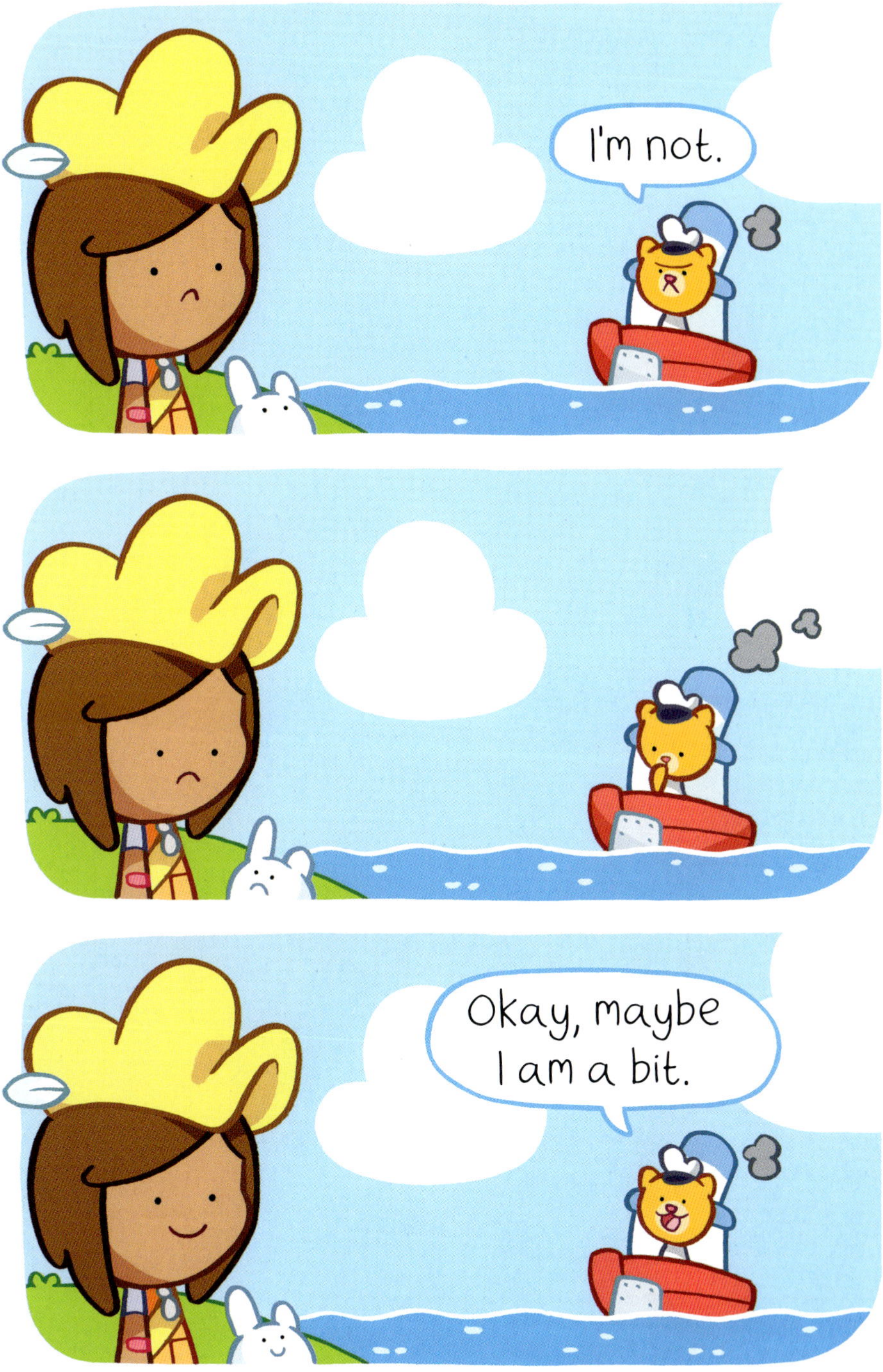
I'm not.
Okay, maybe I am a bit.

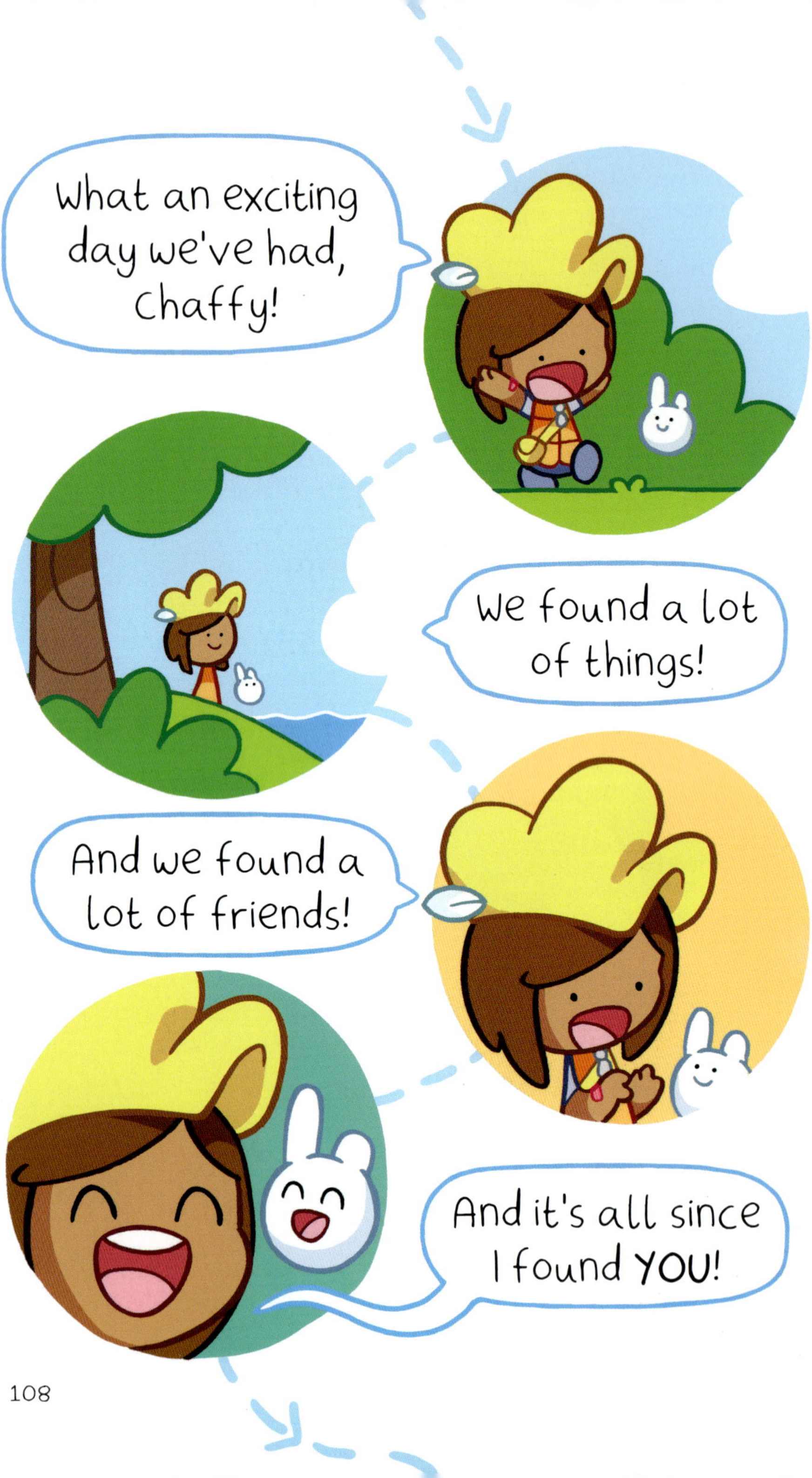
What an exciting day we've had, Chaffy!
We found a lot of things!
And we found a lot of friends!
And it's all since I found YOU!

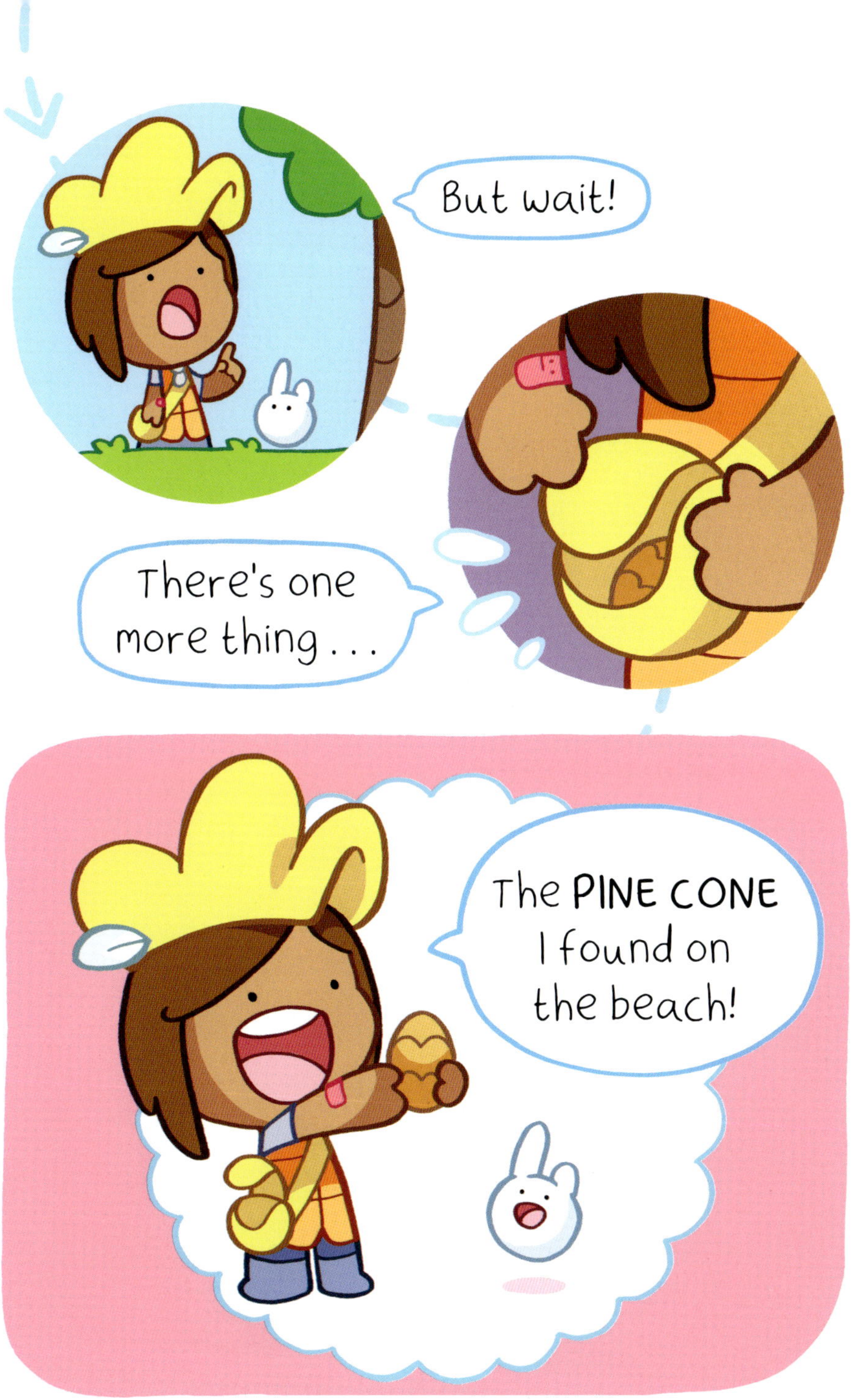
But wait!
There's one more thing . . .
The PINE CONE I found on the beach!

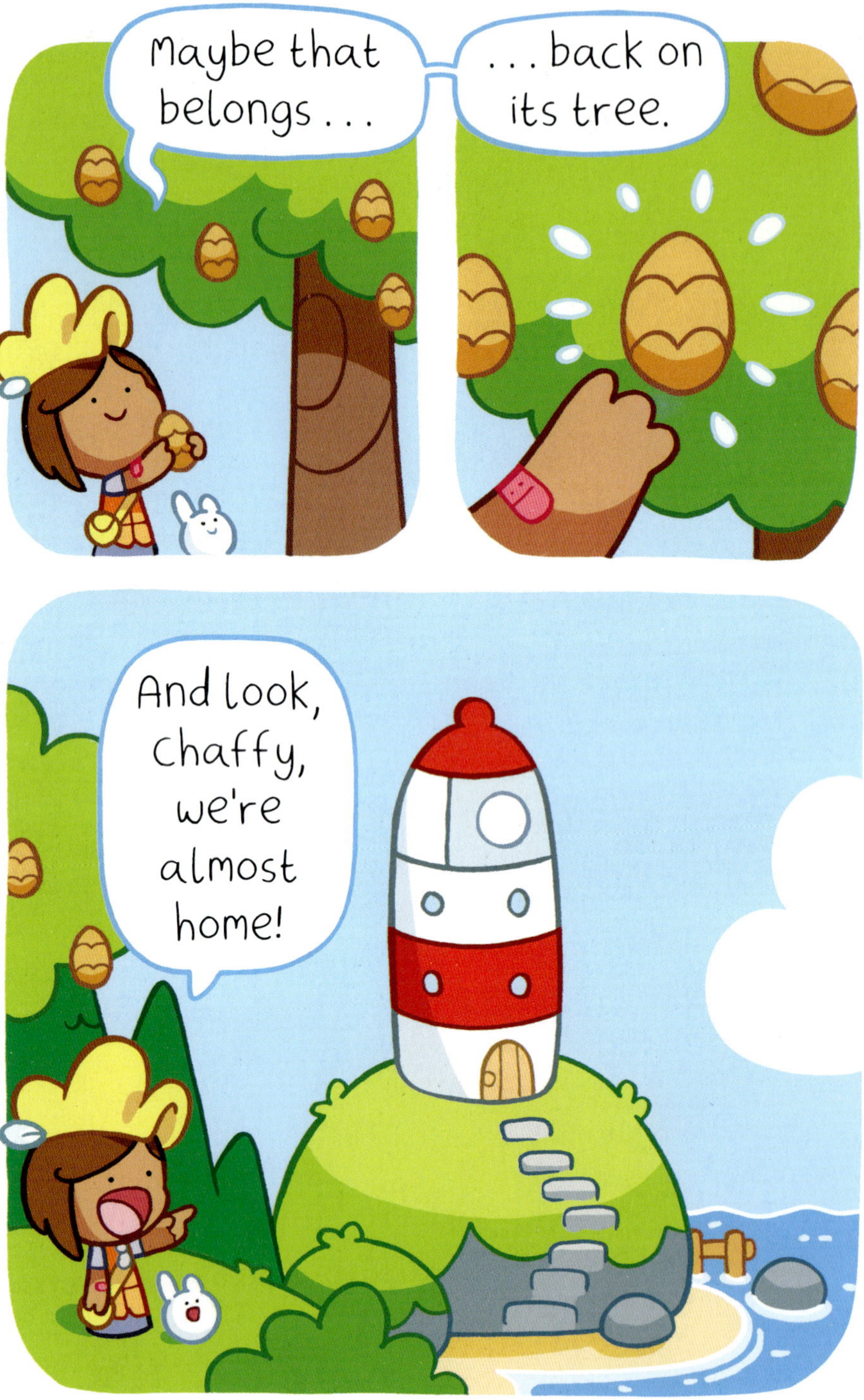
Maybe that belongs . . .
. . . back on its tree.
And look, Chaffy, we're almost home!

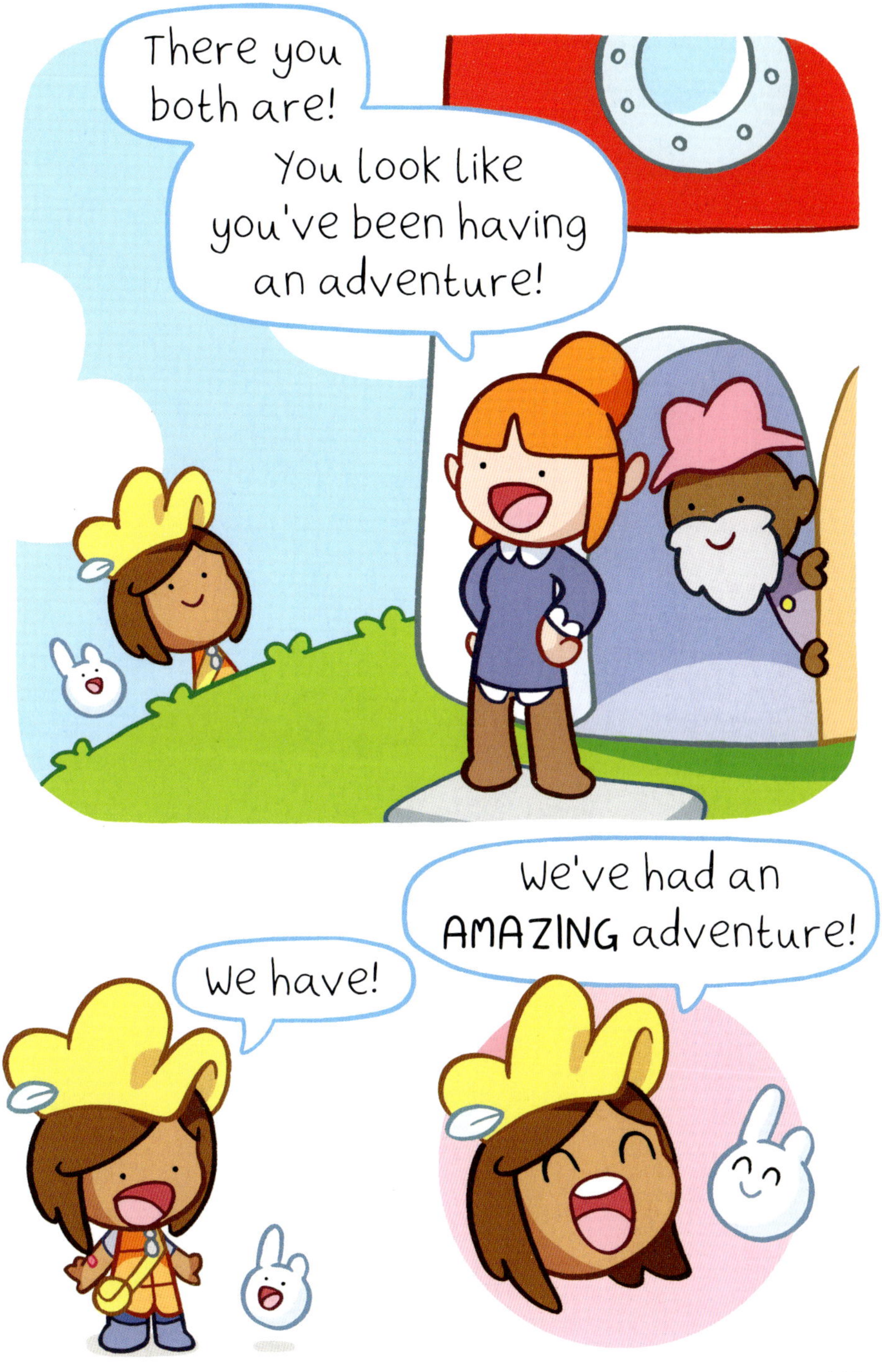
There you both are!
You look like you've been having an adventure!
We have!
We've had an AMAZING adventure!

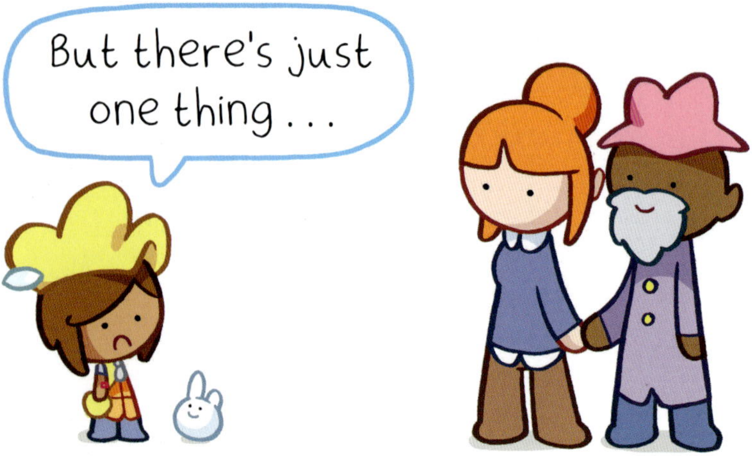
But there's just one thing . . .

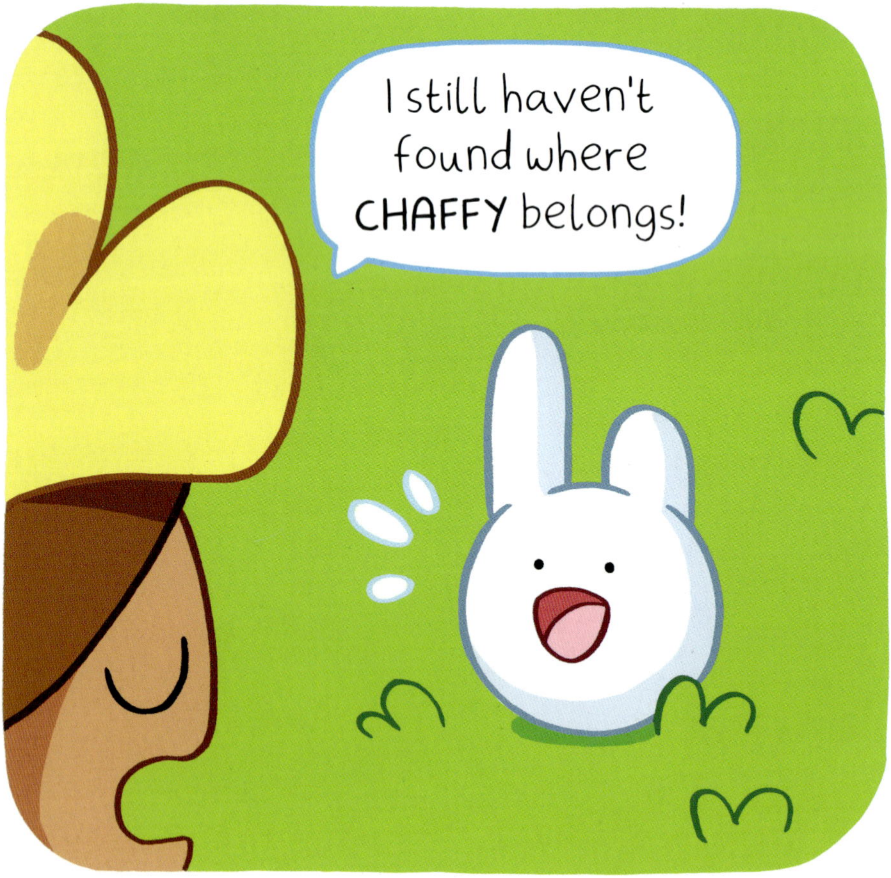
I still haven't found where CHAFFY belongs!

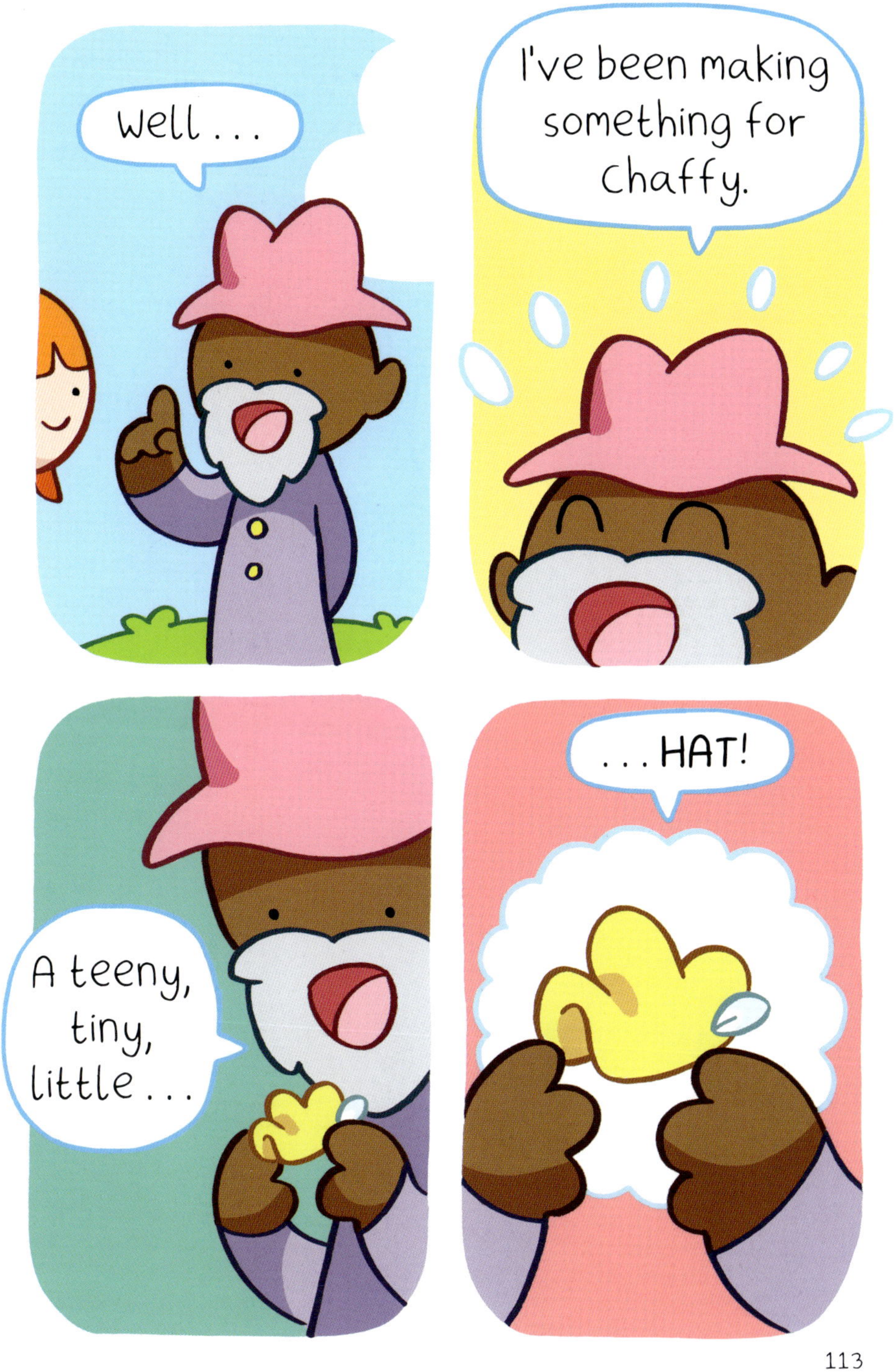
Well . . .
I've been making something for Chaffy.
A teeny, tiny, little . . .
. . . HAT!

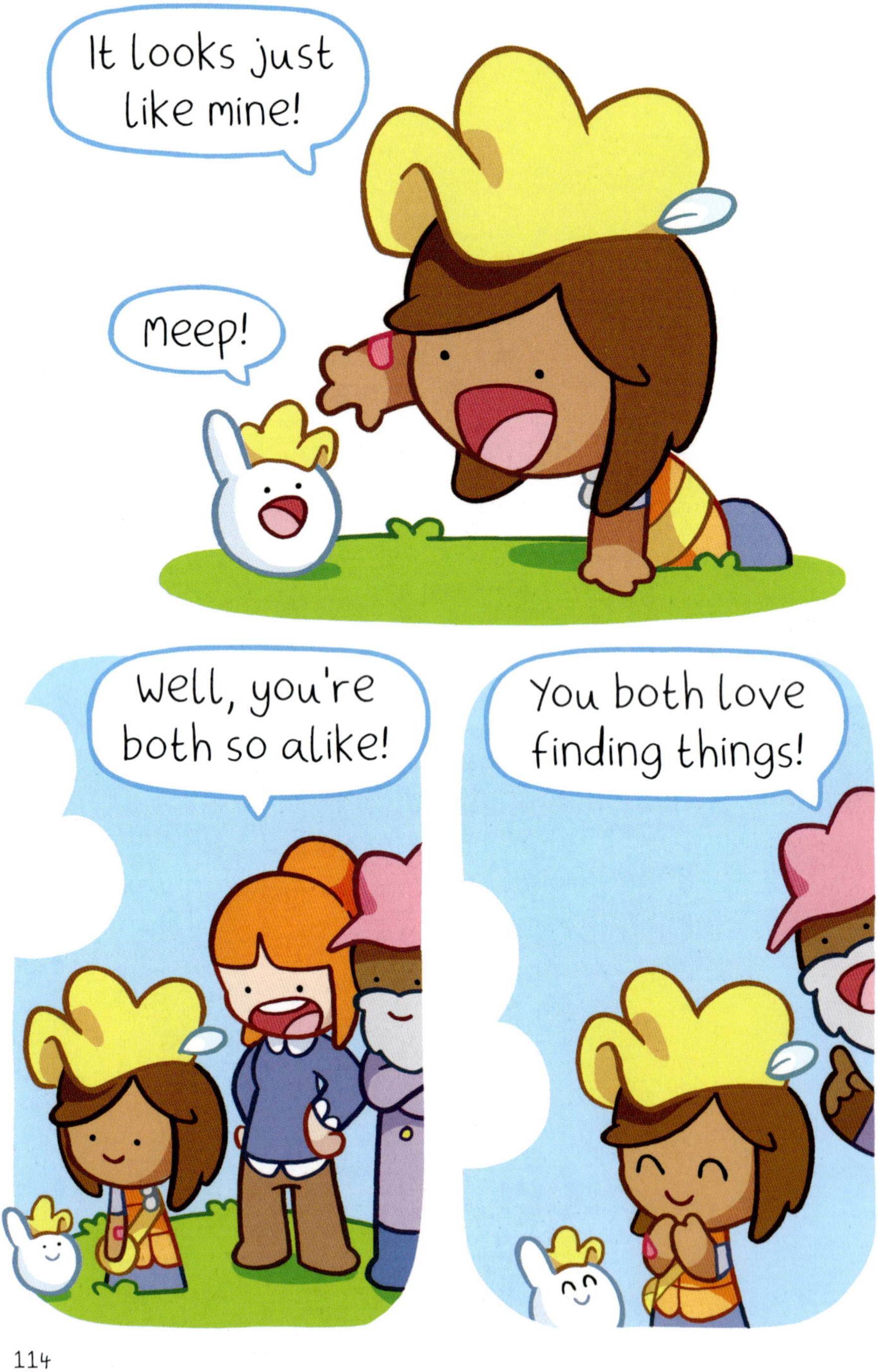
It looks just like mine!
Meep!
Well, you're both so alike!
You both love finding things!

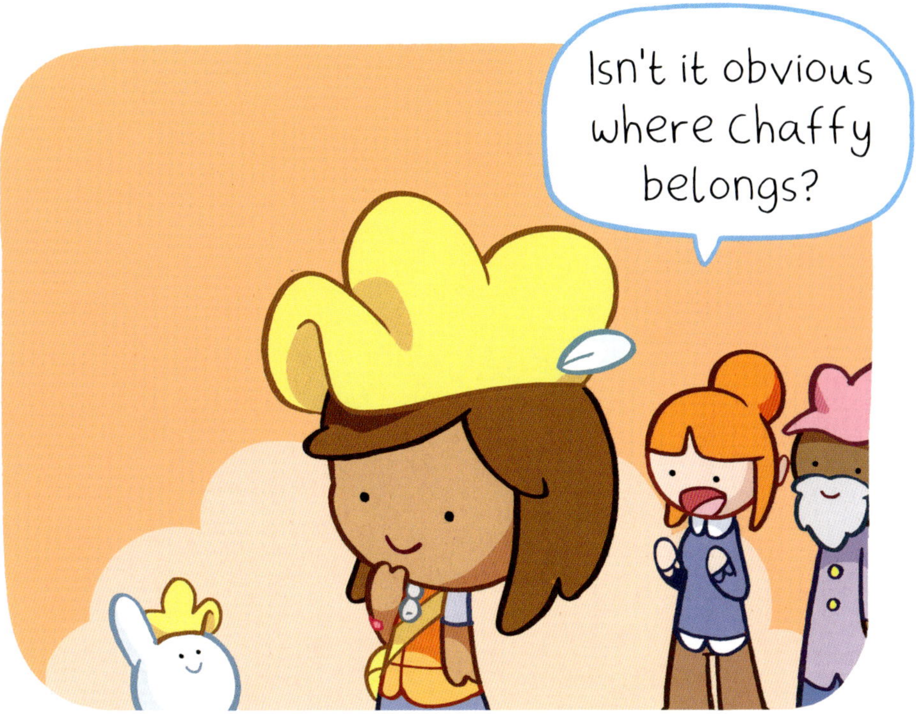
Isn't it obvious where Chaffy belongs?

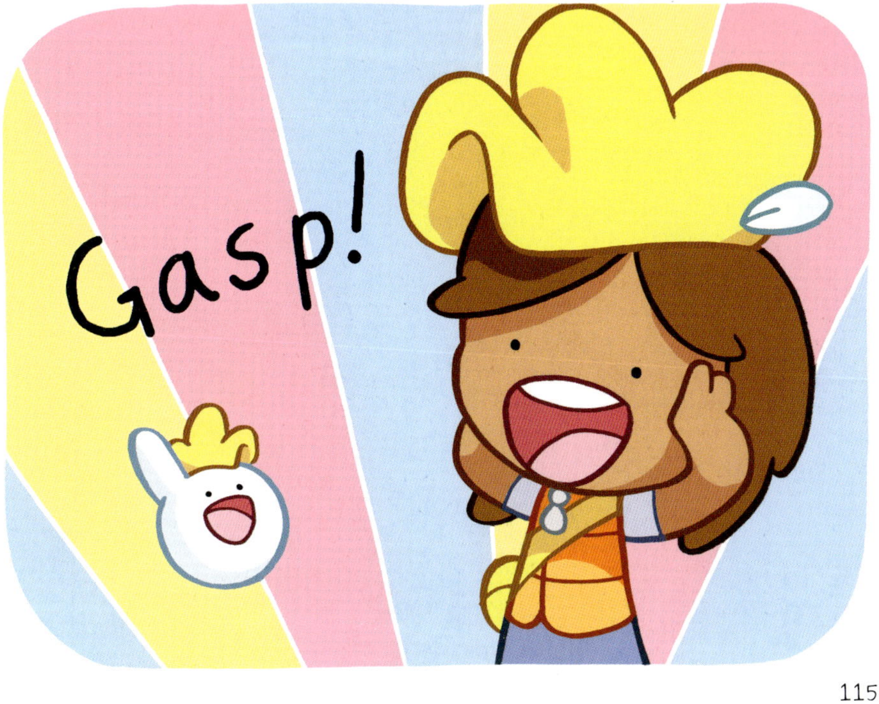
Gasp!

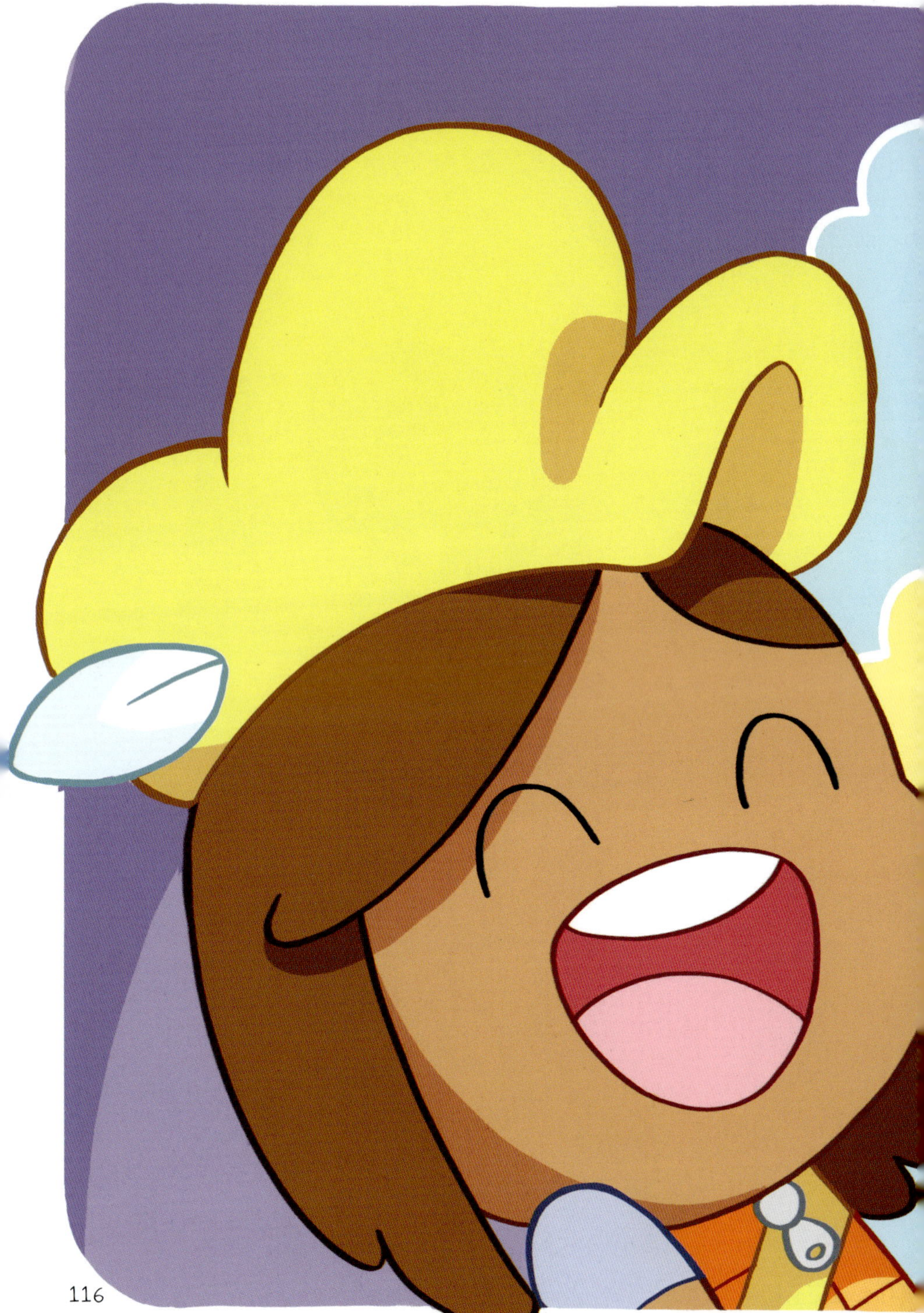

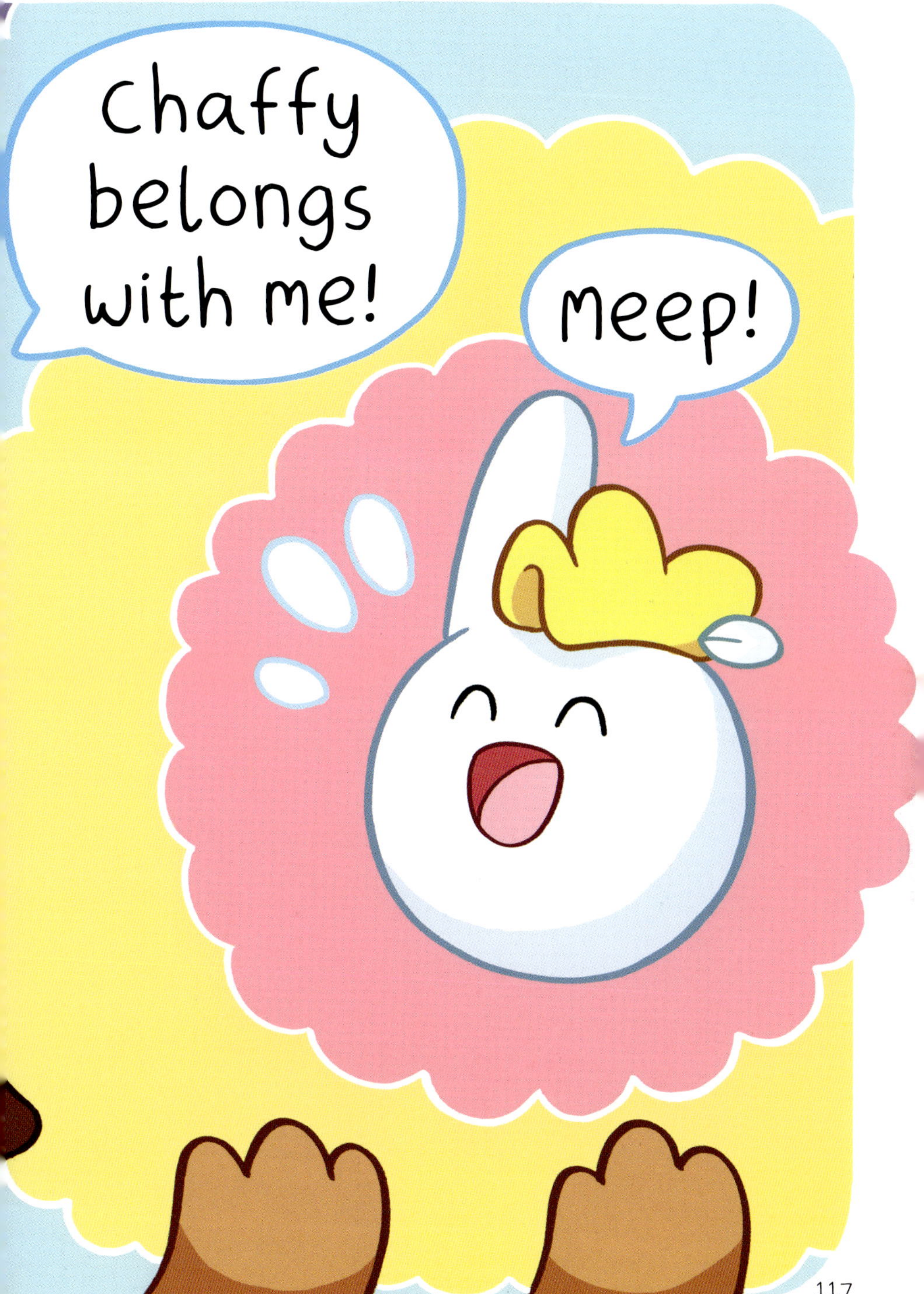
Chaffy belongs with me!
Meep!

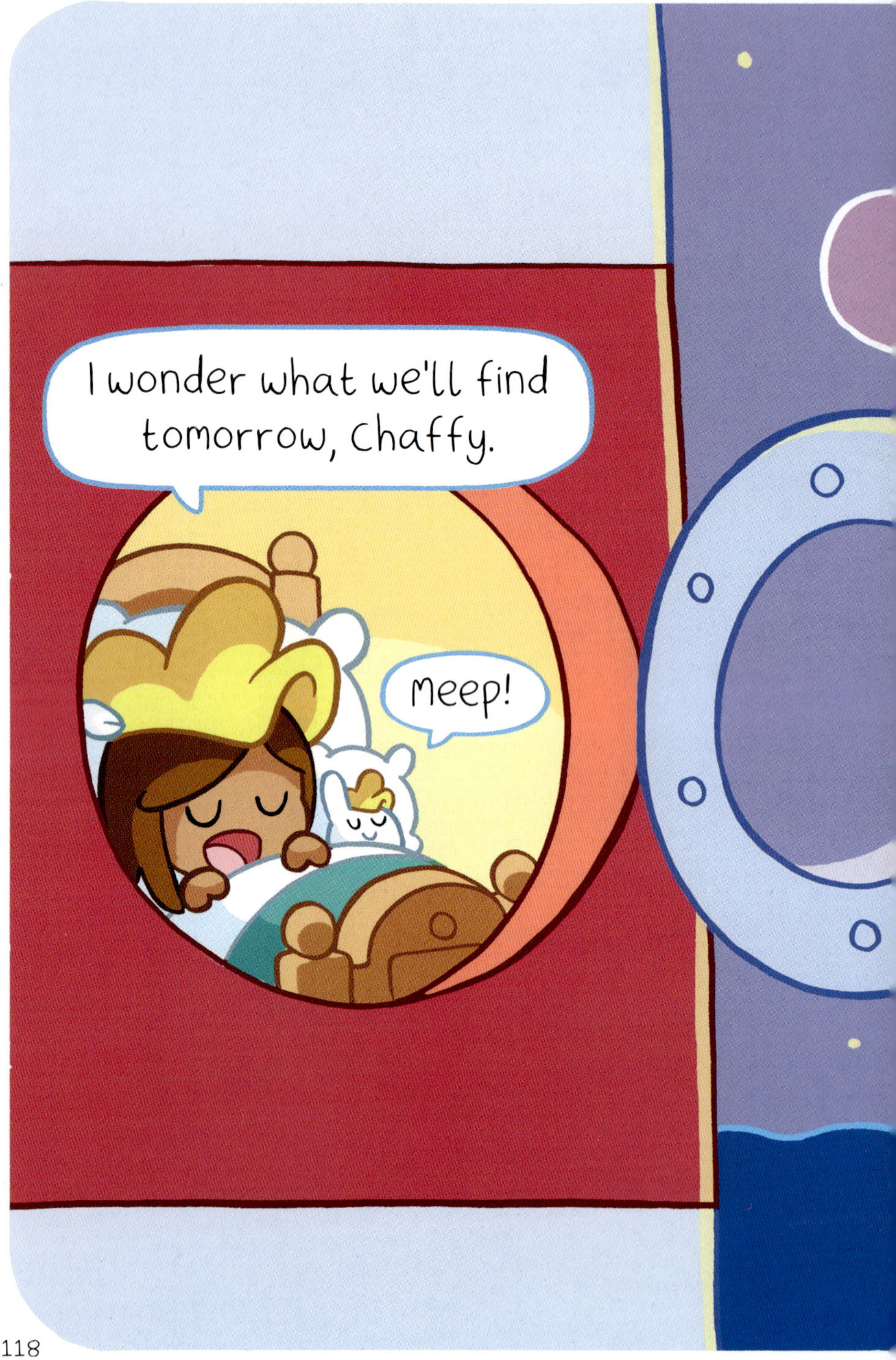
I wonder what we'll find tomorrow, Chaffy.
Meep!

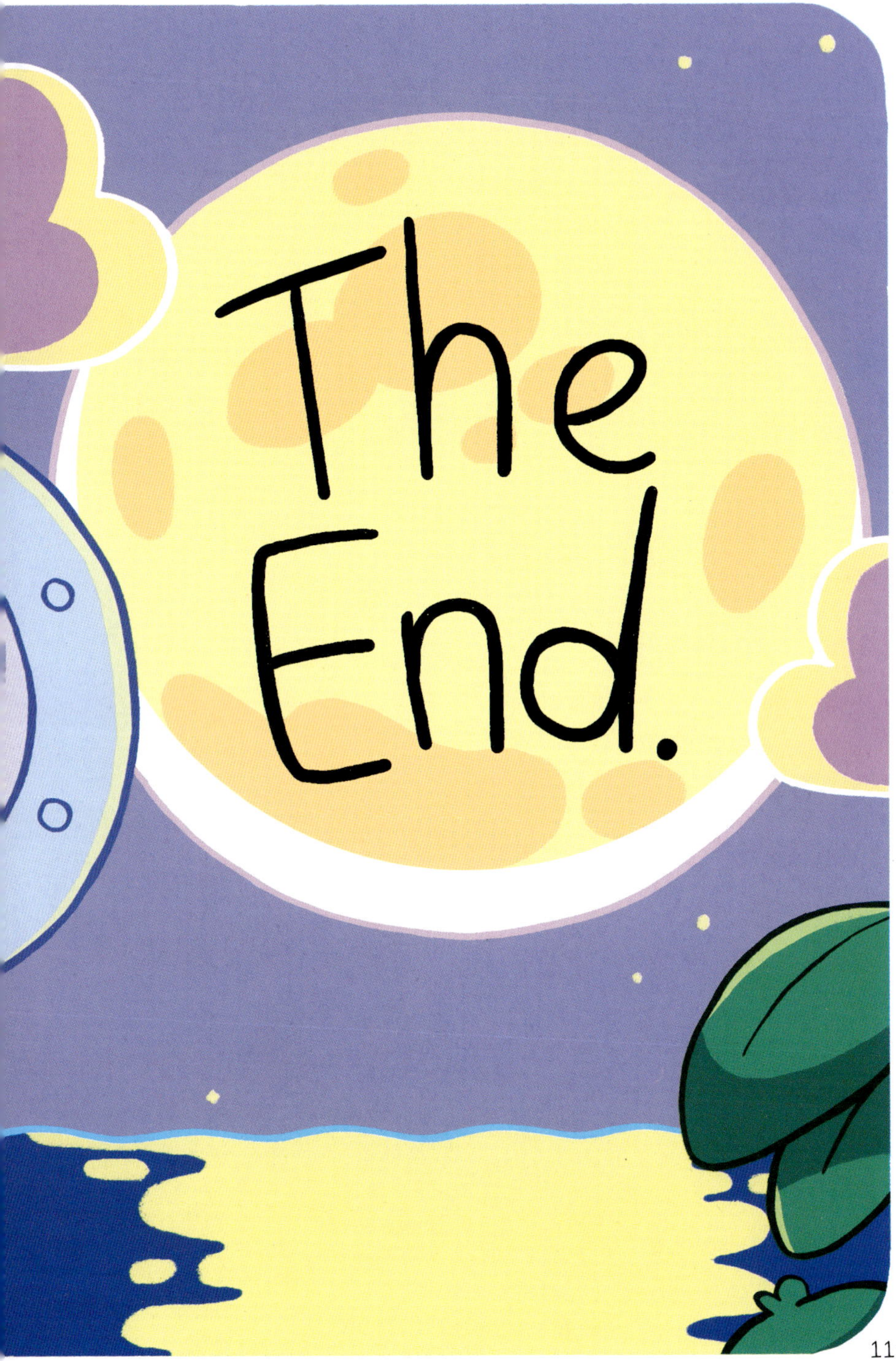
The End.

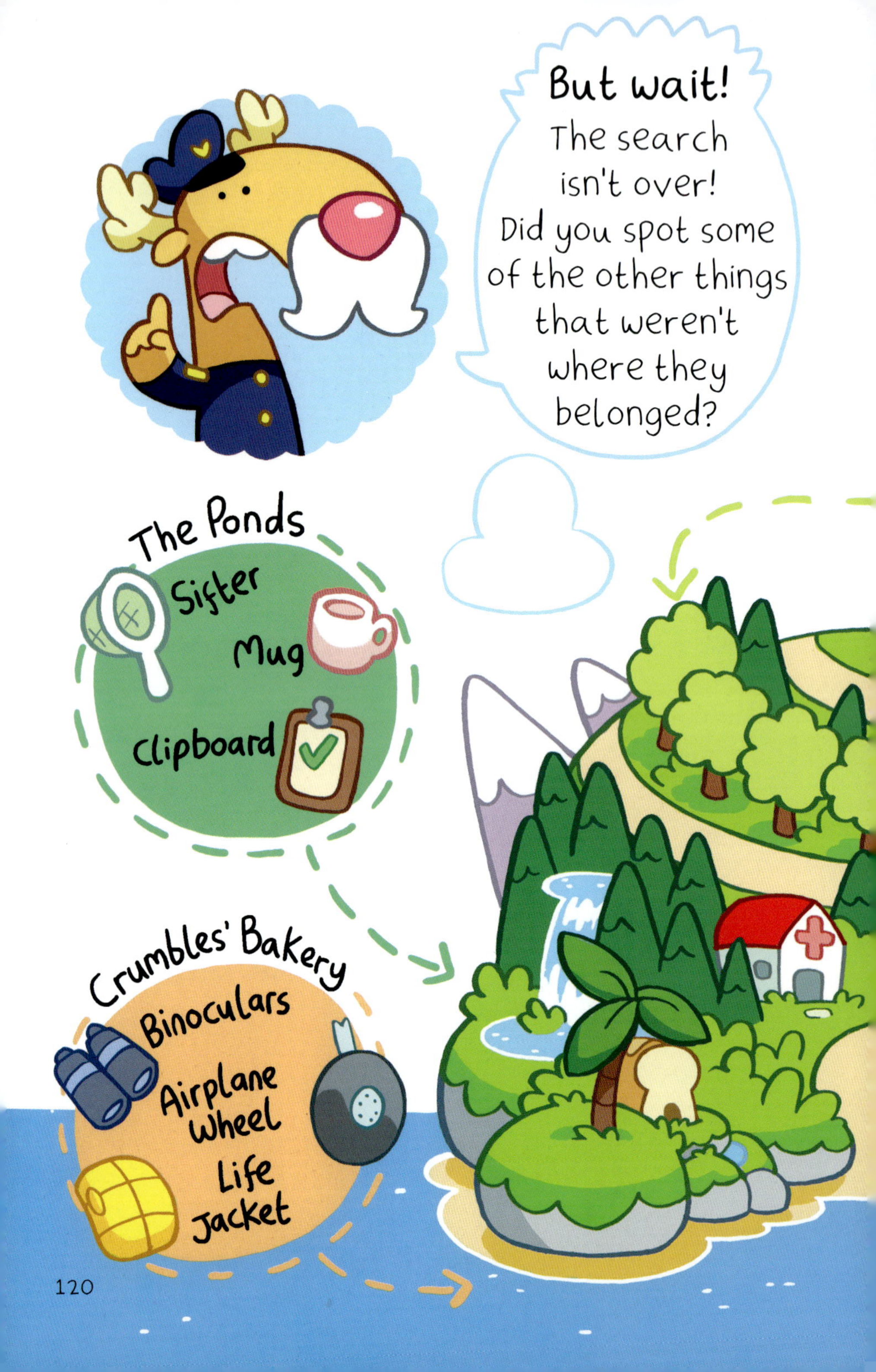
But wait!
The search isn't over! Did you spot some of the other things that weren't where they belonged?
The Ponds
Sifter
Mug
Clipboard
Crumbles' Bakery
Binoculars
Airplane Wheel
Life Jacket

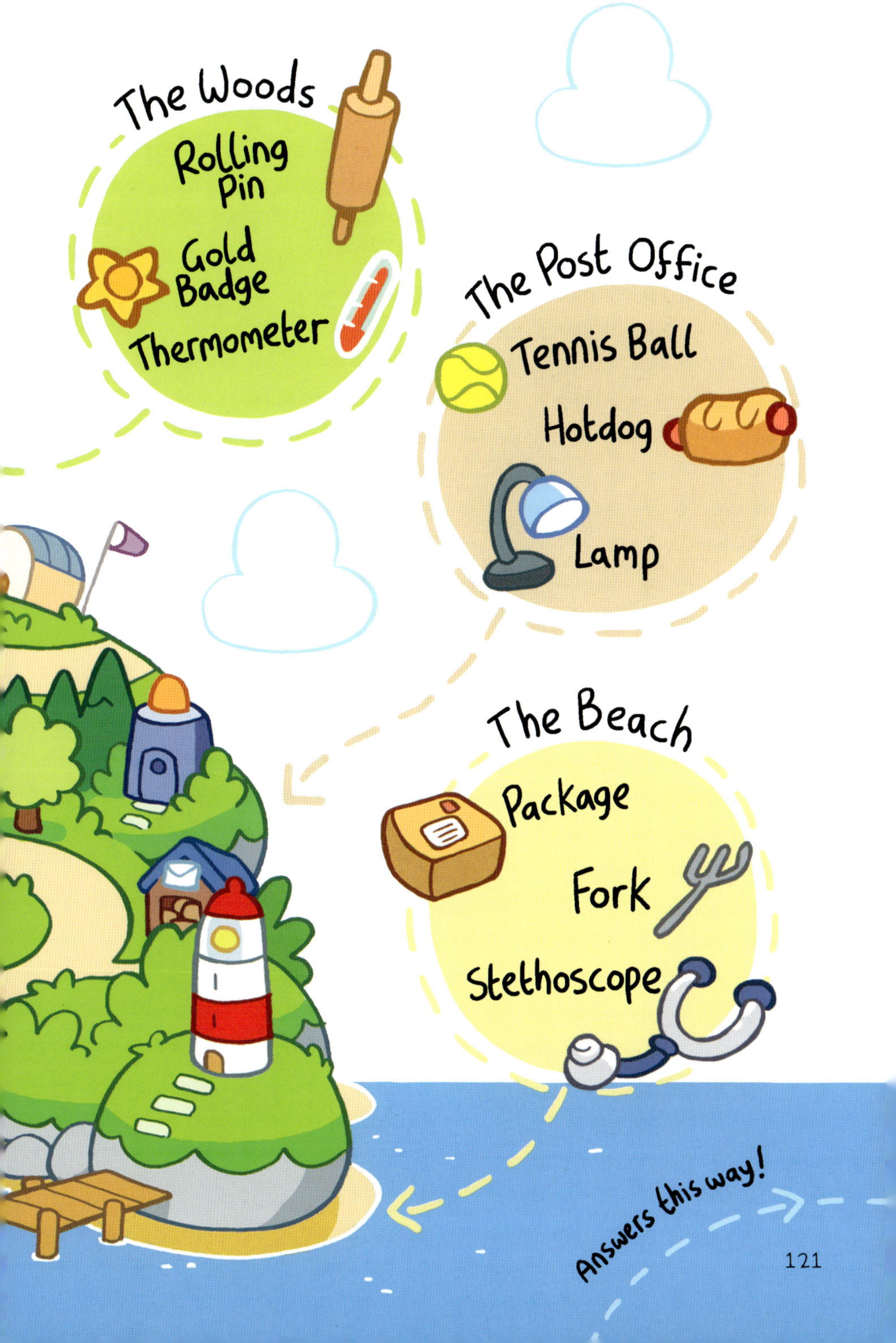
The Woods
Rolling Pin
Gold Badge
Thermometer
The Post Office
Tennis Ball
Hotdog
Lamp
The Beach
Package
Fork
Stethoscope
Answers this way!

Answers

Did you find all the other items? **GOOD JOB!** If you need a little help, here's where everything is!

The Woods

Rolling Pin

Gold Badge

Thermometer

The Beach

Package

Fork

Stethoscope

Crumbles' Bakery

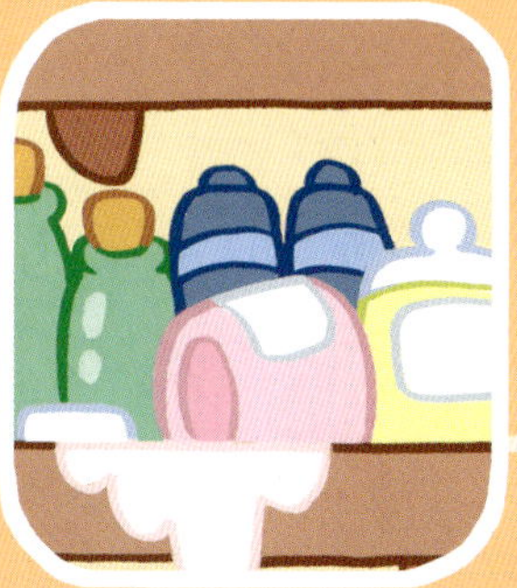

Binoculars

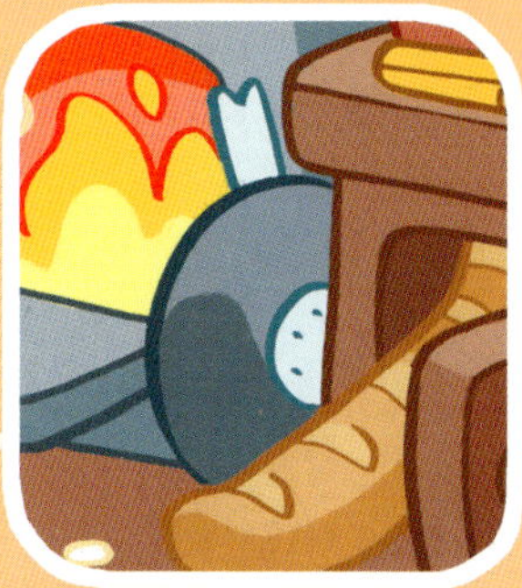

Airplane Wheel

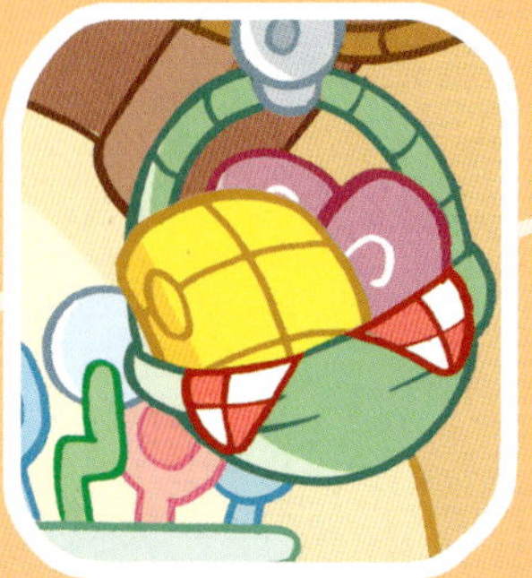

Life Jacket

The Ponds

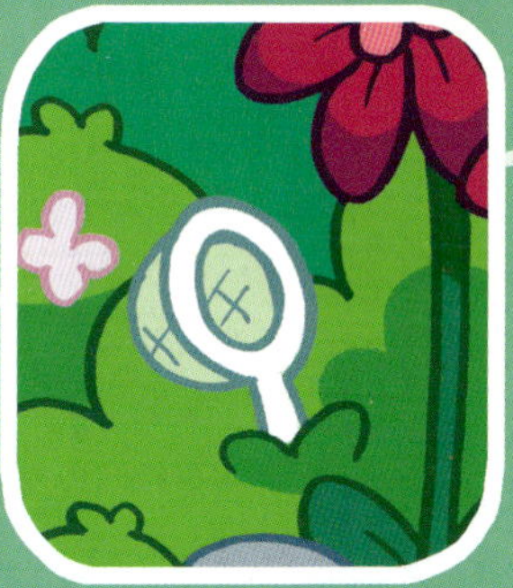

Sifter

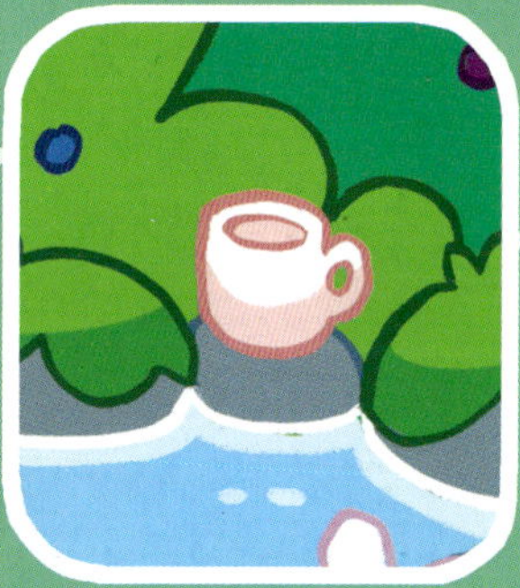

Mug

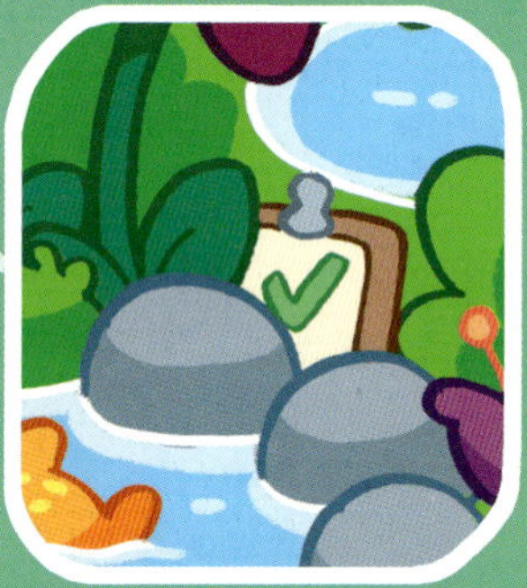

Clipboard

The Post Office

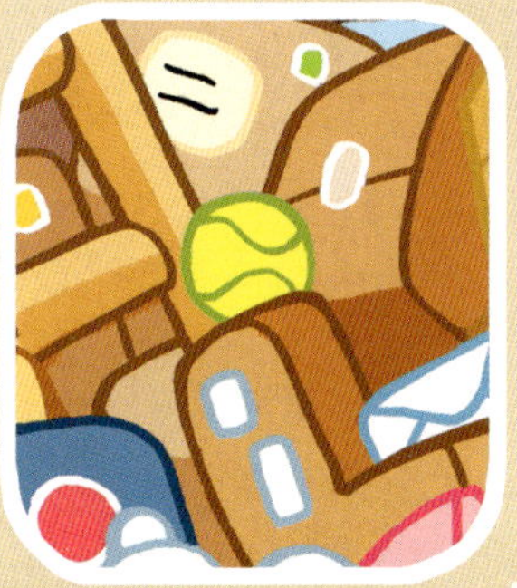

Tennis Ball

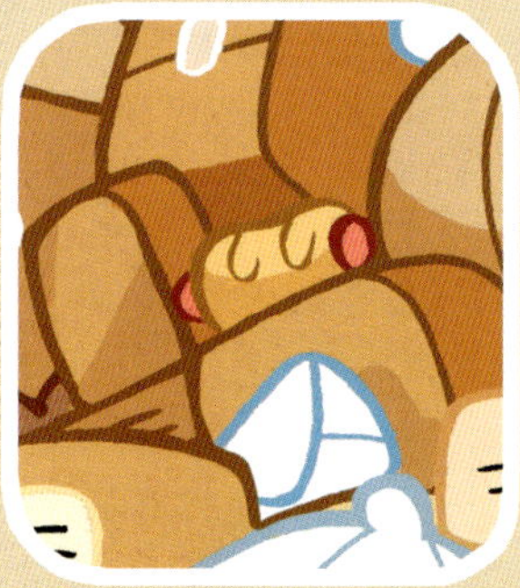

Hotdog

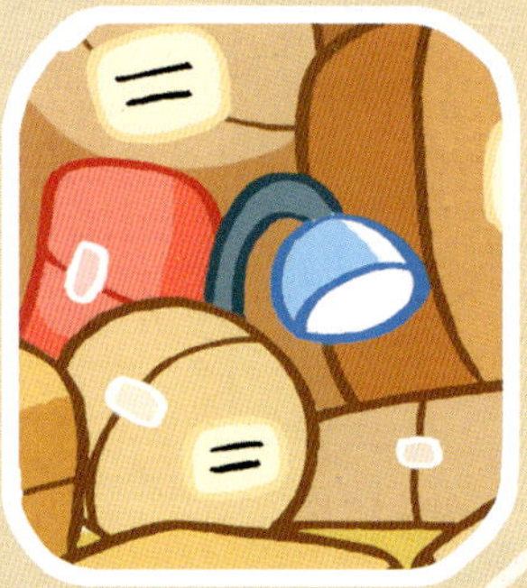

Lamp

More adventures with

MAX & CHAFFY

COMING SOON!

DK
JAMIE SMART'S
MAX & CHAFFY
THE GREAT
CUPCAKE MYSTERY!

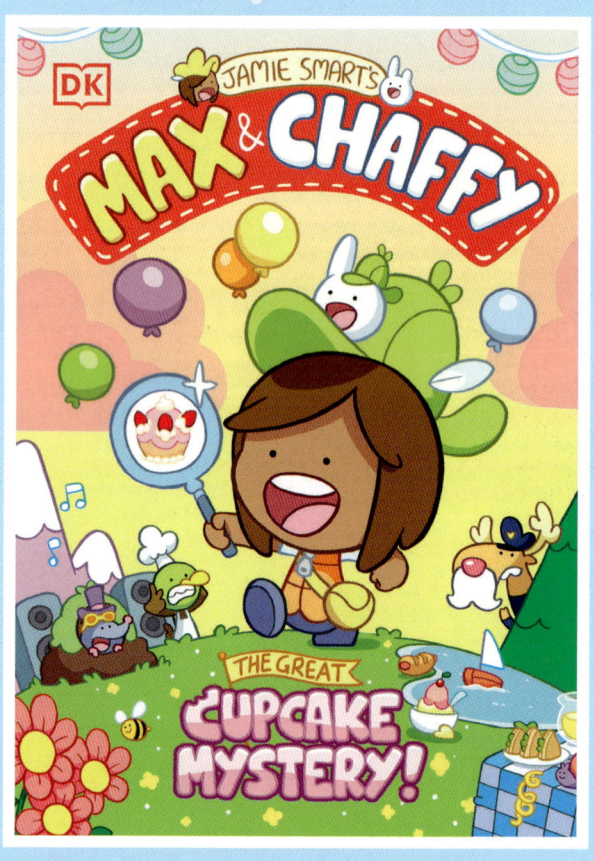

More adventures with
MAX & CHAFFY
COMING SOON!

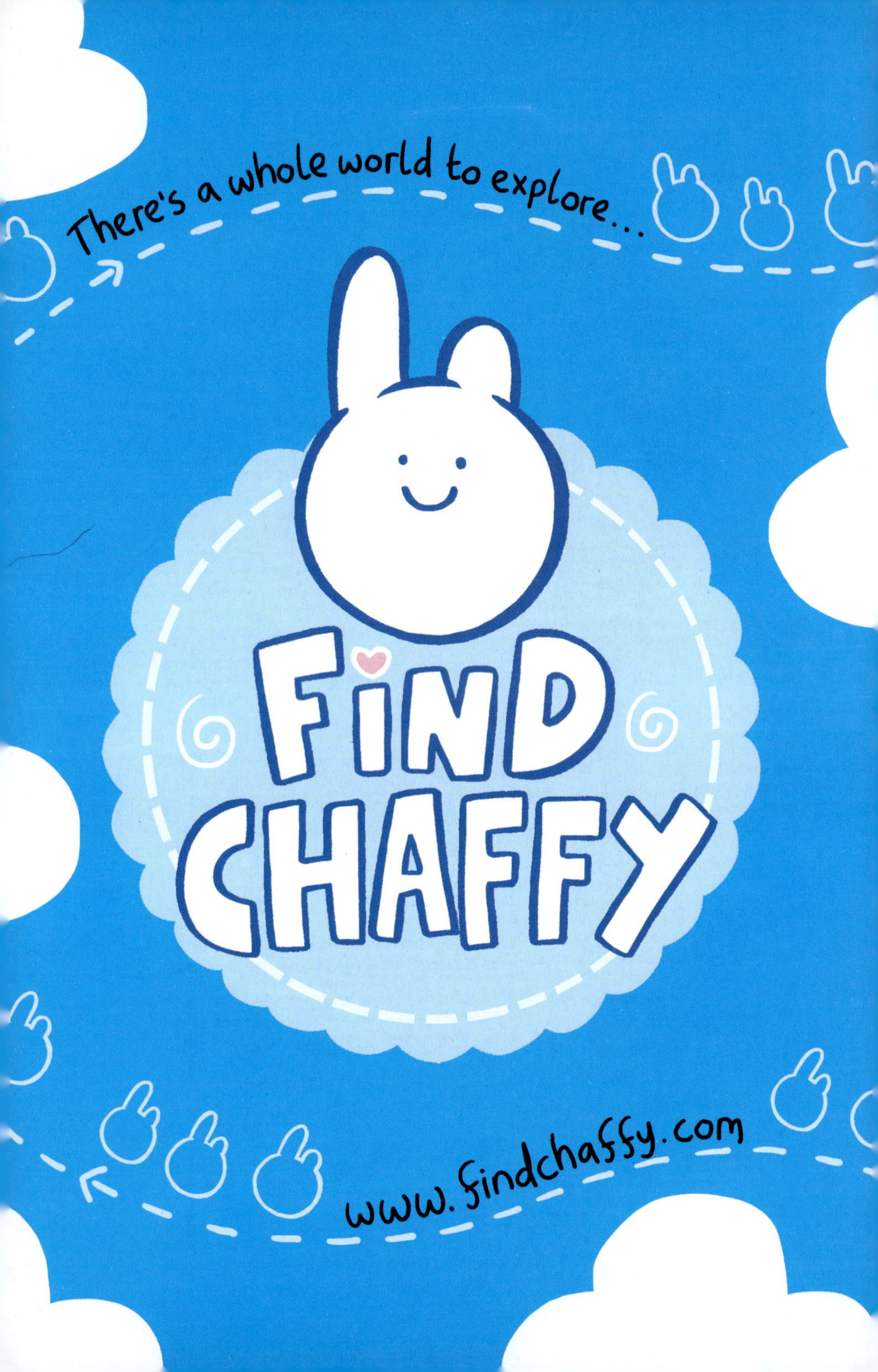
There's a whole world to explore...
FIND CHAFFY
www.findchaffy.com

Hi! I'm Jamie Smart.
I hope you loved reading about Max and Chaffy.
I really enjoyed writing and drawing it.
Thank you to my friends Emily, Rosie, and Katie
who all helped me make this book too!
I've also created other books, like the best-selling

 and

Making up stories and looking for chaffies
are my two favorite things!

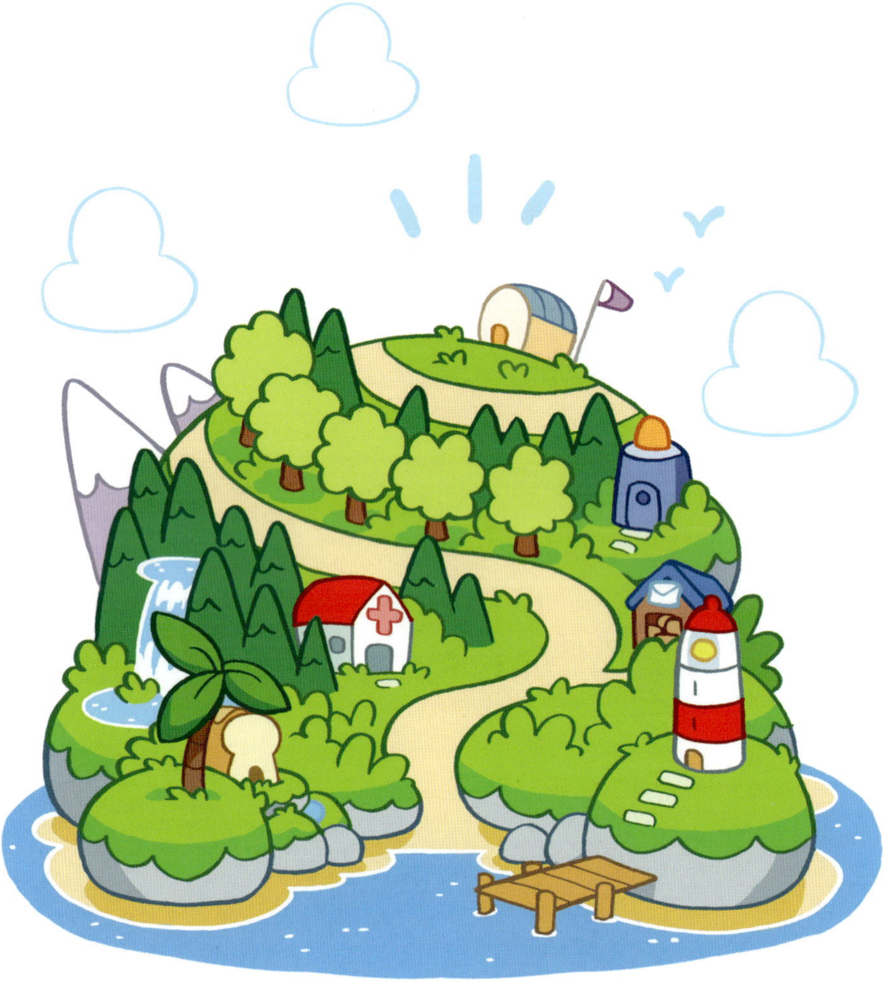

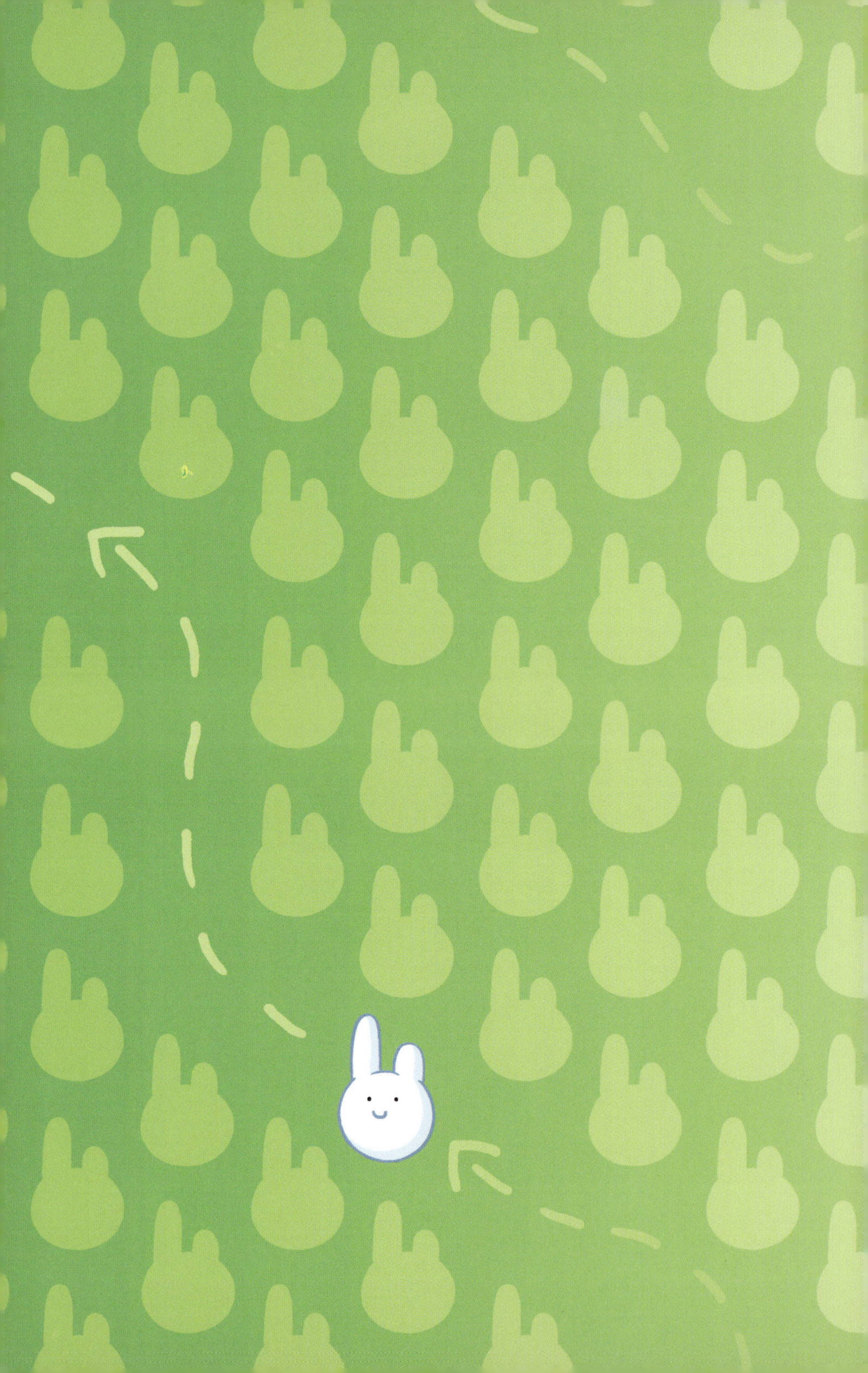